Stella Newman studied English at Sussex University, then went on to work in advertising, at the BBC and then as a professional food taster. She is now a full-time writer, based in London, and has written four novels: *Pear Shaped*, *Leftovers*, *The Foodie's Guide to Falling in Love*, previously published as *The Dish*, and *Seven Steps to Happiness*, as well as the festive e-short story, *A Pear Shaped Christmas*. She blogs about restaurants, food and writing at www.stellanewmansblog.wordpress.com and you can follow her on Twitter @stellanewman.

Praise for Stella Newman:

'I absolutely loved it' Katie Fforde

'Sharp, sweet and satisfying' Kate Long

'Combines our two dearest loves: food and romance' *Cosmopolitan*

'Laura's passion for food somersaults off the page and into your mouth . . . Well written, readable – like a delicious *petit four* . . . leaves you wanting more' *Heat*

'With really likeable characters, a witty turn of phrase, moments of real poignancy and, of course, mouthwatering details of food, it's rather delicious' *Sunday Mirror*

'Deliciously good stuff!' *Sun on Sunday Fabulous* magazine

'This book will leave you happy and hungry in equal doses!' *Take a Break*

'A funny page-turner' *Bella*

'Hugely entertaining' *Lady*

Seven Steps to Happiness

STELLA NEWMAN

REVIEW

First published in Great Britain in 2016 by
HEADLINE REVIEW
An imprint of HEADLINE PUBLISHING GROUP

1

Cataloguing in Publication Data is available from the British Library

ISBN 978 1 4722 2011 0

Typeset in Garamond MT Std by Palimpsest Book Production Ltd, Falkirk, Stirlingshire

Printed and bound in Great Britain by Clays Ltd, St Ives plc

HEADLINE PUBLISHING GROUP
An Hachette UK Company
Carmelite House
50 Victoria Embankment
London EC4Y 0DZ

www.headline.co.uk
www.hachette.co.uk

For my friend
Ali Bailey

PROLOGUE

Nineteen years ago

Lenny sat in the passenger seat of her mother's car on the way to Juliet's wedding, silently regretting her outfit.

'No point looking miserable about it now,' said Gloria, glancing at her daughter's dress, then turning back to the traffic and tutting.

Lenny craned her neck as far as possible and stared out of the window. 'The trees, Mum, look! They're starting to blossom.'

'It's not even lined, it looks tawdry,' said Gloria, savouring the word on her tongue like a sugared almond.

Lenny sighed. 'You can barely see my legs.'

'Like the world needs to see Leonora Dublonsky's knees, your father's calves, not mine.'

'Mum, please.'

Why on earth had Lenny thought that studying up in Glasgow would have mellowed her and her mother's relationship when she was back home? It had merely condensed the time in which they had to argue. Gloria accelerated towards an amber light, changed her mind, then crunched to an emergency stop, stabbing her finger at the Barbra Streisand tape poking out of the car stereo. Enough is enough all right. Lenny should have grabbed a lift with her friend Amy and Amy's new man, but apparently *Ritchie* was driving his Z5, and when Amy had mumbled, 'You could fit in the back, maybe?', her meaning had been perfectly clear.

'Have you and Juliet had a falling out or something?' said Gloria.

'What?'

'Why didn't she ask you to be bridesmaid? Never the bridesmaid, never the bride . . . '

'It's all been very last minute, hasn't it?' said Lenny, gently miming a small shotgun in the hope it might shut Gloria up.

'No *bridesmaids*?'

'Matt's nieces are flower girls apparently. His mum's choice . . .' Now that Juliet's mother was dead, Matt's mother had jumped in to direct the entire show. It wasn't Matt and Juliet's wedding, it was Cynthia Marlow's. Matt was obviously the lead: blue-eyed, six foot two, undergrad at Bristol. Co-starring was the lovely Juliet Field: clever, kind and effortlessly pretty with her big brown eyes and long blond hair. Not quite good enough for Matt, still, *the heart wants what it wants* . . . Of course if Cynthia could've had her way she'd have timed this whole thing rather differently. Juliet was slim, athletic, hardly showing. Nonetheless. Perhaps the photographer could crop out any hint of that déclassé bump?

'What a wonderful day for it,' said Gloria. 'She'll look so beautiful. I would have . . . She . . . Do send her my love.'

My god, if Amy had got up the duff at nineteen and was having a shotgun wedding – a far more likely proposition – Gloria would have spent this entire journey saying, *'Quelle surprise.'* If Lenny had done so, she'd have been sent back to the old country where the baby would have been forcibly removed by mustachioed matriarchs, and Lenny herself carted off for public shaming before drownage in a very deep well. But Gloria hadn't even mentioned the pregnancy. Like everyone else, Gloria thought the sun shone out of Juliet's arse. And it kind of did. (Not literally of course – that would challenge the laws of astrophysics.)

'And do thank her for her card,' said Gloria.

'What card?'

'I sent her a card about her mother – still so shocking. She sent me back a thank you.'

'I'm not bringing up her thank-you card for your bereavement card at her wedding.'

'Don't be stupid, it's been six months. It's polite to acknowledge it.'

'Why don't you send her a thank you for your thank-you card? This could run and run—'

'Oh for Christ's sake, do you want me to pull over right here and you can walk?'

Ha! Gloria wouldn't dare. She'd be hanging round the hotel car park long after drop off, making sure none of the other mothers from school had been invited.

'Next left, Mum, get in lane – and indicate!'

'Why do you have to be so difficult all the time? You're like your bloody father.'

You must be joking, thought Lenny. I learned from the master: you taught me everything I know.

It was kind of a lovely wedding. Juliet looked radiant in an empire line dress, her skin naturally glowing, with Matt standing proudly beside her. The flowers were expensive, the food beautiful – though Lenny noted there'd only been one type of canapé served, good job she'd been hovering by the kitchen entrance and had managed to snaffle several.

The speeches were decent, Matt's surprisingly sincere, his best man's predictably obnoxious – but it was Juliet who brought the house down with a few simple words about her mother. Lenny's throat swelled uncomfortably, like she'd been forced to swallow a grapefruit whole. And then Matt's mum had lanced the sadness, grabbing the mic to propose a toast to the groom and bride – strange how those words sounded in that order.

Lenny couldn't work out why she felt quite so upset as she sat looking over at the happy couple holding hands. Admittedly the seating plan wasn't ideal: to her right was that bozo Danny Freeman, his hand firmly wedged between some girl's thighs. To her left was Amy, snogging Ritchie since before the speeches – though at least she'd given Lenny her bread roll and one of her lamb chops. So no, playing the filling in a gooseberry sandwich wasn't optimum, but it didn't account for the mix of anger and anxiety Lenny felt, when surely she should be filled with unbridled joy?

Could it be envy, or was it jealousy – she could never remember the difference? Certainly no man had ever gazed at her the way Matt gazed at Juliet, with such territorial pride. And Matt was handsome – undeniably so, if you liked chiselled jaws, straight noses and slightly too low hairlines. Juliet could have had her pick of the boys at school

– not that she thought of herself in those terms, but Lenny did, and she thought Juliet had undervalued herself. Sure, Matt was good at almost everything, but he was unremittingly arrogant. Seeing how he fitted into the Marlow family jigsaw, it made sense. He was doted upon, he could do no wrong; irresponsible to bring up a child like that, with no sense of consequences.

You know what? They were still quite young. Nineteen was an adult but maybe not like a proper adult. People always changed in books and films, maybe Matt would grow up and lose the shield of entitlement that radiated off him like a Ready Brek glow.

But it was more than that. Lenny had a sneaking suspicion Matt had impregnated Juliet primarily to limit her possibilities. Juliet could have been anything she wanted, but now she was dropping out of university. Maybe it was her reaction to her mum's death – batten down the hatches, start her own family. Still, Lenny couldn't help but feel that your twenties were designed for making mistakes and figuring out who you were – or would rather be. And Matt was taking these opportunities away from Juliet.

Juliet had always had Lenny's back. Sure, Lenny had taught her quadratic equations, but after school over cheese toasties in Juliet's kitchen, Jules had taught Lenny *life* skills. Foremost was how to avoid being bullied; attacks on Lenny had been multiple:

Scholarship girl = nerd + poor

Dead dad = weirdo

Downside of light moustache > upside of early development. But Jules had taught her other valuable lessons too: how to Immac, blow smoke rings, swear in French. And now Lenny wanted to graduate, have adventures, travel the world. Hell, Glasgow wasn't far enough from Gloria, she'd need a sea between them at least, possibly an ocean. And Juliet would be stuck at home like some boring 1950s housewife.

Of course Lenny would end up marrying one day, and in time have kids, maybe in ten, even fifteen years, but Juliet and she would be entirely out of synch with every passing life stage. Yes, Lenny was being utterly selfish – but . . . well, at least she knew it.

Lenny caught Amy's eye as she unglued herself from Ritchie long enough to grab a drink. Lenny pointed to Amy's plate where a tower of croque en bouche choux buns sat uneaten, mouthed *May I?* then swapped it with her own, already scraped clean. Lenny smashed her spoon through the crunchy caramel barrier, sank it deep into the pastry to get to the heart of the custard. She looked back over at Juliet, beaming with happiness, and a grinning Matt.

Lenny wished them well with all her heart.

Not quite true – she wished Juliet well, and therefore, by association, Matt. She hoped Matt would make her friend happy. She feared he might not.

Lenny often feared the worst.

Lenny was often – but not always – right.

PART ONE

I

Lenny stood at the front of the conference room, waiting for the final stragglers to return from lunch. It was sixteen degrees outside, an unseasonably warm March day in Rome, but even if there'd been snow on the ground Lenny would still have been breaking a sweat. Just because she was good at statistics and analysis didn't mean she had any talent for public speaking. Numbers were her friend, there was safety in them, but standing here with a sea of pan-European colleagues staring at her made her feel quite queasy. Strange really, given how vocal she was in every other context.

Octavia, Lenny's boss, was always pushing Lenny to do things she was rubbish at: 'The twentieth time you do something you're uncomfortable with is when you break through your development barrier.' No, the twentieth time you do something you're uncomfortable with is when it's time for professional psychiatric help. Lenny was more than aware of her limitations: she wasn't good at skiing, crosswords, relationships or public speaking – and she didn't need to repeat any of them twenty times to prove it. Things hadn't improved since Occy had given her some 'friendly feedback': an Occy-oxymoron if ever there was one. 'Are you aware your body hunches right over when you're nervous? Might be wise to consider some power poses or you'll look like Quasimodo.' Nothing friendly about that.

Lenny pushed her shoulders back and glanced at her chest. She had a decent bust which never seemed to cooperate with buttons – but that didn't stop her being drawn to the classic white shirt as a way of making herself feel vaguely professional – and as she looked back up she caught Nick Cooper's eyes, also appraising her chest. Cooper, leaning back in his seat, arm casually draped over his neighbour's chair. Cooper was the cockiest man she'd ever met and she'd encountered many in her time, her data was robust. Yes, he had piercing blue eyes, thick dark hair and a degree of personal charm, and if life were a Hollywood movie – or even a British one – their relationship would play out as follows: initial animosity, a build up of tension, a comic misunderstanding followed by passionately explosive sex and, in the final scene, an admission of mutual adoration. Never going to happen in real life.

Could she imagine shagging him? Yes. Had she already imagined it? Again, yes. But she could imagine it all too precisely. The man – *boy* – was twenty-nine, part of a generation raised on Internet-porn; the sex would be show-offy and all about him. Her mind flitted to Ellis. In spite of his many flaws, his laziness, the fact she had to perpetually 'lend' him the money to top up his Oyster card, she could not fault his generosity in the bedroom.

Lenny glanced down at her list of speakers. After her was little Heinz Werner from the Munich office, presenting on Virtual Instrument Clusters. Last year she'd ended up stuck with Heinz at dinner and as coffees were being served he'd tried to move her hand to his own instrument cluster. Lenny had spilled her espresso on his groin – a happy accident.

People were always telling Lenny her job was glamorous – paid to go to Rome, Berlin, Madrid. Lenny had stopped pointing out she'd rather be paid to go to Milton Keynes, because the reality was she ended up in Rome – in a generic conference room – *giving a presentation* when what she clearly wanted to be doing was drinking cappuccinos, visiting the Colosseum and stuffing her face. On her last trip here, during a snatched lunch break she'd stumbled across an epic queue of locals in a cobbled backstreet. Lenny had joined them and found herself at the door of Pranza, home of the ultimate mozzarella in carrozza – a deep fried golden sandwich that had haunted Lenny like a first love ever since. Just thinking about those springy strings of lush cheese, that golden crispy buttery bread, brought some much needed moisture back to her mouth.

That's what she'd do then. Give her speech and slip out the back to Pranza. She'd leave the networking to Cooper. He'd totally blagged himself on to Euro Conference anyway, always muscling in – the least he could do was earn his keep by pressing the flesh, as long as it wasn't her flesh.

The sooner she started, the sooner that sandwich was hers.

'*Buongiorno*, ladies and gentlemen. I'm Lenny Dublonsky, Head of Research at Wappen London and I'm here today to talk about our latest exciting apps . . .'

Lenny was dreaming she was on a tropical beach, attempting to sunbathe while dressed in an orange prison boiler suit, when she felt, through the haze of alcoholic slumber, something nudge the small of her back. She froze, shifted slightly in the bed and felt it move against her. It wasn't heavy but there was heft to it; long, wide too, like an over-stuffed sausage . . .

Please don't let that be Heinz Werner's *wiener*, she'd never survive the shame – but *please* do not let it be Nick Cooper's. She'd been drunk last night, yes, very – in fact a spinning head told her she still was – but surely not get-into-bed-with-Cooper drunk? Lenny furtively moved her arm under the cover and gave a gentle prod with one finger, then two. The object was soft and smooth, but firm when pushed. What the . . . ?

She hadn't been in bed with Ellis for weeks, still, she hadn't completely forgotten what the male body felt like and it did not feel like this. Further investigation confirmed it was neither penis, nor horse's head – rather a soft tube, seven inches long with a weird foldy-over slightly harder bit at the end.

Lenny drew her hand back sharply, swung her legs out of bed and pulled back the covers. Oh good grief, no! Here? At the Hotel Splendido? On 600 thread count sheets?

This must be Cooper's doing. There was no way she'd have chosen to go that way when in Rome. And even if she had been tricked into it, *absolutely* no way she'd have been so blind drunk that by the time she'd staggered into her room and taken off her clothes . . . Oh, no, she was still wearing yesterday's shirt – though it now had a luminous orange dribble down it. Still, there was *no way* she would have been so drunk that she'd have removed the foil wrapping, got into bed holding it but passed out without even managing a single bite of the burrito currently lying there, unless Cooper had been plying her with booze all night.

She picked up the burrito and stared at it, perplexed.

She remembered giving her speech. Actually it had gone OK, until some researcher from Wappen-Lisbon had asked her to expand on her data parameters. She'd gone into considerable detail, during which time Heinz Werner had walked on stage. He'd publicly invited her to come back up for his own Q&A – thus foiling her escape plans. She'd then been crowd-surfed to dinner with seventeen network colleagues at a musty restaurant near the Trevi Fountain, where the waiters looked carved from the same Travertine stone as Neptune. Afterwards she remembered being force-fed multiple Aperols at a rooftop bar where she'd gone to with . . . Cooper. She remembered him saying she had a beautiful profile, those high cheekbones, that small, strong nose, like Gillian Anderson but with darker hair; how he loved how big Lenny's balls were. Lenny disliked being admired for the size of her metaphorical testicles, but she had been susceptible to the Gillian Anderson comment.

No doubt Cooper's heightened flirtation was part of some larger Machiavellian power play. He'd been Wappen's Chief Disruption Officer barely three months, his only tangible achievement the lunchtime table-footy club, yet already there was talk of him getting his own office if his Wellness Programme took off! Lenny had spent three years earning her office and just as well – where else could she go to, to stick pins in her little Octavia doll that Fran on reception had knitted for her?

She cringed as she remembered sitting close to Cooper, foreheads touching in conspiratorial drunkenness. Oh! And she'd confided in him how Fran had once said that the name Occy sounded like a throat infection and that in relaying this bitchiness like a jubilant baton she was condoning it. Another flashback – of standing in a piazza, a shoe in one hand, marvelling at some huge white monument and singing 'That's Amore' and then, oh Lord, the Gino Ginelli jingle. She had no recollection of the journey from that point to the burrito vendor, nor her return to the hotel, but those events must have happened, because here she was, and here too the snack.

What time *was* it anyway? 6.43 a.m. If she was in a cab to the airport by 8 a.m. she could find a decent bottle of wine in duty free for Juliet's anniversary party tomorrow, even Matt couldn't be snobbish about a Barolo.

She brought the burrito to her nose and gently sniffed it. It was a crime to throw food away. Besides if she didn't do something to soak up the booze raging through her system she was in danger of still being drunk when the plane took off. She'd learned several years ago, when she and Amy flew to Vegas to celebrate Amy's divorce, that being drunk on a plane was *not* actually fun, and had only done it twice since.

Lenny was a thirty-seven-year-old woman wearing yesterday's stained Zara shirt, sitting drunk in a hotel room in Rome, eating a cold chicken burrito she'd been sharing a bed with for five hours, the closest thing she'd had to intimacy in months. And it was missing the guacamole.

This was not how she thought her life would turn out.

Juliet took another look at her to-do list and shuddered. She'd been the one to suggest they had this party at home, Matt had wanted Nobu but that'd seemed flashy and impersonal and besides, raw fish was fine but it wasn't a *party*. Matt was only suggesting it because he'd recently become such a diet bore. Goodness, when she'd shown him her menu he'd made such a fuss! She'd explained that each dish was only bite-sized, and he'd calmed down a bit. 'Look, see? Each one's designed as a tribute to our friends. Dave and Katy love Mexican, so I'm making tiny chicken tortillas. And this is a mini version of the roast beef we had with Jill and Dom in that pub in Ludlow.'

'Jules, if anyone can pull this off, you can, but if you change your mind I'll call the restaurant.' Right now she was tempted to take him up on his offer. Fourteen dishes, plus desserts, was extremely ambitious – still, it would have been OK if Mitchell hadn't requested an impromptu meeting this afternoon. She checked her watch – nearly noon – she needed to get a move on.

She picked up her phone from the hall table and saw another missed call, no number, probably the estate agent, ringing back about their flat. Up until a few months ago Danny Freeman had been staying there when he was in town. He'd come home from Bali in

January and had an epic falling out with Matt; Matt still wouldn't say why – he was so loyal to that man. And Juliet was very fond of Danny but really, would he ever grow up? Surfing his way round the globe long after everyone else had settled down. Did he really finance all that travelling just from odd jobs half the year? Matt claimed Danny had paid him back the £2,000 he'd borrowed to buy the van but maybe he hadn't, maybe that's why Matt was being so cagey? Should she call Danny, see if those two could put whatever this was behind them? Your school friends know you better than anyone and yes, admittedly Danny could be a little bolshy, just like Lenny, but surely he couldn't have done something unforgivable?

She put her phone in her bag. She'd leave it to Matt. You can't go behind someone's back like that, really, it's not on.

Lenny dragged her suitcase into her office and waved to Fran on reception. In the two days since Lenny had been gone the logo behind Fran's head had changed from green to orange: WAPPEN! (Weapon + App + Happen.) Company legend had it the name popped into Jared the CEO's head while he was mid-bungee jump. Strange, as the word that would pop into Lenny's head if she ever jumped from a great height would be four letters long and NSFW.

Wappen specialised in multi-disciplinary solutions. 'Sounds like a brothel,' said Gloria, when Lenny had taken the job. 'It's the full 360 – a one-stop-shop for Concept Development, Big Data and User Experience,' said Lenny, aware as she trotted out these phrases that she understood them only 11% more than her mum. Lenny was still bewildered that she'd ended up working in tech. She clung to her old records on vinyl; she didn't trust Contactless; even now she had a loveless relationship with her phone, could number the apps she chose to use on a V-sign: Citymapper, Uber. Her career, like her life, had been entirely unplanned – jumping ship from one research job to another at the precise point she was too bored or too outspoken. One day she'd figure out what she wanted to be when she grew up; that day had yet to come.

Her current job was assessing all of Wappen's new projects: *Is this app a good idea, will it work?* As Gloria had put it: '*You're* the voice of common sense?' Lenny had wanted to reply: 'Actually it's more the voice of the bleeding obvious,' but on reflection, that would have been an own goal. She could never jack it in though because she had no transferable skills, so in a way she was lucky to have a job she could do in her sleep and sometimes did – red and blue Venn diagrams floating through her dreams, an X-axis chasing her jerkily down a dark alley.

She headed to the canteen, grabbed a Coke, then took the glass lift up – past New Business, then the Programmers aka The Minions, then the Design and Brand Teams, finally coming to rest on the top floor. She'd always dreamed of an office with a view but as she gazed down on to Silicon Roundabout she wondered if perhaps her dreams hadn't been misguided. Google, eBay, all the American tech giants had mythical campuses in California, fibreglass palaces with views of the Pacific. Lenny's visual highlights were Chicken Spot, and last night's sallow club kids gurning their way back to Old Street Tube.

Lenny checked her diary, inbox, voicemail. Status meeting at 2 p.m., three messages from Amy, and an email from Andrew, saying his latest Tinder affair was over. Lenny was craving a pad Thai from Whitecross Street market but she had a niggling suspicion she'd offered to meet with Maureen in facilities, whose son wanted help with his CV. Maureen would never go for foreign food over a free ham sandwich from the canteen, and lunch would mean Lenny restraining her cynicism to the max. Lenny was not in the mood, not in the slightest.

She picked up her bag and made her way down to Maureen's desk, cursing this tiny streak of niceness she must have inherited from her father.

'Mitchell won't be long,' said his receptionist. 'He's just on his way back from The Ivy.'

Juliet wondered whether Mitchell would ever invite her to lunch? She'd been part of Team Celina Summer for five years; she'd ghost-written all six of Celina's bestselling cookery books, was responsible for her every tweet and Instagram. If Juliet thought about it, Celina must have cleared at least three million pounds from her ideas. Juliet chose not to think about it much.

Forty minutes later Mitchell arrived, led Juliet to his vast office, flung his cashmere coat down and stood on tiptoes for a double kiss. He wore an aftershave she recognised from Martha's male friends – the pungent teenage waft of the Abercrombie store.

'Sweetheart, such a busy time! Weber's touring the US next week and visas aren't sorted – can't wipe their own arses these kids.'

Juliet smiled sympathetically. Since Martha had gone to uni Juliet had totally lost touch with the various stars Mitchell represented, was Weber even a person, or a band?

'How's Celina's new book doing?' said Juliet. Every time she saw it in the bestsellers list she felt a small thrill. Sure, Juliet's name wasn't on the cover, she was mentioned in passing in the Acknowledgements, after Celina's personal trainer, her make-up artist and her dog – but still.

Mitchell started to speak but then stopped. His natural inclination was to brag, but he always felt, with these ghosts, that there was such a fine line between keeping them motivated versus keeping them in their place. But then he couldn't help himself. 'Number one, fifth week running!'

'I'm so pleased, I—'

'We're re-negotiating with the publisher, three more books!'

'Great, that's—'

'And we're looking at a possible sixteen page Easter pull out with *The Times*.'

'*This* Easter?' Sixteen pages, thirty-two recipes . . . in twenty days?

'So today we talk – then perhaps you can help out.'

Mitchell made her laugh. *Help out?* More like: create and test every recipe, source props, prepare and style the food on the shoot and then smile when Celina showed up late in her Victoria Beckham sleeveless coat and picked up a wooden spoon for the camera. Why couldn't Mitchell just say 'Perhaps you can do all the work'? Juliet was hardly the type to kick up a stink; she knew what being in the background meant.

'We're desperate to hit mums in national press, Easter's perfect – Jules, we need you!'

That was the thing, they did – and they were all on the same side.

'We could turn Brand Celina global!' said Mitchell, flashing newly bleached teeth.

She could go heavy on breads; or croutons, sweet croutons!

'Sweetheart, is that smile a yes?'

That smile was Juliet imagining a vanilla crème brûlée topped with tiny hot cross bun croutons with orange zest. 'I'll do my best.'

'SUPERSTAR, you *are* the best!'

Mitchell had that rare ability to make you believe he was sincere, even though every inch of you knew he was a cheesy five foot four conman in a shortened Tom Ford suit.

An hour later Juliet was heading through the ticket barrier at East Finchley Tube station when her phone beeped – a breathless voicemail: 'Easter's confirmed! Send Celina the recipes Monday week, shoot starts Thursday.' Well, that was Juliet's life over this month!

Hmm. Mitchell must have known this deal was in the bag before their meeting. If she told Matt, he'd be annoyed she hadn't put Mitchell over a barrel for cash; Matt was always saying she should *learn to play hardball* – such a silly macho phrase.

She rushed to the posh deli to pick up the final ingredients for tomorrow night. They had such fabulous produce in here – today purple globe artichokes, crates laden with round courgettes the size of grapefruits. And their breads! Seven varieties from local micro-bakeries. After Easter maybe she could have a chat with the manager about selling her homemade bread?

In the corner she noticed a basket of fresh dill. She could make blinis with smoked salmon and crème fraîche – just like that *one* canapé they'd had at their wedding. Oh! She hadn't even thought to create a dish just for Matt. It wasn't that she took him for granted, she didn't, but they'd been a couple more than half their lives, and sometimes she didn't think of him as a separate entity – he was as much a part of her as her own heart.

Lenny entered the boardroom and found Occy and Cooper deep in whispered conversation. Occy with her bouncy golden curls and cute button nose. Those cherubic features had never fooled Lenny. The rest of the senior team were sitting in cowed silence. Lenny took a seat between Ravi, head of The Minions, and Philpott, head of design, who smiled at her with watery blue eyes. 'Did you get to see the Pantheon, Lenny?'

'Next time,' she said, wistfully.

'Hush, guys, hush!' said Occy. 'OK, so, Jared's signed off Nick's latest *Disrupt, Innovate, Connect* plans so we'll start with an update on pan-global step-change facilitation from Nick.'

Lenny knew there would come a time when she could take no more of Occy. She prayed that time would come after she'd saved up enough for a deposit on a flat. Just looking at Occy's T-shirt made Lenny feel mild wrath: *Je suis une feministe* in sequins. That was not true, not true in French, not even true in sequins.

'Guys, you've seen the new brand identity?' said Nick. 'It was birthed out of the neuroplasticity colour project I've been doing with the Big Picture team in Wappen-Zurich.'

'Does he mean changing the logo from green to orange?' Philpott whispered to Lenny.

'We'll be trialling it in London, Sao Paolo and Helsinki – the vibrant palette in Bleisure areas, softer colours in Unthinking Zones.'

Lenny hoped her nostrils weren't visibly flaring.

'Nick: brilliant,' said Occy. 'Lenny: crack on with numbers?'

Lenny tried to strip the disdain from her voice as she read out the agency's top revenue generators. 'Daily Diary's exceeding estimate – over eighty thousand downloads.' Lenny had been dismayed when that prototype had landed on her desk. An app that you wrote your appointments in? *That was it?* It was all so imbecilically simple. Lenny had a dozen ideas daily that could make millions, if only she had a decent chunk of seed funding. Even this morning, she'd imagined an app that at the press of one button could deliver a clean white shirt and a bacon sandwich to you as you waited for the Heathrow Express – that was a solid gold commercial idea.

'OK, guys,' said Occy. 'Two new prototypes, first, I had an ideation brainstorm with Wyomie Lex's PR yesterday—'

'Sorry!' said Philpott, raising his hand gently. 'Is he the chap from *Made in Chelsea?*'

'Wyomie runs Dalston's biggest lifestyle blog,' sighed Occy. '*She* is best known for taking three suitcases of shoes to Glastonbury.'

Philpott nudged Lenny. 'There'll be a blue plaque outside her house one day.'

'Her PR team had twenty ideas for brand extensions,' said Occy. 'The one with immediate legs is Get Me Those Shoes Now!'

'Or feet?' said Philpott, chuckling.

'What?' snapped Occy.

'Immediate legs . . . feet . . . Oh, not to worry . . . '

'Imagine this!' Occy fanned her hands out. 'You're flicking through a magazine, you see your dream shoes. With one click the software recognises the shoes, sources them in your size and delivers them to your door, same day! Lenny, I don't mean to tread on your toes – ah, see what I did there, Philpott? – but may I suggest touching base with urban millennials? And the second prototype: Big Sister's back.'

'But why?' said Lenny. 'We agreed it wasn't fit for further qual testing?'

'Jared and I have reconsidered.'

'Can't Cooper trial it? It makes a whopping bulge under your clothes.'

'I'd love to help, Len, but I don't need the extra inches,' said Cooper. Occy laughed and pushed the three-inch plastic monitor victoriously towards Lenny: The Big Sister – a tracking device for heart rate, movement, caloric intake – with all personal data instantly pulsed back to the agency dashboard for public consumption.

Lenny picked up the device and grudgingly switched it on. 'Occy, the wireframe was totally flawed, it makes no sense . . . '

'Functionality is not the point! Just get us a decent UX score.'

Above all else – above the Adult Playpen or the free breakfasts that lured you in early only to serve you a bacon butty made with flabby white bread – the worst thing about Wappen was that Research, the thing Lenny most enjoyed, was frequently manipulated to give the client the result they wanted. Does the consumer like this? No? Ask again: *does the consumer like this?* Keep on asking until the answer's yes.

Lenny clipped the tracker to her bra, then moved it to her waistband. 'It's so obtrusive . . . '

'Due diligence till Easter, please.'

Fine: when it came time for Lenny's management summary she'd detail its multiple irritating flaws and swipe left. (The monitor, not Occy: if only.)

Back at home, Lenny plonked herself on her sofa and groaned as she felt the nub of the Big Sister digging into her waistband. Want to track my every move? Track this! She moved to the kitchen – twelve steps – poured some wine, then returned twelve steps to the sofa. She did not feel any urge to input this data into her phone because it was none of her phone's – nor the agency's – business what she drank in her leisure time. And she was even expected to wear this little snitch in bed! The first time they'd had a sleep monitoring app at Wappen, she'd been astounded at how people could be so navel-gazing. That was three years ago and now there was no bodily function beyond scrutiny and subsequent top trumps, except perhaps farts, and that was only because you couldn't photograph them. That was the million-pound idea – a camera-filter that could capture a Technicolor selfie-fart!

She couldn't be in a worse mood – she might as well call Ellis. She was about to text him when Juliet rang. Ah, such perfect timing – she'd saved Lenny from herself.

'You are still coming tomorrow, aren't you?' said Juliet.

'Of course. Is Martha coming down?'

'No, she needs to finish her dissertation before Easter. She and Nate are going on a road trip to California, three weeks, Route Sixty-six, all the way up to San Francisco.'

'You don't think they're going to go to Vegas and elope?'

'She's not as foolish as her old mum.'

'Nineteen years! I'm so proud of you, Jules.'

'I've been very lucky, that's all.' She hesitated. 'Lenny? I would really love you to bring someone tomorrow night.'

Like who? Ellis would be totally unsuitable. Matt would no doubt start moaning about his bonus and Ellis would go off on some Russell Brand-style rant about rich banker scum.

'I do wish Matt had some nice single men at the office,' said

Juliet, apologetically. 'But most of them are already on their second wives.'

'Huh – the *upgrade*. I don't suppose Amy would be an appropriate plus one?'

Juliet laughed. Before Matt had secured Juliet's affections and been forced to play nice, he used to call Lenny and Amy 'The Witches of Eastbourne' – dumb, really, considering they were all north Londoners and had never even visited that part of Sussex.

'Andrew?' said Lenny. The only liability he posed was staring too adoringly at Juliet.

'I haven't seen him for yonks, yes – and maybe you two—'

'Stop!'

'Well. I hope you like the food, Matt thinks I've gone overboard.'

How was it fair that Juliet stayed forever slim, and Lenny was currently pin-balling between a size 12 and a 14? Juliet had what Lenny had always wanted – more than naturally straight blond hair or long legs, more even than the ability to always see the best in people. Lenny wanted Juliet's most enviable asset: self-control.

By the time Lenny hung up she felt considerably better. She'd leave Ellis for when she really needed him. For now a chicken tikka masala, rice and naan would do.

2

Juliet had woken on her anniversary to a cup of tea in bed, and then at breakfast the perfect gift – the Le Creuset pan she'd had her eye on for ages. Matt had managed to conceal that huge box from her! Impressive, given how well she knew every nook of their home, and how well she knew him. She'd been so lucky – protected from all the romantic horrors Lenny and Amy had endured. Yes, she'd had a rough ride with her mum's death at a young age but Matt had been by her side even back then. That terrible time had taught her a sense of perspective and also an ability to focus on the positives because you'd get swept away in the negatives if you let yourself. Juliet felt that both these lessons had helped her have – well, not a perfect marriage, but a perfectly happy one.

As he was leaving for work, Matt had turned to her in a mild panic. 'Jules, I don't know how neither of us spotted this earlier but we've made a terrible mistake!'

'What?'

'Having this party tonight?'

'Why, what's wrong?'

'It's Thursday!'

'Oh!' She laughed. Curry night – one of their favourite rituals.

'How about later we get into bed, get a curry, then turn out the lights and ignore the front door?' he grinned.

'We'll do that for our twentieth,' she said, kissing him goodbye.

Tomorrow she'd have to switch focus to Celina's recipes but for today she'd been enjoying the luxury of cooking for pure pleasure. By noon she was seven chores down - time for her favourite thing in the world: making bread. Juliet remembered, as a young girl, standing at her mother's elbow, listening to Joni Mitchell, carefully tapping the side of the sieve for her. Nearly twenty years gone and still Juliet missed her every day. The absence was always there but at the same time, standing here measuring the flour by eye with Joni Mitchell playing in the background, she felt her mother's presence too.

She wished Martha had met her grandma. Juliet's mother had given Juliet confidence – in herself, in others, in life. Juliet felt a lot of affection for Gloria but thank goodness Gloria wasn't her mother. That famous Eleanor Roosevelt quote about how no one can make you feel inferior without your consent? Clearly Mrs Roosevelt had not been round Gloria Dublonsky's flat during Lenny's teenage years. Those two had rowed so publically, guts spilling out everywhere. There was love underneath but boy, the surface was rough – no wonder Lenny had turned out so robust. Of course Juliet's family had had their issues but they'd stayed behind closed doors, where they belonged. And as for the Marlows – Matt's father'd had a decade-long affair with his secretary, but Cynthia's approach was to sweep the nasty little facts of life under the carpet. If they threatened to make themselves known in an unsightly bulge like a boa constrictor's lunch, she simply stamped on them.

Juliet finished kneading the dough and was putting a cloth over the bowl when her phone rang: Martha!

'Mum! Happy anniversary. Let me guess, you're in the kitchen, cooking something totally delicious and fattening.'

'Just making bread for the party.'

'Dad'll have a shit fit.'

'Oh he's turned in to such a fusspot. How's the dissertation coming along?'

'Bor-ing! Actually, I'd better go, I've got to be somewhere at 2 p.m. Have a great night, I love you.'

Juliet hung up and ran her finger down her to-do list: meringues for mini Eton mess. Mess, or messes? She took her pencil and carefully added the *e-s*.

She reached for a carton of eggs and a mixing bowl, cracked the first egg on the side and gently separated the sunshine orange yolk from the clinging white.

Lenny stared at the briefs on her desk. It was 5 p.m. now and she really should write up her analysis of Curry Me Badd, an app that mapped out the Indian restaurants in your area that had failed their food safety inspections. What would she put? Dumb, dumber, dumberer . . .

Instead, she took a pencil and drew a circle: a little pie chart of her problems. She drew a line straight down the middle. On the left half she wrote JOB. Yes, her salary was good, but money wasn't everything. Except it did buy her the freedom to go on holidays, be generous with her friends, purchase almost anything she wanted from Topshop.

But there was Occy: Lenny had no problem working for a woman eight years her junior. It was the fact Occy called important briefs 'Biggy Bigs' and lesser ones 'Biggy Smalls', and the fact she insisted Asia was spelled AISA, in spite of considerable evidence to the contrary. Mind you, Lenny would have a terrible boss anywhere she worked, and there'd always be office politics – she'd seen enough wildlife documentaries to know we're all just carnivorous mammals a heartbeat away from ripping each other's throats out.

A lack of fulfilment? Oh how Gloria would scorn that one: *You're not paid to enjoy yourself.* That was work.

In the right half of the circle she drew a line and wrote: ELLIS – then rubbed it out, doubled the area and wrote MEN. She knew she must rid herself of Ellis, and that in order to do so she should go back to online dating – but experience had taught her that Tinder and Guardian Soulmates made her want to kill herself. Not to be over dramatic, but they did. The dating process had become like reverse popcorn for Lenny. Before a date she'd foolishly allow a little puff of hope to swell inside her. But these puffs would shrivel in an instant, turning to bitter, hard kernels of disappointment. Take the most recent, James: on their first date he'd told Lenny he wasn't up for dating, he had *some issues.* Fuzzily philanthropic from the Picpoul, it hadn't occurred to Lenny to ask: *then why are you on a dating website?* James had called her daily to dissect his issues – clearly he *was* interested! Except all it meant was he was interested *in himself.* By the time Lenny figured this out, she realised she must have more issues than he did. Still, it made for a five-minute anecdote down the pub and her friends laughed, commiserated, then went home and thanked the Lord they weren't Lenny.

Not much pie chart left. Lenny's weight: eleven stone. She could carry it – she was five feet seven, curvy – still, there was too much wobble. She'd start exercising, soon, probably.

Another slice: her alcohol consumption. Theoretically she drank more than was strictly necessary according to the *Know Your Limits* pamphlet thrust her way at the GP. But if she didn't drink of an evening, what *would* she do? No, the drink wasn't the problem – the pamphlet was.

Existential angst: that was probably the entire chart if she was honest. She could work hard, have fun, be a good friend but really, what did any of it mean at the end of the day?

By the time she'd coloured each slice in pretty rainbow shades it was time to go home and prepare for Juliet's party.

Matt came home from work early, laden with a bunch of lilies. Juliet loved them, but oh those stamens, prone to falling when you were least expecting and leaving those indelible pollen stains.

'Amazing, Jules, you truly are,' he said, admiring the platters on the counter.

'Gin and tonic?' she said, opening the fridge. 'Oh bugger, I forgot the limes . . . ' She turned to see him looking anxiously at his phone. 'What's wrong?'

'Huh? Oh nothing . . . merger stuff. By the way I saw Caspar earlier – he and Danielle *are* coming after all; the au pair's sister is babysitting.'

Juliet turned back to the salmon canapés.

'Listen, Jules – I know you were fond of Emma, but Danielle's really nice.'

'She's not really a woman's woman.'

'Caspar swears things were over with Emma before they got together.'

'Men don't leave for an empty bed . . . '

Matt frowned. 'It is what it is. Besides, Danielle's a far better match, Emma was always travelling with work.'

As if *that* were an excuse. Still, Juliet must try to be less judgemental. Besides, you never knew what really went on in other people's marriages. She snipped the final fronds of dill on to the salmon. 'Did you speak to Martha?'

'When?' he said, warily.

'Today – she called to say happy anniversary.'

He tapped his pocket distractedly. 'She's busy with her essay. Listen, I've got to pop out.'

'What, *now*?'

'I didn't triple sign the paperwork for the M&A guys; it's sitting on my desk.'

'But it's already five o'clock. The guests will be here at seven thirty.'

'Jules, sorry, but I have to sign it today.'

'Can't they bike it to you?'

'It's quicker if I drive back in. I'll be back by six o'clock, I promise.'

'You won't, it's rush hour – get them to bike it!'

But he was already halfway out the door.

Amy had a habit of phoning Lenny at the most inconvenient times.

'Let me call you tomorrow,' said Lenny, plonking her bag in the hall and heading to her bedroom, kicking a jumper out of her path along the way.

'What are you doing tonight?'

'I'm busy.'

'Doing what?'

Lenny paused. She hated lying, but she knew what would come next. 'Going to Juliet's.'

'Just the two of you?'

'A few others . . . '

It wasn't that Juliet and Amy didn't get on, but had they met as adults they would never have become friends. Lenny was the linchpin of their relationship. Amy had made no effort when she was married, they'd drifted apart, yet she still seemed put out whenever she wasn't included.

'Would it be weird if I came with you?' said Amy.

'Well . . . it's a small anniversary party . . . Plus, you're not invited.'

'She didn't invite me to her *anniversary*?'

Lenny wanted to point out that the fact Amy didn't know it was Juliet's anniversary might be relevant.

'Will there be any nice men?' said Amy.

'Nope,' said Lenny. 'Hang on, what's happening with Seb?'

'Oh, he's still around.'

'When are you going to get rid of him?'

'I'm not the one who's married.'

Lenny had never understood why Amy had embraced mistress-hood quite so readily, given how she'd felt when her ex husband had cheated. 'You don't think you should go on a date with Andrew?' said Lenny, in the tone she normally used when trying to persuade Amy to drink a glass of water after a heavy night.

'A – he loves Juliet, and B – he's a rescuer. I'm a rescuer. You can't have two rescuers, one has to be the victim.'

Here we go again. Amy's mother was a therapist; that woman had a lot to answer for. Amy's view was that as long as she could give a narrative of what she was doing, in quasi-therapeutic jargon, she could do whatever she wanted. *I have low self-esteem plus separation issues and that's why I'm drawn to emotionally unavailable men and that's why I'm shagging my married osteopath – so there's really bugger all I can do about it.* Lenny was of the belief that every emotional mess Lenny had ever made was entirely Lenny's own fault.

Lenny put the phone on loudspeaker and went to her wardrobe. She took out her favourite Whistles dress and had gone as far as putting it on when she noticed a stain on the shoulder. She dumped it in the bag with the rest of her dry cleaning, then reached for a binge-proof loose black number.

'When can we go out then?' said Amy. 'Next Thursday?'

Lenny sifted through her make-up drawer for her eyeliner. 'I'm in Paris, Thursday till Saturday.'

'You're *always* away.'

Lenny turned to the mirror . . . Gillian Anderson, hey? She supposed she did have a similar shaped face: high cheekbones, large grey eyes. But she was willing to bet Gillian didn't have a perplexing new threat of nasal hair.

'Next Saturday night?' said Amy. 'Promise?'

Lenny checked her watch – Andrew would be here in two minutes, and she still needed mascara, a tooth clean, and to locate a pair of hole-free tights. 'Fine. I have to go.'

Lenny scrambled under the bed for the presents – a deluxe cheese knife set from Paxton and Whitfield, and something just for Juliet: a sunshine-yellow leather Smythson notebook with a personalised cover saying 'Bread, and Other Adventures'.

She was biting off the last stretch of Sellotape when Andrew called from outside – he was always so annoyingly punctual!

Six thirty p.m. Juliet had put on her favourite black dress, currently with an apron over the top. The candles were lit, the scent of freshly baked bread was filling the air and Juliet was now preparing to get royally pissed off when she finally heard Matt's car pull up outside.

She smoothed out her apron, reminded herself that being half an hour late wasn't that big a deal and looked down her list to see what was next . . . slice and butter bread for mini toasties . . .

'Sorry I'm late,' said Matt, from the hall. 'I brought you back a little something . . . '

'I hope it's some limes,' said Juliet, putting down her pencil and turning to see Martha, hovering by the kitchen door with a sheepish grin on her face.

'Oh, you little devil, you, and your father!' Juliet felt her heart expand as she put her arms around her daughter's shoulders and hugged her. 'Darling, you're so slim!'

'Mum, I'm so not.'

Juliet stepped back to take a proper look at her. Since the day she was born, all she saw when she looked at her daughter's face was light. 'Can you stay for the weekend?'

'I have to be back for a tutorial at noon tomorrow.'

'And it's OK that you're here tonight?'

'It's totally fine – it's not like I don't ever go out in Manchester. Anyway, I'm handing it in next Friday and then I'm free!'

'And you fly Saturday week, so I won't see you before then?'

'You're seeing me now,' said Martha, laughing.

'Don't forget: lots of suncream. Don't let Nate drive too fast. And call us any time if you need anything at all.'

'Mum, it's all under control. I'll dump my bag and then come and give you a hand.'

Juliet gave her another hug, then marched into the hall to see Matt looking very pleased with himself.

'How long have you been planning this?'

'Is that your way of saying thank you?' he smiled. If anything he was getting more handsome with age. That dimple on his right cheek, his undiminished head of thick dark hair, those clear blue eyes. She moved to kiss him just as his phone beeped and he let out a sigh. 'Bloody merger . . . '

She watched him walk down the hall and felt a profound sense of gratitude.

Lenny and Andrew had been friends ever since they were fourteen and had both been fast-tracked for maths GCSE. Danny Freeman had called them The Mathletes, which was a mild improvement for Andrew on Brace Face, and a definite one for Lenny on Lezzy.

Juliet, ever the romantic, was convinced Lenny would eventually end up with her teenage crush. Eventually had been and gone. There had been an incident, twenty-three years ago, when Lenny had lured Andrew round to 'revise' and they'd ended up in her room, drinking Malibu neat from the bottle. She'd demanded he teach her a complicated hip-hop dance move, conspiring to pull him towards her and in the process he'd tripped hard, chipping his newly straightened front tooth on her desk. The swell of humiliation had lingered in Lenny long after Andrew's lip had stopped bleeding. She'd grudgingly accepted they'd just be friends, and now even though he'd grown into a tall, handsome, successful city analyst, he really was like an annoying kid brother, and whenever anyone said, 'You two'd be perfect together,' she'd reply, 'He'd rather knock his own front tooth out,' and they'd both laugh.

'How are you, Len?' said Andrew, when she finally clambered into the cab.

Lenny pondered the question sincerely. 'Average.'

He laughed and put his arm around her. 'You can just say fine you know, that's all anyone ever wants to hear.'

'Fine then. How are you? Are you over that Tinder girl?'

'Oh, totally – she was bonkers. Anyway, I've got three new dates lined up this weekend.'

'Already? You're a nightmare!'

'Me? Why?'

'London is full of men like you – a hundred girls in your inbox, dumping anyone with the slightest flaw, it's impossible for a thirty-seven-year-old woman in London to find a normal boyfriend: impossible.'

'That's rubbish. Vicky at work's forty, she met some guy on a plane three months ago and now they're engaged.'

'Really?' said Lenny, hope mingling with doubt in her voice. Very occasionally Lenny would hear a story like this and then cling to its hem like a Victorian urchin in a snowstorm.

'Anyway,' said Andrew. 'Your problem is you're too fussy.'

Lenny thought about Ellis. She wasn't too fussy – she was nowhere near fussy enough.

'I haven't seen Juliet since your birthday carnage,' said Andrew. Juliet always showed up at Lenny's parties, invariably making polite excuses for why Matt couldn't join her. Last year the party had been particularly drunken and Lenny had awoken to a flat scattered with Hula Hoops, which was actually quite handy with a hangover.

'I hope she'll serve more than crisps,' said Andrew, as though reading her mind.

'Juliet's an amazing cook, she bakes all her own bread, makes her own stocks.'

'She's basically perfect,' said Andrew, sighing. 'Get her to give you some tips.'

If only Lenny lived in New York, where her lack of culinary skill would be seen as normal or even glamorous, rather than marking her out as a failure of a woman.

'Leonora,' said Matt, giving her a peck on the cheek, and Andrew a firm, matey handshake. Lenny tried to convince herself Matt had forgotten how much she hated being called her full name, but couldn't quite get there. 'Jules is busy in the kitchen, come on through.'

Stepping into Juliet's house always felt like walking into the pages of a magazine – not an impossibly out-of-reach one like *World of Interiors*, more like *Easy Living,* whereas Lenny's flat was more *Smash Hits*. Over the years Juliet had found fabrics and objects others had failed to see the beauty in, and integrated them seamlessly with Matt's taste in expensive mid-century Danish classics. The end result was a happy marriage, stylish and comfortable, all the right boxes ticked with just enough cobalt blue not to frighten the horses.

Wow, Juliet had surpassed herself tonight! The elongated oak dining table looked like a spread from one of Celina's cookbooks, laden with delights: golden mini pizzas, jewelled with olives and sun-dried tomatoes; a sky-blue plate of green cos leaves, brimming with lush coral-pink prawn cocktail; a tower of mini potatoes with chilli and sour cream on the side.

'Lenny!' Lenny turned and did a double take. The girl in front of her looked so much more sophisticated than Martha had done last summer – long dark hair loosely pinned, a simple black shift dress showing off her healthy figure.

'You look stunning,' said Lenny, giving her a hug. 'Jules didn't say you were coming.'

'It was Dad's idea, he wanted to surprise Mum.'

'Well! Nineteen years. It's a miracle in this day and age.'

'Cringey having parents who are so perfect,' said Martha, looking adoringly at her father, pouring drinks at the sideboard. 'Uh-oh. Looks like somebody needs a hand . . . '

Lenny glanced over into the main space. She recognised a few of the couples seated on the sofa: Matt's best friend from work, Caspar, his hand resting on his wife Danielle's straightened back. And another banker, she'd forgotten his name, with his wife. She'd had some work done – the forehead, and possibly the mouth.

Lenny joined Andrew on the sofa where the men were talking interest rates. Lenny's interest rate was minus two per cent, and after smiling into the distance for as long as she could bear, she took her bag and slipped out to the kitchen. Juliet was assembling mini Parmesan tarts in concentric circles on a ceramic dish. When she saw Lenny her face lit up and she pulled her close for a hug.

'A little something for you,' said Lenny, handing her the gift-wrapped notebook. 'My goodness, you've got enough canapés to feed a small army.'

'Oh don't! Matt made a right old fuss about the menu, he's still on this tedious health kick.'

Lenny had noticed the expense account dinners catching up with Matt; she was surprised his vanity hadn't kicked in sooner. 'This is lovely,' she said, admiring the platter's design, white wallflowers with gold corollas on a scarlet background.

'Matt brought it back from Warsaw, some work conference.'

'Polish pottery?'

'I use it all the time on shoots. Actually, if you could pass these round, I can start on the Lenny specials.'

'These are the greatest!' said Lenny, spotting the perfect mini cheese toasties.

'It's tradition, Lenny. How could I not?'

Lenny took the tarts through to the living room where they were met with a chorus of delight. Though why did Matt have to look so irritated with them when three minutes after she'd placed them on the coffee table he'd grabbed two in one hand?

The party was in full swing, the room buzzing with chatter and the occasional guffaw. Lenny drifted around the space, a lonely atom, failing to attach herself to the firmly bonded molecular groups that kept forming and reforming in tight clusters. She didn't fit with the mums; nor with the trophy wives picking at their lettuce leaves; nor the bankers. Cautious of getting too drunk she sought refuge at the buffet, and was in the middle of trying to manoeuvre a mini chilli baked potato into her mouth without spilling sour cream on her chin when Matt came up behind her.

'Canapé chasing again are we, Leonora?'

Lenny smiled weakly and placed the potato back on her plate. 'Great party, Matt. Are you having a good time?'

'Impossible not to!' he said, gesturing towards the crowd. 'What's going on in your life, then? Any more dating horror stories?'

'Nope.'

'How's your mate Amy? Who's she been shagging?'

'How's Danny Freeman? Who *hasn't* he been shagging?'

Matt grudgingly emitted a laugh.

'Where is he?' said Lenny. 'On a beach somewhere, getting a tattoo of Peter Pan on his arse?'

'I don't know,' said Matt briskly. 'So: Juliet said you've just come back from Italy?'

'Rome yesterday, Paris next week. And I hear you had fun in Warsaw?'

'Pardon?'

'Juliet said you were at a conference?'

'Ah, last year. I'm away so often.'

This was something they had in common: every month walking through another airport on autopilot, checking in to another bland expensive hotel that could have been anywhere.

'Do you ever get a feeling of dread, walking into yet another hotel room alone?' said Lenny. 'Or is it different when you've got someone to come home to?'

Matt's brow creased, as if Lenny had asked him how much he earned. 'It is what it is,' he said, then turned to find someone better to talk to.

Lenny picked up her potato again and ate it in two messy bites. Foolish of her to think that after all these years they might be almost-friends. Matt only ever tolerated her for Juliet's sake or when playing to an audience. The only common ground they shared was Juliet.

Lenny headed towards a cluster of Matt's colleagues and their wives and hovered awkwardly on the periphery until Danielle gave her a vague look of recognition.

'Amazing food, isn't it?' said Lenny, looking apologetically at her plate.

Danielle nodded offhandedly.

Lenny persevered. 'Jules is such a domestic wonder woman.'

'I wish I had time to make my own bread.' Danielle's tone suggested that baking your own bread was as peculiar and low budget as crafting your own toilet paper.

'Jules is always telling me it's easier than it looks,' said Lenny warmly.

'I wasn't saying I *couldn't* do it – I suppose one makes time according to one's priorities.'

Matt walked over to the group bearing a magnum of Champagne.

'Are you off anywhere for Easter, Matt?' said Danielle, holding her glass out flirtatiously.

'Sadly not. I'm in Japan, and my clever wife has landed herself a great little gig.'

'Her cooking thingy?'

'Her new book's a bestseller,' said Lenny, pointedly.

'And what will you do in the summer?' said Danielle, turning to one of the other wives.

Lenny listened to talk of boutique hotels, a road trip along the Amalfi coast. All this forward planning. Holidays had begun to fill Lenny with dread. She had no plans for Easter; no doubt it would be spent with Amy – or being ditched by Amy if lover-boy was around.

Lenny noticed one of the platters on the table was empty. She took it through to the kitchen and counted to sixty, slowly. If this was anyone's party but Jules's, she would make her excuses and leave.

An hour later, Lenny was stuck with Danielle again, this time by the dessert platters.

'We have met before, haven't we?' said Danielle, examining Lenny more closely.

'Several times.'

'You work in NPD-tech?' Danielle picked a walnut off a brownie and popped it into her mouth. 'I'm gluten intolerant. You're the one with twins?'

'Yes tech, no children,' said Lenny, taking a large bite of brownie, and wiping her bottom lip with her thumb.

'What will you do about children?'

'*Do*?' said Lenny. 'Did I forget to *do* something?'

'You must want them?'

Lenny hated this question. She had considered having kids with her ex, Toby, in her early thirties, but she hadn't been ready. She had not dated anyone since who'd make a good father. Single parenthood looked hard. She worried she might regret this decision after it was too late. But that didn't seem like a good enough reason to bring a small person into this world.

'Are you SI?' said Danielle, pursing her lips in concern.

'Am I *what?*'

'Socially infertile, circumstantially childless?'

Lenny paused in shock. Are you SI, socially incompetent? she wanted to reply, but reached for a mini lemon meringue pie instead.

'When I met Caspar he had two from his first marriage,' said Danielle, picking the walnut from a different brownie. 'No overlap, obviously!'

No problem stealing other people's walnuts, noted Lenny.

'I'd just been put on the board but I prioritised my ovaries.' She grasped Lenny's wrist, and Lenny felt Danielle's forefinger still damp from where it had been in her mouth. 'I'm like you – a high-achiever, very career focused – but let me tell you, your purpose on this planet is to have children. It's what gives life meaning.'

Lenny pulled her hand back. You are not like me in the slightest, she thought. I would never embarrass another woman by probing her fertility status, nor tell her that her life has no meaning for a choice she might not have made. She swallowed the small burp of indignation that had risen up her gullet and scanned the room for Andrew.

Danielle stared over at Martha who was standing with Matt. 'She's lost her puppy fat.'

'Martha was never fat.'

'She looks so much like Matt: wonderful bone structure.'

'She gets that from Juliet,' said Lenny, curtly.

'Those cheekbones.' Danielle's gaze lingered on Matt's face. 'That's definitely his side of the family.'

'If you'll excuse me,' said Lenny. 'I'm going to check if Jules needs some help.'

* * *

Matt stood by the fireplace, tapping a fork against his wine glass as the guests giggled into an expectant hush. 'Hang on, where is she, I've lost her?'

'Run off with the postman!' said Caspar.

'Do postmen still exist?' said Danielle witheringly, and the crowd snickered.

'Juliet, Juliet, wherefore art thou?' he said, reaching out for her.

She shook her head in embarrassment. 'We agreed, no speeches. You promised!'

'I'll keep it short, two minutes max.'

'Bet you say that to all the girls!' said Caspar.

Matt smirked, then cleared his throat: 'Nineteen years ago, this woman did me the honour of becoming my wife. Look at her, isn't she a knock out? It feels like only yesterday I was sitting behind her in double physics, trying not to stare at her Bunsen burner. Thank you, my love, for being an excellent wife, an amazing mother – a shining example to our beautiful girl. I've bought you a little something for putting up with me for so long.'

'No!' she murmured, grabbing his arm. 'You gave me the casserole pan.'

'It's only small,' he said, taking out a pale blue box from his jacket pocket.

'Open it!' said Danielle.

'I'll do it, darling.' Matt lifted the lid and showed Juliet, and then the group, the necklace – a simple pendant with two interlocking circles in white and rose gold.

'Tiffany's?' said Danielle.

'Only the best,' said Matt.

'Ouch, must have cost a bob,' said Caspar.

'She's worth it,' said Matt.

She's earned it, thought Lenny.

'So, what's your secret?' said Danielle.

'Huh?' said Matt, smiling benevolently at her.

'Your secret? The secret to staying in love so long?'

Matt looked down at his wife as she raised her face to his. He kissed her briefly, tenderly.

Lenny looked at Juliet, radiant in the soft glow of the candles – her heart-shaped face, her wide, generous smile. Lenny was glad, in spite of her childish dislike for Matt, that she had a friend who gave her faith that love and happiness could exist – even if not for Lenny.

'Matt's such a good bloke,' said Andrew, as they sat in the cab on their way home.

'I guess.' Apart from the flare-up at the buffet table, Matt had been on decent form, attentive to Juliet, uxorious, even. But his charm sat uneasily with Lenny: it was too much like a tap – on and off, just like that. She hated herself for needing to find fault with his behaviour, still the words came out. 'You don't think he was rude, being on his phone, literally one minute after he finished that gushy speech?'

'Was he? I didn't notice.'

'He was on it at least half a dozen times tonight.'

'He's working on a huge merger, Lenny.'

'So? He's a banker, not a doctor.'

'It's money, way more important than life or death.' Andrew let out a well-fed, tired sigh. 'I wish I was still married.'

'How are those maintenance payments working out for you?' said Lenny, resting her head on his shoulder.

'You can't deny Charlotte was incredibly beautiful.'

'Incredibly toxic, more like,' said Lenny – then reached out and squeezed his hand in apology.

'I think it's great you and Juliet are still close.'

'Why wouldn't we be?'

'You're so different – she's a grown up.'

'Shut up, dude!'

'Case in point! Who calls people dude?'

She punched his arm gently. He wasn't wrong though, Lenny did think of Juliet as more of an adult because Juliet had done the hardest thing in the world: handled the relentless anxiety and challenges of raising a child. All Lenny had done was take care of herself, and she'd barely succeeded at that.

Lenny yawned and leaned her head against the window as they drove in silence past the Heath. Ah, The Spaniard's Inn! Many a teenage night had been spent in that pub's garden, drinking Archers and lemonade, smoking Silk Cut, looking forward to the day she'd stop feeling left out, boyfriend-less, not enough.

'Lenny – did I snog Amy in that pub?'

'No, that was playing Spin The Bottle at Danny Freeman's house – you kept trying to point the bottle to Juliet, I was pining for Danny . . . '

'What an epic loser!'

'Me, or Danny?'

'Danny! I haven't seen him in years! Is he still working in that pub in Camden?'

'No, but he's still an epic loser. He's now got some dodgy van, does odd jobs.'

'Why wasn't he there tonight?'

'Dunno. Must be away, surfing. Ridiculous, he's nearly forty – *he* needs to grow up.'

'You used to fancy him so much. Do you remember that time you got your fake ID in the name of Lenny Freeman? And then you left it in the common room and Mrs Berle found it!'

'Andrew, don't,' said Lenny, burying her face in her hands.

'Ah poor Lenny,' he said, putting his arm around her. 'You always did have such terrible taste in men.'

When she got home she saw two texts from Ellis, currently saved in her phone as 'Use-ellis': *You out and about? Just finishing a gig in town.* Then twenty minutes later, *Fancy a drink?*

A drink. Why didn't he just say what he meant: 'Fancy some short-term gratification that's physically very satisfying but emotionally pretty damaging for you? Go on, please, because this set-up's pretty sweet for me!'

An overwhelming wave of sheer loneliness crashed over Lenny. Those couples earlier, some on second marriages, some with second homes. Lenny would never catch up with them now. She'd never have a life more together than not, a beautiful daughter to be proud of. Matt's speech had triggered the dull ache she felt in her chest every time she saw couples in John Lewis picking out soft throws.

If Lenny had married when Juliet had, she'd definitely have come unstuck by now. She'd been a mess at nineteen, a barely formed adult, she'd hardly known herself. She had changed significantly over the years, had she not? Learned a few lessons. And she'd made something of her life: she had a good job, great friends, she'd seen parts of the world. She'd never had to concern herself with catchment areas, after-school rotas. She'd built her own permanently single world, no less valid than a shared one. *Socially infertile?* Huh.

She typed a reply to Ellis: *Don't text me again unless you're willing and able to give me more than just sex.* Then deleted it in a panic, and wrote: *Tired. Speak soon x*

She went to the bathroom, squeezed the toothpaste forcefully through the pinhole gap left in the solidified blob at the end of the tube, absolutely nothing to do with her not putting the lid on. She was far too tired to take her make-up off, but crawled into bed and tried to stop feeling so bloody sorry for herself.

Juliet stood in the bathroom, removing the last traces of mascara, replaying the evening. She hoped Lenny had enjoyed herself – she'd seen her with Martha, and Danielle, God, Danielle was hard work sometimes. 'I think it was a success, don't you?' she called out to Matt. There was no response. She walked back into the bedroom to find him frowning at his phone.

'Huh?' he muttered, putting his phone down. 'What, darling?'

She sat and stroked his hair, his forehead felt hot. 'Are you OK?'

He took her hand from his brow and held it over the duvet.

'Matt, please don't be one of those people who works twelve-hour days then has a heart attack the minute you retire.' She squeezed his hand. 'You could change jobs, take a drop in salary. Now Danny's not in the flat, let's sell it? And sell this place, buy somewhere smaller, now it's just us two. Help Martha when she graduates, maybe free up some cash so that we could go travelling . . . '

He let out a deep sigh, brought her hand to his lips and kissed it. 'Darling, I'm tired . . . '

She turned out the bathroom light, then climbed under the duvet beside him.

3

The following Thursday morning Juliet was halfway through making toast when she remembered Matt was off carbs again. When he came into the kitchen he took one look at her plate and frowned.

'Don't panic!' said Juliet. 'It's not for you.' Honestly, he was so unrelaxed about this whole diet thing.

'But you won't eat four slices by yourself.'

'I might do, Carb Cop. Anyway, what are you worrying about? You're looking so slim.'

'But it doesn't help me to see a mountain of carb drowning in butter. You're trying to sabotage my attempts to take better care of myself, can you stop making bread, please?'

Now she was laughing. 'I forgot and they were already—' Hang on. Why was she defending herself over two extra pieces of toast? 'Darling?'

'What?' he said, tapping his jacket pocket. 'Where's my phone? Where is it?'

'Probably where you left it,' said Juliet, getting up from the table and taking another bite. No wonder he was so grouchy, missing out on Marmite and melted butter, all that salty goodness. 'Here it is,' she said, bringing it in from the hall table. 'You've got messages.'

He grabbed it off her. 'Listen, I'm not sure when I'll be back . . . '

'But it's curry night? You don't have to have the rice.'

'I've got dinner with the Germans.'

'*Again?*'

'I did tell you.'

Juliet frowned. 'I would have remembered.'

'Like you remembered about the toast?' He gave her a peck on the cheek. 'Don't wait up.'

Juliet unstacked the dishwasher as she heard Matt rev his engine.

That Porsche – Lenny witheringly called it a menoporsche – it really was such a cliché. Mid-life, though: where had all the time gone? That was a cliché too – but she didn't feel middle aged. Still, she wasn't young any more, maybe she was forgetting things? Only last month she'd forgotten his Geneva trip and had been up half the night worrying when he hadn't come home. You bring up a child, see her safely off to uni and just when you're primed to enjoy middle age doing all the lovely things you've planned together, you get stricken with something like early onset Alzheimer's, how awful would that be? She picked the last plate from the dishwasher and flicked the tiniest fleck of caked-on sauce off it. Enough with such maudlin thoughts.

She looked at her to-do list. Since the party last week she'd written sixteen Easter recipes but she still needed sixteen more for Monday. She spent the day working intensively. At 7.30 p.m. she poured herself a glass of red and thought of her husband, sitting in some steakhouse having to small-talk clients. She took a long sip – the taste of cherries – and watched the liquid slowly slide down the glass. She'd worked ever since Martha started school, she'd have been bored senseless as a tennis-club wife. Still her career – or series of jobs – would never have kept them in wine like this. Last week at the party Danielle had done her usual trick of trying to undermine her – she'd said something so patronising, *how could Juliet feel satisfaction without a career of her own.* Juliet had pointed out that she did have a career, but Danielle had said, 'I meant – you're always in the shadow of that other woman.'

Juliet glanced at the photo on the mantelpiece of Martha with Nate. Nate was a lovely boy, but Juliet's heart ached at the thought that he, or anyone else, might ever hurt her. Still, Martha was resilient, she had more confidence than Juliet ever had at nineteen. If Martha continued to study hard she'd be in a strong position to do whatever she wanted with her life, she'd have opportunities Juliet never had. So really, when Danielle insinuated that Juliet's life had lacked achievement, Juliet pictured Martha – happy, loving, and with her future bright in front of her – and figured: that's achievement enough.

The drink had taken the edge off Juliet's hunger. She ran a bath, leaned back in the warm water, felt the day slip away. She was in danger of dozing off when the phone rang – probably a dropped sales call and sure enough when she finally wrapped herself in her bathrobe it was number withheld. She turned her phone off, climbed into bed. What joy: clean sheets, plumped pillows. She read ten pages of her Anne Tyler, felt tiredness seep through her body. She should wait up to talk weekend plans with Matt . . . Tomorrow . . .

She slept deeply and woke refreshed – except that when she looked at the duvet next to her it was undisturbed.

Her immediate thought was car crash, and as she waited for her phone to come back to life, panic rising, she pictured Matt having one too many drinks at dinner, getting into the Porsche, jumping a red light . . .

No. There was a missed call from him at 11.30 p.m. and a voice message. She listened to it in shock. She felt the blood drain from her face as a sudden dizziness took hold. It was quite lucky she was already lying down.

PART TWO

'Ignorance is bliss.'
Thomas Gray, 'Ode on a distant prospect of
Eton college'

4

That same Thursday morning Lenny was on the Eurostar, entering the darkness of the tunnel, when paranoia closed in on her. Occy had repeatedly talked her up as a rising star but perhaps Lenny had actually been sent to 'Wappen: The Next Generation' as a falling one. The course sub-title – 'Interpersonal Skills 2.0: BE BETTER' – sounded ominous.

As an icebreaker the group introduced themselves by stating the animal they most resembled. If these were the Leaders of the Digital Tomorrow, the future did not look bright. Katja, Wappen-Slovenia, was a cat: 'I'm independent. Beautiful. Also, my name in English is like cat.' Doug, Wappen-Melbourne, was a lion: 'Blatantly head of the pack.' Lenny, who'd done this exercise many times before, chose sloth – she liked the confused reaction this provoked.

The workshop promised a mix of scientific studies, NLP and more practical problem solving in break-out clusters – a phrase which reminded Lenny of the misery of her teenage skin, but also of the strangely addictive smell of Oxy 10 face-cleaning pads. Lenny sat in the back row trying to eat crisps quietly. She became quite absorbed in one case study – 'Dopamine Addiction in Rodents and What It Teaches Us About the Internet'. In the experiment a group of rats were given a lever to access a pleasure-drug: they rapidly over-stimulated themselves to death. The speaker explained that the neural pathways in the rodent brain behaved identically to those in humans online seeking constant new stimulus on Twitter and Facebook. Lenny felt sorry for those poor rats, but also quite sorry for herself because this session was taking place in a basement and she couldn't access the Wi-Fi.

In Friday morning's 'Conflict Role Play', Lenny was playing MD of a failing business. The others had to gang up and attack. Lenny sat calmly as Katja launched into an am-dram tirade and when Doug called Lenny's strategy 'as tired as yesterday's sushi', she'd merely smiled and said, 'Cheers Dougy.' At the end, the moderator commended Lenny on her unfazeability. *Seriously?* Rise to the bait during this piddly classroom exercise? Never. Put me in a room with Occy and Nick brainstorming new beanbags and you'd eat those words with mustard.

In the afternoon there was a session on visualisation, a concept Lenny had long had a major issue with. In her youth she'd occasionally pulled the right end of the wishbone and yet all she had wished for back then – to live in a *Dynasty* style mansion, to be blonde, and for Rob Lowe to rescue her from life's myriad disappointments – all these had yet to come to pass. (Except for a brief encounter with the Sun-In at school, and that had turned out way more ginger than blonde.)

'Visualisation is not about wishing without in-tention or at-tention,' said the session leader, pointing sternly at the group. 'You need concrete examples. What do the next six months look like for my personal brand?'

'Utter bollocks,' said Lenny to Katja, who was scribbling away intensely. 'What have you written?'

'Promotion, twenty per cent pay rise benchmarked against inter-agency peers and Become Industry Role Model. You?'

'Hmm, similar . . . ' said Lenny, scanning her list:

A single adult male boyfriend
Must have proper job (not drummer)
Must like spicy food

Lenny folded the list and put it in her jacket pocket.

When the session was over Lenny saw a missed call from Juliet and tried calling back, but it went straight to voicemail and when Lenny went to supper she had visions of a rat's paws constantly refreshing a Twitter feed, and left her phone in the room. Dinner was interminable: Jon De Jan, MD of Wappen-Rotterdam, showed up to pontificate over a grey regional sausage and Lenny realised that his seminar tomorrow was one she'd already suffered through twice.

That night Lenny dreamed her familiar dream. The plot remained consistent – Lenny en route to sit maths A level having bunked the entire two years of class – but the styling varied. In tonight's version Lenny was sporting a Rachel haircut and bootleg trousers. She always woke from this dream having to kick the anxiety off her like a sweaty polyester sheet. Over breakfast she sat, chewing yesterday's stale croissants, wondering why her subconscious persisted in this fashion – a man in her position wouldn't doubt himself, why *was* that? Did highly educated middle-class female rats dream they were imposters too?

'Is that yours?' Katja pointed disapprovingly to the phone, ringing silently on the table.

Lenny saw Juliet's name on the display and took the call outside. 'Help, I need rescuing!'

'Oh. You're still away?' Juliet's voice sounded unusually flat.

'Why, what's wrong?'

'It's nothing.'

Juliet told her about Matt's message. It didn't sound like nothing to Lenny. She made her excuses, hopped in a taxi and was on the next Eurostar home.

Juliet was sitting at the back of the coffee shop, a glass of water untouched in front of her.

'I'm sorry,' she said, standing slowly to greet Lenny. 'I must look rough.' Lenny would not have gone as far as 'rough'. Even in the throes of labour Lenny suspected Juliet had looked like an Estée Lauder model; still it was fair to say she wasn't looking as radiant as she had done at last week's party.

Juliet shook her head apologetically. 'The minute you said you were on the train back home I realised I've dragged you away from work for absolutely no reason.' She sounded like she almost believed it herself.

'Tell me again,' said Lenny. 'What exactly did the message say?'

Juliet handed Lenny her mobile as if it were a jumbled Rubik's cube. Lenny listened, then pressed repeat. Matt sounded unnatural, rehearsed: 'Juliet: I believe I must take a few days out for myself – to work through some personal development issues. Nothing to do with you and nothing you need worry about. I know you'll understand.'

'I called him as soon as I got it,' said Juliet. 'He just kept saying it's nothing to do with me.'

'Has anything been going on recently?'

Juliet shrugged. 'Nothing I could put my finger on.'

'But . . . ?'

'He's been a little distant . . . '

'Since when?'

Juliet stared up at the ceiling. 'About the time this whole merger started.'

'Where's he staying?'

'Brown's Hotel. What do you think, detective?' Juliet laughed, nervously. 'I'm over-reacting, aren't I? Matt said I have nothing to worry about.'

And if you lived in a world where people said what they meant – rather than the exact opposite – you might be all right, thought Lenny, with a dull sense of dread.

'Actually . . . there was something,' said Juliet. 'He picked this petty little fight . . . said I was "sabotaging" his diet . . . ' She tapped her finger lightly against her spoon. 'Lenny, I think I might have to call his doctor. His irritability, the gym, the Porsche . . . I thought that was him heading to forty, but what if all those are signs?'

'Of what?'

'Something in his brain?'

Lenny looked down into her cup.

'Lenny, I read this terrible article about a man who gambled away all his family's money, turns out he had a brain tumour, it entirely transformed his personality . . . '

To be fair it was a possibility. But Lenny's thoughts turned, as they so often did, to her recent victory in the pub quiz. Lenny had won the bonus round, first to decipher an anagram – Mac Scar Orzo = Occam's Razor: the most obvious solution is usually the right one. Matt loses weight, buys a sports car, stays away from home. Obvious solution = it's not his brain misbehaving, it's an organ considerably lower down.

'What are you doing tonight?' said Lenny. 'Do you want to come out with Amy and me? Or I can cancel her and come round?'

'Lenny, he'll probably be home by the time I get there. And you mustn't say anything, he'll be cross I've made such a fuss.'

Juliet sat back in her car and tried to stay calm. What if it was an aneurism? She clicked her seat belt into place. Someone could go – just like that.

When she pulled up outside her house, the drive was empty. She filled the kettle for two. He'd be home soon, with flowers and an apology. What sort of a neurotic shrew would she be if she hassled him the one time in his life he'd asked for space?

Apparently Amy's poor timekeeping was due to her father abandoning her when she was seven. Lenny had pointed out that she could out-absent-father Amy any day of the week – to no end. Lenny wouldn't have minded so much if she was waiting in a pub, but Amy had insisted on this dreadful Soho members' club, full of people who called themselves 'Curators'.

Ah, finally! Amy, sweeping in with all eyes on her. She wasn't always the prettiest in the room, her brown eyes were small, her chin a little pointy, but she was usually the most captivating. Partly it was her hair, luscious caramel locks falling heavily down her back; partly her legs, tonight sheathed in skinny jeans that would never be Lenny's friend; but mostly it was her confidence. Even guys who found her terrifying (around 40% in Lenny's experience) were incapable of saying no to her. Lenny thought of Amy as a lily, demanding constant attention but rewarding the world with her exotic and obvious bloom. Lenny was more cactus – demanding precious little, with her spikes on the surface for all to see.

'What a day!' said Amy, flinging her jacket down. 'Can I squeeze in next to you, I hate having my back to the room?'

Lenny shuffled along the bench. 'How's your dodgy bloke?'

'Seb? I've just been for an early dinner with him.'

'On a Saturday night? Doesn't his wife wonder where he is?'

'Don't know, don't care.'

'Really? Don't you ever feel guilty about her?'

'Lenny, when I found out Gary had been cheating on me, you

know I blamed The Heavy-Jawed Slut, which frankly wasn't fair because she wasn't the one who'd stood opposite me in church and made vows to forsake all others. It's not my responsibility if Seb cheats on his wife, it's his; besides, men don't cheat unless something's wrong in their marriage.'

'You don't think some men cheat even when they love their wives?'

'Oh Lenny, when were you last in love?'

'Seven years ago, with Toby.'

'And you loved him?'

'I did,' said Lenny, recalling it like a film she'd enjoyed but couldn't quite remember the plot of.

'And how many people did you shag when you were together?'

'None!'

'Right – so unless you're a total shit, you don't shag other people if you love someone. Why are you asking? Have you met a married man? Oooh, you've been naughty!'

'No,' said Lenny crossly. 'I haven't.'

'Well you will one day. And in the meantime, stop being so judgemental. How was Juliet's party then? Is that guy at the bar checking me out?'

Lenny glanced at him: not un-attractive – face like a friendly, intelligent mouse. He smiled in their direction.

'Nearly twenty years,' said Amy, in wonder. 'Juliet's done well to hold on to that idiot.'

'Matt's done well to hold on to her!'

'No, I meant he's so vain.'

'So?'

'It's always the vain ones who stray. Take Seb – says he's a doctor, *no*: he's an *osteopath*, not a real doctor. Speak of the devil,' she said, reaching for her phone.

A 'Girls Night Out' Amy style – Amy on the phone and Lenny nursing her drink alone.

'Oh, nice of you to join me,' said Lenny. 'Ten minutes on that call you were.'

'Chill *out*, Yoda!'

'Why do you waste your time with Seb?' she said, irritably.

'Same reason you waste yours with Ellis. I'm going to the bar to check out that guy.'

Lenny watched as the man at the bar inspected Amy then looked over and caught Lenny's eye. Amy hovered next to him, then shrugged and returned to her seat.

'Waiting for his date,' said Amy.

'Why, because he didn't chat you up?'

'I have a sixth sense.'

'Did you have a sixth sense about Gary?'

'In what way?'

'Did you suspect anything? Was he staying late at the office, that sort of thing?'

'*Gary?* I'd never have believed Gary was working late. He bought some awful lumberjack shirts and changed aftershave. He might as well have worn a sandwich board.'

'So you chose to ignore it?'

'There are strong anthropological reasons why denial exists, Lenny.' For a moment Amy's smile faltered, then returned as her phone flashed again.

Lenny frowned. 'Could you put your phone away, because my whole life is phones and I'd like two hours where we interact like humans used to before smartphones existed?'

'You're just pissed off no one's texting you,' said Amy, heading back outside. The man at the bar's gaze followed her thoughtfully, then he slowly made his way over to Lenny. Up close he looked like a slightly sexier woodland creature than a mouse – inquisitive warm brown eyes, more like a badger.

'I couldn't help noticing your friend's disappeared again.'

'Her name's Amy. She's head of a PR agency. What else do you want to know?'

'Your name?'

'Lenny.'

'Ben.'

She gave Ben her firmest *don't mess with my friend* handshake.

'Can I sit with you till she's back?' he said.

'She may be some time – I hope your line in patter's good.'

He laughed. 'Does Amy do this often?'

'Yep,' said Lenny, regretting she'd allowed him to sit, when all he was doing was ingratiating himself while fishing for information about Amy.

'Are you guys coming upstairs to eat later?' he said.

'No.'

'Definitely not tempted by the menu?'

'My friend already ate,' said Lenny, raising her eyebrows.

He relaxed back into the seat. 'So – what do you do, Lenny?'

'Boring research stuff, and you?'

'Not boring research stuff! I'm an epidemiologist.'

'Viruses?'

'That's the one.'

'When I was young, I watched this TV show about rabies – it was terrifying.'

'*The Mad Death*! That's what first got me interested in the subject. You don't look old enough to have watched TV in the early eighties.'

A charmer, thought Lenny. But handsome when he smiled.

He glanced at his watch.

'Are you waiting for someone?' Maybe he'd have a friend, and Lenny wouldn't have to play gooseberry on Amy's return.

'Just a mate. They're late. I'd better see if they've gone straight up to the restaurant. Sorry I can't wait till Amy's back.'

'Do you want to leave me your number and I'll pass it on?'

'To Amy? No! Not at all.'

'Oh. I thought . . . ?'

'Why do you think I came over?'

'Oh!'

'Do you by any chance like curry?'

'I love it.'

'Me too: if you're free next week maybe we could go for a bite to eat?'

Interesting job, single, likes spicy food . . . Not that Lenny believed in visualisation lists, but that didn't mean she didn't *want* to believe in them! Ben wasn't as physically attractive as Ellis but still, Lenny had known from the moment she met Ellis that a hot drummer who'd never had a day job would not end up being the future Mr Lenny, no matter how sexy he looked sitting on the side of her bed, slipping his white T-shirt back on over his lean, muscular torso. Ben could be the solid, stable slow-burner you're meant to end up with. If she could start dating a man like this then maybe she could be free of Ellis and the bad feelings he brought with him once and for all!

'What are you looking so happy about?' said Amy.

'Huh?' said Lenny, shaken from her fantasy.

'Why the grin?'

'Because! That guy *you* said was waiting for his date just asked me out, Miss Know-It-All.'

'Really? I just saw him go up to the restaurant. With his date.'

Lenny's brand new balloon went pop.

'Oh,' said Lenny. 'Well he did say he was meeting a friend . . . '

'Friend in a tiny red mini dress?'

'Friends wear dresses . . . '

Amy shrugged. 'Now listen, don't go mental but I might have to go.'

'*What?*'

'Seb's having drinks at The Groucho, I said I'd join him.'

'If you ditch me to go back and see that cheating nob-head—'

'Fine, I'll get him to come here then. I'd like to know what you think of him.'

'I just told you what I think of him. And then it'll be just like at Juliet's wedding and every other time you and some boyfriend spend the whole night ignoring me.'

'I didn't even have a boyfriend at Juliet's wedding!'

'That guy with the quiff? Robbie?'

'Oooh, *Ritchie*? Christ, you really do hold on to stuff. I wonder if Ritchie's on Facebook?'

'Maybe he's unhappily married and now would be the ideal time to start an affair with him?'

'Maybe you should mind your own business. Now listen, if you can pick up the tab—'

'I *always* pick up your tab.'

'No, you just think you do because you're a bit tight – I promise I'll shout you next time.'

On her way out Lenny popped up to the restaurant. Sure enough there was Ben at the corner table with a blonde, and even from Lenny's awkward angle in the shadow of the doorway she could see their fingers were entwined in a distinctly non-platonic way.

Often when Lenny was upset she'd drink but just as frequently she'd eat. She headed north, to Bar Italia for one of their gigantic mozzarella sandwiches – twice the price of a regular sandwich, but four times better. She sat at the side counter, her gaze fixed on the mirror in front of her, reflecting the life being lived all around her. She ate the sandwich till her stomach hurt.

On the bus home Lenny leaned her head against the cold glass of the window. A long time ago she'd imagined things would work out for her and she'd find someone she'd want to wake up with every day. It had been too long now, with nothing good looking like it could ever happen.

Wanting things and not getting them was painful; it was easier to stop wanting them in the first place.

5

Lenny woke up in the same mood she'd gone to bed in. She stared at the gap between the curtains: sunny out, blue sky – the type of day that if you failed to spend every available minute enjoying London's outdoor spaces it would add to your toxic sense of loser-dom.

The Savage Sunday App – maybe that could make Lenny her fortune? An app that suggested things to do, would factor in your food preferences and discern your mood. Today would be: stay under duvet, watch *Bridesmaids*, eat Ben & Jerry's.

She called Juliet, pausing before dialling. She was far too familiar with that feeling of your phone ringing and the caller not being who you were hoping for.

Juliet sounded tired. 'We spoke last night, he needs a little more time.'

'OK . . . Do you fancy going to Maltby Street later?'

'I can't, I've a dozen more recipes to write by tomorrow.'

'Would company make you feel better or worse? Do you need anything – papers, coffee, food?'

'I'm not in hospital, I'm fine, please, forget it.' Lenny could be so dramatic. Juliet hung up, regretting the fact she'd made a big deal to Lenny about what would end up being nothing.

There were only two things Lenny wanted to do today. Both of them were bad ideas; she simply needed to figure out which to choose. If she called Ellis, she could persuade him to go to Maltby Street, they could eat posh Scotch eggs, stroll by the river and have a lovely time. She could keep it platonic. Just because her hormones were doing a last-minute frenzied twerk for attention didn't mean she had to obey them.

Or she could put on sunglasses, head down to Brown's Hotel and spy on Matt. But what if he was with another woman? It wasn't that she'd be embarrassed to be caught. She would, of course, but she could endure that. It was the fact she'd then have to pass on the message to Juliet. Amy was right: other people's affairs were none of her business.

Decision made.

Lenny stood at London Bridge station with her arms folded, waiting for Ellis. For three years they'd been 'hooking up' – how she hated that phrase, with its suggestion of a sharp metal curve piercing the soft flesh of an aquatic animal's minuscule brain. When she'd first met Ellis she'd been amazed he was interested. He was like Danny Freeman, the exact type who'd have ignored her at school. Tall, dumbly handsome, totally comfortable in his skin. They'd gone on a 'first date' to a shitty dive bar, then had had a heated kiss in the street before he'd dashed off to a gig he was drumming at. On the next date they'd gone to her favourite burger place and their chips had grown cold as they'd talked and talked. He was easy-going, funny, not an ounce of spite in him. They'd kissed all the way home, then spent all night having sex that was, unfortunately, better than any sex Lenny had ever been involved in. The following morning he'd told her she was beautiful and great and he'd love to do this regularly but he didn't do relationships – never had, never would.

This had set the pattern for the last three years. Lenny trying to force Ellis into being more boyfriend-like, or at least more of a well-rounded fuck-buddy in the hope of showing him how much fun life outside a bedroom could be – with a view to eventually penetrating his dumb, commitment-phobic skull. Sometimes they'd spend entire weekends together in a bubble of bliss – country pubs, walks, lying in bed, telling each other their secrets. She'd feel pure happiness pulsating through her. But at these precise moments when she felt closest to him he'd gently stroke her hair and say things like 'Baby, you know this can never be anything more', and then he'd leave, with a vague 'See you when I see you', and she'd feel like a full-body-plaster was being ripped off and realise that their set-up was actually the opposite of everything she wanted.

But inevitably, a month or two later, after a date with a coke-addicted banker or a man wearing a trilby to hide the fact he was four inches shorter than he'd claimed, she'd feel that Ellis was her best, sexiest, most comfortable bet – for now – and she could of course totally handle it.

Here he was, heading towards her with that smile. His mouth always made her heart flip. He had the most beautiful eyes, blue-green like the sea, so open, so honest – and that's how their relationship felt: transparent. He'd always been clear about his terms, he'd never lied. And she held up that truth to the light like a diamond ring, admired it with some pride: at least he doesn't deceive me. She did not dwell much on the fact she was deceiving herself.

Even though she hadn't seen him for weeks, the minute he linked arms with hers it felt like they'd never been parted and never should be. If only it was just sex and they didn't get on. But they had such a familiar, comfortable rapport. He was funny and smart and sexy and he thought she was those things too, and they both loved watching good TV and eating curry, so really, what was his problem?

They stood waiting for a traffic light to change, feeling the early spring sun on their faces. Ellis squeezed her hand, then pulled her close and kissed her passionately and she could feel him, already hard through his jeans.

'You really are in a good mood, Ellis.'

He swooped in to kiss her neck. 'It's been too long.'

'I'm sure you've kept yourself entertained,' she said, pushing him away.

'Don't be like that. You're the one who keeps me at a distance,' he said, pulling her back in. This was the most messed-up thing about their whole relationship! Ellis pretended he liked her more than he did, and she pretended she liked him less – and only in this way could their status quo be maintained.

'Where are we going, anyway?' he said, the first signs of resistance in his voice.

'The Warhol exhibition, at Tate Modern.'

'Can't we eat first?'

Lenny's convoluted plan had involved an hour at the Tate, lunch and a soft drink by the river, a stroll back to Bermondsey and then perhaps one – *one* – drink at that cosy wine bar near Borough. Then she'd hop on the Tube, *alone,* having had an action-packed, well-balanced day. Still, she was hungry too . . .

The Hope was one of her favourite gastropubs, but it was only after they'd been seated in a cosy corner and handed the wine list that she remembered how good their selection was – a shame not to honour such delicious food . . .

They ordered and talked. Ellis had been offered some session work with El 212, a band Lenny had actually heard of. She was genuinely happy for him but the thought of him being on tour plagued her. Insane but still, as a surrogate boyfriend he gave her so much less than she wanted, it only underlined her loneliness. They ordered another bottle, settled in, and before she knew it, it was 5 p.m.

'We'd better get to the Tate,' said Lenny, gesturing for the bill. 'They shut at five.'

'At six.'

'Oh baby, my back's hurting,' he said, his shoulders drooping.

'Since *when?*'

'Like, Wednesday?'

'Ellis, the Warhol's only on for another week.'

'But you'll be too rushed now. Go next weekend, it's a big show, it's across six rooms.'

Ellis's knowledge of the exhibition's layout was surprising and yet not: he always seemed armed with the perfect facts to get his way.

'But we should do *something,*' said Lenny.

'Like what?' He grabbed her hand. 'Baby, I promise, I'll come with you next weekend if you really want. But please, can we go and chill? Is that OK?'

And an hour later, when they were back at hers lying naked in bed, she thought, Yep: that's OK.

Lenny always wanted more than she was allowed. She needed to lower her expectations. The problem was her.

6

'Someone's had a late night,' said Cooper, breezing into Lenny's office on Monday morning and plonking himself down opposite her.

Lenny rapidly turned her gaze from the list on her computer: 'Reasons Never to Shag Ellis Again'.

'According to the Big Sister dashboard, you didn't register any sleep!' said Nick, smirking.

'Oh bollocks,' said Lenny. 'I forgot to press the sleep monitoring button, but see *this* is why it'll fail – it needs far too much manual input.'

'So you weren't getting lucky?'

'Nick,' she said, blushing. 'Do I walk into your office and ask you obnoxious questions about your personal life?'

'You might do, if I had an office,' he said, sniffily. 'Lenny, I'd like your opinion.'

'Should you have your own office? Definitely not. Philpott deserves one far more than you.'

'Your opinion on my new Project: Kinfolk. Occy and I have been brainstorming Graduate Recruitment. We always end up hiring Oxbridge types but I'd like to revolutionise the process by creating a proprietary app.'

'Go on . . .'

'Neuroscientists have identified the key factor for work happiness is collegial interaction – how much you like your co-workers.'

'You need a neuroscientist to figure that out?'

'And anthropologically, we tend to gravitate to people like ourselves.'

'And again: der!'

'So let's look at candidates more laterally – think who we'd like to be stuck in a lift with. Get them to list their likes and dislikes – not obvious stuff, but smells, textures—'

'And anyone who likes the smell of Justin Bieber?'

'Exactly! Then The Minions can map sub-clusters based on our own preferences.'

'So we end up being cultural narcissists rather than socio-economic snobs?'

'Basically.'

'Meh.'

Cooper's smile drooped.

'OK, Nick, it's not your worst idea. What do you want, a medal?'

'Yes! But failing that, your list by end of play.'

'I can't just drop everything!'

'What are you up to, anyway?' he said, craning his neck to see her computer screen. 'Ooh! Who is Ellis?'

'I'll have it for you in an hour,' said Lenny curtly. 'Shut the door on your way out.'

Lenny grabbed a Chipotle receipt from her desk and started scribbling on the back. Where to start? *Dislikes* – there were way more of them than *Likes*. OK, first and foremost: *corporate life*. Also *management meetings; made-up words, i.e. imaginate; working for a fake-feminist who constantly seeks to undermine me.*

Impolitic to bring any of those to the Wappen table.

How about *the polishing tool at the dentist* and *Coldplay songs apart from 'Yellow' and the one with all the strings in it?*

As for *Likes? Curry,* obviously. And: *reading Nora Ephron in bed on a rainy afternoon while eating Nutella from the jar; melted cheese in all its permutations; the ground when it's frosty, seen from above, but not underfoot when you're actually slipping on it* – now stick that in your algorithm, Cooper!

On second thoughts, Lenny wasn't convinced she'd want to recruit an army of mini-Lennys. Maybe Lenny at twenty-one but not the current jaded incarnation. If she could choose anyone to employ tomorrow it would be a Juliet – someone smart and positive. What might a Juliet put? *Likes: honesty; sunshine; The White Company; tidiness; toasted cheese sandwiches; making people happy; Bake Off.*

Lenny crossed out *tidiness*, no one would buy that from Lenny.

Dislikes? Juliet really didn't moan about much . . . *mess? Supermarket bread!* And *discourtesy.* Yes, that would do.

If they could recruit someone with Juliet's creativity and gentleness and Lenny's . . . Lenny's . . . well, Lenny was good at maths, then that would be a start.

Juliet had come a little unstuck on Sunday speaking to Matt, when he claimed he couldn't understand why his continuing absence was problematic.

'Martha called to say she'd landed – she asked where you were, Matt, I don't want to lie.'

'Say I'm out, there's nothing sinister. I'll give her a call later. Listen, I have to go, I've got a conference call—'

'On a Sunday *night*?'

'Yes, on a Sunday night! Darling, let's speak tomorrow.'

She returned to her desk to review the recipes: Asparagus and Bacon Tartlet; Asparagus Arancini; Asparagus and New Potato Salad. She'd stuck asparagus in too many recipes. Plus, she'd been so preoccupied, those sweet croutons had entirely slipped her mind.

Focus! She turned over to a fresh page in her notepad and worked till 3 a.m., then spent Monday morning editing the ideas, and finally sent the recipes off to Celina at noon.

Not a good day to have time to kill. She tidied the house then took a coffee out to the garden. The magnolia buds had finally appeared – their petals tightly furled, like bandaged fists thrust up to the sky.

At 5 p.m. she opened a bottle of wine, drank a glass and then another, then called Lenny before she could pour herself a third. 'I think I'm going ever so slightly mad. I don't suppose you could pop over after work?'

Lenny was standing with her coat on at 7 p.m. when Occy slipped into her office with a pained look: the onset of a migraine.

'Are you off right now, Lenny?'

No, I was planning on promenading round my desk in my coat till the stars come out. 'Is there something you needed?'

'I wanted to ask how your Leadership course went?'

'Yup!' said Lenny, in a voice squeakier than she'd anticipated. 'Very educational.'

'And how was your final session?'

'Final session . . . visualisation!' said Lenny, putting her hand in her pocket – that stupid list was still in there; she must remember to shred *that*.

'Visualisation was on Friday. I meant Saturday's session. Imagineering?'

How did Occy know Lenny had bunked off? Could the Big Sister be monitoring *sound*? Occy would have had an earful of her and Ellis last night.

'You look confused, Lenny?'

'No . . . Saturday . . . I did skip that final hour but only because—'

'Lenny, I know you struggle with me being younger than you but you do need to ask my permission for a schedule change. As a cheerleader for the Wappen brand, you're supposed to embody our values.' Lenny struggled quite hard to imagine the word *Cheerleader* on her business card. 'Leaving a workshop, even on a Saturday, is not in line with my expectations,' said Occy.

'Occy, I've done that session twice; both times it was identical.'

'Lenny, stop resisting feedback. You can be so confrontational.'

'I'm just trying to explain myself,' said Lenny, quietly.

'See? There you go, saying what you think without thinking. If you want to be a team player, you'll need to adapt your personal style.'

It was true, Lenny invariably did say what she thought. It was also true she disliked team games – redolent of the horrors of being the weakest on the B-team.

'Lenny, there are big changes coming this side of Christmas. Personally I'd like you to head up a bigger team and give you more responsibility – '

What? A pay rise? This year? And then Lenny might get close to six figures by the time she turned forty, and then she might finally be content?

' – but only if I see a major shift in temperament,' said Occy, shaking her head.

'Occy, you're quite right. I'm sorry, I should have let you know.'

'Fine. And don't look so wounded.'

This look isn't wounded, thought Lenny. It's merely despair.

Lenny headed down City Road, through the sea of commuters surging to the Tube. A man twenty metres in front of her was walking towards her, head down, clasping his iPhone tightly in front of him like a prayer book. Lenny watched him. She could be naked or pointing a gun at him – either way he was in no danger of looking up! Was he really just going to carry on looking at that screen? She stayed still as he continued his beeline, then smacked straight into her.

'What the fuck is your problem?' he said, staring at her in disbelief.

'*You* are,' said Lenny. 'This is a *street* – look where you're bloody going!'

'Bitch,' said the guy, shaking his head and carrying on. 'You weird, crazy bitch.'

Lenny walked on, her heart thumping. She probably should have walked around him but damn it, she was in the right! She waited until she was safely inside the florist before taking out her own phone. No text from Ellis – there never was after he'd got what he wanted. There would be, in due course, next time he wanted it. She felt violently annoyed at herself for being weak yesterday. How could she have felt so good last night when she felt quite so bad right now?

There was a text from a number she didn't recognise and when she clicked on it her irritation mounted. *Fancy that curry, Research Girl? x*

There would be no nicknames here. Before she could apply any self-control she texted back: *Will your hot blonde date from Saturday night be coming too?* Her shame amplified in the silence of his non-response as she sat in a taxi all the way to Juliet's house.

Juliet tutted when she saw the bouquet in Lenny's arms. 'I really am going to feel silly . . . '

'Stop!' said Lenny, giving her a hug. 'I'm allowed to buy you flowers.'

They sat in the kitchen. Lenny ate while Juliet picked at her food and they both drank steadily. Every so often Juliet's gaze would flick to her phone, then she'd look away, embarrassed.

'You might think I'm naive, Lenny, but I know him better than I know anyone but you.'

Lenny sighed. 'I really think you should insist on seeing him this week. He owes you some sort of an explanation.'

Juliet took another sip of wine and smiled gently. 'He isn't the type to cheat, Lenny, he hates men who do . . . ' she said, her voice trailing off.

Lenny poured the last of the wine into Juliet's glass. 'So if it was an affair?'

Juliet closed her eyes and when she opened them again she looked exhausted. 'We're human; we make mistakes. A one-night stand isn't worth throwing away a life together over.'

'You'd forgive him?'

'You're an idealist, Lenny – and maybe that's why you've never settled, but marriage is all about compromise.'

So, Juliet had a plan – to deal with one short, sharp shock.

Lenny said nothing. She cleared the plates and stacked the dishwasher.

'Don't be disappointed in me, Lenny, if it comes down to it?'

'Jules, I'd never be disappointed, I'm worried about you, that's all.'

On the way home Lenny sat in the back of the cab and tried to forget the look she'd just seen on her friend's face. Whatever this was about – if Matt hurt Juliet, Juliet might forgive him, but Lenny never would.

7

Juliet turned the shower on full blast, tipped her head back and felt the needles of hot water against her skin. Of course Lenny was right. The last five days had been so confusing, and last night Juliet had drunk too much and succumbed to a spiral of pessimism based on no evidence whatsoever. Yes, she would respect Matt's privacy but enough was enough.

His mobile rang out unanswered, so she left a message and sent a follow-up text. She made fresh coffee, and was in the middle of working out a list of kitchenware for Thursday's shoot when her phone rang: Celina.

'Hey, Celina. How were the Maldives?'

'STUN-NING, babe! We had our own butler, click your fingers and he did whatever you want. I've told Mitchell I'm getting him a little bell to wear round his neck, ha ha! Listen, these recipes are amazing – that hot cross bun brioche loaf is ridic! Now you know I can't do close-ups till after my cleanse but we're shooting food from Thursday? And I was thinking, I've been inspired . . . maybe I could do my next book on bread? It's commercial, right?'

'Oh sure, with *Bake Off* and everything, absolutely.'

'But could I have enough ideas to fill a whole book?'

Juliet bit the inside of her lip to avoid laughing. 'I'm sure you could have lots of ideas.'

'Like . . . what sort of chapters would I have?'

'Ooh . . . well, you might want classics, then more speciality loaves – but start very simply so it's accessible to all your readers. A chapter on sandwiches?'

'Great. You flesh out my ideas and I'll tell the publisher – if you think I can make that work?'

'Celina, I think you can do whatever you want. See you Monday,' she said, shaking her head as she hung up the phone. Celina's ability to believe Juliet's ideas were her own never ceased to amaze Juliet. It was uncanny, the way she'd flip the language so fast it can't even have been conscious. Celina had no *compunction* – that was the word: *compunction*. A pleasing word, displeasing quality.

Her phone was ringing again: Matt.

'Jules, I'm in back-to-back meetings, can it wait?'

'No it can't. Are you coming home today?'

'I thought we agreed not to put a timeline on this.'

'No, you agreed that. I'd like to see you. Today.'

'Impossible, tomorrow's out too—'

'Why?'

'Because! I'm taking the bloody Germans to Hakkasan and dropping three grand on noodles!'

'Don't take that tone with me. This has gone on for nearly a full week.'

'Fine, it'll have to be Thursday then, around 8 p.m. Listen, I'm being called back in, I've got to go.'

It wasn't ideal, Thursday was day one of the shoot. Still, she could be patient for another forty-eight hours. Things would become clearer soon enough.

8

Juliet had been at the photographer's studio on Thursday since 7 a.m. She'd spent the first two hours prepping the trifle, first casting the perfect raspberries, then painstakingly defuzzing them with micro-tweezers before painting them redder with a tiny make-up brush till they were fit for the cover of *Vogue*. Now the crew were preparing to do their first shot with the hand model – a luscious, caramel-dripping-off-the-spoon set-up. Terry, the photographer's assistant had just called three minutes. Juliet turned the heat up under the pan and was watching carefully as the sugar melted from white granules to nothingness, then just as quickly started to reform as a dark bubbling liquid, when her phone rang. She glanced at the screen, number unknown, went to push divert but accidentally pressed answer, then made the tiniest of fists as she heard a woman's voice, and hurriedly picked up.

The woman sounded surprised. 'Is that Juliet Marlow?'

'It's me,' she said, trying to sound patient though if this caramel seized because she'd lost control of it she'd be rather cross with herself.

'Oh . . . Hi . . . My name's Angela; I work with Matthew.' Juliet could hear the woman's nerves, strung thin, down the telephone line. She lifted the pan off the hob, felt heat in the handle as cold fear ran through her body.

'What's wrong?' She'd had a brief chat with Matt yesterday about their health insurance – he'd wanted to drop their level of cover, but the policy was in her name and she'd insisted they keep it at a higher level and now she said a silent prayer of relief as she pictured him, having dinner with the Germans, then returning to the office and being found slumped over his desk this morning. She felt her mouth go dry. 'Is Matt OK?'

'I haven't seen him recently. We don't sit on the same floor anymore.'

'You're not HR?' Juliet put the pan back on the heat and carried on swirling. She felt a vein in her forehead pulse. 'I'm at work actually – is this urgent?'

'I shouldn't have called.'

'It's fine, if you can be quick?' The liquid was bubbling, on the point of turning.

There was a deep breath in, and then Angela's voice in a blurted, panicky rush. 'There's no easy way to say this so I'll just say it: I've been having an affair with your husband, and I'm sorry but you married a liar and you don't even know the half of it . . . '

Juliet felt a burning desire to drop the phone into the saucepan and watch it melt into dark, smoking plastic. From the bustle behind her she heard Terry's voice. 'Thirty seconds on caramel, darling!'

'Juliet? Are you there?' said Angela.

'I'm sorry, Angela, did you say you were or you are?'

'Were or are *what*?'

'Involved still, with Matt?'

'Jules, darling!' shouted Terry. 'Hurry it up!'

'It's over,' said Angela. 'That's the reason I'm calling you.'

Juliet looked down at the dark mass solidifying in the pan as Terry headed across the studio towards her. 'Angela, I can't talk. I literally have a hot pan in my hand, I'm going to have to call you back.'

'I shouldn't have called . . . '

'No, please? I want to speak, today if possible. Can I call you at lunch?'

'I'll be in a meeting . . . '

'After work then, any time before eight p.m?'

'I'm with Mum tonight.'

'Just a quick call, ten minutes?'

'I really can't.'

'Tomorrow then? Or, actually, could we meet?'

'Yeah, I guess. Tomorrow?'

Jules checked her schedule – she was shooting all day Friday and Saturday. 'Sunday's the earliest I can do?'

She wrote down Angela's details, the sweet acrid smell of burning sugar filling the air. 'Can I ask – have you tried calling me before and withheld your number?'

There was an embarrassed pause. 'You never answer.'

'Jules, babe? Time, money, caramel!' said Terry, coming up behind her.

'Angela—'

'I'm sorry, I'm so sorry.'

'I'll see you on Sunday.'

She hung up. Counted to ten. Felt a buzz of chaos in her head. Felt nausea rise, took a deep breath and turned back to the hob.

'Everything OK?' said Terry.

Jules shook her head. 'Terry, I'm so sorry, I've cocked this caramel up royally. Give me three minutes, and I might need a new pan.'

Matt was already waiting at the table in the restaurant off Charlotte Street. He looked slimmer and well rested, he didn't look like he'd been losing much sleep at all.

'I ordered a few bits,' he said, pouring Juliet some wine and pointing at the plates on the table. 'Sea bass, tuna, seaweed salad . . . '

Juliet had lost her appetite and shrugged her indifference. 'Matt,' she said, reaching for her wine, then resting her hand on the stem of the glass. 'I had a call today. From a woman.'

He shrugged.

'About you,' she said, trying to keep her voice steady. 'She said you'd had an affair.'

'*What?*'

'She said you'd been—'

'Hang on, rewind. Did she give you her name?'

'Oh!' said Juliet, with a nervous laugh. 'Is there more than one?'

'Who was it?'

'Angela. From your office.'

'Ange? *Big* Ange, from *work?*'

'Yes.'

'*What*, and she said we'd had *a thing?*' He squinted as if listening to directions in a foreign language.

'That's the reason you left, isn't it?'

'You don't actually believe her do you, darling?'

'Why would she make that up?'

'Well . . . Ange is someone with a serious alcohol addiction, severe . . . ' She saw Matt teetering on the verge of responding to a further accusation she hadn't even made, then backing himself away from the ledge. 'Her mother's a manic depressive. She's probably inherited her mental health issues.'

'But she's well enough to be employed?'

'Not in my team, no, in a different department.'

'OK . . . '

'I mean, it would cost a fortune to fire her – you know how these things are – but my point is, she's a mess.'

She sighed. 'Don't you think it's a little far-fetched that you leave home with no explanation and then Another Woman turns up, and those two things are not connected?'

'Tell me, what exactly did she say?'

'Not much; I'm interested in your version.'

He brought his fingers to his lips as though trying to recall the vaguest of memories. 'Big Ange . . . I think she first flirted with me at the Christmas party. She's forty, kind of a crazy look in her eye – I should have realised she wasn't right in the head. I felt sorry for her, she seemed very . . . lonely.'

He was talking rather a lot for a man with nothing to hide. 'I didn't ask about her emotional history,' said Juliet. 'I asked about her history with you.'

'I'm about to tell you – I'm merely trying to explain that she's a fantasist. Besides, what happened has nothing to do with what I'm going through.'

'What *are* you going through?'

'I'm trying to figure out *my* needs going forward, to be happy!'

'Matt, something happened with this woman, didn't it?'

'OK. Well . . . there was an incident.' He leaned forward, lowering his voice. 'But I'd really rather not discuss it here.'

'Oh please, you know I'm not going to cause a scene.'

'Jules, she's been threatening to call you because she's angry that . . . well . . . I should never have done it, she's clearly insane.'

Juliet shook her head in disbelief. 'It's a mistake because of her reaction? Not because your marriage means something?'

'Hang on, I'll show you her texts.' He scrolled through his phone impatiently. 'Here, look!' he said, triumphantly. *You can't just walk away – WHY SHOULD I PROTECT YOU NOW?* 'She's one of those bunny boilers!'

Or someone who's been extremely poorly handled, thought Juliet. Her head was throbbing. Matt was sitting there looking as though not only had he explained himself amply, but as if he was the victim in all this.

'Matt, to be clear – you did actually sleep with her?'

He moved his chin an inch towards his chest. There it was. She'd thought she'd steeled herself so that an admission wouldn't hurt. She'd thought wrong.

'What's done is done, Jules. I swear on Martha's life it's over.' He reached for her hand, then stopped himself.

Juliet took a deep breath. 'The diet, the sports car . . . has this affair been going on for months?'

'Oh, Jules – an affair is when you're in love and I never had *feelings* for her.'

'Then why did you do it?'

He opened his palms to the ceiling. 'A moment of madness – she's not even my type.'

Was he trying to make her feel better? He should try a bit harder. 'What does she look like?'

'*Ange?* How would I *describe* Ange? Mousey brown hair? Dumpy? Not beautiful like you. She looks . . . weathered. She's borderline alcoholic.'

'So why did you choose her?'

'Jules, she chose *me!*'

Juliet had seen it many times, a predatory woman at a party standing too close, seeing his wedding ring as a challenge. Matt was normally adept at slipping out of the tightening loop of flirtation without leaving egos bruised.

'And you slept with her just once?'

'Honestly, the fact she even has your number terrifies me. She must have stolen it from my phone.'

Juliet thought about the logistics of this: a women being left alone with her husband's phone on a one-night stand? While Matt was taking a shower? Before coming home to her? She reached for her wine glass.

'If she calls again, Jules, promise you won't speak to her – and let me know immediately.'

'Why, what are you so worried about?'

'I'm worried she's crazy! I might need to think about a restraining order.'

Her husband's face seemed suddenly unfamiliar; his expression – one of a wounded little boy – she found unspeakably unattractive. She gripped her glass so tightly she feared it might shatter. 'You might need a restraining order on *her?*' said Juliet. 'Sounds to me rather like you're the one who needs the restraining order.'

'*What?*'

'On your groin, Matt.'

'Oh Jules, please,' he said, shaking his head. 'That's hardly necessary, is it?'

It was peculiar. She'd expected him to ask for forgiveness and talk about what next for them. Instead, he'd attempted to seize the moral high ground and was now loading slightly too much sea bass carpaccio on to his fork as though the entire matter were put to bed.

She was glad she'd arranged to meet Angela on Sunday. Would Matt consider it disloyal? If so then tough: they still wouldn't be remotely even on that front.

9

Well! This wasn't how Juliet had planned to spend her day off – camped out in a basement bar in The Strand, waiting for a rendez-vous with The Other Woman. She was grateful the lighting was so dark, she could hide the evidence of the three sleepless nights she'd had since Thursday. Once she'd got the measure of the situation she'd call in Lenny, but if she'd told her straight away, Lenny would have demanded firebombing Matt's office as her opening gambit.

Juliet wasn't sure what she was expecting, but when an attractive woman with dark hair in a low ponytail came down the steps, spotted Juliet and did a double take, she figured that whatever Angela was going to tell her was true. *Big Ange?* The woman gripping the leather strap on her handbag so tightly it might snap was a size twelve, at most, with the smallest waist Juliet had ever seen.

All the cool, clipped sentences Juliet had practised were forgotten the moment Angela looked her in the eye and burst into tears. Juliet felt compelled to put her arm around her, sit her down and order a bottle of wine.

Closer up, her face did look . . . what had Matt said? Weathered? Juliet would have said weary. She had intelligent brown eyes, a natural high arch to her brow suggesting she was always in on the joke, and a slim top lip, unbalanced by a far more generous lower one.

'I don't know how we do this,' said Juliet, her smile as half-hearted an offering as a stale custard cream.

Angela shook her head apologetically. 'Honestly, I've never been in this situation before.'

A little late in the day to start caring about my opinion of you, thought Juliet.

'It's weird,' said Angela, staring at her. 'I always considered you the enemy, but we've got more in common than I thought.'

Juliet shifted in her seat. She and this woman opposite her were not on the same team, why would she even begin to think they were?

'Has Matthew told you I drink?' said Angela.

'Matt said you had a few issues . . . ' Juliet ran her finger slowly along the crease in her paper napkin.

'Did you tell him we were meeting?' she said, warily.

'No. Did you?' Juliet pressed down firmly, turned the napkin over, and pushed it to one side.

'We don't speak anymore.'

'When did you last speak?'

'Not since it ended.'

'Which was when?'

'November the thirtieth.'

November made no sense. 'I thought it was at Christmas?'

'*It?*' Angela's face crumpled in disbelief. 'What exactly did Matthew tell you?'

'Not much,' said Juliet, unnerved by Angela's reaction. 'So I'd appreciate it if you could!' She could hear sharpness in her tone, as alien as her own reflection the time she'd had a heavy-handed free makeover.

'Listen,' said Angela, standing abruptly. 'I'm sorry but I don't want to be the person who tells you these things. Go home and ask your husband.'

'Wait,' said Juliet, reaching out. 'I won't get angry. I just . . . I need to know. Please?'

It took the whole bottle – not long – to hear everything she didn't want to. The relationship had started five years ago and had carried on for two years before Angela had called it a day.

'My friends told me I wasn't doing anything wrong. I was single and I wanted to believe them, but . . . Do you believe in karma?'

'Me?' said Juliet, whose brain was spinning out, trying to process this timescale. 'I guess I believe in trying to be the best person you can be.'

Angela nodded forlornly. 'He used to say I was the only person who understood him; the only one he didn't have to lie to. So even though you shared a house, I knew things about him you never would

– and I suppose that made me feel like I had an advantage. Which in retrospect I can see was incorrect.'

Juliet filled her glass and tried to drink but there was acid rising up her throat.

'I can't believe I'm admitting this to you – but I'd look at your photos on Pinterest. You had this picture-perfect life, but the more I looked the more real you became. I ended up seeing your side of things: he'd say you'd neglected him since Martha was born, and I'd tell him he sounded like a spoilt child.'

Juliet listened with interest. It was like listening to a story about a man she'd never met – he even had a slightly different name: he sounded like a cad.

'My therapist told me I was being manipulated, that Matthew was toxic, but when you're in love, you don't see that.'

Juliet wondered, was that what love boiled down to? Re-inventing facts so they were easier to live with?

'I tried to finish it: I changed departments, ignored his calls, six months cold turkey. I was starting to get over him, I was, but then Mum got ill . . . and I felt like he really cared.'

'This was when?'

'December, three years ago. I'm not saying none of this was my fault, I'm just trying to explain – to myself, I suppose – why I went back for more punishment. On Christmas Day I was in hospital with Mum and I thought of you playing happy families in your matching cashmere socks . . . and if anything, that should have been a turning point . . . But it actually made me feel weaker, so when he came sniffing . . . Anyway,' said Angela, swatting away the memory. 'He swore it would be different, he took me on work trips, to Japan, Warsaw—'

'You *travelled* together?' For some reason Juliet had pictured them snatching time in the office after hours. She couldn't figure out why the thought of them walking through an airport together, taking their time, made her want to tear her own skin off.

'He *said* that as soon as Martha left home he'd leave. Then he said you had empty nest syndrome, you were too fragile, he'd have to wait. Eventually I realised I'd fallen for the oldest line in the book.' She emptied the wine in her glass, then headed abruptly to the bar.

Juliet watched her frantically tapping her fingertips on the counter. Maybe Angela was an alcoholic, and clearly she was in emotional distress. But she wasn't lying.

It occurred to Juliet, only as Angela made her way back with a miserable look, that Angela wasn't aware Matt had left. Why was she here today, fizzing with her need to connect over shared outrage?

'Angela, why did it end?'

'In one phone call, that's it! No explanation, he says he can't do it any more!'

'*Matt* ended it?'

'*Yes!* But here's the thing, and this is why I rang you,' she said, now looking at Juliet with utter conviction. 'I know Matthew. I know the way he thinks. The only reason he'd have left me . . . it's not because he felt guilty, that never bothered him . . . I think there's someone else. In fact I'm sure of it. I genuinely feel bad for you, I do. You gave him the best years of your life and I think you and I are now in the same boat. Which I'm sure you'll agree is an extremely undesirable place to be.'

Juliet did not want to be in the same boat as Angela; she did not want to be in the same bar as her. She wanted to be far away – preferably waking up from this nightmare or, failing that, lying down in a darkened room. She left Angela and walked out into the piercing light of the April afternoon, crossed the road to the Savoy and handed them her credit card. She checked herself into a luxury room, drew the curtains and felt her brain fizzing like a snow globe with the glitter travelling upwards.

I have been married to a different man. This is not the same man. I don't know this man. Her self-protection mechanisms were putting up anti-riot gear.

She must have dozed off, because when she opened her eyes and checked her watch it was 7.45 p.m. She picked up her phone and called Lenny.

* * *

Lenny lay fully clothed on the king-sized bed, staring at the ceiling, her half-drunk Martini clutched in one hand. She wasn't sure if she'd blinked the entire time Juliet was talking. Juliet lay beside her, her gaze also fixed unblinkingly upwards.

'You definitely don't think Angela is lying?' said Lenny.

'Why would she?'

'Matt said she's a liar. Or maybe she's exaggerating, to hurt him?'

'There's too much detail. There's too much pain in her eyes.'

Lenny let out a low growl of rage. 'Your husband is a complete bastard.'

'Yup,' said Juliet, so softly it was little more than a breath. 'It's just . . . '

'What?' said Lenny, hoping Juliet might have discovered a sharp little rock in the story, to rip the threads of it apart.

'It's just I can't believe it. I do. I'd just rather not.'

Lenny sat up in bed, frowned, and punched the top pillow into a better state of pouffiness. 'I am going to kill him. Mum knows some dodgy Albanians at the car wash she claims are Mafia.'

Juliet took a large sip of her cocktail, then shuddered. 'I don't think Matt – *Matthew* – is worth doing time for.'

'Can't we maim him, at least? A little Bobbitt?'

'It's a generous offer but . . . well, I'm sure there's a reason not to.'

'How about we kill Angela?'

'It's weird, my instinct was to blame her, but that rather lets him off the hook.'

Lenny took a sip of her drink and winced. 'What she did was completely unsisterly.'

'Mostly it was un-husbandly. Marriage vows are supposed to mean something, Lenny,' she said, shaking her head as though movement might jolt the facts to her brain.

Lenny looked at Juliet – pale, puffy-eyed and in shock. 'You're not going to work tomorrow are you?'

'I'm on set at seven a.m.'

'Can't you call in sick?'

'There's no one else they could get at short notice, plus Celina's on set,' said Juliet, draining the last of her drink.

Lenny bit the edge of her nail, then dialled room service and ordered two more Martinis and club sandwiches with extra crisps. 'So . . . if Matt comes home tomorrow, and begs your forgiveness?'

Juliet sighed. 'If it had been a one-night stand . . . Yes, forgive, move on. But it's not the sex – it's all the lying.'

'Will you confront him tomorrow?'

'He's off to Tokyo, but anyway I don't want to speak to him till I have more facts.'

'Shall I get one of the programmers at work to hack his computer? They can do that same day, it's totally untraceable.'

'Thanks but there's no need. I have a hunch Danny might know something. It's just whether or not he'll tell me.'

By midnight they were both so drunk they couldn't figure out which switch related to which light in the hotel room and passed out with all lights blazing. Lenny woke at 3.23 a.m. with the first crack of a hangover. She tiptoed to the window and looked down on to the Thames at the dark water flowing by. A feeling of dread rose up in her. There was something even worse out there waiting for Juliet.

Brace, brace.

IO

Juliet's first shot on Monday morning – raspberry bunny-face cupcakes – had gone royally pear-shaped. She'd put the finishing touches on: flaked almonds for eyes and swirls of sticky jam to define their features, but the jam looked like blood, the poor bunnies like they'd been involved in a pub brawl. She had to redo the entire batch, and once she had, Celina could not get her shot right. She made 'seductively bite the ear of a bunny' look more challenging than 'broker peace in the Middle East'.

They stopped for lunch and Juliet ventured outside. It was drizzling and she pondered whether to pop back in and forget about calling Danny. Maybe he didn't know anything. Then again, Danny knew Matt almost as well as she did – perhaps better.

Her heart sank as she heard the elongated ringtone. It was probably 3 a.m. in Mexico or Bali or wherever he was. She was about to hang up when he answered, hesitantly.

'Danny, sorry to bother you – are you somewhere exotic?'

'Donegal, rain coming down in sheets, at a funeral.'

'Now?'

'We're on our way to the wake. My old boss from the pub's dad . . . eighty-nine or ninety-three, no one seems to agree.'

'I wondered if we could talk . . . '

'About Matt?'

'I know it's unfair to put you in this position.'

'He's not my friend anymore.'

'I know you guys had a falling out. What happened?'

'Ah – it's not really one for the phone, Jules.'

'No?'

'No,' he said, and his voice was suddenly serious.

'OK, well . . . when are you back in town?'

'I'm off to Bundoran tomorrow, back in London with Dad for

Good Friday, then off to Thailand for six months on Saturday, my last big trip for a while.'

'Oh Danny, I really need to see you before then . . . when exactly are you back?'

'I think my flight lands at Stansted around three p.m. on Thursday?'

'Shit. It's the last day of the shoot, I'm working till eight.'

'Then swing by West London after, we'll have a drink? I think you might need one.'

Things like this happened every day. When Martha was at school, Juliet used to meet with the other mums regularly for coffee. Every so often one of the mums would tell a horror story about someone else's husband having an affair with the Latvian au pair *under the wife's nose*, or an *entire secret second family in Chichester*. The collected wives would shudder over their skinny lattes then return home to be extra vigilant around their spouses. Things like this happened every day: to other people.

Juliet was thankful the shoot had been so intense. Every night had run to overtime, and her limbo was restricted to her commute and the brief minutes after her head hit the pillow. Finally it was Thursday and a particularly painful one, Juliet counting the hours till she was due to meet Danny. Celina had been partying the night before with Serafina, her yoga teacher, and consistently messed up every shot. Seriously, how hard *was* it to bring a spoon to your own mouth?

'Jules, babe, you're amazing!' said Celina, when they finally wrapped. 'Make sure that hot hubby of yours serves you breakfast in bed this weekend.'

'You coming for a drink?' said the photographer, as Juliet wiped down her work surface and filed her paper copies.

'Thanks, but I already have plans.'

She took the Tube to Kilburn, pictured herself staying on to the end of the Jubilee line and back again. She'd like to go home, get into bed and pretend all of this was a bad dream; she hadn't truly processed Angela's story yet, she'd been putting it off till Easter weekend, like a chocolate egg filled with maggots.

Danny had suggested one of the many pubs on the High Road. She walked past the dismal stretch of loan shops, pound stores and fast-food joints – the smell of fried chicken making her queasy. She walked into the pub, past two glaring fruit machines, a dart board, and the slow-eyed stares of old men, and found Danny in a back room seated at a rickety table, rolling a cigarette. He seemed surprised at the sight of her, as if he'd come home to find a well-loved object turned upside down on the mantelpiece. He stood and gave her a hug. He had that familiar smell – not unpleasant – of smoke and washing powder and the sea. He looked good: tanned and relaxed, the ends of his wavy blond hair almost white from the sun. Though the evening was cold, he was dressed only in jeans and a white T-shirt that showed off his bronzed arms. At school he and Matt had been equal in terms of looks and brains and popularity, and Matt had gone in one direction – the house, the family, the job – and Danny had stayed more or less put: never tried, never had to fail. He was halfway down a pint and Juliet offered to buy him another, but he insisted on going to the bar and returned with a bottle of wine. 'Not up to Matt's exacting standards I'm afraid.'

He sat and rolled another cigarette, listened carefully while Juliet told him of Matt's departure, and then of Angela. Juliet's voice was gentle but there was an unmistakeable wobble to it and Danny found himself unable to meet her eye.

'Angela thinks there's *another* woman . . . and I thought of all the people who know him . . . '

'Christ, Jules. I don't know what to say,' he said, running his hand through his hair. 'I thought he was my best mate, but he doesn't know the meaning of loyalty.'

'Why did you fall out? I thought maybe . . . ' Her gaze turned to the nearly empty pouch of tobacco on the table.

Danny laughed bitterly. 'I know you've always thought I was a bit of a waster but I've repaid Matt every penny I ever borrowed.'

'So it wasn't about money,' she said glumly.

Danny looked at Juliet and felt a surge of rage towards Matt for a multitude of reasons – but primarily for being such an ungrateful shit who could marry one of the two loveliest girls at school, then proceed to treat her with so little respect. And now Matt didn't even have the balls to fess up, it had somehow fallen to Danny to enlighten her.

'Danny, I know you don't want to betray him . . . '

'It's not that.' He didn't care about betraying Matt, but he *really* didn't want to be the one to devastate Juliet.

'Please, Danny? If I know the facts at least I can figure out what to do with them.'

Danny shook his head in quiet surrender. Juliet was too good for all this – she deserved the truth.

Danny hadn't known about Angela, but he'd known about another mistress, years ago – a three-month affair, one of the secretaries at work. Juliet vaguely remembered her – dyed red hair, pale eyes. She remembered feeling slightly unnerved by the way the girl had stared the few times they'd met in Matt's office.

'Maybe I should have told you back then, but I thought it was a one-off. Plus Martha was only little – that's a family you're potentially breaking up.'

Juliet felt the tears rolling down her cheeks. 'I guess we married so young, he never had a chance to sow his wild oats the way you did . . . ' She looked down, embarrassed, wiped a teardrop from the table's surface. 'Boys will be boys.'

Danny took her hand gently. 'He's a man, not a boy. I've seen him live his whole life with other people making excuses for him.'

Matt and Danny's fall out? Was that the worst part? Probably. Danny had taken the van in for a service and had a few hours downtime in the flat when he'd normally be at work. He'd heard a key in the door, then Matt's voice, accompanied by the sound of a woman's laughter. Danny had gone to the hall to greet him, and while Matt's smile had only temporarily faltered, and he'd introduced Tasha as a girl from the estate agent, that night he and Danny had come to blows. 'He must have thought I was born yesterday! This gorgeous blonde – sorry, Jules. It couldn't have been more obvious. He tried to explain that it wasn't what it looked like – but it was exactly what it looked like.' The absolute hat trick of clichés – Matt joins a gym, buys a fast car, then visits an Exclusive Gentleman's

Club in Mayfair with clients one night and falls head over heels for the hostess, a hot twenty-two-year-old blonde. Matt Marlow, Olympic Asshole – Gold medallist.

'I told him to end the affair, have counselling. He couldn't throw away nearly twenty years of marriage for some bimbo. Anyway, not to put too fine a point on it, Jules, he told me it was none of my business. I might have called him a certain word which he took objection to, and he told me to get out of the flat by the end of that week. That was three months ago, I haven't heard from him since.'

Juliet closed her eyes. There was a dull, high noise in her ears, like a speaker about to blow. She stood up, her head violently spinning as Danny reached to steady her. He led her outside, hailed a cab and sat with his arm around her all the way home.

Danny sat in the Marlows' living room, his foot tapping nervously against the solid oak floorboards, looking at the empire of middle-class perfection Matt had built – and now destroyed.

Meanwhile in the upstairs bathroom Juliet was on her knees on the black and white tiled floor, head over the toilet being violently sick.

PART THREE

'Happiness ain't a thing in itself, it's only a contrast with something that ain't pleasant.'

Mark Twain

Hot cross buns?

How about the Extra Fruity ones?

Could Waitrose's poshest, most deluxe Hot Cross Buns – toasted, with a lot of unsalted butter – help your friend get over the discovery that her husband of nineteen years was a liar, philanderer, coward and all round creep? How about these cute pink cupcakes topped with chicks hatching out from under white icing duvets?

Lenny pushed her trolley further down the aisle. It was day two of the meltdown. Danny had called her first thing yesterday: 'Lenny DuBee – it's been a few years! I'd say Happy Good Friday but it's not turning out to be the best . . . '

She'd gone straight round to the house to find Juliet in her bedroom in the most impenetrable of sleeps.

'I think it's that post-traumatic shock thing,' whispered Danny who, in spite of sleeping on the sofa and suffering a little creasing around the T-shirt area, was looking remarkably well. Lenny hadn't seen him for several years but he hadn't aged at all. She caught herself staring at his green eyes and his glowing skin – not a trace of a wrinkle, the jammy bugger! Small wonder though – all Danny ever did was go on extended holidays and muck about in that van.

He made Lenny a pot of strong tea and gave her the low-down and when Lenny heard the details she dug her nails into the arm of the sofa with rage, sadness and a fair bit of hate.

'So do you think he's shacked up in the bloody flat with this slapper?' said Lenny.

'What difference?' said Danny.

'It's their marital property. It's even more disgusting if she's living there! You need to go round and check.'

'Firstly, I haven't got keys anymore; secondly, I'm not Miss Marple; thirdly, what do you want me to actually do if she is there? And fourthly,' he said, checking his watch, 'I'm flying to Thailand tomorrow morning and I haven't even packed yet.'

'Oh Danny, please, change your flight! You've got to stick around while we figure out what's going on.'

'I can't change it last minute, it costs a bomb.'

'I'll pay. But please stay with me and help her – help me! I need an extra pair of hands, please, just for forty-eight hours.'

In the end he'd changed his flight to one on Tuesday, which involved a lengthy stopover in Guangzhou. He'd refused to let Lenny pay and she'd felt temporarily guilty, not least for re-routing him via some random Chinese city, but then she'd become so preoccupied with checking Juliet was still breathing, she'd forgotten about it.

Last night Lenny had lain awake in Martha's room, staring at the ceiling, thinking: How dare he, how dare he? On Saturday morning Juliet had come down to the kitchen where Danny and Lenny were having coffee and claimed she was better – but shortly after had burst into low, aching howls that lasted so long Lenny had considered calling an ambulance, until Danny came to the rescue with a large whisky and some dodgy valium he'd picked up in India.

So yes – it was probably going to take more than Hot Cross Buns.

Lenny wheeled her trolley round the corner. There were excellent deals on roast lamb, and she was sure the doctor would have prescribed Juliet something nutritious and protein-based. 'If you can read you can cook, unless you're a half-wit,' said Gloria – but the one time Lenny had roasted a chicken, she'd proved herself the half-wit. There was one dish Lenny could pull off – the toastie. Lenny piled the trolley high with Cheddars, Gruyère, various posh breads. Maybe something sweet would cheer Juliet up? My goodness, so many different Easter eggs! All these new variants – Teasers, Scratchers, Triangulons – the novelties made her feel old. Lenny picked up a chocolate rabbit covered in gold foil with a red velvet collar. It came with a free set of bunny ears, rather like those of a hostess at the Playboy mansion; possibly not the best choice for Juliet, all things considered.

Lenny chose a bittersweet dark mint egg from Green and Blacks and hurried her trolley over to the booze aisle.

Lenny returned to find Juliet in her dressing gown, sitting on the sofa with a barely sipped cup of tea. Her cheeks were flushed high pink, as though she'd stolen the rouge from her mother's dressing table.

'I'm not fine but I am fine and I'm going to be fine,' said Juliet.

'I know you are,' said Lenny, sitting down beside her.

'She's not in the flat. He isn't either, he *is* in Japan. Probably. Somewhere abroad at least. Could be in Japan *with* the girlfriend, or on the moon, I mean who actually knows at this point?'

'Danny's been to the flat?'

'He's on his way back now. I've asked him to buy cigarettes, I feel cigarettes might help.'

There was a slightly crazed spark in Juliet's eyes. Lenny wondered if she should ask Danny to source some marijuana too, strictly for medicinal purposes.

'So what's the deal with the flat?' asked Lenny.

'Danny said it's empty.'

'And you called your husband?'

'Danny did, blocked his number . . . it rang a foreign ring tone. I made him hang up.'

'What are you going to do?'

'I imagine I'm going to get divorced, then try not to become bitter, possibly take up a new hobby – hopefully not *Hating Men* – and then in about forty years' time I suspect I will die alone.'

'Hmm,' said Lenny, taking the shopping through to the kitchen. 'I was thinking more in terms of this weekend.'

Easter to-do list: drink, cry, realise you're drunk, eat a toasted cheese sandwich, feel temporarily better, have a cigarette, feel temporarily worse, repeat.

Juliet, Lenny and Danny sat on the floor round the fireplace on Monday afternoon, crumb-covered plates, empty cups of tea, an ashtray and wine glasses piled at their feet.

'I can't even begin to unpick it,' said Juliet, her eyes drifting to the wedding photo on her mantelpiece. 'Even back then – was he ever who I thought he was? Have I been entirely stupid? Is this *my* fault?'

'Of course not!' said Danny, outraged.

'You trusted him, that's all,' said Lenny. 'You're a trusting kind of a person, that's a great quality. Just not with regards to that dickhead.' If Matt had been in front of her now, Lenny honestly thought she'd be capable of bodily harm – somewhere around the midpoint of actual and grievous.

Juliet sighed. 'In a way I'm a tiny bit grateful – that it's all so brutal.'

Danny shot Lenny a look of concern.

'I mean, it makes it easier – slightly,' said Juliet. 'If it had been a fling, I'd have given him a second chance – I know I would have – and then what? A third? No – this is better. Not less painful. Just clearer.'

'When's he home from Japan?' said Lenny.

'Wednesday. I have this morbid curiosity to find out what he'll do next. At what point is he going to tell me? But then I think: I will not sit here waiting to see how much more disappointing he can be.'

Lenny's brain kicked into overdrive. 'Maybe he planned the timing – knowing he had the trip coming up, and knowing Martha would be abroad too . . . to make the transition smoother.'

'Maybe he's going to claim I made it all up because I'm jealous,' said Danny, shaking his head.

'Maybe he's going to claim Tasha's a delusional alcoholic, like Angela . . . ' said Juliet.

'Maybe he'll claim he only just met Tasha on the flight back from Japan . . . ' said Lenny.

'Well he can say whatever he likes.' Juliet reached for another cigarette as Danny held out a light on auto pilot. 'There was a Matt I was married to, and he can stay as that person until the day he left. And now there's this new, other Matt,' she said, inhaling deeply. 'I don't even know him – and that's just the way it is.'

You can make divisions in your mind, with words, clearly marking out what you want the facts to be. It doesn't make them true, and it doesn't make them hurt less.

1 2

At the crack of dawn on Tuesday, Lenny borrowed Juliet's car and drove Danny back to his dad's. Danny was strangely silent as they drove through North London, his face a mixture of anger and something Lenny couldn't quite put her finger on.

'So, what's your plan?' asked Lenny, glancing at him. 'How long are you away for this time?'

'It's my last big trip. I'm back in the summer, then I'm sticking around. Dad's getting older . . . and I've got plans for my business.'

'Your business? What exactly is this business?' The last she'd heard, he was doing random house moves for a tenner a pop, and the odd bit of botched plumbing.

'I've got the van now. I'm going to get professional, have a website, do some branding.'

Sounded suitably vague and Danny-like. 'What are you going to call your "business" then?' she asked. 'The Dan with the van who fixes your pan . . . '

'It's more than plumbing now – I do electrics, a bit of carpentry, heating. When I've done my next stage of night school I'll be gas safe.'

'Gas safe?' said Lenny, trying not to smirk. 'Does that mean no more farting?'

'No, Lenny,' he sighed. 'It means I can do jobs involving heating, ovens, boilers.'

Oh dear, now she'd hurt his ego. Still, he'd be doing something far more high-powered if he hadn't mucked about when he was at school first time round.

'And besides,' he said, his voice softening. 'I think that would be wind safe.'

She giggled: 'Listen – I feel bad about you paying for that ticket change. Will you let me pay you back? I know you're not . . . you know, financially . . . '

'Lenny, please do not patronise me, I can afford two hundred pounds.'

'I'm not patronising you, I'm trying to say thank you.'

'Yeah, well . . . it was the least I could do, given the circumstances.' Lenny caught something in his voice and turned to look at him, but he'd turned away again.

Lenny thought about the ties that bonded people: having things in common, having each other's backs, having mutual secrets. That look on his face just now, it was guilt! That's why he'd paid for the ticket change – out of *guilt*! He'd known about that first affair, he probably *had* known about Angela, how could he not have?

'You and Matt were like twins at school,' said Lenny rolling down the window as anger heated her face, then quickly rolling it up again as she felt cold air hit her cheek.

'Yeah, well.'

'But you're so similar. That's why you stayed so close. You're both kind of irresponsible, both womanisers . . . '

'Lenny, don't tar me with that brush!'

'I remember now! You two-timed Ellie Gorman with Stacey Shelton, then you cheated on Stacey with that slutty Goth who worked at the Odeon Camden Town.'

'Give me a break, I was seventeen!'

'And all the women you've been through in the last twenty years—'

'I've just never met the right one. Anyway, I'm not the one who was married.'

Huh, maybe he had a point. 'Straight ahead or left at the junction?' she said, irritably.

Danny thumbed to the left.

'Anyway,' said Lenny. 'Whatever. You *should* have told her about this girl back in January, when you first found out.'

'That's why you're picking a fight?'

'I'm just saying.'

'Lenny, do me a favour? Pull over here, would you?'

'Why?'

'Just do it.'

Lenny moved to the left lane and turned the engine off.

'Look at me,' said Danny.

Lenny turned to him and felt her face flush.

'Lenny, if you'd found out that Juliet had been having an affair—'

'Don't be ridiculous.'

'Answer me honestly – would you have told Matt?'

'That's a stupid, hypothetical question.'

'Lenny, would you have snitched on your best mate? Think about it for five seconds. If you're angry with anyone, be angry with Matt – not me,' said Danny, opening the car door.

'Danny, it's only another five minutes, get back in the car.'

'You're all right, Lenny. I need a bit of air.'

'But it's cold.'

'Don't worry,' he said, giving a tight smile. 'This time tomorrow I'll be on the beach.'

'Well . . . but . . . look,' she said, leaning across the seat, trying to catch his eye. 'I'm sorry, OK. I'm just upset for Juliet. And for Martha. This whole thing is just so, so . . . '

'Yeah, I know,' said Danny. 'I care about them too.'

She watched with a frown as he walked away, his hands thrust deep in his jeans pockets.

Back at the house, Lenny found Juliet lying on the sofa with her eyes shut. 'Honestly, Lenny,' said Juliet, without opening her eyes. 'I am going to be fine. I won't have you miss work on my account, I'll call you if I need anything.'

Lenny headed to work, stony-faced. It was so bitter out it might as well have been February and Lenny cursed the fact that she hadn't taken one of Matt's finest Italian cashmere jumpers, which she could then have set fire to once safe and warm inside Wappen. Well, not inside the building itself – that would be a safety hazard – but outside, by the recycling bins, preferably along with Cooper's Subbuteo balls.

In the management meeting when Occy asked for her feedback on the Big Sister app, Lenny realised that in light of the weekend's events she no longer gave a flying fuck either way. 'Yep,' she said to the team. 'This will be right up there, top three revenue generator alongside FishSelfie.' Occy gave her such a warm smile, Lenny thought she might gift her a shiny star sticker.

That afternoon Lenny sat at her desk, her fingers twitching over her keyboard. Should she email Danny an apology? He'd been so supportive all weekend, and she had been a bitch earlier. Still, she couldn't get past the fact he should have done something to stop this happening. Juliet's was by far the most epic relationship break-down of any of her friends, with a cherry on top. Juliet was the kindest, fairest person Lenny had ever known, and though Lenny had grown up in a household where Gloria's constant refrain was 'life isn't fair – get over it', Juliet had inhabited a different world. And what was happening now was so deeply, profoundly unfair. Lenny was well aware how entirely inadequate and juvenile the word 'fairness' – or even the concept of it – was, at a time like this.

So sod it: no point apologising to Danny. By the time he was next near a computer, he'd be eyeing up some surfer-chick. He might have helped out these last three days, and that was great and all, but now he was heading for sunshine, and Juliet for nothing but a storm.

Juliet stared numbly into her garden. The wind had taken its toll. The daffodils' stems were bent and broken; the magnolias had turned from tightly closed buds to a mass of crumpled pink and white petals, a thousand wet losing lottery tickets scattered across the lawn.

Matt would be back tomorrow and then regardless of how busy he claimed to be she would make him look her in the eye. How could he do this, how? She felt confusion and misery rise up again, felt tears threatening. Coffee! All she needed was strong coffee. She was always emotional when she was exhausted, and she really was exhausted; all that sleep at the weekend seemed to have left her more tired.

Sod Matt's stupid over-complicated state-of-the-art espresso machine. She put the kettle on and checked her emails. One from Danny with his details in Thailand. One from Martha with photos of her and Nate on the Golden Gate Bridge. And one from Mitchell

– the pull-out had been a triumph, he'd like to catch up to talk about the new bread book.

She hadn't even thought to buy the paper yesterday. She'd worryingly lost track of what day it was, and now Mitchell wanted a catch-up? In person? Which would require getting dressed and leaving the house? These things simply were not possible, not until she'd actually had a conversation with her husband telling him the game was up. Game! Her entire marriage had apparently been a game – and one she'd just lost. What on earth would they tell Martha when she came home? Did Matt think Martha would believe his lies too?

In fact why *was* she waiting till tomorrow? He'd probably be too cowardly to meet her gaze or – worse! – he'd look at her brazenly, like he had when he'd lied about Big Ange. No. She didn't need to sit in purgatory a minute longer.

She must have put too much coffee in her cup because her hand wouldn't stop shaking as she dialled. She listened as the foreign ringtone went unanswered. A text arrived: *Still with clients – speak when I'm back tomorrow?*

She replied: *I know about Tasha. I know Angela's entire story – including your trips to Japan, etc. Shame on you.* She'd forgotten where else Angela had said they'd been but that didn't matter. *I would appreciate you phoning me to discuss how we handle this with our daughter.*

She wasn't sure what response she expected: a degree of apology, some element of denial, surely?

Martha's an adult now. We'll simply tell her that it is what it is – we've grown apart. But perhaps not just yet? Think about it, J, you don't want to ruin her trip, do you?

Juliet opened a kitchen cupboard and reached for the canapé platter he'd brought back from Warsaw – *that* was where Angela had been with him – and raised it high above her head. She took a deep breath in, blew it out.

On second thoughts, the dish was far too pretty to smash. She'd give it to the charity shop. Instead she turned her attention to his coffee machine, ran her hand over the sleek surface then attempted to snap off the stainless steel milk frother – bloody German engineering: solid, unbreakable. The most she could do was throw away the detachable metal filter, which did not seem an appropriate and proportional gesture.

No: she would not let him reduce her to a crazy person. If she couldn't even break Matt's coffee machine, there was no way she'd let him break her.

This was not the worst thing that had ever happened. This was not her mother being destroyed by cancer in the space of two months, while she and her dad stood by helplessly watching.

She would get through this.

13

The following Tuesday, Juliet woke with a dull pain in her stomach and a desperate urge to ask Matt why he'd timed his departure for the week after their anniversary. Surely he'd decided he was leaving her before their party?

She hoped this urge would pass once she'd had a shower but as she slowly shampooed her hair, she felt the pressure of curiosity swell in her brain, then spread through her body so that by midday it was all consuming. If she didn't ask him today – *face to face* – she might implode or explode; preferably implode, that'd be easier to clean up.

Why had she left it a whole week to have this conversation? Admittedly these last seven days she'd spent most of her time staring into space, or in bed, sedated by Danny's valium, but she was on the mend now, she definitely felt strong enough to see Matt. Besides, how could she truly move on without facts? Knowledge would help shift the pain, the truth would set her free.

The Juliet of two months ago would never have turned up at Matt's office unannounced, she would have considered it unseemly, but appearing unseemly was of minor concern as she hovered by a pillar outside the thick glass doors. Did she look mad in the reflection? Her hair was neat enough, scraped back into a ponytail; she looked tired and pale, but she'd managed to apply make-up. She could pass for normal.

The receptionist called through to Matt's department and after an evidently confusing conversation asked Juliet to take a seat. A few minutes later Matt appeared, looking flustered.

'What's happened? Is everything OK?'

'I've come to speak to you,' she said, firmly.

'Now? I've got a squash game with Caspar – I'm borderline late already. Why are you looking at me like that, Jules? If you'd told me you wanted to see me, I could have rearranged Caspar or something,' he said, throwing his hands up in confusion.

'You can't just walk out of a marriage without expecting to talk about it at some point face to face like an adult.'

'Of course, but can we talk at the weekend?'

'Matt, I know you obviously aren't too bothered about my opinion, but you might be bothered by your receptionist's – she seems intrigued and, quite frankly, who can blame her! Our neighbours are all talking, you think people don't notice but they do.'

'Juliet,' said Matt, lowering his voice. 'Please. Not here.'

'Then come round the corner with me now.'

'But I haven't even got my jacket.'

'You don't need a bloody jacket.'

Juliet was trembling with rage as they walked in silence to a coffee shop. She shouldn't have come, she should have done this over the phone because looking at him sitting with his arms casually folded, as if waiting for an inevitable bollocking from teacher for not doing his homework, she realised she'd never disliked anyone quite as much as she disliked him now.

'I know Danny's given you some sob story,' said Matt, stirring a sugar into his espresso. 'But he had no right to tell you anything.'

'If he hadn't told me, I'm not sure where we'd be right now!' said Juliet. She thought she'd be able to stay calm, but already her voice was shrill. 'Would you have come home? Or were you always planning on leaving for good that day?'

'I—' Matt opened his mouth then promptly shut it. He hadn't had anywhere near enough time to work out a response that would make him look good.

'What was going on in your mind that morning? You said you had a dinner with the Germans, presumably that was a lie?'

Matt shook his head. 'You're over-thinking all of this, making out like I had some master plan. I simply woke up that day and couldn't do it anymore.'

'Do *what* anymore?'

'Live in that marriage. All that talk at the party of another Bank

Holiday weekend, another summer, trapped with those same people doing those same things again . . . '

'You mean our *friends*?'

'Juliet.'

'So to be clear: you'd been seeing this new person – the one *after* Angela – for *how* long at that point? Danny said he caught you in January.'

'Her name is Tasha,' he said tightly. 'And this isn't about Tasha – please don't drag her into this.'

Juliet shook her head. 'You must think I'm the stupidest woman on the planet.'

'What? *What*? OK, fine, yes, I had *met* her already. But nothing had happened physically, I was just helping her with her CV—'

'Oh for God's sake!' said Juliet, pushing the table an inch away from her. 'Don't you want to tell the truth? Don't you think it might help you as well as me?'

'Fine, OK, what do you want me to say? The truth is Tasha and I fell in love the moment we met. It literally felt like I'd been dead these last few years and suddenly I felt alive again.'

Maybe the truth wouldn't set Juliet free; maybe it would actually hurt more.

'Do I feel bad about you? Of course!' he said, shaking his head, and for a moment looking sincere. 'I'm not a monster, but I can't apologise for my feelings. I refuse to! Life is short and I deserve happiness just as much as anybody else does.'

Juliet took a deep breath. 'So did you feel alive all those years you were having sex with Angela? Or did you feel dead with her too?'

'See? I try to be honest and you try to twist my love for Tasha into something cheap – but you can't. I hope one day you'll feel about someone the way I feel about her because you deserve to Jules. You're still attractive. There's nothing to say it can't happen for you too now you're back on the market.'

'Does this girl know about Angela? That you have form? It doesn't bother her that you're a liar?'

'Look, you're angry. I get that. But I've been completely honest with Tasha from the start. She understands that sometimes people do things because they're driven to it—'

'*I* drove you to the affairs?'

'I'm not saying *you* per se – more unconscious drives. My struggle against suffocation, the tedium of domesticity—'

'Good grief, Matt – I didn't realise you were the one at home doing the ironing!'

'Tasha practises self-forgiveness daily.'

'I bet she does!'

'She is wise beyond her years. I'd like to think one day you two could . . . well, if not be friends . . . I do think you'd like her.'

Juliet rubbed her brow. Over the last five minutes she'd developed a nauseating headache above her right eye. 'I think you've actually lost your mind, Matt. I think you're so blinded by sex or whatever this is you've completely lost touch with reality.'

'I'm sorry you're upset.'

'Not sorry *you* upset me?'

'You know what? I possibly do owe you an apology. I think at some level I thought that if I left *after* the anniversary, this should be easier for you.'

She felt her shoulders tense with loathing. 'Easier for me?'

'I didn't want to ruin the party; you were looking forward to it so much. But I see, in retrospect, perhaps I should have told you earlier. That *was* a misjudgement,' said Matt, with a nonchalance that made Juliet fear she might smash his face in. 'I suppose there's never a good time to leave.'

Now would be a good time: leave now, leave now, leave now. But she didn't. Instead, as if in slow motion, she reached out for her cup of now-cool tea and flung it straight in front of her, watching, mesmerised as the pale brown liquid spread itself over Matt's crisp white Savile Row shirt. Her aim was true, she'd hit his sleeves, his torso, his chest, even the tops of his thighs.

He was right, he should have brought his jacket.

It was one step up from throwing away the filter on his coffee machine, yet still this act did not feel much like victory.

14

Spring that year turned into a time of hibernation. As the days became warmer and the nights longer, Juliet went into a state of slow, still shock. Every morning she'd wake and for the first two, or sometimes three seconds, she felt OK. Then the weight of unhappiness would crush her.

Matt picked up most of his things the week after they'd met up, while she was out. She returned to find the place changed from a home back into a house – like a body once the soul had left. The whole experience reminded her of death: the initial shock, the busy aftermath; then the noise finally fading and leaving you with the cold, permanent reality of loss.

They communicated by email.

What should we tell our friends? They're asking us round for dinners.

Nothing – it's not their business.

Matt, do you envisage *ever* telling the truth?

The effort of stripping away her anger to preserve her dignity was debilitating. The only thing they agreed on was waiting until May to tell Martha when she was back and settled from her trip. Matt was protecting himself; Juliet was protecting Martha.

Juliet and Matt's lives were a patchwork she now unpicked alone. Once she started looking at the layers of betrayal, examining both sides, analysing the subtle and more obvious faults in the fabric, she felt herself coming apart at the seams. She was stuck in the middle of a shared life. She had their past: love, marriage, their home, their daughter – every significant thing together; and then all the joys to come – and that was the tricky part. Juliet didn't know how to grieve for her lost future.

Her two consolations were that at least Martha wasn't still living at home and also, thank goodness, her own mum hadn't lived to see Juliet struck so low. As consolations go, they weren't the greatest.

She tried to keep busy. She spoke to Mitchell, agreeing to discuss the new book when she was over this really nasty virus. She tidied, she cleaned, but where could she file all these messy feelings? One Friday afternoon at the end of April, she found herself curled up in a ball on the kitchen floor, holding a photo taken the day Martha was born, unable to stop sobbing.

It was only Lenny, arriving after work with yet another takeaway and flowers, that forced Juliet to pick herself up off the ground, legs shaking as she walked to the door.

Lenny had spent most of her weekends since Easter at Juliet's. Like a couple in the first throes of love, their time was spent in a haze of wine and talking – but with zero sex and way more revenge fantasies.

Juliet had decided to start seeing a therapist, but Lenny knew people who'd been in therapy for years and still all they did was blame their mothers. The only thing that could help was time, but time seemed to have frozen for Juliet. So much of her energy seemed to be taken up with the business of getting out of bed and pretending to be OK, she seemed to do everything else at half speed.

Juliet was in the habit of washing her face with a rose-scented cream she'd rub into her skin, then wash off with three separate rinses of a muslin cloth. But recently she'd taken to standing, staring at her reflection and thinking: Did Matt see something in my eyes that made him think I was easy to fool? She'd barely pass the cloth over her skin.

Lenny caught her one Sunday morning in front of the glass. Juliet had never been vain, but Lenny saw her transfixed by her own reflection.

When she saw Lenny behind her, she turned her gaze downwards. 'How do you cope with the loneliness? Lenny, I don't know how to do it. Please tell me how to do it.'

Lenny pulled her close and held on to her. 'You just have to get on with it.'

Which was a better answer than the truth, which was: some days I don't.

15

Saturday afternoon of the May Bank Holiday, Juliet stood in the kitchen with her back to Matt. Martha would be here any minute, and Juliet was ragged with nerves. Perhaps she should have warned Martha there was bad news coming, but then Martha would have demanded to know on the phone. Maybe she should have asked Martha to come down earlier, but she and Nate had been busy every weekend since they'd been back. This was the first weekend Martha was in London alone. Oh, what was the point of agonising over the logistics? There was no right time to have this conversation.

'She's not expecting a full cream tea,' said Matt softly. 'You don't need to make sandwiches.'

Juliet scraped the knife across the butter; damn it, why hadn't she taken it out of the fridge earlier? 'Don't tell me what I should and shouldn't do.'

'Look, I'm just saying . . . Oh, forget it. OK, so I'll explain it in broad terms and, as agreed, no need to touch on any other factors.'

Juliet dragged the knife over the Hovis. 'We're calling your girlfriend a factor now?'

Matt sighed in frustration. 'Why can't you accept that Tasha has nothing to do with me leaving – she was a catalyst, not a cause.'

The same reason I can't accept anything that comes out of your mouth, thought Juliet, but instead took a sharp knife and thinly sliced the cucumber.

'This is hard for me too, you know – I'm losing my best friend,' he said, then was saved from Juliet's furious response by the doorbell. 'OK, darling, let's keep this as unified and reassuring as possible.'

Unified and reassuring? A catalyst, not a cause. Christ, was he standing for local by-election?

'Please, Juliet, for Martha's sake.'

The only reason she was doing *any of this* was for Martha's sake.

The only reason to pretend some semblance of unity was so that her daughter wouldn't hate Matt as much as Juliet currently did. 'Matt, our daughter is young but she's not an idiot. If she asks me directly I will not lie to her face.'

'She's not going to *ask you directly*. It's fine, I'll handle it.'

Juliet stared at the sandwiches. Martha would probably take one look at shop-bought bread and know something was seriously wrong.

'Are you pranking me?' said Martha, looking first to Juliet and then to Matt, sitting together on the sofa, Matt's hands clasped tightly between his knees.

Juliet smiled in an attempt to be reassuring, but immediately saw Martha's face crumple into confusion.

'But why? What's happened?'

'Darling,' said Matt, tenderly. 'Your mother and I, we got together when we were terribly young. At your age we were already married, with you on the way.'

'What's that got to do with anything?' said Martha.

'I suppose . . . ultimately . . . we've grown apart. There's no "reason" as such, but you'll understand when you're our age that who you are at nineteen is not the same person you are as you're nearing your forties.'

Juliet felt her top lip twitch in irritation.

'But . . . that doesn't make any sense. You guys are one of the happiest couples I know. Something must have happened since the party.'

Matt rubbed his forehead slowly with his palm. 'I moved out a month ago,' he said, sorrowfully. 'I'm renting a place in Clerkenwell, it's very small—'

'A *month* ago and neither of you thought to *mention* it?'

'There was no point telling you while you were away,' said Juliet. 'You were having such a lovely time.'

'So you left a giant shit bomb for me to come home to? So hold on, Dad, you've actually moved out? Mum! What has he done?'

'Darling, I haven't done anything,' said Matt, patiently.

Juliet listened to him with fascination and disgust – he really was a most excellent liar.

'Mum? Why have you done this to him?'

'Martha,' said Matt, reaching for Juliet's hand. 'There are things that might not seem to make sense now, but longer term they're ultimately for the best – for everyone.' Juliet stared at his hand. She had not signed off on any politician's wife fake hand holding!

'Why are you defending Mum if she's made you leave for no reason?'

Juliet removed her hand from under Matt's and folded her arms tightly.

'Darling, it's not your mother's fault. It simply is what it is.'

'No, what it *is* is bullshit!' said Martha, as tears started to form.

Juliet rose to comfort her, but Martha pushed her away and stormed out. Juliet and Matt waited in silence as they heard her footsteps overhead and then the slam of her bedroom door.

Juliet's voice trembled with rage. 'You have got to tell her something. Maybe if you're honest now there's a chance she might respect you for it down the line.'

'You just want her to think I'm a complete arsehole!'

'I'm not taking the credit for that. You go up there right now and make this right!'

'You've put me in an impossible situation.'

'You've put *yourself* in it.'

'I'm not telling her, I can't. It will hurt her.'

'Yes, of course it will hurt her,' said Juliet, choking back her own tears. 'It already has.'

How very young Martha suddenly looked, lying on her bed, her cheeks pink and blotchy, her hair swept over her face. Juliet sat by her feet, reached out and gently rubbed her calf. Martha feebly kicked her away. 'Leave me alone, Mum. I don't want to speak to you, or him!'

'Martha. We both love you very much. Please remember that.'

'Oh my god!' Martha suddenly scrambled to sitting. 'Danny!' she said, in disgust.

'What about Danny?' said Juliet, warily.

'They had a fight but Dad wouldn't say why. You had a thing with Danny! That's why they fell out, and that's why he's left you – you and Danny had an affair!'

'Martha, stop this right now!'

'Well then . . . tell me what's going on, please?' said Martha, her body shaking into sobs. 'Has Dad done something awful? He has, hasn't he? Is it Danielle? She's always flirting with him, that horrible bitch!'

'Martha!'

Martha reached for her mother's hand.

Juliet looked into her daughter's eyes, her lashes heavy with tears, and felt her own heart break all over again.

'Please, Mum, don't lie to me.'

Juliet couldn't do it; she could not sit here and lie. Was that a sign of weakness or of strength? What difference. Martha deserved the truth, if not all the grimy details.

16

It was the start of October, the days draining of the last hope of warmth. Six months had passed, the lows of which had been bountiful: finding out from Matt's credit card statements that he'd been spending a lot of time, and their money, in Prada and Agent Provocateur. Discovering couples you'd been friends with half your life didn't want to take sides, but nor did they want you round for dinner – a good-looking soon-to-be-divorcée posing an overwhelming threat. These paled in comparison to the fallout with Martha.

Juliet had told Martha the bare minimum: Matt had met someone else. She hadn't told Martha about Angela, nor the previous affair, nor Tasha's age. Still, Martha's father had been Martha's hero; these facts were enough to sink her. She'd insisted on coming home to see Juliet every other weekend during the summer term, and now she was going back to university lugging with her anger, distrust and sadness.

Matt had called Juliet in a rage. 'I cannot believe you did this to her – you are so selfish.'

Juliet could no longer handle these conversations where he turned facts on their head. Since then, Martha hadn't spoken to Matt, Matt had barely spoken to Juliet, and when Martha spoke to Juliet, she sounded permanently bruised. Only three weeks ago, she'd threatened to defer her year, to come home and spend it with Juliet.

'Mum, I don't want you to be on your own.'

'I'm fine, darling, honestly. Martha, I dropped out of university and limited myself, you can't do it too. What your father's done . . . in the scheme of things . . . well, you cannot let that get in the way of your future.'

Thank heavens for Celina, a phrase Juliet rarely employed. Juliet had started on the new bread book, and every day the necessity of working towards a deadline had forced her out of bed. She'd worked solidly, steadily, and created sixty recipes. In the kitchen her focus moved mercifully to her fingertips and away from her brain. There was much comfort in her work, its precision. The ingredients of bread-making were few, simple and honest. If you followed Juliet's recipes things worked out and if you didn't, they didn't. They were due to shoot this book in November. There was less daylight to work in than for Easter's shoot, so it would be physically less intense – and short of Matt announcing he was trans-gendering, it couldn't be as stressful emotionally.

Six months had passed. She *had* made progress. Lenny kept telling her six months was nothing, it had once taken Lenny two years to get over a relationship, but that was Lenny.

But sitting here today, waiting for final feedback from Celina, staring out of the window at the autumn leaves starting to turn, it did not feel much like progress. It felt as though the day she'd found out the truth she'd been in a car accident. Bang, crash, impact! She'd been in shock, suffered cuts and bruises and a few broken bones, but she'd been able to walk away from the wreckage – she had.

But it had taken her all this time to realise that inside she was still bleeding – she wasn't free at all.

Six months for Lenny and nothing much had changed. She'd been to Wappen's offices in Stuttgart, Mumbai, Berlin, Antwerp and Dubai, spending barely a night in each city. In August she'd turned thirty-eight at a conference in Bratislava on Haptic Comms – Touching The Future. The only thing she'd touched that night were some disturbing Slovakian dumplings.

DogAndJog had been Wappen's big hit of the summer. They'd employed two new cookie-cutter Oxbridge types. Cooper continued to make his mark – only last month he'd introduced Adult Colouring In Books for all staff, and was laying plans for an agency Water-Pistol Championship come next spring.

In her personal life it was business as usual too. She'd endured seven colossally dreadful Tinder dates, and after each had ricocheted straight back into Ellis's consoling arms.

Lenny was weary, she was tired, but more than anything she was worried about Juliet.

Juliet had once said that losing Matt felt like a living bereavement because unlike normal grieving, the person you'd lost was still alive. Lenny thought she'd got it the wrong way round. Matt was the one so un-dearly departed, but it was Juliet who'd turned into a ghost.

Lenny sat at her desk on Friday morning, three pages into her report on FangClub – another facial analysis app from the same client they'd worked with on Highbrow-Eyebrow. 'The app demonstrates how the user will look with various dental enhancements – straighter teeth, a gum reshape' . . . Lenny ran her tongue over her right incisor; gum reshape sounded positively medieval. She let her mind drift to all her future happiness. Next year she'd save up and go to South America, have a proper holiday! She'd have lost weight by then too, though you were allowed a sizeable bottom in your bikini in Brazil.

She looked up as Occy entered the room. 'Can I borrow you a moment?'

Lenny's stomach dropped. What now? She hadn't even done anything!

Occy tipped her head to one side. 'Lenny, I've noticed you've been very quiet recently.'

'Oh. Have I?' said Lenny, straightening up in her chair.

Occy's brow wrinkled, as though she could hear a distant mobile ringing. 'You're subdued.'

'Possibly . . . I guess . . . The thing is . . . '

Occy smiled. 'I sense a new maturity in you. I don't know whether it's something in your personal life making you happier – I shan't pry – but anyway, long may it continue.'

Wow, thought Lenny. My best friend's heartbreak, and the commensurate squelching of the last smidgen of faith I had left in the universe, is clearly a winning look.

'Lenny, there's a key Personal Development app proposal pending. I want you to embrace the project two hundred per cent.' Occy smiled her perfect little white teeth. 'If you do, I guarantee you'll be pleased with the outcome.'

Mathematically you actually mean one hundred per cent, thought Lenny, but decided it wiser not to heckle.

Lenny turned up at Juliet's that night and found her already in pyjamas.

'Fancy the pub?' said Lenny. 'You can wear that dressing gown, it kind of looks like one of those nice MaxMara coats.'

Juliet held up the belt strap dubiously. 'The neighbours will have a field day. Sorry . . . ' she said, heading through to the sitting room. 'I've had such an annoying day. I took five boxes of props round to Celina's house to sign off for the shoot and it turns out she's gone to Ibiza with Serafina, the make-up artist. I confirmed that meeting with her on Wednesday! And now my lawyer says Matt's Form E makes no sense and he's hiding half his bonus payments.'

He's such an epic wanker, thought Lenny, though what was the use of saying it? It gave her minus pleasure to witness how much greater a pillock Matt was than she'd ever envisaged. 'Jules, if I ever bump into him, do I have your permission to tell him exactly what I think of him?'

'Do whatever you like,' said Juliet, picking at the corner of the cushion she was hugging. A loose thread had started to unravel and she wrapped it tightly round her fingertip till her skin turned white.

On Sunday Lenny tried to drag Juliet to Columbia Road market but Juliet had slept badly and decided to stay put. As Lenny browsed the stalls full of light and life and colour, she thought of Juliet, depleted back home, and it made her furious; she felt so powerless to help.

She returned festooned with delphiniums, and fresh bread from St John. Juliet had been picking at her food for months but when Lenny came through to the living room with two plates of Welsh rarebit her eyes lit up and she took a bite. 'You know, you've really mastered your craft.'

'Actually it's a challenge knowing exactly how much Worcestershire sauce to sprinkle in.'

'I wasn't being sarcastic – you've found your forte.'

Lenny laughed. 'OK, so, there's a Danish film on at the art house cinema with that hot guy from *Game of Thrones*? We could sit and perv on eye candy while eating actual candy? Or how about we drive to a country pub? I made a list, it's in my bag somewhere . . . '

Juliet reached out her hand to stop her. 'I promise I'll be livelier soon. It's just coming off the sleeping pills has left me tired . . . '

'Please! Matt gives you a metaphorical punch in the face and you're not fully back on your feet yet. Don't beat *yourself* up.'

'But you should be out enjoying your weekend.'

'Jules, I don't care if we sit here for two years. I want you to know that things will get better.'

'I know they will, I do. I just could really do with a timing plan.'

'Let's do something practical? We could clear up the spare room? Or hack Matt's Facebook account, make a public service announcement.'

'Lenny, the best revenge is living well.'

No, the best revenge is shagging someone younger and hotter and not giving two hoots what your ex thinks. Lenny was about to say as much, when she realised this was exactly what Matt was up to.

'How about a classic DVD?' said Lenny. 'And I'll pop down the offy and buy us booze to match. *The Godfather II* and some Sicilian red?'

'Too bloody.'

'*Casablanca*? Do Moroccans make wine? Or something funny or adventurous? *Nymphomaniac*? Weird sex, Fran at work saw it, said it was so bad she laughed the whole way through – though I'm not sure what we'd drink with it.'

'I'm not really in a sex mood.'

'I've got it: *Thelma and Louise!* With a nice bottle of bourbon to see us through the afternoon?'

'That is not the worst idea you've ever had,' said Juliet, and Lenny was relieved as hell to see the trace of a genuine smile – albeit small – on her friend's face.

'I think we've done ourselves proud, Thelma,' said Lenny, holding the bottle of amber bourbon to the fading light.

'I always thought Louise was the cooler one,' said Juliet, taking the bottle from Lenny and pouring herself another thumb's worth.

'Thelma's the one who gets to shag Brad Pitt. Plus you have that big Geena Davis smile.' Or at least you used to.

Juliet pressed pause and turned to Lenny. 'We should do something like that.'

'Oh Jules – it does not end well.'

'I don't mean the Grand Canyon part. But we should have an adventure, just take off somewhere fabulous one of these days.'

One step at a time, thought Lenny. First I have to figure out a way to get you out of your house.

PART FOUR

*'The spring seasons are hidden in the autumns,
And the autumns are charged with springs'*

Rumi

17

'It's like a flipping circus in here today,' Philpott muttered to Lenny as he cast a glance round the boardroom table.

Lenny wasn't sure if he was referring to Occy's clown-striped playsuit or Nick's latest plans for a giant indoor slide, but either way, all she was focused on was the Vietnamese spicy sandwich she had planned for her lunch.

'Word up, guys, got a Biggy Bigs on the pad today,' said Occy. 'But first, the Biggy Smalls But Perfectly Formed. Celebulist! – a subscription-based app, offering curated lists of celebrities' favourites: Gisele's favourite jeans, Alexa's favourite muses. Everybody loves lists, everybody loves celebrities: it literally is a no brainer.'

So it is, thought Lenny. Where could she borrow fifty grand? An app that matched your film to your booze – that *was* a million dollar idea, maybe she could get it co-funded by her two beloveds, Oddbins and Netflix?

Lenny sensed a shift in the room's atmosphere and hurriedly tuned back in to hear Occy saying ' – client briefing literally gave me goosebumps, European roll-out is practically bullet proof!'

This must be the app Occy had mentioned. What did bullet proof mean exactly, did it involve a Kardashian?

'Lenny, what's the number one growth area in apps?'

Porn. Seven hundred per cent uplift and rising energetically. And it didn't rule out a Kardashian. Would Wappen tackle a porn brief? Lenny didn't want to – and as for Occy The Feminist?

Cooper was straining to contain himself: 'Wellness! Sorry, Lenny – it's what I do.'

Lenny narrowed her eyes.

'Wellness – specifically happiness!' said Occy. 'Happiness is *the* number one socio-political and economic lifestyle trend and HappyGuru is a problution-focused human-first-designed technically pioneering enabler of personal growth, offering transformative paradigm change, it's taken the client's unicorn.'

Philpott turned to Lenny in confusion. 'It's taken the client's unicorn?'

Lenny shook her head. 'Client's now a unicorn.' Philpott still looked confused.

Occy continued: 'The genius of HappyGuru is in its holistic approach. For example "Running" – you'd traditionally measure success in terms of the physical, the effect on body fat, but HappyGuru also measures the effect on your soul, so no more soul fat either!' She read from the press release: '"HappyGuru's architects have travelled the four corners of the earth . . . "'

Earth's round, thought Lenny, round things don't have corners, in the same way souls don't have fat, or at least she hoped they didn't.

'"We've gathered golden nuggets of happiness to fast-track your empowerment – "'

Ooh, perhaps she fancied fried chicken for lunch instead of Vietnamese . . .

'" – and make each day a day filled with sunshine from within."'

Lenny's gaze drifted outside – it was pissing down out there, in fact, was that hail?

'"Erasmus said: 'Happiness is reached when a person is ready to be what he is.' We think Erasmus was trying to say that true happiness comes from being your authentic self."'

Lenny turned to see Cooper nodding ostentatiously. As if Cooper even *had* an authentic self, the chameleon! She'd seen him briefing the design team, dropping his 'ts' – all *awight guv'nor* – then channelling full Bullingdon Club around senior clients. And as for his hair! One week, Brooklyn-man-bun, the next, a shaved head and a beard so manicured it was like he'd measured each hair against some GQ dapper barometer.

'"HappyGuru is a self-improvement enabler for all",' read Occy. 'So, Entry Level is freemium, but for a three pound ninety-nine upgrade to Platinum Access, the app literally guarantees happiness – but only on an iPhone at the present time.'

'There's money in them thar hills,' said Philpott, wearily.

'Exactly – the perfect hybrid of spirituality and business!' said Occy, handing the file to Lenny with both hands. 'So Lenny – the full three sixty? Two hundred per cent? Bring your A game?'

'Consider my A game brung,' said Lenny. 'I mean brought. I mean brung.'

Lenny had tucked herself away in the Free-Me Zone in an attempt to concentrate on the HappyGuru bumf. It appalled her that as a thirty-eight-year-old woman, she could not be alone in a room with Wi-Fi and exercise sufficient self control not to Google *Will it stop raining by tomorrow? Is Ryan still with Eva? What is 143lbs in kilos?*

She was readjusting her bottom on the beanbags when the door opened and Cooper appeared. Lenny shook her head. 'This room is for quiet contemplation only, I was here first so unless you're here to take my coffee order, please leave.'

'Your aggressive flirtation is fooling no one,' said Cooper, taking the beanbag next to her. 'If I didn't know better, I'd say you were in love with me.'

'Nick, if you were this funny in real life I might be.'

'So,' he said, leaning back and resting an exposed ankle on his knee. 'What do you think?'

'I think you should never wear skinny cropped jeans unless you're Italian – and in Italy – and even then exercise caution.'

'I meant of the brief?'

Lenny shrugged. Before the Mattastrophe she'd have said that HappyGuru was cynical – happiness was not a business but a wondrous, joyful, transitory human emotion to be cherished during the fleeting moments it appeared. She'd have said attempts to measure it were tyrannical, and that a failure to achieve peak happiness 24/7 was yet another inadequacy-shaped stick for people to beat themselves with. And for good measure she'd have added: spending *more* time hooked on your phone is *not the point*. But she'd spent her entire journey into work haunted by how lost Juliet had looked at the weekend. So now Lenny thought: if this app can guarantee even a five per cent uplift in happiness then it's worth a try.

'What are you disrupting today anyway?' said Lenny. 'Other than my concentration?'

'I'm planning a major revolution in this workplace.'

'Start with the bacon sandwiches. The bread's a disgrace.'

He proudly handed her his folder: Disrupt, Innovate, Connect, Kinship. She flicked idly through his plans for a revamped Game Zone.

'Subbuteo and ping-pong feel too nineties,' said Nick. 'I reckon we go old school on games, symbiose with the new eighties sweet shop pop-up in reception and get a floor-to-ceiling giant jelly bean dispenser.'

'Your acronym says it all,' she said, wearily handing it back. 'Nick, this is an office, not a playground.'

'A happy worker's a more productive one.'

'Yes? And how's this for a revolutionary thought: a happy worker's one who's paid a fare wage?'

'Ah, Lenny The Leninist – *so* twentieth century. Also, I'm thinking – how about we turn the top floor into a NERF Centre? You know, adult toys?'

'An entire floor of adult toys?' said Lenny in disbelief. 'The Americans will never sign off on that, they're far more conservative than we are, and wouldn't you need to black out the windows?'

'Lenny, do you even know what a NERF is?'

'Yes and you're getting on mine.' The beanbag made a tired shluffing sound as she stood. 'Cooper, happiness is not about jelly beans and stupid adult whatevers. If you'll excuse me, I'm going to take my research elsewhere.'

In fact to The Shepherdess – the local caff and Lenny's traditional hiding place. This was how she remembered Old Street before the hipsters invaded with their ironic everythings and their tattoos and their intimidating drip-fed coffees. In here, Radio One jangled away in the background, copies of the *Sun* decorated the tables and there was no bothersome Cooper.

She settled herself in the corner with her phone, a mug of strong tea and a fridge-cold Kit-Kat. OK then, HappyGuru, let's get to work . . .

The landing page showed a beatific blonde wearing a bikini, sitting in the lotus position in front of a liquid sunset of impossible beauty – pink and lilac and gold. Huh, thought Lenny, stick blondie on the Northern line in rush hour and we'll see how orgasmic her smile is . . .

On the next screen were the words: 'Happiness is a Choice'. Or a warm gun . . . Lenny entered the user name: Lenfer – and password: NickIsABellend5 – then swiped to the contents page: 'HappyGuru has been designed to dramatically enhance happiness in seven steps. Disclaimer: If you are suffering from moderate to severe emotional problems please consult your physician before starting.'

She flicked through the inspirational quotes section – the usual suspects, from Confucius to Clint Eastwood with a heavy smattering of Gandhi. One day Lenny would write a book of quotes and on the first page would be the distilled essence of all the wisdom Lenny had gleaned in her thirty-eight years on the planet:

Shit happens.
Then more shit happens.
As long as you don't expect shit not to happen, you'll be fine.

Lenny spent an hour investigating the prototype, paid her bill, then rang Juliet as she meandered back to the office.

'Jules, I have a proposition for you – please don't say no.'

'Depends what it is.'

'I have to test drive a new app for work, and I need a friend to help.'

'OK . . .'

'Amy's too flaky, Andrew's out of the question – there's Lycra involved – and actually bits of it might be fun, so I need you to commit to doing these things with me and you will occasionally have to leave your house at the weekends, and also your post code.'

'This isn't a dating app is it? I'm not quite ready to get back on the horse or whatever it is people ride nowadays.'

'They ride fixies – bikes with fixed gears – but no, this isn't a dating app.'

'So what is it?'

'It's smushed together the greatest hits of Buddhism, philosophy, self-help, diet, fitness and a bunch of mystical hippy crap. We're test driving the UK version because the Americans are worried Brits are too cynical and all we do is drink and moan about the weather.'

'Did you *see* that hail this morning?'

'Balls the size of Maltesers!'

'I'm debating turning the heating on.'

'So anyway, what do you reckon?'

'About my heating?'

'About the app!'

'But you haven't even told me what it does?'

'Oh . . . Well, it suggests activities – the usual bollocks: reiki, hugging strangers, scented candles – and by the end of seven stages it promises . . . well, it promises to make you a little bit happier.'

There was a pause on the line followed by gentle laughter. 'Lenny Dublonsky, why on earth would you think I might need to feel any happier? My life is so entirely fabulous right now, why, only this afternoon I spent two hours working out where to put my suppressed rage – Cath Kidston don't seem to make a box file big enough.'

'The app's not for *you*, obviously!' said Lenny, laughing. 'It's for *me* – strictly work! So . . . please? Help me?'

'Well, if it's to help *you*, how could I possibly say no?'

'Yay!' said Lenny, punching the air. 'Right, what's your diary like for the next few months?'

'I'm shooting the bread book in November but my nights and weekends are pretty free.'

'Great! So, first things first, there's a short questionnaire. OK, number one: "What is your current state of happiness?", one being "Can't get out of bed"; ten being "Bursting with fruit flavoured joy". Lordy, we need to get the copywriters to de-Americanise this . . . '

'Um, I *can* get out of bed. Though I wouldn't say I'm entirely the fruit thing.'

'I'll put happiness level four? Age – thirty-eight, gender – female . . . Next: which of the following currently makes you happiest?

Family
Friends
Food
Water sports
Religion / Belief in a Higher Power
A Sense Of Purpose
Helping Others'

'All of them bar religion and water sports,' said Juliet.

'OK. That's it? That's such basic data input,' said Lenny, making a note. 'Right, the app will suggest actions based on your data – follow the action, the app assesses your mood change then suggests further actions, so it's tailoring content all the way through The Journey – *Journey*! *So* American. So, let's see . . . today's October the sixth so, according to my phone, by the end of November we should be at least sixty-five per cent happier.'

'Or your money back?' said Juliet, laughing.

'No,' said Lenny. 'It doesn't mention anything in the small print about refunds.'

18

Lenny woke the following day feeling the tiniest bit encouraged. As soon as she was on the bus to work, she clicked on the smiley face icon to start:

> Congratulations on committing to achieving your goals. Your Personal Best Happy (TM) starts in your head. Positive Thinking is proven to be the foundation of the world's happiest people. Find a Positive Thinking workshop, show up with a smile! Check back in and tell us how you got on! Happy Days!

Ooh, and now it was going all highbrow:

> *'There is nothing either good nor bad, but thinking makes it so'* – William Shakespeare

Ah! If only Hamlet had downloaded this app, his life might have worked out a whole lot peachier . . . Positive thinking . . . *Seriously?* Juliet was the original positive thinker and look where it had got her.

Lenny googled and found an eight-week course, starting that Friday in Camden. Eight Friday nights, sitting in a circle with a bunch of North London yuppy self-help bores? Eight Friday nights that could be spent out on the lash, or watching Netflix, or doing anything *but* sitting in that circle?

Ah, this was better – a two-hour session for Time-Poor Professionals, tonight, £20 a head. Lenny hurriedly bought two tickets then texted Juliet, who immediately rang back.

'I'm so sorry, I should have said – Wednesday is therapy night.'

'My fault. I forgot. I'll see if there's another session.'

'No, you go. Take notes, you have to do it anyway, right? Or is this whole thing a ruse?'

'Not entirely,' said Lenny. 'How is the therapy going?'

'It's kind of interesting, I think we might be getting somewhere.'

When she was sixteen, Lenny had been to see a counsellor at the GP, when she was going through a particularly fractious time with her mother. The therapist had reminded her of Gloria – same hair, same deep-set frown lines. She'd suggested that Lenny was feeling a little angry and if so, why might that be? Lenny had reeled off the first thirty-two reasons that sprang to mind, starting with the list of nicknames she'd been called at school and finishing with 'being forced to see you because Mum thinks there's something wrong with me when actually I'm *just a normal teenager*, you have heard of *hormones*, haven't you?' The therapist had finished the session by telling Lenny that if she hoped a white knight was going to gallop in and rescue her from her life, she'd be waiting some time.

Fine. Lenny had become her own white knight. As for her jousting skills? She was still honing them.

Juliet had always thought therapy was a little self-indulgent, unless you were depressed. When Matt left her she hadn't been depressed, just paralytically sad, in a way that had annoyingly interfered with her ability to leave the house. She'd been too embarrassed to ask anyone she knew for a recommendation and instead had googled and found someone who looked impressive. If Matt could afford £450 Prada loafers and £395 G-strings for his girlfriend, he could damn well afford her Harley Street shrink.

She liked her therapist, Joan, a sharp-bobbed brunette with large brown eyes behind dark-rimmed spectacles. She didn't confuse Juliet with lots of jargon, and only occasionally replied to one of Juliet's questions with her own 'What do you think?'

Over their sessions they'd established that Juliet had come from an exceptionally happy, loving background which had created a secure sense of self. She was almost abnormally free of neuroses, had healthy boundaries and had – until recently – dealt with her life-traumas well.

'The thing I'm struggling with is why I didn't spot anything,' said

Juliet in her first session. 'Other people look at me like I'm entirely stupid, that I didn't see it coming.'

'You learned from your parents that it was safe to trust. If you're unfortunate enough to find a mate who is intent on deception, they're often adept at hiding it.'

'Do you think perhaps I *was* in denial?'

'What do *you* think?' said Joan, tipping her head to one side.

Juliet shrugged. 'I thought I *really* knew him, and I realise I didn't . . . How could I stop that happening again?'

'We can't control others, only ourselves, and you seem to do that admirably.'

'But what if I turn into a man-hater? My friend Lenny's mother became so embittered when her husband left, it poisoned every part of her life.'

'And before this woman's relationship ended, what was her outlook?'

Juliet had only known Gloria after Lenny's father had died. Gloria was not only a man-hater but a hater of many things, including kittens. 'I think she was built differently from me in the first place.'

Joan nodded. 'That's the thing about personality. By the age of seven, you basically are who you are.'

As Juliet sat down today she had a thought: they'd talked so much about Matt during these sessions, but she didn't want to spend a minute more with him in the room.

'Joan . . . I can see how I had a blind spot in my marriage, and I know Matt's deception wasn't my fault. But I'm not sure what I do next.'

'What would you like to do?'

Juliet looked to the ceiling, such beautiful cornices in these town-houses. 'I'd like to move on but all I see is this gaping abyss in front of me. I'm so used to being part of a couple, I feel like something's missing all the time.'

'Your whole adult life has been taking care of other people's needs – your daughter, your husband, even in your career. Take this current period of recovery to reflect on your own needs. Do some things purely to please yourself.'

Juliet considered this. 'Isn't that selfish?'

'Self-centred is not the same as selfish. Long-term relationships are based on constant compromises. Now's the time to explore your own world. You are the most important person in your life. Would you want your daughter to make herself happy?'

'Of course – all I want is for her life to be filled with things that are exactly what she chooses.'

'Right, so how about you start thinking about yourself in those terms too?'

The first hour of the positive thinking workshop was 1.4 times worse than Lenny had predicted: new age twaddle, with a few pertinent facts Lenny extracted for Juliet. She tried to concentrate but the speaker, Dr Durcat, reminded her of Elliot Sands from school, skin the colour of wet paper and a very thin nose, although Dr Durcat had a look of self-satisfaction poor Elliot had lacked, due to Danny spreading a rumour that Elliot had lost both testicles in a tragic boating accident.

Lenny's first question was borne out of professional curiosity, honestly. Dr Durcat had just made a point that negative thinking was a learned behaviour. 'As babies, we are all full of positivity but very quickly we learn negativity from those around us. By the time a child can verbalise, they've already picked up the habit of negative thinking.'

Lenny thought of Gloria and then of Juliet's mum and whether her and Juliet's lives would have turned out differently if they'd done a mum-swap. She wasn't sure if Dr Durcat had a point but either way, how could anyone prove it? Lenny raised her hand, gingerly.

Dr Durcat looked at her with a benign smile. 'Yes, lady with the dark ponytail?'

'How do you know babies are born positive?'

'As I just said, by the time they can talk, they're displaying positive or negative traits.'

'Right. But maybe babies are born neutral? Maybe they learn positivity and / or negativity?'

Dr Durcat looked down at his notes and frowned.

'I mean they're babies – they can't explain themselves,' said Lenny. 'Sorry, it's just that I'm a researcher and I think what your example actually demonstrates is that babies learn from their environment – full stop. What exact methodology was used?'

'It's not really important,' said Dr Durcat.

'It kind of is,' said Lenny. 'I mean they're babies: babies don't spend their time filling out questionnaires.'

'Perhaps you did when you were a baby . . . ' said Dr Durcat, smiling as the audience laughed. 'Let's move on,' he said, reshuffling his notes. 'The average individual has fifty thousand thoughts a day and naturally, if the bulk of those are negative – worrying about what has happened, or what may happen – the individual will experience negativity.'

Lenny didn't have anywhere near 50,000 thoughts a day – after a heavy night it was more like seventy. Maybe she had rotted her brain cells with wine? Should she go back to the GP and get a liver scan? Was she drinking too much? Could you get a liver scan on the NHS merely by asking for one? Was she nearly out of that nice Malbec? What time did the offy shut? Would that cute Italian be working there tonight? Or would it be that blonde cow who never wrapped the bottles nicely, was she dating the Italian and *that* was why she was always so unfriendly?

'The world is made up of energy and vibrations – it's essential that what you put out into the universe is positivity.'

Game over. Anytime there was talk of mystical vibrations, Lenny went into meltdown.

'If you send out negativity, you get it back. Yes?' he sighed. 'Another question?'

'So! I have a friend who's the most optimistic person I know, she only ever thinks the best of people, yet something very negative happened to her. Are you saying that's because she wasn't thinking positively enough?' Because that, Dr Durcat, is bullshit.

Dr Durcat gave a smug smile. 'Who knows how much worse things might have been if your friend wasn't such a positive thinker?'

'You mean she got off *lightly*? Because of her *vibes*?' Lenny tried to strip the scorn from her voice.

Dr Durcat shrugged. 'Who knows?'

'*Clearly* not you!'

'Moving on,' said Dr Durcat. 'Lady at the back with the scarf?'

'Doctor Durcat, when genuinely bad things do happen, how do you stay positive?'

'A problem is a solution waiting to happen. Often we find life's greatest challenges are an opportunity to grow. When it looks like we're facing a wall, the question to ask is not, "How do I get over this wall?", but rather: "Is this wall really a wall or is this wall a door?"'

Is that door really a door? thought Lenny, looking longingly towards the exit.

19

Juliet was in her kitchen the following afternoon, measuring out the spices for a chicken curry. Lenny was coming for dinner and a debrief and Juliet couldn't remember the last time she'd actually cooked for pleasure. Oh. Oh yes she could, for her anniversary.

She was levelling off a teaspoon of furious orange turmeric when her phone rang: Mitchell.

'Jules, sweetheart, Celina had a few thoughts when she was in Ibiza.'

What? Other than 'Will I get papped doing drugs?' and 'Which bikini best showcases my new breasts?' thought Juliet, then scolded herself for being so uncharitable.

'She thinks you've missed a trick and haven't put enough greens in the book,' said Mitchell. Juliet had only noticed, on this recent book, that when Celina loved an idea it was Celina's, but if she wanted a tweak then the idea reverted to being Juliet's. Perhaps she'd always been like this but Juliet had never noticed before.

'Greens?' said Juliet. 'Green *bread?*'

'Veggie stuff. She says Nigella's planning a veg book and Jamie's doing one, and can we add stuff to the sandwiches chapter, stick some greens in?'

Vegetables with bread. Juliet remembered a perfect plate of grilled flatbreads with spinach and feta on a family holiday in Crete years ago. A lazy afternoon in a taverna, Martha playing with the owner's son, she and Matt enjoying a few snatched glasses of wine. Only now when she thought back to it, her memory derailed itself as she started to wonder whether that holiday was before or after Matt's first affair.

'Can you turn around a dozen recipes and still shoot in November?' said Mitchell.

Juliet forced her attention back to the call. 'End of next week all right?'

'Superstar, Jules, you're always so accommodating – there's no one like you.'

She wondered if all of her happiest memories would suffer from a retrospective taint. If so, that would be a shame.

'It doesn't sound like I missed much,' said Juliet, pen in hand, as Lenny squinted to decipher her notes.

'What's that notepad?' said Lenny.

'It's the one you bought me!' said Juliet, holding up the cover: *Bread and Other Adventures.*

'Ah, well, there was definitely no bread, and even fewer adventures,' said Lenny. 'Let me see what I wrote . . . Basically the guy said "Think less, do more" . . . What else? "Turn thoughts around – don't think what you've lost, think what you've gained", so I guess don't think: "I've lost a husband", think "I've gained the rest of my life back". "Turn doubt into possibility" – so when you were saying you can't imagine loving someone that much again, just, like, try to?' Lenny blew out in frustration at how unhelpful she sounded.

Juliet wrote it all down. 'It sounds like common sense really, doesn't it?'

'I suppose it's just the first stage. What shall I put the score down as? You were a four.'

'I had an OK session with Joan yesterday so maybe a five?'

'Fine, so what it should do now is take the data and suggest the next action,' she said, tapping her phone. 'Gratitude Lists. Oh. Apparently you're meant to do these daily, in which case that should have been first,' said Lenny, irritably scribbling: *Navigation out of synch.* 'OK, so it says: "Before you go to bed write down everything you're grateful for." Hmm, well today that'll be the fact Occy was in Milan for a conference, and also this delicious takeaway.'

'Takeaway? I'll have you know I made this curry!'

'You did? Oh you *did*!' said Lenny, high-fiving her. 'Back in the game.'

'So – what's next?'

The sunshine icon spun round on Lenny's screen, then stopped in tandem with Lenny's smile.

'Yuk. "Sweat it out!"' said Lenny. '"Mainline your way to happiness with nature's Prozac – Endorphins! Boga, Discyco, Crossfit . . ."'

'What are they?'

'Boga is yoga meets Jamaican sexy dancing, Discyco is disco meets cycling, and Crossfit is weightlifting but modern and too hard.'

'How do you know all this?'

'The twentysomethings I work with do this for fun. So does Amy – she belongs to some "boutique" gym in Chelsea, two hundred pounds a month she pays! Hmm, maybe she can get us guest passes? I'll ring her.'

'Can't we just go for a jog in the park?'

Lenny was fully aware that in the park, with its wide open spaces, there was nowhere for her to hide, but in the back of a crowded exercise studio there just might be. 'It's good to try something outside your comfort zone,' said Lenny, scrolling for Amy's number.

'Chelsea's a bit poncy,' said Juliet.

Lenny shrugged. 'It's ringing at her end now, too late . . . Ah, Amy! Jules and I want to come to your gym with you, please?'

'Really? All right, I'll get you passes – if we can go out on the lash after,' said Amy.

'Fine. Saturday afternoon? Class wise, I'd rather not sweat too much, my hair goes frizzy.'

'Ha! Do you remember that time in Mexico, you'd forgotten your straighteners and that guy asked if you'd stuck your finger in an electric socket?'

'I do vaguely remember a very rude man yes. In fact, didn't you cop off with him?'

'Right, so . . . Saturday at four p.m., Studio A – Brutal Body Beasting?'

'Er, no.'

'Studio B, Abs Attack and Terror Thighs?'

'No!'

'Or Studio C, Ballet-Barre-Core-Flex? That's mainly floor work.'

'Floor work, excellent: lying down is my thing.'

'You'd better dress for it, Lenny, you can't just wear any old track-suit in that place. And be warned, if you don't work hard the trainer picks on you – it's worse than PE ever was.'

20

Lenny had insisted on a trip to a patisserie on Saturday afternoon, to give them the energy to face buying sportswear. She'd chosen poorly, and wrinkled her nose as she took a second bite of her carrot cake. 'Too sweet, don't you think?'

Juliet scraped the tip of her fork along the icing. 'They've just mixed icing sugar and butter, it needs cream cheese,' she said, taking out her notebook and scribbling, *Spinach and cream cheese sandwich?*

'How's Martha doing? Is she feeling any better?'

'She's OK,' said Juliet, though the question made her heart hurt. 'She's getting back into her studies, that's the main thing. She'll come down one weekend before Christmas. It would be nice if she could see Danny, too.'

'Danny? When's he back?'

'Oh, he got back a few weeks ago,' said Juliet, poking her fork warily into her own chocolate cake, dry as an old sponge and slightly less tasty.

'Did he?' said Lenny in surprise. 'Have you seen him?'

'He's really busy working, and back at night school, but he's called a few times, he wants to hang out.'

'Oh. My. Goodness!' said Lenny. 'Do you think he's going to try it on with you?'

Juliet put her fork down and stared at Lenny. 'Danny? With me? Not in a million years!'

'He's always had a little thing for you.'

'We had one tiny snog when I was fourteen.'

'Oh, but you should though,' said Lenny, debating whether to leave the rest of her cake, it really wasn't worth the calories.

'With *Danny Freeman?* Are you mad?'

'Oh, I know he's a total waster but he's got such beautiful eyes.

And that body! Plus it would annoy Matt so royally,' said Lenny, glowing with pleasure at the thought.

'Danny is my friend, he was Matt's best friend.'

'Exactly!' said Lenny. 'He's perfect: he's hot, he's not the type of guy you could ever fall in love with, and some meaningless filthy sex might do you good.'

Juliet shook her head. 'I'm not a meaningless filthy sex kind of girl.'

Lenny stared at the cake, it really was horrid. She hurriedly finished it and signalled for the bill. 'Why do you think he's so keen to see you then?'

'It's just Danny being sweet,' said Juliet, pushing her barely touched plate to one side.

Juliet could be a little naive sometimes, thought Lenny; men like Danny didn't waste their time being sweet.

Juliet browsed the racks of patterned Lycra in Strong Fit Sally while Lenny examined a pair of orange and fuchsia leggings. Lenny didn't get it: if you were a Large – which she was in this terrible place – why would you wear anything but the blackest of blacks on your lower half?

Lenny zipped up the waterproof jacket in the changing room and turned to look at her Lycra clad arse in the mirror. Not great, but a considerable improvement on her real one. 'How are you getting on?'

'It's a bit jazzy,' said Juliet. 'Come see?'

Lenny pulled back the curtain. Juliet was facing the mirror, wearing purple cycling shorts, a green sports bra and a luminous-pink vest. Lenny found herself staring at Juliet's toned legs, her absolute lack of cellulite, and she suddenly felt fourteen again, which for Lenny was never a good feeling. Lenny had been in the locker room one afternoon after netball, staring at Juliet's bottom. Well, not so much her bottom as the sides of it, what Gloria called her haunches. Lenny's haunches were displaying the first worrisome signs of dimpled flesh but Juliet's looked like she was born of an entirely different species. They were actually sculpted, like that Olga Korbut. On that long ago day, Lenny had suddenly felt the awkward sensation of eyes on her. She'd turned abruptly to see Annalex Williams looking at her shrewdly. Please, anyone but Annalex. She could imagine Annalex rushing to the common room, frothing at the mouth with Sapphic breaking news.

If Annalex had challenged her she'd have tried to explain: Yes, I want to look like Juliet, and be able to flit like she does – effortlessly between cliques – rather than be labelled geek till the day I die. Yes, I want to *be* Juliet – not because I'm in love with her, but simply because I don't want to be me. But fortunately Mandy Mullwood had bent to tie her shoelaces and farted like thunder, which had created sufficient stimulus for shaming to last until the bell rang for geography.

'What do you think?' said Juliet, adjusting the bra strap. 'Is it a bit tight?'

Lenny had stopped comparing herself physically to Juliet when she was fourteen, when she realised that every time she did, it made her feel rubbish. She must try to remember not to start again now.

Amy's gym was like an after-show party at London Fashion Week: a DJ, strobe lights, and dozens of abnormally long-limbed, hungry-looking women with voluminous Middleton blow-dries and fully contoured eye shadow. Lenny lost count of the number of large diamonds on display. Chelsea was a different world, one where women spent their husband's cash, and entire days making themselves look just like the woman next to them, only thinner.

Amy was at the bar area flirting with the instructor, a six foot two, broken-nosed hulk in shorts. She greeted Juliet with a long hug: 'Jesus, I'm still in shock! I was utterly devastated when I heard.'

'That's right,' muttered Lenny. 'Make it all about you.'

Juliet smiled gently at Amy. 'It's not been my favourite year . . . '

'Come with me,' said Amy, grabbing her arm and leading her into the studio. 'We'll do this class, then go drinking and I'll tell you how to take that rat to the cleaners.'

'Ladies!' shouted the instructor. 'Grab the dumbbells, straight into ten burpees, ten reverse lunges then ten push-ups to a T-stand.'

'The only T-stands I'm interested in hold scones,' said Lenny as they hurriedly arranged themselves on their mats.

'Thirty kettle bell sit-ups – faster, *faster*!'

'This is impossible,' said Lenny, whose face had already turned the shade it normally did after an hour's exercise.

'It is intense,' said Juliet.

'Ha!' said Amy, over her shoulder. 'This is just the warm up.'

The problem wasn't that Lenny was unfit – she was unfit, but it was more that she was mal-coordinated.

'Hands off the bar, engage glutes, sexy deep plié, bend left on one leg, right arm over, elbow twist, switch, reverse and switch again!'

Of course Juliet had been good at sport, whereas Lenny had expended all of her excess energy begging Gloria for sick notes. Lenny's periods had been ferocious, and the thought of some heinous incident like Lisa Rochman had suffered in the netball match against Camden High? You *never* got over that sort of trauma. 'Wear an extra pair of knickers if you're that worried,' said Gloria. 'I suppose my ovaries are Dad's fault too?' screamed Lenny in response. Lenny would rather be back on a netball court right now than in this over-priced swanky gym, burning with teenage inadequacy at the age of thirty-eight.

'Take that squat to the floor, hold, pulse, feel those legs burn!'

Around her, the women of Chelsea squatted and pulsed, their collagen pouts as bored as if they were flicking through *Tatler* in a Harley Street dermatologist's waiting room. Lenny was drenched in sweat, her thigh muscles were on fire and she was straining to breathe. 'Going . . . to . . . puke,' she said, emitting a grunt of pain before finally sitting in defeat.

'Over in the corner: failure is not an option!'

'Clearly it is!' shouted Lenny.

'Go into full body push-ups, come on lightweight – smash it!'

'I'm going to . . . do myself . . . an injury . . . '

'Lower, come on! Head to the floor.' The instructor bent down till his face was an inch from Lenny's. 'MAN UP OR SHUT UP!'

Lenny's arms were shaking violently. She felt her wrist about to snap, and chose instead to pitch forward and land on her face.

Part of her was secretly gratified to see a drop of blood fall from her nose to the mat.

'Oh Lenny, it's only a stupid exercise class,' said Amy.

'You said it was mostly lying down, you lying cow.'

'I guess it's different every week.'

'It's humiliating,' she said, touching her nose tenderly.

'Since when do you care what a bunch of trophy wives think?'

'So they *were* laughing at me?'

'They're just jealous,' said Juliet. 'We're obviously women who eat and they haven't tasted bread since the nineties.'

'Never again,' said Lenny.

'I think we should go for a run on the Heath tomorrow,' said Amy.

'Sounds good,' said Juliet. 'Lenny?'

'Nope, go without me.'

'Suit yourself,' said Amy. 'Right, let's shower and go for a drink.'

'Oh good grief!' said Lenny, catching her reflection in the changing-room mirror.

'You do look rather puce,' said Amy. 'Maybe Peter Jones stocks balaclavas. We'll go for a drink and text you where we are. Join us when you're looking human again.'

An hour later, Lenny walked into the bar in Sloane Square to find Amy and Juliet laughing over a bottle of wine.

'Cheers for the text,' said Lenny. 'I had to call Juliet to find out where you guys had sloped off to.'

'I did text you! By the way, you do realise you still resemble a beetroot?'

'I do realise, yes, thanks. What are you guys talking about?'

'I'm just trying to persuade Juliet to use my lawyer, he's a total Rottweiler.'

Juliet shook her head. 'I can't afford it, plus I only want what's fair for Martha and me.'

'If Matt's anything like Gary, he'll try to shaft you,' said Amy. 'If he's already lying on his Form E, you'll have to threaten court.'

'Court will cost thousands and I can't bear the thought of an ugly fight.'

'You deserve a fat maintenance package. Go for the jugular,' said Amy, shaking her head.

'It's not who I am,' said Juliet. 'It just isn't.'

It was none of Lenny's business how Juliet handled proceedings, and on one level she was proud Juliet was not avaricious. Still, she couldn't help feeling that Matt should be punished – and punished where it would hurt.

21

Juliet drew back the curtains on Sunday morning. Outside the sky was blue, the leaves were golden, and it wasn't until she'd showered and finished her second cup of tea that she felt the first pang of something missing from her life.

Amy had texted her and Lenny to meet at noon. She tried Lenny but couldn't get through, so drove over and met Amy at the north entrance to the Heath.

'Any word from Lenny?' said Juliet.

'Probably avoiding us – you know she hates running.'

They started jogging, down from the Vale of Health, through the light-dappled woods. It really was the most glorious autumn day, the sun making a rare blaze for glory. The light, the leaves, the colours were dazzling. Juliet had been worried she wouldn't be able to keep up but they were all the way to Kenwood before she realised she hadn't had to stop for breath.

'You're a natural,' said Amy.

'I prefer this to yesterday's class – the fresh air, nature – it feels freer.'

'Shall we go for lunch?' said Amy, when they were back at their cars. 'Call Lenny again?'

Juliet tried but it went straight to voicemail, so they headed into town. 'I hope she doesn't think we've left her out.'

'I've sent her a text – she's probably seeing her useless fuck-buddy.'

'Have you ever met him?'

'Once, at some awful gig. Very sexy but an utter dick – she's totally wasting her time.'

Lenny's first thought on waking was that she must have got into a fight last night. Every part of her ached but particularly the sides of her stomach, her ribs, and the front and back of her thighs. Imagine going for a run! She could barely hobble to her kettle.

Eleven forty a.m. She rang Juliet, Amy, Andrew, then made a strong coffee. She thought about tidying her wardrobe, thought better of it, then waited for someone to call her back.

Time passed. Lenny picked up an old copy of *Wired*. She tried to read an article about Pi, but it kept going on and on. She made another coffee, pondered Nick Cooper. Was he really that ebullient all the time? How could anyone with multiple fake selves be truly happy? At best he must be Facebook happy. No one on the planet was happy every single day.

Perhaps her phone was on silent? No. Huh. It seemed like Lenny's whole life had been spent waiting for phones to ring: the heavy landline of her teenage years; the exotic hands-free at uni that always seemed to go AWOL; the ever-evolving mobiles she'd had in the last decade – her current iPhone, with its Eurythmics 'Sweet Dreams' ringtone, or absolute lack thereof.

Waiting for the phone that never rings . . . wasn't there a similar song, about a train? Yes, that's right, by Madness – how apt: an insane waste of time, all those hours, no, *years* of waiting. She could have taught herself Spanish in that time. Or Japanese.

A watched pot . . . She left her phone in the flat and went out for bread and the papers. She came home, made two rounds of peanut butter on toast, then a third.

An hour later she double-checked her phone had not developed artificial intelligence and a malicious personality and suddenly switched itself to silent mode.

It was 4 p.m. She had to *do* something with today. Fine. There was one person who always got back to her, because of the incentive.

Fancy the pub / a movie?

If Ellis didn't reply she might actually jump from her second-floor window.

She really should do a business plan for the Savage Sunday app – there must be thousands of lonely Londoners just like Lenny. Surely she couldn't be the only one in this vast city feeling the blues?

At 7.30 p.m. Lenny ordered enough takeaway curry for two – someone would surely get back to her soon?

Ellis, are you on tour already? If not, phone me!

Of course she wouldn't kill herself if Ellis didn't reply: she'd just eat enough curry for two, and drink most of a bottle of wine.

Lenny always felt her friendships were the consolation prize for the kids and partner she'd failed to have. But on days like today, when not one person called her, she felt like she was floating on pure loneliness and that the only reason she had friends was because she was the one constantly putting petrol in the friendship tanks.

22

Six fifty-eight a.m. on Monday morning, Lenny checked her phone. Still nothing! But then an email popped up on her screen, sent from Juliet last night:

Hope you're OK? Can't get through on your mobile? X

Lenny rushed to her landline, phoned herself, then let out a small growl.

She hadn't expected to get through to her phone company immediately – she was not naive – but she was still on hold by the time she reached the bus stop. How dare they sully Lenny's love for Taylor Swift by playing her as hold music!

Two coffees and fifty-three minutes later, Lenny was still on hold, but now at her desk, browsing winter coats on Topshop.co.uk, when she was startled by a voice. Lenny had only had the chance to say 'I've been on hold for one hundred and five minutes!' before the other person, sensing fury, hung up. Well, you would, wouldn't you?

Second time round she'd only been waiting an hour when someone answered. She hurriedly grabbed for the phone, swallowed her anger like an illicit sweet and got as far as, 'Hello' when her door opened and Occy walked in. Lenny froze and did a rapid calculation:

Maintain new calm persona Occy is so enamoured with = my life better in a myriad ways vs. chat with phone provider = lose rag = P45 + would you like fries with that?

Lenny hung up and smiled gingerly.

'Oh don't worry, if you were on a personal call?' said Occy sweetly.

'Not a problem. How can I help?'

'I just wanted to say you're doing a great job, Lenny.'

'Oh! Thanks,' said Lenny, smiling briefly before an alarm bell started ringing.

'I'm delighted with the step-change in your performance,' said Occy. 'So much so, I was hoping you could do me a little favour. There's a board meeting in New York next week and Jared's insisting I fly over – we're discussing Global Expansion, he needs my perspective. I was meant to be guest speaker on Friday at the Visionaries day at Wappen-München, it's like a mini-TED, but I really need the time to prepare strategy for Jared.'

'OK . . . '

'So, would you mind going to Munich for me? You have so much energy for all the international stuff. Take an eight a.m. flight out, get the five p.m. back, easy peasy.'

'OK . . . what were you due to speak on?'

'The challenges of being a female leader under thirty-five – obviously you'll have to do something else. What was the last presentation you gave?'

Lenny frowned. 'Measuring the effectiveness of proximity based user-interfaces.'

'Oh,' said Occy, wrinkling her nose. 'Is that . . . what does that . . . ? You know what, I'm sure it's fine. Just make it, you know, interesting, relevant, dynamic, and if you can give it some sort of feminist angle, that would be amazing.'

'Er . . . I'm not sure . . . '

'Is that OK?' asked Occy. 'I mean we can always ask Nick to do something on *Disrupt, Innovate, Connect,* but . . . well, I'd rather give you the opportunity. At this stage . . . '

'Sure,' said Lenny, tightly.

'Great! I'll let you get back to your personal call.'

Lenny picked up the phone for a third time. What was four hours spent waiting for your mobile company in the scheme of life? *Four hours too many, that's what!* Lenny explained to the poor man on the line the repercussions on her equilibrium of not having had incoming comms for the last day and a half: she omitted the Ellis part but didn't spare him much else.

'I do understand how you feel,' he said.

'When can you fix it?'

'I can't actually give you an actual time.'

'But I can't *actually* function without my *actual* phone.' Lenny knew she sounded like an arse of the highest order – a fact she blamed on him.

'I understand it's frustrating.'

'You can drop the empathy script, buddy. Just fix the phone . . . please.'

'I'm sorry you feel that way and I understand completely.'

'I don't care if you understand me better than Sigmund Bloody Freud, when will my phone work?'

'Our technicians are on the case.'

Lenny closed her eyes and pictured the A-list celebrity who starred in her phone company's adverts. She'd have pocketed a million for selling her soul like that – a million that should have been spent on Lenny's network's infrastructure!

'Put me through to your boss, please?'

If there was a heaven and Lenny ever made it to the gates and they played back the conversation she had with the call centre manager, she'd be in real trouble.

An hour later her texts from the day before started pinging through in a hailstorm of missed opportunities:

Juliet: *Come for a run, we miss you!*

Andrew: *Yeah, well up for something, I'm bored too x*

Amy: *Get your arse down to Marylebone, Michael Fassbender is here – I swear he just gave me the eye.*

Fran: *Hubby's got man-flu, got a spare ticket for Springsteen at the Roundhouse tonight if you fancy?*

Ellis: *Meet you in The Duke at 5 p.m. x*

Ellis: *I'm in the pub. Baby, pick up your phone?*

For a moment, Lenny felt almost overwhelmed by relief, gratitude and love.

The feeling was sadly temporary.

Juliet had developed five vegetable-based sandwiches already but on Monday afternoon she decided to head to Borough market for inspiration.

The mushroom specialist had a beautiful display of the season's finest: chanterelles, like exotic corals; girolles, with their dark honeycomb lattices. Texturally though, mushrooms didn't lend themselves well to a sandwich, even in more chewy bread – though hot-fried they'd stay firm. Maybe add bacon, parsley, crème fraîche? Though that somewhat defeated Celina's healthy brief . . .

She was heading over to the spice stall to think more about flavours when Lenny rang.

'This is your happiness officer, checking in with you,' said Lenny.

'Hey! I was just thinking how much clearer my head feels after all that exercise. Put me down as a happy seven?'

'Excellent. What's next . . . Hold on, my phone's jammed . . . I hate this phone, I hate it . . . '

Juliet scanned the spice jars while Lenny hated her phone for a while. Moroccan, Cajun, Indian! She could do veggie curry in a flatbread.

'*What?*' said Lenny. 'This won't solve anyone's problems: "Happiness starts from within. Nourish your flesh without flesh. Meat free is good for the earth and the soul."'

'Your app is learning to read minds! I'm just researching veggie recipes.'

'It's not veggie!' said Lenny, desperately. 'It says go vegan.'

'What, *forever?*'

'For a *whole day*. "Celebrity vegan chef Moet Farn has devised twenty bespoke recipes." Lord help us.'

'Oh Lenny.'

'No milk in your tea? No cheese on your anything? Whoever designed this app knows nothing of human nature – the removal of cheese is a fast track to unhappiness.'

'This is only step three – give it a chance,' said Juliet, and the hint of melancholy in her voice made Lenny think that a happy seven was probably more like a faking-it five.

A thought popped into Lenny's mind – quite a positive one. 'How about a little vegan dinner party at yours on Saturday night? Invite Danny?'

'Lenny, you're not trying to match-make, are you?'

'No! You invite Danny, I'll invite Andrew. It'll be fun.' And if Juliet didn't get closer to Danny, Juliet could get closer to Andrew, thought Lenny, hanging up the phone in satisfaction.

Juliet headed further into the market and discovered a stall run by a good-looking blue-eyed man selling beautiful savoury pastries. One in particular, a bacon and Gruyère spiral, had the most extraordinary plaited twists.

'I hope you don't mind me asking,' said Juliet, 'but were you an origami master in a former life?'

The man laughed. 'I used to be a head chef – though that pastry is kind of tricky.'

'A head chef? You gave that up to run a market stall?'

He laughed. 'Don't get me wrong, it's bloody hard work, but I never regret it. I get to wake up every day and decide what I do. I have freedom.'

'Do you by any chance have any pastries that are vegan and, if so, would they keep till Saturday?'

'Double no, I'm afraid,' he said, sweetly. 'Everything I make has a shed load of butter, and shelf-life wise, I don't think anyone's ever gone to sleep with one of my pastries uneaten.'

'Well then, I'd better buy one for my tea,' said Juliet, taking out her wallet.

23

'I know you like The White Company, but this is next level,' said Lenny, as she and Andrew walked into Juliet's kitchen and saw a spread of grey, putty white and beige bowls on the counter.

'It's been quite "The Journey",' said Juliet, giving them a hug. 'I didn't fully appreciate butter till I tried making it from curdled wet cashews.'

'Well, I guarantee this is one hundred per cent animal free,' said Lenny, handing her a bottle of Champagne.

Juliet popped the cork and poured them a glass. 'Danny will be down in a minute, he's just upstairs in the bathroom.'

'*Is* he now?' said Lenny, with barely controlled glee.

Juliet tutted. 'He's having a look at the toilet – it's making some rather unhappy gurgling noises.'

'That'll be our stomachs in an hour,' said Lenny, poking her finger into a bowl of wet mulch.

'Lenny, you are so rude,' said Andrew.

'Jules knows I'm only joking! I'm sure it will be delicious.'

Danny came into the kitchen wiping his hands on an old towel. He was looking remarkably well – it was partly his tan and partly, unlike the other three, he didn't look London-tired. 'All right, Andrew, it's been a while,' he said, shaking his hand warmly. 'Lenny, nice to see you,' he said, more guardedly. 'How've you been?'

'Yep, business as usual,' said Lenny, kissing him hello and moving quickly away.

'You've been in Thailand?' said Andrew.

Danny broke into a grin. 'I had the best time, man, the people are so laid back and friendly. The guy who runs the surf shop taught me how to cook Thai food properly.'

He was like a blond version of Ellis, thought Lenny, irritably: both guys so unthinkingly handsome, with such a casual attitude to life, both so lazy. 'OK for some – swanning around, learning to make curries!' said Lenny, rolling her eyes.

'I can teach you sometime if you'd like?' he said, smiling.

'I don't cook.'

'Really? Not at all?'

'What? I'm supposed to know how to cook just because I have ovaries?'

'No, Lenny, you're supposed to know how to cook because you have a mouth and a stomach. Anyway, Jules, let me give you a hand.'

Lenny watched as Danny helped Juliet out with plates and cutlery. The way he looked at her was so respectful, and to Lenny's mind, slightly guilty. Lenny watched him reach up high for a serving dish and couldn't help but notice an inch of tanned stomach revealed at the top of his white boxer shorts. Yeah, he was lazy and lairy and borderline rude, but it would be a shame to let such a nice body go to waste. Juliet should definitely shag him.

Juliet lifted a forkful of sludge to her mouth, then put it despairingly back on her plate.

'What is this again?' said Andrew, politely.

Juliet laughed. 'Soufflé, the main ingredients of which should be eggs, butter and cheese,' she said, scribbling in her notebook.

'Take something wonderful and try to change it to a paler, less interesting version of itself,' said Lenny. 'Superb idea.'

'Sounds a lot like marriage!' said Danny.

'Like you would know,' said Lenny, laughing.

'I have eyes, don't I, Lenny?'

You do, thought Lenny. Two green ones, with flecks of hazel right near the pupils.

'Danny's right,' said Andrew. 'My ex-wife once told me I made too many jokes and I was too sociable.'

'Matt once told me I should stop being so generous,' said Juliet, laughing.

'What a dick,' said Lenny.

'Utter dick,' said Danny.

'Yup,' said Juliet. 'What an utter dick.'

Juliet dubiously placed a casserole dish with the main course down on the table. What should have been a bubbling and golden surface was slimy and greige. 'I could have done a delicious veggie curry, but all this trying to copy meat just doesn't work.'

'It's like being blessed with chestnut hair and bleaching yours blond,' said Danny, giving Lenny a sideways look.

'All right, Mr Metaphor, I hope you're not referring to me in the sixth form are you?' said Lenny.

'Your run in with the Sun-In,' he giggled.

'A poet . . . ' said Lenny, witheringly.

'I don't suppose you have a spoon?' said Andrew, attempting to fork food into his mouth as thin, off-yellow liquid dripped through the tines.

'I'm so unspeakably sorry,' said Juliet, laughing louder than she had done in ages. 'I'll make omelettes.'

'Hold on,' said Andrew, fishing out his phone. 'Just gotta make a quick call.'

'Get off your phone,' Lenny shouted after him as he disappeared into the hall. '*You* are the one who's rude!'

'Be thankful I spared you the cabbage brownies,' said Juliet.

'What was that?' said Lenny, when Andrew returned. 'Buy, buy? Sell, sell?'

'I take it that means you've no interest in the two large meat feast pizzas and barbecue chicken wings I've just ordered?' he said, winking at her.

'Top man,' said Danny.

Juliet flashed Andrew a smile. 'You are a good man,' said Juliet, and Andrew beamed in response.

Juliet had replaced her yellow happiness notebook with an A4 pad and was on the sofa with Andrew, taking notes.

'How do you think she's doing?' Lenny whispered to Danny. 'She says she's OK, but I don't think she is.'

'She's got a good head on her shoulders. It was always going to take time. What's the knob-end up to anyway?'

'No idea, you guys haven't spoken at all?'

'Why the hell would I?'

Lenny nodded in approval. She was surprised Danny was as intolerant as she was when it came to forgiving Matt.

Danny leaned back on the sofa, looked over at Juliet and Andrew, heads bent close, then turned to Lenny with a wry smile. 'So it seems we're the only two who haven't managed to get divorced yet. Does that make us the winners round here?'

'Huh,' said Lenny. 'I'm sure we would have got divorced if we'd been married.'

'Ah, you never know, we might have made it,' he said, taking a sip of red wine. 'I like the fiery ones.'

'*What?*' said Lenny, practically spitting out her wine. 'I didn't mean if we were married *to each other.*'

'You'd have to tone down your mouthiness, of course.'

'Me? Mouthiness?'

'Oh for goodness sake, Lenny, calm down, I'm only joking. You do take yourself rather seriously, don't you?'

'*Me?*'

'With your power suit and your kitten heels. "I just got back from Munich yesterday, blah blah blah." It's all a load of bollocks, you do realise that?'

He was looking at her with those big, mesmerising eyes – the idiot hadn't the slightest idea what he was talking about.

'First of all, Danny, I don't even *own* a power suit. Secondly, I wear high heels or trainers; kitten heels do my ankles no favours. Thirdly, giving a PowerPoint presentation on User Interface to a bunch of code-obsessed tech-nerd German dweebs is not remotely glamorous, and fourthly I am the *least* corporate person you've ever met.'

'Sure,' he chuckled. 'You're a maverick.'

'I *am*, I *hate* my job! Anyway, that's easy for you to say, you're just an overgrown beach bum. What's so wrong with having gainful employment? Does that make me square, because I actually get out of bed every day and go to an office, rather than swanning round the globe like some giant man child?'

'Oh good grief,' said Danny. 'Look what I've unleashed.'

Danny was *exactly* like Ellis, worse than Ellis. 'You've just done what you've wanted your entire life,' said Lenny. 'Surfing, partying, enjoying yourself—'

'And what precisely is wrong with enjoying your life?'

'What indeed!' Lenny found herself explaining to Danny exactly why work wasn't meant to be fun and how freedom and happiness were bad. She realised shortly into her diatribe that she didn't believe a single word she was saying, but she had far too much momentum to stop. Besides, Danny was looking at her like she was a moron, how could she possibly back down now?

'Oh Len, there's me thinking you'd grown up and you're still exactly like you were at fifteen.'

'*I'm* the immature one? I'm not the one who's still at school!'

'Meow! Put the claws away,' said Danny, shaking his head.

'You started it!'

'Everything OK, guys?' said Juliet.

'Keep it down at the back of the class,' said Andrew. 'I'm trying to explain to Juliet the finer points of spousal maintenance.'

'Just reliving happy school memories,' said Danny, smiling at them, then turning back to Lenny. 'Lenny, I'm not who I was at seventeen and the only reason you think I am is because you always think you know everything. You always did, and you still do.'

'You have no idea what you're talking about, Danny. I've barely seen you in the last ten years.'

'Then why do you think you know who *I* am?' said Danny. 'Anyway, I've got a meeting with the bank manager on Thursday. Next time you see me, I'll be a limited company.'

'You already *are* limited company,' said Lenny, crossly.

'You really are a grumpy cow sometimes,' he said, laughing to himself, then heading out to the garden for a roll-up without even asking if she'd like to join him!

One thing was for sure: she did not want Juliet shagging Danny after all. Andrew would be a far better prospect all round.

24

'The way Occy's carrying on, you'd think she's got an audience with Bill bloody Gates,' said Fran, who was sitting at her desk in reception, putting the finishing touches to a knitted Berlusconi doll. 'Do you think this orange wool is too orange for his face or not orange enough?'

'He's perfect.'

Fran's brow furrowed. 'Do you think Occy's shagged him?'

'Shagged Berlusconi? Shagged *Jared?* He's far too geeky. She'd go for someone more alpha.'

'More alpha? Have you seen the size of Jared's yacht?'

'Have you seen the size of his feet? They're smaller than mine.'

'Oooh. Then maybe she wants the New York job? Yeah, all this talk of restructure, that's it!' Fran's eyes lit up. 'If she leaves then *you* could run the London office!'

'Don't be ridiculous.'

'You're the only one here who doesn't bullshit all the time.'

'Hence I'd make a terrible MD.'

Fran tutted. 'Shame. You could have introduced a skateboard ban, or better yet, a Cooper ban. Meanwhile, who are *you* shagging?'

Lenny shook her head violently.

'What about dating apps? That's how I met Paul,' said Fran, waving her ring finger at Lenny.

'You got lucky, as did Paul. I hate dating apps, I want to meet someone in real life.'

'Then come out with me and the girls. We're in Clapham Friday night – bar crawl. Come!'

'Paul not coming?'

'He'll be home in bed with the crossword, he's such a geek, I love it.'

'Hold on, two minutes?' said Lenny, picking up her phone to Juliet.

'Hey, Len, I wanted to say thanks again for suggesting Saturday – it was fun, and I'm sorry the food was inedible.'

'The pizza was good.'

'You and Danny, meanwhile?'

'What?'

'You guys were flirting outrageously!'

'You mean fighting?'

'Same difference with you, Lenny. You know what? Danny's a good guy.'

'He's utterly obnoxious, he was totally picking on me.'

'He likes you.'

'Oh Juliet, stop. I already have one useless himbo on speed dial, I do *not* need another.'

'Danny's really not a himbo, he's very capable. And reliable.'

'And he's thirty-eight years old and sleeps on his dad's sofa, case closed.'

'Whatever. Anyway, put me in the app as an eight. In fact Saturday night has given me an idea for work. I'm seeing Mitchell on Friday.'

'Friday?' said Lenny, at the sound of which Fran's ears perked up and her fingers did a little disco spin. 'Swing by here afterwards and we'll go for a drink with Fran and her mates.'

'Maybe . . . '

'A night out will do you good. We'll just have one or two? Go on, please? Say yes, go on! It'll be fun. Say yes, you have to, say yes!'

'Sounds like I don't have too much choice in the matter,' said Juliet, smiling as she put down the phone.

25

'Jules, sweetheart, forgive me, but I'm meeting Tafi at The Groucho at five p.m.; that only gives us twenty minutes,' said Mitchell, pushing a plate of chocolate biscuits towards Juliet, then pulling it back briefly to grab one.

'That's fine,' said Juliet, taking out her new ideas notebook. 'You mentioned Celina wanted a book for next summer?'

'Go on,' said Mitchell.

'Well . . . I made some rather horrid vegan food last weekend, and it got me thinking: the cookbook market is flooded with books on healthy eating using all these faddish ingredients but I'm not sure anyone ever truly craves a cabbage-agave brownie.'

'I'm listening,' said Mitchell, though by the looks of it his concentration was solely focused on which biscuit to eat next.

'But fashion's cyclical, and I think we're due a return to real ingredients, simpler stuff. I know it's not original but I think someone like Celina might reach a new audience if she focused on comfort food. Winter classics – everything from shepherd's pie to the perfect toastie.'

'Keep going,' said Mitchell, breaking another biscuit and offering Juliet the smaller part.

'We could do it in a stylish, modern way,' she said, showing him a list of potential chapter headings. 'Good stuff on toast, pota-to-topped winter warmers . . . There's a certain integrity, an honesty to that style of cooking.'

Mitchell raised his eyebrows, then grabbed his fountain pen. 'The latest research from the ad agency says Celina's brand *lacks* integrity . . . so that integrity thing – say it again?'

Juliet tried to repeat her pitch word-for-word as Mitchell scribbled it all down.

'Integrity . . . honesty . . . ' said Mitchell, putting the lid back on his pen with a satisfied smile. 'Those are the qualities you cannot fake and, Jules, you're just the woman to deliver them! You know what, sweetheart?' He stood to kiss her goodbye. 'I think we're long overdue a spot of lunch. Week after the shoot any good for you?'

Juliet left Mitchell's office and headed up towards Piccadilly. She couldn't remember the last time she'd felt this energised! Momentum pushed her down the street; she couldn't wait to start writing down recipes. She'd head up to the café in Waterstones and do an hour's work, then go and meet Lenny for a celebratory drink.

Her phone was ringing: her health insurer. She and Matt had argued about keeping their cover – he was claiming he couldn't afford it but he'd grudgingly agreed to keep the family policy until Martha finished university.

'Mrs Marlow? This is Lorraine, calling about a query on your policy.'

He couldn't have gone behind her back and stopped the direct debit, surely, she was the named policyholder, the rat!

'Hi Lorraine – thank you but we're definitely not looking at changing our cover yet.'

'That's fine, Mrs Marlow, I'm actually calling with regards to your consultant's referral letter. I wanted to confirm your options with regards to the procedure for Mr Marlow . . . '

Juliet stopped walking, and covered her other ear with her hand. 'Which letter?'

'The urologist's referral? Dated October the fifth?'

'Oh that letter . . . '

'We've spoken with the consultant and he has confirmed that until Mr Marlow is in theatre, it's unclear whether a vaso-epididymostomy will be necessary, but if so that's a more complex procedure with an overnight stay involved which would not fall under the current terms of your cover, so you'd need to authorise payment directly with the clinic.'

'Sorry, say that again?'

'Micro-surgical reversal *is* covered under the existing terms, but if it is necessary to perform a vaso-epididymostomy, you'll be liable for the excess.'

'Sorry – one more time, I always have trouble with that word!' said Juliet, laughing nervously.

'It has got rather a lot of syllables, hasn't it?' said Lorraine. 'Va-so-e-pi-di-dy-most-o-my. So *would* you like to confirm the treatment, with yourselves meeting any excess?'

'Lorraine, there's no health risk in delaying?'

'No, it's an elective procedure.'

'Fine, then let's put it on hold. I think I need to speak to my husband.'

Juliet took a deep breath. She was pretty sure she could guess what a vaso-epididymostomy was but she googled it anyway. Huh. She struggled to find the gratitude in this situation. At least she was the policyholder, which meant she currently had Matt's balls – well, by the balls.

Lenny had made her change Matt's name in her phone to Wanker. As she scrolled to the letter W, she felt her body hijacked with rage – a feeling she'd been free of for at least several weeks now.

'Jules, listen, I'm rushing between meetings.'

'Oh of course you are, you're always such a busy man.'

'Why are you saying it like that?'

'I'm saying it like that because your work has always been more important than mine – which means I've traditionally run our household.'

'Jules, if this is about interim maintenance payments, can it *please* wait till the weekend? I've told you I don't know why that last transfer didn't come through on time.'

'It's not about cash, it's about your genitals.'

'Excuse me?'

'Because I run the household I run our health insurance policy, which means that if you wish to modify your nether regions, I'm the one who gets the phone call. What, nothing to say? Well I have: given how tight you say money is, I don't think now's the best time for your little procedure.'

'Jules . . . tell me you didn't mess with that surgery date.'

'You can always pay for it directly, outside of our insurance.'

'But obviously I'm the one paying for it either way. It's petty of you, really, you're better than that.'

'Yes I am, but I have to say I find it a little challenging, you contemplating fatherhood again, given how extremely adamant you were about only wanting one child.'

'Oh, Jules! You're not going to have a problem with that now, are you? After all these years?'

Lenny had just calculated she had only 74 minutes – 0.024% of her working week – left, until she could legitimately be seen to leave the office, when Fran rang up from reception.

'Tell me that's not a client?' said Lenny. 'I spilled chilli sauce all over my white top at lunch.'

'Your friend Juliet's here early. She wondered if you could pop down?'

'What's wrong?' said Lenny, leading Juliet over to the Free-Me Zone. 'You look pissed off.'

'Just when you thought you were making progress,' said Juliet, slumping down on a beanbag and rubbing her eyes. Please don't let her slip backwards, thought Lenny, she's been doing so well recently.

'It's pointless getting upset now,' said Juliet. 'I entirely accepted it at the time. I was happy – I *am* happy with one child, Martha's my life – but Matt's the one who made such a big deal about the financial strain of more kids. The thought of him being a dad again . . . going through all those joyous events with *her*, it makes me sick, Lenny.'

'Hold on – him booking the surgery doesn't mean anything. They'll have broken up by Christmas.'

Juliet shook her head distractedly. 'And Martha hates him so much right now, this will devastate her.'

'Right,' said Lenny, standing abruptly. 'Is he at work?'

'What are you going to say to him?'

'I'll think of something en route.'

* * *

153

'I'm sorry, what did you say your name was?' said the receptionist.

'Say it's his old friend Leonora.'

The receptionist spoke softly into the phone, then smiled nervously. 'He's busy, I'm afraid.'

'Funny, I thought that might be the case. Tell him it's a rather sensitive personal matter – feel free to use that phrase?'

The receptionist murmured into the phone again. 'Apparently he has meetings till late.'

'Oh. Then perhaps explain to him that I myself have no plans for the rest of my life, and I'm more than happy to wait it out in your reception.'

'I'll pass that on,' she said. 'Nope. Apparently still busy.'

Lenny smiled sweetly. 'Maybe just say I've come to congratulate him on his reverse vasectomy and I hope that he and his lap-dancing, barely-legal stripper girlfriend will be inviting me to any forthcoming christenings.'

Lenny took a seat and flicked casually through the *FT*. A minute later, Matt came storming out.

'Matt!' said Lenny, moving to give him a kiss, which he sidestepped. 'I haven't seen you since your wedding anniversary, what a lovely night that was.'

'Leonora, you can't do this.'

'Do what?'

'It is not appropriate,' he hissed.

'I'd say you're the last person on earth to judge what's appropriate.'

'Did Jules put you up to this?' he said, grabbing Lenny's arm and leading her out of the door.

Lenny wrenched her arm from his. 'Believe it or not you can't control what other people think of you, Matt.'

'What are you even talking about, and what do you want?'

'Oh Matt, don't be stroppy. I wanted to congratulate you and the stripper.'

'Firstly, she is *not* a stripper, she's front of house, and secondly, why don't you mind your own business?'

'Because this is my business – you've ruined my friend's life.'

'I bet you're loving this.'

'Yeah, nothing makes me want to do cartwheels more than seeing Juliet suffer.'

'You never thought I was good enough for her.'

'And *clearly* I was wrong!'

'Leonora, you have no idea what goes on inside a marriage. All those years, standing on the sidelines with your nose pressed to the glass. You could never keep a man and now you're pushing forty you can't even get one, you just want everyone else to be as miserable as you are. Well I don't give a shit what anyone thinks – least of all you – because I have real love in my life.'

'Yeah, she's definitely not a gold digger, Matt. She's definitely not shagging some hot guy her own age behind your back and laughing about you.'

'You really are a bitter, loveless little witch.'

'And *you*,' said Lenny, feeling rage pulse through her entire body, '*you* are an epic coward.'

'I'm a coward because I had the courage to leave a marriage that had run its course?'

Lenny felt herself trembling with hatred. 'The nerve of you! People fall out of love – I get that – but it's the way you handled everything, letting your mistress and Danny be the ones who told the truth because you didn't have the balls.'

'Oh I forget! You're the one with the balls, aren't you, Lenny? You're more of a man than most around Jules.'

'*What?*'

'You always were so jealous. When we were young I thought you were jealous of her, because you wanted to fuck me. But over the years I've realised you were jealous of me! You want to fuck her, you're in love with her, you always have been.'

'You think calling me a lesbian is an insult? Are you twelve? You are the most path-et-ic man I have ever met,' said Lenny, her hands balling into fists. 'You're a disloyal wanker. You robbed Martha of a sibling, and now you want to have babies with some stripper who's the same age as her? You're a disgrace.'

'Tasha is *three and a half* years older than Martha and she is *not* a stripper!'

'I hope when they reverse your vasectomy they cut through the wrong tube and you end up having to piss out of your bum for the rest of your life.'

Matt shook his head in disdain. 'Lenny, you clearly have no idea how the male body works, which just goes to prove what a massive dyke you are,' he said, turning to walk back into his office. 'If Juliet's that bothered about another baby at her age, why don't you guys have one together? Isn't that all the rage with you lesbos nowadays?'

'Hah! Because *that's* entirely how the female body works!' shouted Lenny, flipping the V-sign at Matt's retreating back.

'If you follow me into my office, I'll call the police,' shouted Matt.

Lenny reached frantically into her jacket pocket. What could she chuck at him? Her iPhone? She hadn't got round to insuring it. Or a packet of Orbit with two pellets of gum in it? She threw it towards the back of his head, and missed. She never was any good at netball.

'How did it go?' said Juliet, looking anxious as Lenny stormed back into Wappen's reception.

'As well as can be expected,' muttered Lenny. 'Right, we're going to Clapham and we're going right now. I need a drink immediately, probably a double.'

The summer they were seventeen, Lenny and Juliet had gone on holiday to Rhodes. Juliet remembered one particular carnage-strewn night, which started with an electric-blue drink served with a sparkler fizzling in it. Lenny, tipsy from an afternoon of Sangrias, had mistaken the sparkler for a straw, yet burns on her fingers had not put her off her stride. The girls had snogged two Geordie lads, shied away from a group trip to the tattoo parlour, and later Juliet had held Lenny's hair back in the toilets of Pedro's, a putrid karaoke-disco bar. The Buzz Lounge reminded Juliet of Pedro's, the air humid and smelling un-naturally sweet, heaving with semi-clad drunks – though in Rhodes it had been thirty degrees and outside on Clapham High Street it was a rainy ten.

'Welcome to the Jungle, indeed,' Lenny groaned, as they weaved their way to the bar through the mess of Friday night drinkers screaming along to Guns N' Roses. 'What are you drinking?'

Juliet looked as the girl beside her wiped her mouth with her forearm, then plonked her glass down and laughed uproariously. 'I'll have what she's having.'

'That way madness lies,' said Lenny, shaking her head but ordering the Jäger Bombs anyway.

They were halfway through double gin and tonics, backs against the wall, fending off men. Three pairs of idiots had already been despatched by Lenny, two more were en route. School years had immunised Lenny to her sidekick status. Pre-Matt, Juliet would drag her on double dates to the cinema or bowling alley and Lenny would invariably get stuck with the fellow sidekick who would, by end of play, aim his tongue hopefully at her mouth. Times had not changed nearly enough.

The guy currently chatting up Juliet was blandly handsome, the sidekick less so. For the last ten minutes he'd been telling Lenny how mental his exes were. Lenny had stayed silent because Juliet needed some male attention, and Lenny knew the moment she responded to this odious man there'd be trouble.

'My ex once found a photo of another ex – topless but not sexual – and she smashed my phone up.' He took a swig from his beer. 'It was an old photo! Her dad came out as a poof when she was twelve, and I reckon it destroyed her self-esteem.' He glanced briefly at Lenny's cleavage. 'I think girls who don't have a strong relationship with their father end up messed up and insecure.' He smiled. Lenny did not. 'So are you close to your father?' he asked, giving her a look she suspected was intended to convey emotional intimacy as a prelude to the physical kind.

Lenny shook her head.

'Really? You seem normal to me, ha! So, you aren't close or you're just not a daddy's girl?'

Why did he have to ask twice? Lenny sighed. 'If you must know, my father left when I was two, moved to Leeds with his mistress, then died of lung cancer when I was four. So no, we weren't the closest.'

'Christ, is that *true*?'

'No. I'm lying,' said Lenny, rolling her eyes, then realising from his appalled expression that he now thought she *had* made the whole thing up, rather than was merely being difficult. 'No, I'm not making it up! Why would I lie about my dad dying?'

'Er, to get attention maybe? Christ, you're weird.'

Lenny looked to the ceiling. 'Don't ask a question if you don't want the answer,' she said, then stormed to the bar. Where was Fran? She checked her phone. *Change of plan!!!! Meet us at Be At One.* Plus a text from Ellis: *Thinking of you. About later if you fancy hooking up? xxx*

Why did Ellis always have to text her at the precise moments she was feeling crap, disgruntled, lonely? Hmm, possibly because these points weren't isolated, but accounted for thirty-five per cent of her waking hours.

She was paying for another gin when Juliet found her.

'Where's Fran?' said Juliet.

'In a bar round the corner.'

'Well let's neck this and get going,' she said, grabbing the drink from Lenny and tipping it down her throat in a distinctly un-Juliet-like manoeuvre.

They stood in line outside Be At One as the drizzle turned to a more determined shower. The constant stream of drunks 'wayhey-ing' past them was draining Lenny of her party spirit.

'Oy!' called a man from across the street. 'You in the white top! Nice tits for a forty year old!'

'I'm thirty fucking eight!' Lenny shouted back in outrage.

'Then nice tits for a thirty eight year old!' he shouted, howling with laughter.

The bloke in front of her turned round. 'Take the compliment, babe, they are nice tits.'

It was only Juliet's arm on Lenny's that restrained her.

'I'm never going out in Clapham ever again,' said Lenny. 'Never.'

Oh, but the night was still young.

At 1.30 a.m., Lenny found herself in the queue for the toilet at Good Times. She and Juliet had queued to get into Lux, queued twice at the bar there, then moved on and queued to get into Good Times, queued for the cloakroom, and at the bar four times over. If she'd plotted their night on a histogram it would demonstrate an inefficient use of their leisure time.

They'd had to pay a fiver to get in – rich, given that Good Times was the type of place Lenny would happily pay a tenner to escape. It held in its foundations the heady smell of Red Bull, bleach and vomit. The dance floor was sticky underfoot; the bodies grinding against them no less sticky. It could not have been more like the school disco: groping, lip gloss, the DJ playing MC Hammer, the soundtrack to Lenny's youth. The bass was so loud you could feel it in your larynx. She'd left Juliet on the dance floor with some young guy, executing a low booty-squat similar to the one that had toppled Lenny at the gym.

Lenny finally entered the cubicle, holding the door shut with one frantic outstretched arm. She grimaced as she realised, too late, that if she wanted the luxury of toilet paper, she'd come to the wrong establishment.

Juliet couldn't imagine a cleaning product potent enough to banish the noxious smell in this club. She pictured a detergent ad in reverse: brown molecules of stench penetrating the fibres of her dress. She'd have to risk a sixty wash tomorrow. Still, she was enjoying herself, definitely. She was drunk – good drunk, happy drunk, not thinking about her life drunk.

Matt had never liked dancing – other than lap-dancing apparently – so they'd rarely gone clubbing and as the opening beats of 'Raspberry Beret' came on, she remembered how much she used to love dancing! Why had she not made more effort to go without him? She took another swig of mojito. Man-boy was leaning in, telling her how beautiful she was. *He* was beautiful. Dark hair, high cheek-bones, a little stubble – a relief because otherwise she'd have sworn he was almost a boy, but apparently he was twenty-five, considerably older than Matt's girlfriend. Man-boy, what *was* his name? Will? Yes, Will's lips brushed her ear. Did she want to go outside for a cigarette?

Yes she did. Fresh air good; cigarette-y air even better. She followed

Will outside, accepted a place on his knee, and his arm around her waist.

'Oh!' said Juliet. 'I thought you meant a real cigarette.'

'I'm sorry,' he said, nervously. 'I usually vape.'

Modern options, thought Juliet. She patted his arm. 'These are healthier, right?'

'You are so gorgeous – did I already tell you that?'

Juliet nodded. She wished her husband felt the same way.

Where was everybody? Lenny did a circuit of the room, found a text from Fran who'd moved on to The Grand, and eventually found Juliet outside

'Will, this is Lenny, she's currently saving my life. Sit!' She tapped the wall next to her.

Lenny whispered, 'I don't want to cramp your style.'

'Not at all! Do you want to go home? We can go?'

Lenny's feet hurt and she'd managed to spend £80 to feel rotten and dehydrated. It was 1.50 a.m. 'Soon-ish?'

'You go. I'll be fine.'

'Are you sure?'

'Totally!'

Lenny gave Will a stern look. 'Put this woman in a cab safely. Actually, I'll call an Addison Lee to pick her up at three a.m. You can take it back to his,' she whispered to Juliet. 'But this way you have the option, if he's a weirdo.'

'He should be more scared of me right now,' whispered Juliet, wobbling on his lap and laughing.

Lenny ordered the cab and one for herself to pick up immediately, then she gave Juliet the last £20 in her purse and strict instructions to text when she got home.

'Thanks, Mum!' said Juliet, giving her a long hug goodbye.

Will bought Juliet another drink and they returned to the dance floor, and she danced and danced. She felt so carefree, so alive. Will seemed almost in awe of her; she had forgotten how it felt to be looked at with such longing. She wanted him to kiss her but he was shy and eventually she leaned into him. She had not kissed anyone but Matt for years, yet three minutes later she had Will up against the wall. He was holding her face gently in his hands; her hands were rather less gently pulling him to her, kissing him like it was their last goodbye, like it was both their hearts that were breaking.

She dragged him to a seat in a dark corner. When her cab arrived she was on the verge of inviting him home, except she realised – quite suddenly – that she did not want to wake up next to him. So she was sensible – ish – and stayed with him until the cab called again, then she hurriedly kissed him goodbye.

She sat in the back of the cab, her head spinning, giggling at what she'd just done.

Those last ten minutes in the club had been a bit of a blur. She was pretty sure at one point her hand had been down his trousers, she was a hundred per cent sure his hand had been up her dress, and for a millisecond she'd thought, Someone might see, but then she'd thought I don't care at all.

By the time the cab pulled up outside her house, her mood had turned from jollity to shame. She'd realised that letting some random young guy, even a beautiful one, touch you up inside a nightclub, doesn't make your husband start loving you again, it doesn't make his new girlfriend not twenty-two. It doesn't change anything.

Her yellow notebook lay on her bedside table. She scribbled a few words on her gratitude list, including *Addison* and *Lee*.

She lay back on her pillow, closed her eyes and thought: I am in pain.

Lenny stared out of the cab window at the purple and yellow lights of Blackfriars Bridge reflected in the Thames. Pretty, this city, even at 2 a.m. in the rain.

It had simply been one of those nights where you'd frantically chased Fun and it had eluded you precisely because it knew how desperate you were for it. It was foolish to take any of it to heart. Juliet had definitely had a good night. But 'Nice tits for a forty year old?' Positive thinkers might argue it was a compliment but to Lenny it meant 'It's all over'. There were many quotes about the impossibility of a woman over forty finding love, none of them remotely uplifting. Less than two years to find this elusive soul mate who would make her happy, tick tock, tick tock . . .

Her phone beeped. Juliet, wanting to get her cab earlier? No, Ellis. *Leaving a gig in Soho, you about?*

She'd be home in fifteen minutes. That would give her just enough time to shower and touch up her make-up.

It had been a month since she'd last seen him and when she opened her front door the look in his eye suggested he'd spent every minute of it craving her. He kissed her deeply and her heart skipped a beat. She never was sure whether this was her mind saying bad idea or her body saying good one, but either way, she let him lead her to her bedroom and her hastily made bed, where he lifted her skirt, pulled down her knickers and within moments was inside her. He'd had a lot of sex in his life; he was very good at it. He knew how to give pleasure and how to take it.

For several minutes after she felt so happy, so full of contentment, she thought she could almost die right now and it would be OK, to go out with a bang like this. He draped his arm over her waist, kissed her neck. She ran her palm over the top of his thigh, heard him sigh with satisfaction. She felt so close to him, and was about to ask if he'd like to come to the pub quiz with her on Wednesday when he casually mentioned he was off to Scotland with the band on Monday – for a few weeks, possibly longer, it was still undecided.

She swallowed her sentence before it made it into the universe. Once again she was reminded of the space she inhabited within this relationship: a malformed pen. She'd been aware since day one of how tiny this space was, but she'd bent herself to fit it. But at moments like this it felt like Ellis was moving one side of her cage inwards, constricting still further a space she could barely exist in – yet couldn't quite escape.

It was 3.40 a.m. She got out of bed, ran a bath, sat in it and stared at the water. Her eyes focused on the surface, the panes of the bathroom window reflected at an angle, the silly little head of her electric toothbrush. Relaxing her eyes she watched, mesmerised, as the soapsuds swirled chaotically around her knees.

She had no grounds to feel this bad. He'd never lied to her. She'd signed up to his terms, she knew what she was getting – and more importantly what she wasn't – so for her heart to ache at this point, well, she had no one to blame but herself. The fact that what she said, what she did, and what she felt did not match up was not Ellis's fault. She must harden herself, become one of those girls who could have sex and not feel the need to attach any stupid emotions to it.

Lenny used to think that the way she and Ellis made each other feel – not just physically – must mean something to him. It *must* because it meant something to her. Now she thought that particular theory was wrong. She had spent considerable time figuring out why Ellis was the way he was: his mother ran off when he was young; his older brother left too, when Ellis was only ten. Naturally Ellis was terrified of real intimacy – he couldn't let himself get close. He'd never known healthy, functional love, so no wonder he was incapable of giving it.

She had so many of these tricksy little theories, which she'd worked out alone in her bed at night, or in boring meetings at work, or anytime there was a clearing in her mind.

Yet she had spent precisely zero hours thinking about the only angle on Ellis that actually mattered: which was not why he did what he did – but why she let him.

26

'Happy Monday, Lenny,' said Occy, swooping into her office like a disco bat. 'Biggy smalls favour to ask. I'm meant to be in Lisbon next Monday, delivering a talk on Wappen's expansion plans for Eurasia – '

I *love* Erasure, thought Lenny. I must fish out my old vinyl from the cupboard, I haven't listened to them in years.

' – Jared's summoned me to New York *again*,' continued Occy. 'Restructure. I don't suppose you could step in for me, could you?'

That's a rhetorical question. Still, Lisbon had been on Lenny's hit list for a while, apparently the food scene was great. Perhaps she could stay the night and have a decent meal, carve out a small chunk of excitement for herself.

'The speech is scheduled for twelve p.m., so you can grab a sandwich at the conference and get the five p.m. flight home,' said Occy, as if reading her mind. 'You won't need to stay for dinner.'

'Sure. Not a problem,' said Lenny, watching Occy's back as she walked out the door. Occy would not beat her! Lenny was determined to do at least one fun thing while she was there involving her stomach. She set to googling and had just located the world's finest custard tarts when her phone rang.

'Jules! How's it going?'

'Busy. Celina wants to expand the sandwiches chapter to encompass sweet so I'm trialling brioches as we speak,' she said, gently easing a loaf out of its tin. 'Could you pop by one night this week for an eating session?'

Another rhetorical question, Lenny preferred this one.

'And listen – what's the next step for the diary so I can plan my weekend? I want to get organised.'

'Hang on,' said Lenny, grabbing her phone. Ah, that was more like it. '*Travel and change of place impart new vigour to the mind* – Seneca.

Expand your horizons, open your eyes to the world' . . . Bad timing though. 'Jules, we have to fly somewhere for the weekend.'

'Is this our Thelma and Louise moment? I like it – two one-way tickets to the Grand Canyon,' said Juliet, laughing.

'I can't do Arizona but I do have to go somewhere. I need to file my report next month.'

'Lenny, I can't go anywhere this weekend, I have to go to Homebase.'

'Jules, you always said you envied my freedom to get on a plane. You can't let a trip to Homebase stop you.'

'Lenny, I'd love to but my shoot starts in a week.'

'That's a whole week away! It's only one night, we'll be back Sunday afternoon.'

'Where would we even go?'

'Brainwave! I've got to be in Lisbon on Monday so why don't we go there? Then I'll stay on and you can come back Sunday night? Homebase will still be there on Monday morning.'

'Oh. Lenny, I'm sorry, but we went to Lisbon last year . . . Matt and I . . . ' Juliet was still getting used to consciously uncoupling herself from a 'we'. 'Maybe somewhere else?'

Lenny pictured flying back to London on Sunday night, then having to head straight back to an airport the following morning. She just wanted to stay still for one minute.

'You know where I've always wanted to go?' said Jules, giving the top of her brioche a squeeze. Perfect! 'Amsterdam.'

Lenny's nose wrinkled. 'You don't think it'll be full of drunken stag dos?'

'It's a cultural centre, there are world class museums and galleries, canals.'

Lenny quickly checked more flights – oh fine, Schiphol was a central hub so that could work. 'Jules, are you OK to fly home alone and I'll fly straight from Amsterdam to Lisbon?'

'Of course.'

'Great. I'll pick you up in a minicab at seven thirty a.m. on Saturday morning.'

27

Forget Amsterdam, Stansted Airport was like one giant stag do! In front of them a group of ten lads in tight Superdry T-shirts and skinny jeans were holding up security, fiddling with their over-stuffed bags of toiletries.

'We're going to miss the bloody flight,' said Lenny, staring at her watch.

'We'll be all right,' said Juliet, trying to figure out if this was true or merely wishful thinking.

'Seriously, look at that idiot – four full-sized bottles of Lynx,' said Lenny, rolling her eyes. 'Decant, man, for goodness sake! And an entire bag *just for hair product*. When did men become so vain?'

'Ladies, I'm glad I'm not in front of you,' said a man behind them.

Lenny turned to scowl at the eavesdropper.

'At least I wouldn't be guilty of too much hair gel,' he said, pointing to his bald head.

Juliet couldn't help but giggle.

'Yeah, well, we're going to miss our flight due to metrosexual grooming, so I'm sorry but I'm a little stressed.'

'Which flight are you on?'

'Amsterdam, ten fifteen.'

'I'm on it too, don't worry, they won't fly without me.'

'Why? Are you the captain?' said Lenny. He looked vaguely Italian, big, gentle brown eyes, light tan, a smart navy suit, a crisp white shirt.

'I'm their Head of Operations.'

'Then can't you jump this queue?' said Lenny. 'And take us with you?'

'It's not my style,' he said. 'Besides, I like to understand what our customers go through, I like getting feedback.'

* * *

'And another thing, Robert!' said Lenny. 'These seats are like rocks covered in cardboard. Also, your food is grim. And *four pounds for a cup of tea?* It's insatiable greed!'

'Bet you're glad you sat with us,' said Juliet, taking two foil-wrapped packs from her bag, and handing them to Robert and Lenny. 'Brioche with smoked ham and tomato on the left, smoked salmon on rye on the right.'

'Thanks, Mum,' said Lenny.

Robert took a bite, then looked at Juliet as though he'd just fallen in love. 'These are fantastic sarnies!'

'She made the bread and everything! Tell him what you do,' said Lenny.

'Are you a chef?'

'God no. I'm just an amateur.'

'Nonsense! She trained at Cordon Bleu, then worked at a food mag. She's been a recipe developer for years, and now she's the ghostwriter behind all the recipes for that awful celebrity chef—'

'Lenny!' said Juliet, firmly.

Robert took another bite. 'Do you make sweet stuff too or just savoury?'

'She does everything,' said Lenny. 'She's the greatest!'

'Interesting,' said Robert. 'Have you ever considered hospitality?'

'What, like restaurants?' said Juliet.

'Like airlines . . . '

Juliet laughed. 'I'm not sure I'm up to making ten thousand sandwiches a week in my kitchen.'

'I was thinking more of a consultancy role. The catering team are looking at making our current range more premium. Do me a favour? Email me on Monday?' he said, offering Juliet his business card. 'I think you could be exactly what the guys are looking for.'

'Oh, thanks, but no. It really isn't something I'd be any good at.'

'Take the card,' said Lenny. 'Take it!'

'Where are you staying?' said Robert, as they joined him in the queue for taxis at Schiphol airport.

'Da Pijp,' said Lenny.

'I'll give you a ride, I'm near the Rijksmuseum.'

'That's kind,' said Juliet. 'What are you in town for, anyway?'

'My son Jack's studying here. I've come to check he's not having too much fun.'

'Where's your wife?' said Lenny, wondering if Robert had slipped his wedding ring off for the weekend.

'His mother lives in Paris. We're divorced. Why do you ask?'

'No reason,' said Lenny. Other than that you've been looking at my friend rather frequently these last two hours, and I want to make sure you're not another love-rat.

'Ladies, it's been a pleasure. If it's not already on your list, make sure you visit the Van Gogh museum, there's a painting up on the third floor, it's quite something. Oh, and buy a timed ticket online to avoid the queues. And if you get into trouble in a coffeeshop, call me.'

'We're a little old for coffeeshops,' said Juliet, smiling.

'Speak for yourself,' said Lenny.

'You've got my card,' he said. 'It would be great to talk.'

'He was pretty cool in the end,' said Lenny, as they headed for their hotel's reception.

'He was,' said Juliet, finally turning her gaze from Robert's cab as it disappeared round the corner.

In their room, Juliet spent five minutes cross referencing the to-do list she'd made hurriedly the previous night with a map, while Lenny busied herself figuring out which hotel toiletries she could smuggle back in her hand luggage.

'Listen,' said Juliet, coming into the bathroom to find Lenny taking the shower caps for her collection. 'Shall we start at the Rijksmuseum? Or there's a food hall in the west that sounds good?'

'Let's just get out and explore – turn right and see where the road takes us.'

Not very far, as it turned out. Five minutes later, the two of them stood in the coffeeshop next door to their hotel, inhaling the sweet ripe fug of marijuana.

'It's not illegal in Amsterdam, it's a very permissive society,' said Lenny encouragingly.

'Lenny, you know I'm not moralistic but the drugs out here are meant to be extremely strong.'

'Nonsense. They have every type under the sun. Look, fifty different varieties!' she said, inspecting the display case, row upon row of pale green buds in tiny plastic bags. 'How about that one? *Mellow and very light*. We'll buy one spliff, we don't even have to smoke the whole thing,' she said, handing over a five euro note.

'I don't even think it's working,' said Lenny, taking another puff, and staring at the couple opposite. The guy was fast asleep on his girlfriend's shoulder, snoring and dribbling gently – it was two in the afternoon. His girlfriend was sitting, eyes closed, giggling to herself. 'We should have chosen a stronger one,' said Lenny. 'Like whatever those guys are smoking.'

'What?' said Juliet, staring straight in front of her at the purple and yellow Jimmy Hendrix poster on the wall which was hovering in mid-air. 'Did you say something?'

'I said it's not working,' said Lenny, inhaling deeply and shaking her head. 'Have another drag?'

'I've had enough.'

'Well there's no point wasting it,' said Lenny, chuffing till all that remained was a crinkly grey stub. 'Easy. All done. Right. So, it's two oh five p.m.,' she said, attempting to stand, then sitting straight back down again.

'Are you OK?' said Juliet, reaching to steady her.

'Totally. I'm just going to sit still for a moment,' she said, smiling, as she leaned back in her chair and felt a beautiful, gentle numbness flooding through her. Oh, but it was lovely! Mmm, taking the edge off things, not in an out-of-control way, but simply mellow, a bit soft . . . like a nice cup of tea, and a duvet and fluffy slippers . . . mmm . . . marshmallows . . . clouds . . . softness softness . . . softness . . . softness . . .

'Lenny? Lenny! Do you think we should go and do something?'

'Huh?' said Lenny, grinning into space. 'What?' She opened and shut her mouth several times, someone had suctioned all the moisture from it, the impertinence! 'Jules, I need lemonade.'

'Lenny – it's four thirty p.m.'

'What?' she said, giggling. 'Scottish dentist time?'

'What?'

'*What?*'

'*What?* Lenny, it's *four thirty p.m.*'

Lenny grabbed Juliet's wrist and stared at her watch as the second hand did one long full rotation. 'We only got here ten minutes ago?'

Juliet stared at her watch in confusion. 'It's not four thirty p.m., it's *five thirty p.m.* I forgot the time difference.'

'Oh. Whoa. Oh,' said Lenny.

'Should we try and go to a museum?'

'Tomorrow,' said Lenny, slowly rising to her feet. 'Right now I've got a bad case of late-onset munchies.'

'Then let's get a cab to that Foodhallen place.'

Juliet popped to the loo as Lenny hovered by the counter. There were so many varieties of cannabis, even more than of chocolate Easter eggs. The Dragon? That sounded a little fierce. Afghan Haze? Old Jamaican? *Super sweet and happy.* On brief! Lenny took another note from her wallet and handed it to the woman behind the counter.

The food hall was housed in a 19th century tram shed, a vast brick-walled space with dozens of food stands lining the sides, surrounding a central bar area bustling with a lively crowd.

'Look at all this,' said Juliet. 'They've got Mexican, Vietnamese, Spanish hams, Belgian frites, oooh – I think they're doing sushi.'

'Smell that!' said Lenny, following her nose to a queue waiting for a vast pot of smoky barbecued meat.

'What are those?' said Juliet, pointing to the stall next to it, piled high with round golden croquettes. 'Bitterballen?' She read from the chalkboard: 'Deep fried crunchy balls filled with—'

'Stop!' said Lenny. 'You had me at deep fried and crunchy.'

They bought a selection of food, and wine, then took a seat in the bar area and happily watched the world go by.

'Look at those guys,' said Juliet. Lenny followed Juliet's gaze towards two tall blond men working at full speed making deluxe cheese toasties for a huge queue. The man on the left was operating a giant panini-style toaster while making fresh sandwiches as the bread was grilling; his partner was taking orders and cash, and serving drinks.

'Fit,' said Lenny.

'I was actually admiring their production line.'

'They are both super hot though, the Danish have such great bone structure, that's why they're so in demand as donors.'

'Lenny, you do realise Danish is not the same thing as Dutch and we're not in Denmark?'

'Oh,' said Lenny, in confusion. Maybe the weed was quite strong after all. She headed over to the bar for a glass of water and another bottle of wine, then settled back next to Juliet as they merrily drank their way through it.

'It's coming up to nine o'clock, what do you fancy doing?' said Lenny, yawning, and picking at the last of the crumbs in front of her.

'I guess we should go to a club, but I'm knackered. I just want to go back to the hotel and pass out. If we're in bed by eleven like a pair of grannies, at least we can get up early and have an action-packed day tomorrow.'

Lenny smiled with relief. 'Would it be wrong to share one of those toasties for pudding?'

'I'm pretty full,' said Juliet, rubbing her stomach, then catching Lenny's plaintive expression. 'Oh go on then. Let's live a little.'

In the cab back to the hotel, Lenny made a mental note to flesh out an alternative happiness app, revolving around melted cheese, chocolate, wine and friendship, with hot Dutch / Danish men involved in some capacity too – her greatest new business idea yet!

The following morning Juliet woke early and checked her itinerary. 'OK, here's the plan: we hire bicycles, cycle to Vondelpark, get to the Van Gogh by ten a.m., do ninety minutes there, grab lunch, then see some canals, an hour's shopping in The Nine Streets and if we have time pop to the Rijksmuseum on the way back.'

'Sounds good,' said Lenny, who was rooting around in her handbag. 'And we can smoke this little dooby first!'

'When did you buy *that*?'

'On the way out of the coffeeshop yesterday.'

'But *why*?'

'Because!'

'But it's total wipe-out stuff.'

'Let's have a little toke in the park, it'll make the paintings even better.'

'No.'

'If we don't smoke it, I'll accidentally leave it in my pocket and get busted at the airport and banged up abroad, and it'll be like *Orange Is The New Black*, except way less funny.'

'Or you could just throw it away?'

'You know I never throw anything away.'

'Oh Lenny, you're so silly sometimes. Fine, you smoke it, I'll enjoy the scenery. Come on, let's get bikes, it's already nine o'clock.'

Half an hour later Lenny was lying on her back in the park staring up at the clouds, smiling. Juliet was sitting next to her looking rather cross.

'Seriously, go without me, go, I can't move right now,' said Lenny, giggling.

'Lenny! We can't come all the way here and you spend the entire weekend stoned. You're behaving like a fourteen-year-old boy.'

'I know,' said Lenny, laughing. 'It's baaaad, isn't it?'

'Yes, Lenny, it is! We're meant to be opening our minds and seeing new things.'

'And believe me, Jules, I'm doing both those things right now. Is that my voice? It sounds weird. How *do* you spell weird – is it i-e or e-i or e-a-r-d?'

Juliet sighed. 'Fine, I'm going.'

Lenny felt the blades of grass under her fingers. They felt cool and squeaky and she imagined she was lying on a bed of chives, which would make her some kind of fish? Oh now that was a wierd, weird, weard thought . . .

'Lenny, are you sure you'll be OK?'

'Yeah, yeah, yeah, yeah, yeah, yeah, yeah. Look, Jules – at that cloud! It looks like a . . . like a cloud!' said Lenny, and burst into hysterical laughter.

'Oh Lenny,' said Juliet, shaking her head. 'Meet me at noon at that nice looking coffee shop by the hotel.'

'A coffeeshop?' said Lenny, giggling again. 'I thought you said drugs were bad.'

'I meant coffee as in beans, not drugs. Jeez, Lenny, just make it the waffle place instead.'

Juliet rode east from the park through the wide elm-lined streets, past rows of handsome houses with their prettily patterned brickwork. Such tall wide windows! Each one looking like it had been cleaned and polished especially for her this bright, blue-skied morning. She parked her bike, then found herself at the back of a serious queue. There were at least three hundred people in front of her, none of them going anywhere fast. But then she remembered Robert's advice about buying a timed ticket online – might that work right now? Yes! What a great tip, and wasn't technology brilliant? She walked straight to the front and up the stairs into the museum.

Juliet knew a couple of well-known facts about Van Gogh's tragic life – depression and the ear – and was familiar with a handful of his most famous works. These paintings had hordes of visitors in front of them taking photos – a few had actual checklists of Greatest Hits they were crossing off efficiently. She waited patiently until there was a space so she could see better. There was something incredible about the work close up: the brush strokes, the colours, the emotion. She was quietly moved. Then less quietly moved by a group of sharp-elbowed Chinese tourists intent on getting their selfies dead centre in front of each masterpiece.

Leisurely she wandered to the next floor. She hadn't had any idea how prolific Van Gogh had been in his short life – two hundred paintings in one year alone! And he wrote, a lot – letters to his beloved brother, and his family. Lenny would laugh if she were here. Of course she would, she was currently laughing at clouds. But she'd also laugh at the framed pages of handwritten letters, because Van Gogh's writing was small and neat and precise and not unlike one of the many pages in Juliet's own notebooks.

She headed up another flight of stairs and her eye was immediately caught by a vivid blaze of colour on the wall. In the painting a solitary reaper, scythe in hand, was hard at work harvesting a field. Above him the sun was heavy in the sky, beating down on an abundance of golden swirls of wheat. Over in the far distance was a line of rolling hills, green and purple and blue. There was so much feeling in front of her it took her breath away. She leaned in closer to read the sign. This was the view from Van Gogh's room in the asylum in Saint Remy. The following year he was dead by his own hand, but for this still small moment he sat and looked out from his prison window, attempted to paint his way out of misery, a shout of joy in the dark.

Juliet felt her throat well up. She couldn't take her eyes from the canvas. She stood, absorbing the sensations in her body. She felt close to breathless, felt a surge of hope rise up in her chest. She was astounded to feel tears rolling down her cheeks.

When she finally did force herself to walk away, she felt like something inside her had shifted.

Juliet arrived at the waffle shop to find Lenny sheepishly eating a plate of pancakes. 'Lenny, are you still high or are you back on planet earth?'

'Oh the buzz has definitely worn off,' said Lenny, putting her fork down. 'Are you OK?' she said, noticing Juliet's smudged mascara. 'You haven't had a call from Wanker have you?'

'No,' said Juliet, shaking her head gently. 'I went to the museum, Lenny, I saw these stunning paintings. I realised how extraordinary the world can be and I've made a decision. I want to get back on with the rest of my life. I'm ready for it.'

PART FIVE

'Most folks are about as happy as they make up their minds to be.'
Abraham Lincoln

28

Lenny woke up severely dehydrated and confused, thinking at first that she was in her own bed, then in Amsterdam, before finally realising it was 5 a.m. and she was in a hotel room in Lisbon. It had been silly of her to fly from Amsterdam to Lisbon last night – or rather, silly of her to visit another coffeeshop after Juliet had headed home. Still, positive thinking . . . She didn't have to give her speech till noon, which meant she *could* visit the famous custard tart place after all!

She was first through the door of Pasteis de Belem, and her research proved accurate: these were the greatest custard tarts in the universe – heavy custard with the crispest, crunchiest flakiest pastry. She'd wolfed down two, taken a savoury break with an exceptional ham and cheese toastie, then gone back in for more sweet, when her work phone pinged an email alert. An all-staff memo from Occy: more new Wappen offices, spreading pan-globally like the plague.

> To celebrate the opening of our 25th office, in Kyoto, all staff will be given a free sushi lunch and a selfie stick. Shoot your favourite Wappen moment – submit with the hashtag #iheartmyjob to appear on our virtual Wall of Selfies and you could win an Apple Watch.

That had Cooper's paw print all over it. She was drafting a reply, suggesting The Wall of Selfrees – photos of anything but one's own face – when Juliet rang.

'Eight thirty a.m.?' said Lenny. 'You're keen!'

'I want to get cracking – what's our next stage, guru?'

Lenny clicked on the app. Hmmm. '"Let your body take risks and your mind will follow. Try sky-diving, trapeze, parachute, or find the tallest building in the city and head to the roof." I presume that doesn't mean to jump off. OK, so I think the Shard has a restaurant at the top?'

'Come on, Lenny, let's be more ambitious!'

'Let's not.'

'SJP did trapeze in *Sex And The City* and it looked fun.'

Lenny thought back to the episode. SJP had been fearful at the start, but she'd learned to let go – it was all some big metaphor to do with Big or Aidan, she forgot which one.

'And Martha's friend had her eighteenth at some circus school in Bromley,' said Juliet. 'I'll google it.'

'No, don't. Trapeze is too dangerous.'

'Their website says they've been in business for twenty years, accident free.'

'They're hardly going to advertise the broken limbs.'

'Lenny, we're doing it.'

'We're not.'

'You owe me.'

'For what?'

'Yesterday? Being totally useless and getting stoned when you should have come with me and looked at some amazing paintings?'

'Oh,' said Lenny, sadly, reaching for another custard tart. 'I suppose that is one way of looking at it.'

Juliet hung up from Lenny and booked two tickets for trapeze class on Saturday. She looked out of the window – it was about to rain, but she'd go for a run anyway, it was only water. Then she had two more brioches to finalise, but all she could think about was making the phone call . . .

She took his card from her purse and dialled, her heart quickening as it rang.

'Robert Kirk.'

'Robert - it's Juliet Marlow, we met at the airport.'

'Indeed we did!'

'I wondered if we could have a coffee?'

'When are you around?'

'I'm shooting a bread book next week,' said Juliet. 'But I'm pretty flexible before then.'

'Would four o'clock this afternoon be too soon?'

Not soon enough.

'How was your trip?' said Robert, greeting her in his office reception and leading her over to a coffee area.

'Lenny took her own little trip,' said Juliet, laughing. 'But actually it was great – surprisingly restorative. How was your son?'

'Oh, to be twenty-one again and have your whole life in front of you, all those mistakes you haven't yet made.' Robert looked at her warmly. 'What can I get you? The coffee's OK but I'm embarrassed to offer you one of our cakes.'

'No need,' she said, reaching into her bag and bringing out a cardboard box she'd wrapped with ribbon. 'Here's one I made earlier . . . '

'I probably shouldn't say this out loud but I already think you're too good for us.'

She tried not to stare too obviously as he ordered their coffees. He was taller than she remembered, she guessed from his laughter lines a few years older than her, though he looked so relaxed and content he could easily have passed for early thirties.

'Our head of hospitality's keen to meet you,' he said, returning with their drinks. 'We're looking for someone to do ten days a month developing recipes. The day rates are higher than industry standard – we have a pretty crappy reputation, historically deserved, I fear.'

'How long have you worked here?'

'Seven months. I was with an airline in New York but these guys offered me silly money to move.'

'You gave up Manhattan for West Acton?'

He smiled. 'My life in the last five years has been full of change; I suppose I felt ready to put down roots again.'

He talked her through an outline of the role, which would start in January, and gave her a list of people he'd like her to meet. Then he wrote down a figure for a day rate which was higher than what Mitchell paid her in a week. 'Can you get back to me by next Friday?'

'Absolutely.' Juliet stood and smiled as Robert helped her with her coat.

'So, did you make it to the Van Gogh in the end?'

'I did! Thanks for the ticket tip – that was genius.'

'And what was your favourite picture?'

'Oh, I loved them all so much,' she said. 'The cherry blossoms . . . And there's a little painting of a blue horse that was wonderful, but there was one – on the top floor I think – of a wheat field. It was just . . . It was the most extraordinary painting I've ever seen.'

Robert's whole face lit up. 'The harvester, reaping the corn?'

'You know the one I mean?'

'I do,' he said. 'It's my favourite too.'

29

This was a terrible idea of Juliet's. The journey alone took Lenny far beyond her comfort zone, all the way to zone six. The unwritten law of taking no more than two types of public transport had been broken: the Northern line, the DLR, a bus and then another? She should have put her foot down and insisted on cocktails in a skyscraper.

Half a mile down a street full of deserted buildings they eventually came to a five-storey warehouse with a small orange sign: Carnival Recreational Arts And Play Space. Juliet pushed the door open and stepped inside. Lenny took another look at the sign: CRAAPS indeed – then followed her through.

'So! To recap – climb the ladder, Ru will strap you to the safety wires, then grab the bar and swing. If that goes well, second time do a knee-high: hoik your legs up, engage those calves 'cos your calves are what's keeping you suspended. Drop backwards, and if you're feeling brave we'll aim for a catch. And remember, what's the four-letter C word we don't use up on the platform? CAN'T!' said Jay with a well-practised laugh as he stood before the motley crew sitting cross-legged at his feet.

Lenny shivered. It was cold in this vast space, plus she was profoundly terrified. Her *calves* would keep her suspended? She'd never been a fan of them – she hoped they hadn't taken the years of dislike to heart and were planning their revenge by releasing her from a great height on to her head.

'OK,' said Jay. 'First up – Stephanie!'

'What's eight metres in feet?' whispered Juliet.

'Dunno,' mumbled Lenny. 'Twenty-six?' It sounded scarier in imperial. She watched, transfixed, as Stephanie, high above them on the platform, panicked. Lenny could practically see the molecules of fear radiate off her, travel through the air and finally hover like a swarm of wasps around Lenny before being absorbed into her skin.

'You're perfectly safe,' Jay called up.

'I can't,' said Stephanie. 'It's too scary.'

'Bend your knees, then just a small jump.'

Stephanie inched to the edge. Lenny checked her watch. The communal sense of anticipation was morphing into boredom. Watching someone not jump off a platform. Woo-hoo! What a way to spend your Saturday.

'I'm glad she went first,' Lenny whispered. 'At least now I won't look like as much of a chicken-shit as she does.'

'Stephanie: bend those knees and *jump*,' said Jay.

And then she did! She jumped, and it was exhilarating to watch, because if Stephanie could do this anyone could! The small crowd breathed a sigh of relief as Stephanie floated back to the net, puffing her cheeks out in amazement.

'Lenny, you're next.'

Lenny took a deep breath and walked to the ladder. Wow, rickety! She'd only taken three steps but it was creaking, wobbling. She couldn't be the heaviest person ever to have climbed it, but maybe ladders – even metal ones – were like socks and wore thin over time. She hadn't realised until this moment quite how much she despised ladders.

Don't look down. Or up. Lenny's heart was booming as if through headphones. By the time she reached the top her mouth was retchingly dry.

'Face the front,' said Ru gently, but when Lenny forced herself to make the turn she was hijacked by a panic so immense it stopped her breath.

'It's fine, you're safe.'

The only body part Lenny could move was her head, which was shaking violently.

'Toes over the edge, go forward, FORWARD,' said Ru.

Lenny thought she might vomit – an inelegant cascade of lunch arching through the cold air to land in a splatter on the mat.

'Reach and grab the bar,' he said.

'The bar?'

He pointed to the pole swinging in the air.

'But it's nowhere near me?'

'It's coming your way,' said Ru, pulling it closer with a makeshift hook. The hook reminded Lenny of the one used to snare rubber ducks at the fairground, the shonky fairground, where crappy rides fell apart and freak accidents killed people.

'Right arm on the bar, *come on*,' said Ru.

She reached forward, flailing wildly. After several false starts she stood, unbalanced, toes over the edge, one fist frantically clutching the bar.

'Now let go of the other rope, reach forward and grab the other end,' said Ru, as innocuously as if he were saying: take out the teabag, add milk, stir.

Nothing happened.

And then nothing.

Still nothing.

Lenny's left hand clung to the rope, her knuckles popping out of her skin. She attempted a swallow, produced a small choking noise.

'Let go of that rope!'

Lenny wondered how her right arm was capable of such frantic trembling yet her left was sticking out as unnaturally as a ventriloquist's wooden one. Sweet Lord, she was making Stephanie look like Bear Bloody Grylls.

She willed her arm to move, staring at it urgently as if it were a glass on a Ouija board. Un-clench! That's it, un-grip those fingers one by one . . .

Seven minutes later Lenny was still standing, frozen, at the edge of the abyss. What would they do if she couldn't move? Carry her back down? Push her off?

'Just fucking jump,' said Ru under his breath.

Lenny looked down 26.2 feet to the ground below and saw the group chatting. One woman was curled up on her side, asleep. Only Juliet was looking up at her with a huge, encouraging smile. Juliet gave the smallest of nods, and then Lenny jumped!

Oh my! She was flying! Through the air she whooshed, she actually whooshed in the most tremendous arc, her legs dangling, fists gripping on for dear life – but she was doing it! Aaah, it wasn't so bad, it was sort of OK, yeah, it was fun. Was it fun? She didn't know what she felt but she was all the way over to the other side of the room just reaching the highest point when she happened to look down and realise the madness of trapeze and the next thing she knew her grip was slipping, slipping, and she dropped like a rock, skimming her arse royally along the safety netting as she landed with an ignominious dull bounce.

'Shit,' said Lenny. 'Ouch. Sorry.'

'Not a problem, let's get you down.'

Juliet was already rising to her feet. 'You were great!'

'It's vile up there. You're braver than me though, I'm sure you'll be OK.'

She watched nervously as Juliet lightly climbed the ladder, stepped confidently on to the edge of the platform, leaned forward, grabbed the bar with her right hand, then her left, and on the first call of jump watched her glide through the air, legs perfectly together with pointy toes and everything.

'Brilliant,' said Jay. 'Exactly how it should be done.'

'Weren't you scared?' said Lenny.

'I really liked it,' she said, apologetically.

I'll do better next time, thought Lenny. But as she climbed the ladder again she was gripped by the certainty of failure. All that was keeping her safe from a four-storey face-plant was Ru, but she couldn't feel nor see him so he was a little like a god, though surely a merciful god would never have let Juliet book these tickets in the first place.

'Lenny, just jump!'

So she did, telling herself, I CAN AND I WILL, but she couldn't, wouldn't, didn't. Her clammy hands released the bar like a burning metal rod.

'It's fine,' said Jay, but it wasn't really because Lenny was the only one who'd fallen once, let alone twice. Whereas Juliet, second time round, swung through the air, executed a perfect knee-high, then without hesitation let go, arching backwards into nothing, the void! Juliet's face looked like the sun was shining directly on to it after a cold winter. Her arms – flung out in confident trust – met Jay's and as she unhooked her knees and gently flipped herself into space, he swept her high up into the air, flying, flying, before landing her, most elegantly, back on the mat like Superman.

Lenny clapped with sincere admiration and tried not to think about her nausea, which should have passed now the threat of humiliation had.

The sick feeling stayed in her body during their odyssey home, and in the pub later. Juliet had filmed Lenny's inglorious attempts, but even watching herself on Juliet's phone brought back a heightened state of terror; and while Juliet was all for encouraging Lenny to go back next week, to conquer her brand new fear, Lenny felt cowardice and failure solidify in her like stones.

30

'You're here crazy early?' said Terry, as Juliet walked into the photographer's studio at 7 a.m. on Monday with a smile on her face and two loaves of freshly baked homemade bread in a bag.

'I thought I'd make bacon sarnies for the crew – help sweeten those Monday morning blues.'

'Jules, where do you get your energy from?'

She didn't know what was making her feel better – time or therapy or the app – but it didn't matter. All that mattered was the pain was fading. She was beginning to see possibilities.

When they broke for lunch she found an email from Robert, checking she was still thinking about their conversation. She had spent a lot of the past week thinking about their conversation.

If she was supremely disciplined, she'd surely be able to free up ten days each month for the work he'd proposed.

The money was fantastic. Andrew had advised her that the fact she'd worked throughout her marriage meant a smaller settlement than if she hadn't. She'd need a regular income.

And the commute was OK, an hour's drive round the North Circular.

Consulting for an airline was a big stretch, but she felt ready for a challenge, and what better way to start a new year? They were a big business: a big, corporate, multi-layered, bureaucratic business . . .

With layer upon layer of yes – men . . .

She thought back to the pastry chef she'd met in Borough market. There was something about the lightness in his expression when he'd talked about the freedom of working entirely for himself.

She called Robert on her way home.

'I didn't expect to hear from you so soon.'

Juliet could hear the hope in his voice. 'I wanted to thank you for championing me.'

'I think you'd be great for the role.'

'It's a very generous offer . . . '

'Why do I get the feeling you're about to say *but*?'

'But I think there's something else out there with my name on it. I need to find some headspace to figure out what that is. Do you think I'm mad to turn down such a generous offer?'

'I think you're brave. So is there nothing we can say that will change your mind?'

'I don't think so.'

'Oh, that is a shame; personally I was rather hoping you'd be interested.'

Lenny frowned at her phone. She'd just hung up from Juliet who was still so high from trapeze she was claiming a happiness nine! No way would Lenny input a nine. Firstly, she was pretty sure it was Juliet's adrenalin talking, and any day now Matt would do something horrific and she'd plummet again. And secondly, Lenny herself seemed to be down to a five. She'd input a seven. It would be wise to test if the app understood the concept of a setback.

Uh-oh, your happiness seems to have stalled! Might be time to offload some baggage?

She heard her door open and looked up to see Occy hovering. 'Lenny, is now a good time?'

Occy's new civility was beginning to freak Lenny out. She was almost treating her like an equal, rather than like a seven year old who didn't have English as a first language.

'Have a seat,' said Lenny. 'I'm just trialling the penultimate stage of HappyGuru.'

'Show me,' Occy said, coming round to Lenny's side of the desk.

'OK: if we go to the dashboard here you see my Buddha's currently yellow, he shines brighter the happier you get. And over here in the Rewards area is my tree of enlightenment – you grow another branch after each stage. So, I'm testing what happens if you take a step back: the algorithm's factored in the regression and now . . . ' She handed the phone to Occy.

'"Your home is a reflection of your mind. Only have within eyeline objects you are passionately in love with." Ooh, I like that advice,' said Occy. 'Professionally and personally . . . ' She paused, as though counting silently to ten. 'Lenny, Nick is convinced this app's going to be our primary revenue generator next financial, but I sense you're not on the same page.'

'What do you mean?'

'He's far more enthusiastic.'

'I wouldn't say I'm not enthusiastic,' said Lenny. 'I'm circumspect.'

Occy blew out a slow puff of breath. Lenny smelled cinnamon chewing gum, and the faint tang of menthol cigarettes. 'I suppose Nick does have that incredibly positive energy.'

'Positive energy . . . ' said Lenny, trying to keep her voice neutral, and failing.

'What, Lenny?'

How to keep this diplomatic? Perhaps make it into a metaphor?

'You know, Occy, it's a bit like cats and dogs. Nick's a dog: you throw a bone, he bounces after it with boundless unthinking enthusiasm, tail wagging, ears flapping.'

'Uh-huh, I get that,' said Occy, nodding.

'Whereas I'm a cat: I like to sit back and consider something thoroughly, let my whiskers do the twitching . . . '

Lenny felt the last fragment of her soul wither as she voluntarily compared herself to a domestic house pet, and one with a facial hair problem.

'Lenny, you're so smart. You're becoming more Wappen every day.'

And bingo! There it was, it was official: soul not fat, but dead.

31

'Your place is bigger than mine, Jules, let's start there?'

'My stuff's pretty under control, Lenny – let's tackle yours.'

'OK,' said Lenny, reluctantly. 'Sunday morning?'

'Martha's coming down for Sunday lunch. I was going to invite Danny – and you, if you're free?'

'Oh,' said Lenny. 'Danny?'

'It'll be fun. I'll do a roast with all the trimmings.'

'You know what? I'll let you guys get on with it. I guess Danny hasn't seen Martha for ages.'

'You're not avoiding him are you?'

'No! But I'll leave you guys to it. Saturday morning instead?'

'I'm doing a five-k run – if you'd care to join me? No? OK, well I'll come to yours at two o'clock, but promise me you'll actually throw stuff away, not just move it from one pile to another. I mean it, Lenny. Do it properly or there's no point.'

'Wow, Lenny, you have a lot of junk,' said Juliet, hands on her hips surveying the mess.

'You say that, but there is a reason for keeping it all.'

'Yes, but not necessarily a good one. What's this?' she said, picking up a pale pink baby-doll minidress.

'Don't you remember, I used to wear that to Camden Palace?'

'In 1990. Try it on.'

'I'd never wear it now.'

'So why have you kept it?'

'It reminds me of the good old days.'

'And this?' said Juliet, picking up a pair of flared leggings. 'And this?' – a cropped T-shirt with *Kiss FM's Bobby & Steve – Ibiza '94!* written on it.

'Reminders.'

'Lenny, memories live in *you*, not scrunched up in your wardrobe. *This* skirt?'

'Saving it for a mid-nineties-Russian-hooker-themed fancy dress party.'

'And this milkmaid wig?'

'Farmyard-themed fancy dress.'

'And what's this?' she said, holding up a moth-eaten, curry-stained purple jumper.

'It's nice and soft. I only wear it round the flat.'

'And this? And this?'

'The purply blue one was expensive, the bluey purple one was a total bargain.'

'Lenny, you can have a stay of execution on one jumper only. You need a pile for junk, one for charity and one for dry cleaning.'

'And a pile for keeping.'

'Yes, Lenny. I didn't think there was much danger of you becoming a minimalist. Right, I'm going into your cupboards. See you in an hour.'

Lenny had grudgingly amassed three piles and was working through the pockets of the clothes for the dry cleaner. In her one good work blazer she found the crumpled Visualisation list from Paris. She re-read it: 'Man – with job – who likes spicy food.' Apparently too vast a demand upon the universe. The list went in the bin, the jacket in the dry cleaning pile.

Lenny's hand hovered near the baby-doll dress. She'd kept that dress for the memories, but also if she ever had a daughter, her daughter might want to wear it to go clubbing. Mind you, it was insanely short. On second thoughts, she didn't want any imaginary daughter of hers leaving the house showing that much flesh.

Lenny lay down on her bed. Disaster: the transformation was complete. She had finally turned into her mother.

'Lenny! This is no time for a nap,' said Juliet, coming in armed with bags of Lenny's life debris. 'Get up and tell me honestly – are you passionately in love with this flyer?'

Lenny took it from her hand. 10% Off Your First Haircut at Richard Clive, 14 Bermondsey Square.

'Ah!' said Lenny, tenderly. 'That's from when I worked down in Southwark. And ten per cent off makes a difference you know.'

'Sure it does, however I've just googled it and that address is now a Sainsbury's Local. So do you think you could possibly bear to part with this clearly definitive part of your self?'

Lenny tutted.

'And you can keep these only if you can tell me what they are,' said Juliet, handing her a small silver foil pouch containing two black circles.

Lenny turned the pack over. The circles resembled flat pills. She squeezed them. Squidgy. What on earth . . . ?

'No? Time's up,' said Juliet, putting them in the bin. 'And I'm getting rid of your collection of shower caps, and your cassingles too – they can't have been played in forever.'

'I'm keeping the Rebel MC,' said Lenny, flicking through the box. 'And Beats International. That's a total tune!'

Lenny surveyed the nine bags on her floor and shook her head. 'I'm done.'

'Fine, let's take this lot round the corner,' said Juliet, refolding Lenny's work jacket and her Whistles dress neatly on top of the bag.

'Let's just take the recycling – it's too much all in one go.'

'You promise you won't wake up tomorrow and start taking clothes out of the bags?'

'I promise.'

'Good. Now don't you feel lighter, mentally?'

'Oh my goodness!' said Lenny, her eyes opening wider.

'What? Are you experiencing enlightenment as we speak?'

Lenny scrabbled in the bin bag. 'I've figured out what those squidgy black things are: ear-bud covers for those crappy headphones I got free with my old Nokia.'

'Lenny,' said Juliet, shaking her head in despair. 'You really need to learn to let go.'

32

Lenny had just returned from lunch and was standing looking down on to Old Street. She'd stood at this window countless times, tracking the ever-evolving styles of beards and unflattering jeans; it never ceased to amaze her how bad people were willing to look in the name of cool. Having this thought made her feel old.

'Nick, you'd make a terrible spy, I can see you in the reflection.'

'What's going on down there?' he said, coming to join her. 'Man, I'd love to have this view. You can see for miles!'

'Nick, if you've got designs on my office, I warn you the view is overrated,' she said, returning to her seat with a sigh.

'So, what's the dilly-o?' he said, coming to sit opposite her, picking up her empty coffee cup and flicking his finger against it in an annoying drumbeat. 'You still doing HappyGuru?'

'Final step tonight and then I'm sending my report to Occy tomorrow. Why?'

'I'd say from your negative energy you seem to be getting grumpier by the day. Are you sure you're not actually on an OscarTheGrouch app?'

'Nick, this whole quantified self movement—'

'Why are you pulling that face?'

'It's so tedious,' she said, rubbing her forehead. 'People don't exist anymore unless they're measuring their lives digitally, sharing their data – how far they've run, what they've just eaten. It's relentless self-obsession; no one's that interesting, Cooper – not me, and *definitely* not you.'

'Ah, Granny Luddite – time to get a job at the dinosaur museum.'

Lenny grunted. 'Haven't you got some jelly-bean flavours that need urgent curating? I think toasted marshmallow is off brand, more Google than Wappen . . . '

'Lenny, did you know that the part of the brain which reacts to threat or fear – such as competition from a younger male in the workplace – is the same part of the amygdala that's stimulated when—'

'Nick! I've been meaning to ask you a question for some time. It's rather a personal one.'

'Yes, Lenny, the rumours are true – I'm hung like a moose.'

'It's actually pronounced mouse, but no, that wasn't my question. Do you ever have a conversation that doesn't come with some faux neuro-science bollocks attached?'

'You do know I have a 2.1 in psychology from Durham, don't you?'

'But perhaps *you* are not aware that *I* have a PhD in Advanced Bullshit Detection.'

He smiled. 'That's the thing I love about you, Lenny. You're so smart about certain things, yet you don't even know how to begin to play the game in this place. So what *is* your final stage? Pagan goddess workshop? Inner-city weeding project?'

Lenny held out her phone wearily as Cooper read from the screen. '"Stop your thinking process and troubles will come to an end – Master Bhaizang",' he said, nodding knowingly. 'Been there, done that, got the T-shirt. I've been meditating since 2013, I can literally empty my brain—' He clicked his fingers: 'Like that.'

'I'm surprised it takes you that long,' said Lenny.

33

Lenny was in the meditation and yoga centre gift shop, breathing through her mouth to avoid the tang of sweaty feet barely masked by the waft of ayurvedic twig tea. She picked up a mug and read: *The best things in life aren't things* – then nearly dropped it when she saw the price tag. The best things in life aren't £20 mugs either!

She took a seat in reception and searched her bags for her HappyGuru report. Pages 1–2: Executive Summary – she'd tweak that tonight. Pages 3–5: Information Architecture and Navigation Glitches. Pages 6–9: Tone, Brand, Feel. Pages 10–13: Usability vs. Utility, and pages 14–22: User Experience Summary.

There was no denying Juliet was definitely on the mend, almost her old self: positive, funny, buoyant. As for Lenny? She couldn't say she was happier; in fact she was at least 30% less happy and she remained dubious that an hour's silent meditation with a bunch of Primrose Hill fake-hippies would tip her over the edge into Nirvana.

Still – what to write? Occy was so clearly a fan. Lenny would use Juliet's view. Yes, she was going straight to integrity-hell, but isn't that what success in a corporate world boiled down to? Relentlessly pretending to be someone you weren't?

'I'm sorry I'm late,' said Juliet, sweeping in, her hair glistening from the rain. Her skin was glowing. All that running really was working for her. Lenny should think about some exercise . . . soonish, maybe next spring, when the weather improved.

Lenny thought they were probably ten minutes into Mindfulness for Beginners, but you were meant to keep your eyes shut and if she opened them to check her watch, she'd see the session leader's judgemental eyes boring into her.

'Sit in stillness. And breathe.'

Lenny swallowed loudly. It was too warm in here. They must have crammed fifty people into a room for twenty and at £20 a pop, that was £1,000 for that guy to just sit there reminding everyone to breathe. Dream job – literally paid to do nothing!

'Focus on the breath: in, out . . . '

Juliet took a deep breath in, then slowly let it out. She was tired but good tired – hard work tired. That Welsh rarebit they'd photographed this afternoon, with the golden bubbling cheese spilling on to the blue glass plate – that had looked totally mouth-watering.

'The aim of meditation is to calm the mind.'

Who was that whistling through their nose? And where was Lenny's locker key? Had she left it in the lock? Her handbag was at the side of the room but her laptop, her work papers, all that stuff was in the locker. This place probably attracted a *load* of opportunistic thieves; they must see the clientele coming, £20 mugs indeed. Lenny quietly patted her jacket pocket. Ah, thank goodness.

'Sit in stillness. Be in the moment.'

Juliet started to run through tomorrow's shot list in her head – then stopped herself. And breathed.

'If you want, choose a mantra, a phrase you repeat in your mind . . . '

This is my idea of hell . . . my idea of hell . . . my idea of hell . . .

'A single word is fine, something meaningful to you – perhaps Love . . . Peace.'

Progress, thought Juliet. Progress.

'Do not get frustrated if the mind wanders. Observe your thoughts, watch them come and go like clouds.'

Those clouds in the park in Amsterdam . . . Lenny had spent such a happy few hours staring at those clouds. Maybe that was what meditation felt like, if you actually managed to do it properly, like being stoned, but without the fear of a cavity search. Surely an hour must nearly be up?

'Return to full focus. Be at one with the breath.'

Be At One! Juliet thought back to that boy in Clapham – adorable, but so young. That was only a month ago but she really had turned a corner since then.

'Be at one with the present, your thoughts neither in the future, nor the past.'

Be At One – forty-year-old tits. Lenny sat up straighter. Posture was key when gravity started winning. Posture and expensive bras. She should probably buy another good bra – the woman in the posh bra shop said it was best to buy a new one every six months, but she would say that, wouldn't she? Lenny still owned bras she'd bought in the twentieth century. It would take more than a posh bra to get her happy at this point. What she really needed was something random and excellent to happen to her.

'Breathe. Breathe.'

Juliet breathed in – and out.

'Stress free, your mind is still.'

Everyone else was probably meditating perfectly. Lenny was crap at it, though unlike trapeze at least no one could *see* how crap she was. Aha! Now *that* was positive thinking . . . Oh, for goodness sake! What cretin had left their mobile phone on? Oh. Ah. Er. That would be a Lenny-shaped cretin . . .

'Feel a space clear.'

For almost a whole minute Juliet's mind was still. And then a memory floated in – of the day before her anniversary. She'd gone to the posh deli, she'd meant to go back in to ask them about selling her bread . . . She could do that once the shoot was over . . . maybe she could contact other delis too. Oh right, yes, back to the breath . . .

'If your attention has wandered, notice where your attention is – honour it – then move on.'

Hang on a minute: what was that weird throwaway comment from Nick about her *not knowing how to play the game*? And why had Occy insisted she send this report to her in New York? She could have waited till she was back, surely? Was she trying to prove to Jared how useless Lenny was? All that nonsense Occy was spouting about Lenny being good at international, and her second in command. No doubt she was lulling her into a false sense of security – she was about to fire her! Lenny couldn't help herself: she opened her eyes. Oh thank goodness! Only three more minutes. Come on then, happiness – you've got 180 seconds to show up. No? Not coming? Still not coming? No? Thought not.

* * *

'Enough with the mindfulness,' said Lenny, struggling with her umbrella as she hoiked her bags over her shoulders and they headed out into the rain. 'I could do with some stomach-fulness.'

'Do you think we'll ever get a cab in this weather?' said Juliet. 'I'm not walking to the Tube in these heels.'

They stood looking hopelessly up and down the street as the rain started falling more heavily.

'Do you think my laptop's going to get wet?' said Lenny. 'This bag isn't very waterpr—'

'Hang on – is that one there with its light on?'

'Where? Yes! Yes it is!' said Lenny, rushing forward. 'Stop, stop!' She ran towards it with her arm out and just at the moment the driver saw her, she felt her foot leave the curb, her heel slip, and her ankle turn from under her as she fell to the ground, hard.

'Jesus, Lenny, are you OK?'

'FUCK! Ooh, that properly hurt. Shit, is my laptop OK?'

Juliet gathered Lenny's bags and helped her back up. 'Your laptop's fine. Oh no, your knee, it's bleeding – and your hands!'

'Oh bollocks, these were brand new tights.'

Juliet held her arm out for Lenny as the cab pulled in and Lenny brushed the wet dirt from her skirt.

'Are you sure you're OK?'

'Embarrassed, that's all,' said Lenny, wincing as she tried to put weight on her left foot. 'Let's just get in the cab and get some dinner.'

'Lenny, you're not eating?'

'I'm not very hungry,' said Lenny. Even her wine was making her nauseous but surely it was an analgesic.

'So, will you finish your report tonight?'

'I'll get up early maybe,' said Lenny quietly, pushing a cube of chicken tikka across her plate. All she wanted was to go home, take the maximum amount of ibuprofen and put some ice on her foot.

'Lenny,' said Juliet, laying down her fork and looking at her with concern. 'I think we should go to A&E.'

'*What?*'

'In all the years we've been friends, I've never seen you not eat your dinner.'

'I'm fine.'

'Let me see your ankle.'

'No,' said Lenny, who could feel something extremely untoward happening at the bottom of her leg. 'Look, if it was broken I'd know about it.'

'Don't make me crawl under this table.'

'Oh, all right,' said Lenny, rolling her eyes. 'I'm not going to take my tights off in here though.'

She didn't need to. Even through sixty deniers it was clear that a medium-sized grapefruit had replaced Lenny's left ankle.

'Cankle-tastic!' said Lenny, feeling her stomach flip

'Lenny! I'm getting the bill and calling you an ambulance.'

'Oh don't be ridiculous, we'll get a cab,' said Lenny. 'And at least let me finish my wine.'

Lenny had been sitting in a wheelchair in A&E with her leg elevated, hypnotically monitoring her ankle for the last two hours. It had swollen and swollen from grapefruit to honeydew melon, the skin morphing from red through blue to a deep purply black.

Five drunks had slurringly told her how sore her foot looked. Three medical professionals had asked if she'd been drunk when she fell. Two of them had gently prodded her ankle and when their fingers had made contact with Lenny's skin, her eyes had watered and she'd almost passed out. When the nurse had given her a tetanus jab, then cleaned up the grit-crusted grazes on her hands and her knee, Lenny had wept at the sheer shooting pain – and the tenderness of their care.

'Oooh, that does look sore,' said the doctor, returning to the cubicle in Minor Injuries and sitting down next to Lenny. 'So, Leonora, you have a rather nasty haematoma.'

'Haematoma's a bruise?'

'Exactly – imagine squeezing a tube of toothpaste but the lid's on. Your blood is the toothpaste, it can't circulate around the wound, it has nowhere to go, so it gets squeezed into the dermis, then gets old – that's why it's discoloured.'

Lenny blew out a puff of air in lieu of retching.

'But see here on the posterior X-ray?' said the doctor. 'The bones are intact – there's no dislocation, no fracture.'

Lenny glanced at the image, then turned away.

'Ah, that's a relief,' said Juliet, patting Lenny's arm. 'Lenny? It's not broken.'

'Actually a bad sprain can feel even worse than a fracture,' said the doctor cheerily. 'The key thing is keep all weight off it for the next forty-eight hours.'

'You mean I can't go to work?' said Lenny, hopefully.

'Keep it elevated till the swelling goes down. Alternate paracetamol and ibuprofen. We'll give you a compression bandage and crutches, then at the weekend try putting partial weight on it to encourage healing.'

'OK, let's go,' said Lenny, pushing against the side of the chair, and holding on to Juliet with one arm. 'Oh, doctor?'

'Yes?'

'How do I get up the stairs to my flat?'

'You don't have a lift?'

Lenny sighed.

'You don't live with anyone who could help?'

Lenny stared at the doctor.

'Going down, you go on crutches – slowly. Up? Remember when you were little? Shuffle up the stairs backwards on your bottom.'

HappyGuru – the final stage: pain, humiliation and climbing up stairs on your arse.

Lenny wanted a refund and she wanted one now.

34

Juliet had helped Lenny set up her bedside table with the essentials: chocolate, drugs and water. Lenny's adrenalin had worn off before her paracetamol kicked in, and she'd been in dull pain – mostly in her foot but also in her arm from the tetanus jab – till 2 a.m. She'd slept heavily, then woken to find her ankle still grotesquely swollen and almost entirely black but with some new yellow bruising along her foot.

She'd necked some painkillers, then determinedly finished typing her report:

HappyGuru is the future of mood-curated User Experience. We should embrace the digital takeover of the human spirit.

She'd even quoted Buddha:

'Happiness comes when your work and words are of benefit to yourself and others.'

Occy's ego would adore that.

Lenny had sent off the report at 11 a.m. and celebrated with a double helping of ibuprofen. It was now 2.45 p.m. and Lenny was going stir crazy. Juliet had offered to pop round after the shoot but Lenny had a desperate craving for a Mint Aero, a posh coffee and some company *now*.

'Baby, that looks really sore,' said Ellis, carrying Lenny's coffee as she hopped on her crutches back to bed. 'Is that a drinking injury?'

Lenny gently lifted her leg back on to a pile of cushions. 'Meditation should come with a health warning.'

'Wow, it's so swollen!'

'They said the swelling will go down if I keep it up for two days.'

He grinned and lay down next to her. 'That's given me an idea . . .' he said, kissing her neck.

She batted him away.

'Not in the mood?'

'No, I am not! I want to watch TV.'

Ellis looked at his watch. 'Sure, baby.'

'I don't get what all the fuss is about,' said Ellis, fidgeting with the pillows and wriggling annoyingly next to her.

'Seriously, you don't like Tina Fey?'

'She's OK.'

'Oh Ellis,' said Lenny, shaking her head in disappointment. 'Make me a cup of tea would you?'

'Yeah, OK. I'll pop out for a fag and make you one in a sec,' he said, grabbing her keys.

Lenny readjusted her pillows and peered at her ankle: possibly eight per cent less swollen than it had been this morning. What was the time in New York? Nearly noon. Occy should have received her report by now. Lenny checked her phone, ah yes!

Fantastic research – I've shared it with Jared and Canyontech – we're all INCREDIBLY impressed. Sorry to hear you've hurt your foot but can you make it in to work on Monday? I have a very exciting reward. (Even more exciting than another branch on your virtual tree of enlightenment!!)

Lenny felt a rush of relief – she was finally getting that pay rise!

She heard the front door open again. 'Ellis,' she called out. 'Forget the tea, let's have some wine. Do me a favour – take my wallet from my handbag, go round to the offy and buy us a bottle of Malbec. My pin number's 4240. Oh, you know what? Can you do me an even bigger favour, there's a bag of dry cleaning at the bottom of my wardrobe. Grab my work blazer, would you?' Lenny could hear Juliet's voice in her ear. 'Actually, take the whole bag – and there are two other bags in there.'

'What did your last slave die of?'

'Unoriginality. Bring them here?' said Lenny. 'Right, the blazer bag is for the dry cleaners, the one with those two purple jumpers on top – that goes in the Oxfam dumping bin, and the one with the baby-doll dress goes to the charity shop – got that?'

'This pink dress looks pretty foxy,' said Ellis. 'Try it on.'

Lenny shook her head. 'Ask the dry cleaner to fast-track it, it costs extra but that's OK. For Monday morning. Don't forget, my PIN number's 4240.'

'OK, OK – I'm not stupid.'

'Don't let the bank machine swallow my card. And pink dress bag to the charity shop, right?'

'Pink dress – charity shop!'

'You can carry it all?'

'I'll be fine,' said Ellis, loading the bags into his arms.

Bless him, at least he was there for her when she needed him.

'What are you doing this weekend?' said Lenny, pouring the last of the wine into his glass.

'Going to a rave down in Sussex tomorrow, our guitarist's dad owns some mega pad with a hot tub and pool.'

'Oh. That sounds nice,' she said forlornly. 'Will you be back in London on Sunday?'

'Why? Do you want me to come round and keep you company?'

Lenny looked at him tenderly. 'You'd come back early to help me?'

'I mean, if you can't find anyone else . . . '

'No,' Lenny sighed. 'That's fine.'

'I'll come by one night next week? That'd be better – you'll be on your feet by then, they said try walking this weekend, right?' He checked his watch. 'It's nearly seven o'clock!'

'So?'

'The guys are jamming down in Brixton and I thought I'd go hang with them, if you're not up for, you know, anything more fun?'

Lenny felt hurt, in the form of anger, flare up. She had a violent urge to tell him to piss off and never call her again. But then an overwhelming weariness silenced her and she closed her eyes. She'd want him back, if not next week then next month, and then she'd look doubly stupid and weak.

'I'm pretty tired anyway,' she said. 'Thanks for taking my stuff round. See yourself out.'

'So what's this meeting on Monday?' said Juliet, standing by Lenny's side as Lenny hobbled with her crutches through to the living room on Sunday afternoon.

'I'm not sure yet,' said Lenny, hoiking her leg up on to the coffee table, then picking at the corner of the plaster on her right palm. Her hands were still so sore, and now they were starting to itch. 'I'm hoping it's a pay rise that comes hand in hand with less travelling and less responsibility.'

Juliet laughed, then checked her watch. 'Does your oven run hot or cool?'

'No idea.'

'I'd better check.'

She opened the oven door and inspected the ciabatta – perfect! She transferred the loaf to a rack, blowing in an attempt to fast-cool it, then brought it through to Lenny. 'Are you sure you don't want anything more exotic?'

'Warm bread and butter – what's finer than that?' said Lenny, ripping a chunk off the loaf.

'I wish I could give you a lift to work tomorrow but I'm on set early.'

'Don't worry. I'm not due in till midday, I'll take a cab.'

'But you'll need help going downstairs on the crutches.' Juliet took her phone out and dialled. 'Danny, it's me . . . '

Lenny shook her head violently.

'Can you do me a favour? Pick Lenny up tomorrow at eleven a.m. and drive her to Old Street? Thanks.' Juliet hung up and smiled.

'Jules, I can get a cab.'

'They're not a hundred per cent reliable.'

'Nor is Danny.'

'Lenny, you're so hard on him. He really has grown up a lot this year.'

'If you say so,' said Lenny. 'How was lunch, by the way?'

'Oh, it was good,' said Juliet. 'Danny might stay in the spare room for a few months.'

'What?' said Lenny, pausing mid chew.

'Just till he finds somewhere decent and affordable. I won't ask for rent or I think I'd have to give Matt half, but Danny will chip in for bills and housekeeping and help out around the house. Martha thinks it's a good idea too.'

Danny Freeman, freeloading, as ever. Fine, well, Lenny's original view still stood. Good for a shag, but not much else.

35

It was surprisingly tricky to apply make-up while standing on one leg with both hands covered in plasters but Lenny made a valiant effort, and by the time Danny rang her doorbell she was looking almost normal.

'Ouch!' said Danny. 'Had a few too many Babychams and took a dive, did you?'

Lenny smiled sweetly. 'I tripped in the street. Perhaps if I'd been wearing those kitten heels you think I'm so partial to, it might not have happened. Anyway, it's very kind of you to give me a lift – you claimed you had a full-time job though.'

'I work Saturdays and take Sundays and Mondays off.'

'Oh,' said Lenny. 'This is your day off?'

'Happy to help. Do I give you a fireman's lift then or what?'

'Not unless you want to end up in hospital too. I have to pop round the corner to the dry cleaner and pick up my jacket, then we can head into town.'

'Steady now,' said Danny, as Lenny gingerly attempted the stairs. She was more nervous than she thought she'd be – the memory of the pain too fresh, the thought of falling without a safety net too scary.

'Hmm. Hold on a sec,' she said, clinging to the bannister to calm her nerves.

Danny raced down the stairs, dumped Lenny's bags on the floor, then raced back up. 'Go on, I'll give you a piggy back.'

'I'm too old and too heavy.'

'Get back up those stairs and we'll give it a shot.'

Lenny rolled her eyes, then sat down heavily on her bottom.

'Why are you sitting on your arse like a fool?'

'It's how you get up,' said Lenny, shaking her head in annoyance as she hefted herself up and Danny tried not to laugh. Finally at the top, she clambered on to Danny's back. Ooh, he was strong! His upper body was so much more muscular than Ellis's.

'Are you touching me up back there, Lenny?'

'What? No! Just be careful with me.'

'Please. I'm used to handling precious surfboards – a Lenny Dublonsky's a piece of cake.'

'You're speedy on those crutches,' said Danny, as Lenny hopped round the corner to the dry cleaners, then stopped abruptly outside the window of the charity shop.

'I don't believe it,' said Lenny.

'What?'

'That's my dress, my pink dress. They've put it on the mannequin!'

'You used to wear that when you and Jules went out on the razzle, didn't you?'

'It's so pretty,' said Lenny. 'Maybe I should go in and buy it back.'

'Another time,' said Danny, racing in front of her to open the door to the dry cleaner's.

'Right, here we go,' she said, passing the ticket to the man at the counter. 'Actually, Danny, I've got a load of stuff – any chance you could run it back to my flat? We don't have to leave for half an hour.'

'Sure.'

The dry cleaner emerged from the backroom carrying ten clear plastic bags of clothes.

'That's great, thank you,' said Lenny, taking out her wallet, then glancing down and catching sight of the garment on top . . . a bluey-purple jumper.

'Hang on,' she said, shaking her head. 'I didn't have any jumpers. Mine's a navy blazer, a navy silk dress, a black wool dress . . . '

The guy checked the name on the ticket. 'Lenny Dubonkee?'

'Dublonsky.'

'Flat Three, 145 Glenmore Road?'

'That's my address, but this isn't my . . . shit!' Lenny lifted the top jumper and underneath saw a clear plastic bag, containing another purply-blue jumper, also with moth holes. Underneath that were the free nylon pyjamas she was given on a business-class flight six years ago which she never wore because they brought her out in a rash. Underneath that the rest of the battered, moth-eaten clothing destined for the Oxfam bin.

'What's wrong?' said Danny.

'Is something wrong?' said the dry cleaner.

'Yes,' said Lenny. 'Can you check? There must be a second bag here, with a navy blazer, a really expensive Whistles silk dress, a black Reiss dress . . . '

The guy disappeared behind the counter and returned three minutes later. 'Might it be in another name?'

'Yes,' said Lenny. 'Maybe under Ellis? Or Ellis Davidson?' Or Ellis Complete and Utter Fuckwad-Shit-For-Brains.

'There's nothing back here I'm afraid,' said the guy, returning to the till. 'So, are these yours or not?'

Lenny shook her head in despair.

'They're not yours?'

Lenny squeezed her eyes tightly shut. When she opened them again, nothing had changed. 'They are mine. But there's been a terrible mistake.'

'OK, but not at our end I'm afraid, so that'll be one hundred and forty pounds. Will you be paying cash or card?'

'How could you do this?' said Lenny, grasping her phone tightly as she felt her face flush with fury.

'Baby, I've literally just woken up from the rave, don't do this to me!'

'Ellis, I was extremely clear – baby-doll dress bag to charity, blazer bag to the dry cleaners, and all the dodgy stuff in the Oxfam bin!'

'You made such a fuss about your pin number, I had so much to remember—'

'*Where* are my smart clothes?'

'I did take one of the bags to the Oxfam bin. So maybe go and see if they're still there?'

'You'd have me clamber into a bin, would you? Even if they are still in there, they'll be covered in tramps' piss by now.'

'Baby, don't be annoyed with me. I was only trying to—'

Lenny hung up.

'You look like you're having a coronary,' said Danny, taking the clothes as Lenny stabbed in her pin number and felt her eyes about to drop out of their sockets with rage.

She tried to focus on her breathing but instead felt tears of frustration spring forth.

'Oh Lenny,' he said, putting his arm around her. 'Is there anything I can do to help?'

Lenny sniffled and swallowed a huge sob. 'I don't think so, no, not at all, well, actually maybe . . . '

Lenny stood on one leg, desperately clinging to Danny's arm while he poked deeper into the metal slot of the clothing bin. He'd fashioned a tool out of one of her crutches, a wire hanger from the dry cleaners plus some twine from his van; it was a surprisingly excellent contraption – but it didn't help.

'You're sure this isn't yours?' he said, fishing out a Winnie-the-Pooh babygro, its little legs blowing in the wind.

Lenny shook her head in despair: 'Try again! We have to leave in five minutes.'

Danny poked the crutch back in and fished out an old lady's one-piece orange swimsuit, complete with swim-skirt. 'You don't want to wear this at your swanky trendy digital agency? You sure now?'

'Danny, it's no use, they're gone forever, gone!'

'Oh Lenny, it's only stuff. You need to learn to let go.'

Lenny wobbled on one leg and grabbed Danny's arm tighter. 'I really do wish people would stop telling me that.'

'Ew,' said Occy, her lips pursing as if she were about to suck on a barbed-wire straw. 'That looks sore.'

'It's OK,' said Lenny. 'It's less painful than it was.'

'When are you off those crutches?'

'Mid-week, hopefully.'

'That's great,' said Occy, rubbing her hands together. 'I've got the perfect tonic. I was worried the crutches might impede, though actually the timing is probably perfect. So, obviously HappyGuru has been a key project for you – '

Lenny relaxed back in her seat and nodded patiently. Would her pay rise kick in this side of Christmas? She sincerely hoped so, then she could treat herself to some new smart clothes to replace the ones she'd just lost . . .

' – I did express concern you weren't as enthusiastic as Nick – however! Your report reflects a whole-heartedly positive attitude. The client was delighted and has offered us a seven-day immersion at a premium wellness retreat in southern Spain that's on their partner-brands roster—'

'Hold on, it's a *holiday*?'

'You'll have to write a short report about the place, but no more than a one pager. It's more an act to show willing – the final rubber stamp on the client-agency relationship.'

'Oh,' said Lenny, shifting in her seat.

'I thought you'd be pleased?' said Occy. 'It's recognition of a job well done.'

'It's just . . . ' It's not a pay rise. And an *immersion*? That sounded closer to waterboarding than to a holiday.

'It sounds fabulous – extremely luxurious, integrative, holistic, totally off-grid. The programme itself is life-changing,' said Occy. 'Given how run-down you must be, I'd have thought you'd embrace it. I mean perhaps I should let Nick have it? He probably does deserve it.' Occy's gaze shifted back to her screen. 'And well-being's more his thing. He's really been performing at the highest level these last few—'

'I'll take it,' said Lenny. 'I'm in.'

36

Juliet was carving shapes out of dark chocolate with a scalpel blade to decorate a toasted almond brioche loaf when she noticed Celina, over the far side of the studio, with Serafina, the make-up artist. Those two had become inseparable recently. Juliet had tried to make friends with Serafina, she really had – but Serafina was one of those ombre-haired party girls who looked permanently unimpressed by other women unless they were famous. She'd been the fashion stylist on set two years ago, had reappeared last year as a yoga teacher, and had now reinvented herself as a make-up artist. Serafina caught Juliet's eye, whispered to Celina, then headed over to Juliet's prep area.

'Hey, sweets,' said Serafina. 'What are you doing?'

'Just finishing off these chocolate leaves,' said Juliet, carefully curving the blade in a perfect arc.

Serafina peered into Juliet's utensil crate. 'What's *this?*' she said, picking up a long glass tube with a narrow neck at each end.

Juliet looked up. 'A vintage ice-water rolling pin.'

'Why do you need *that?*'

'It's helpful when you're making certain types of pastry,' said Juliet, gently tweezering the final leaf on to a plate. 'It keeps the dough cold.'

'Oh, right,' said Serafina, suddenly bored again. 'Where's your shirt from?'

'*This?* Er, Zara, maybe?'

'Hardcore-normcore!'

Juliet wasn't sure if she'd just been complimented or insulted.

'Hey, babes,' said Celina, coming over to join them and surveying Juliet's handiwork. 'These leaf things are beaut! I don't know what we'd do without you, Jules – you know that, right?'

Juliet shrugged awkwardly. 'Celina, did you get a chance to speak to Mitchell about the new book?'

Celina clapped her hands together. 'Love, love, *love!*'

'I've got some ideas for the cover,' said Juliet. 'Shall I take you through them at lunch next week?'

'Great.' Celina ran her finger down Juliet's shot list. 'How long till the brioche shot?'

'You've got ten minutes – they're still shooting close-ups of the soda bread.'

'Seffie, darling, can you come to the bathroom and help me powder my nose?'

Even an eight year old knew enough about natural lighting to appreciate that the studio toilets were the least well-lit environment in which to apply make-up. Still, Celina's nose powder was none of Juliet's concern.

Lenny had suffered a mini-meltdown when Occy had mentioned the retreat was Wi-Fi free, but now she thought about it peace, quiet and a digital break would be ideal. She gazed out of the window as the taxi took her from the airport on a spectacular two-hour drive through Andalucía, past unspoilt white villages, giant sequoias, broad oaks, and up into the mountains. The last roadside café they'd passed was forty miles back, the only living creature she'd seen recently a lone mountain goat.

Finally the taxi turned left up a long drive lined with palm trees and arrived at a low modern building made of steel and glass. Oooh, it did look luxurious! She pictured herself at happy hour by an indoor pool with a glass of cold white wine and a bowl of salted almonds – heavenly.

At reception, a smiling Spanish lady greeted Lenny warmly and poured her a glass of chilled water with lemon and mint. Nice touch, flavoured water. Lenny would wait until 6 p.m. for her first glass of wine. Her stomach was rumbling though – she'd misjudged the extra time she'd need to get through the airport with her ankle, and had been forced to buy a vile, dried-out sandwich on the plane. When she got to the room she'd order a few little bits to tide her over till dinner.

Lenny squinted at the girl's name badge. 'Estella! Thank you.'

'And your Serenity pack,' said Estella, handing her a brochure, along with the room key. Lenny smiled. As long as there wasn't enforced trapeze or veganism she didn't care what was in this brochure. Her plan was to sit with her leg up ordering club sandwiches, cocktails and the occasional warm chocolate brownie with vanilla ice cream. An immersion in salt, fat, carbs and booze was just what the doctor had ordered.

Her room was beautiful! A vast bed with six giant plumped pillows, a view of the far-off mountains, and a marble bathroom with ultra-fluffy robes. Why had she put up the slightest resistance to coming here? She settled in under the huge duvet and opened the brochure.

> **Seven-Day Nourish and Healing Immersion at Casa Movada.**
> The Spiritual Awakening Programme operates on four foundational principles: love, kindness, compassion and forgiveness, to return The Self to serenity and wholeness. There are twice-daily lectures with guru Ian Bottomsley, author of the e-book *Conscious Spirituality in Action*. We much recommend attendance: toxicity is not unique to the processed foods we are consuming but also found within our processed, negative thought patterns. Alongside our magical cleansing programme our guests find also greatly helpful a daily coffee colonic.

Coffee colonic? A translation error, surely? She looked at the original Spanish – 'colónica café' – must be some locally brewed nutritious drink. Speaking of which! Lenny pulled open the drawer of the bedside table: the Bible, a notepad, a pencil – no room service menu. Nothing in the desk drawers either, apart from a map of local hikes.

She called room service and five minutes later a young boy knocked.

'*Gracias*!' said Lenny, flicking the menu open. 'Oh, hang on – this is just a vegetable juice menu. Could you bring me the food menu, and the wine list? *Vino*? Alcohol?'

The boy's eyes widened in confusion.

'Er – *mangiare*? Food. To eat?'

The boy shook his head.

'Tapas? Patatas bravas?' she mimed eating, and the boy giggled.

Lenny laughed. She was no good at Spanish, why should he be any better at English? 'Don't worry,' she said, cheerily. 'I'll grab one at reception.' Chorizo, she'd definitely order chorizo – perhaps a tortilla?

Lenny went back through to reception and spoke, increasingly heatedly, to Estella.

She returned to her room ten minutes later, lay on her bed and let out a long, low howl.

'You'll be OK, Lenny – you've already made it through two hours.'

'Jules, look up return flights, leaving tomorrow. Call that Robert guy, see if he can help?'

'Hang on in there.'

'You don't understand – *therapeutic fasting* – it's enforced detox! There's no food whatsoever, I've checked the surrounding trees, not even an olive on those branches.'

'Surely they can't starve you?'

'No, they're torturing me instead. Three green juices a day, liquid broccoli, and the only way I can have coffee is if they stick it up my bum.'

'Oh don't, Lenny – it can puncture your bowel.'

'Juliet, do you think I would voluntarily let someone put a hose in my rectum and fill it with Nescafé? The other guests have paid four grand for this, the guys running this place must be laughing – four grand and they don't even have to feed the inmates!'

'Lenny, I'm sorry but we're on the final day of the shoot and I have to get back to my baguettes . . . '

'Do not speak to me of freshly baked bread.'

'And then I have to make a round of Coronation chicken sandw—'

'Hush now.'

'And a stack of grilled cheese—'

'Stop!'

'We might even have a glass of cold Champagne, you know, to celebrate . . . ' said Juliet, trying to suppress a laugh.

'Jules, I seriously properly hate you right now.'

* * *

Juliet relaxed into the back seat of the taxi home. She'd had a couple of drinks with the crew after the shoot had wrapped, but she wanted to go for a run in the morning and was looking forward to the peace and quiet of an empty house and a long bath tonight.

It had been a great shoot – such a contrast to Easter. She still felt mildly sick at the memory. She switched her thoughts to the present, closed her eyes, then opened them suddenly and grinned. What the hell, she had a little Dutch courage, ha, Dutch – how apt! She took out her phone and dialled, hoping he wasn't out on a date – maybe he had a girlfriend? She'd never thought to ask.

The phone rang a foreign ringtone. He picked up sounding pleasantly surprised.

'Robert? It's Juliet – from the plane.'

'Juliet From The Plane – or, as I like to think of you: Juliet.'

'I'm sorry, you're abroad somewhere, aren't you?'

'In Geneva – at a week-long Corporate Governance Seminar. I am living the dream!'

'Not to worry. I'll speak to you when you're back in town.'

'No, you have perfect timing. I know the team interviewed a couple of chefs but they weren't that impressed. We could look at getting you in for a chat next week?'

'Ah, no, that's OK. But thank you anyway.'

'Oh. Right. I thought you'd changed your mind?'

'No. I haven't. I'm sorry.'

'Oh. OK. So . . . I'm confused. You're *not* interested in the role?'

'I'm not,' said Juliet, feeling a barrier of nerves suddenly rise up, and forcing them to one side.

'You're *not* interested? OK . . . Then why are you calling?'

'I'm not interested in the role. But I am interested in you.'

There was a very long pause. Juliet held her breath, then felt a flood of relief as Robert came back on the line. 'To be honest,' he said, 'that suits me even better.'

37

Lenny was broken. She'd spent all weekend pacing her bedroom, dreaming of escape. Eighty-eight hours till her flight home on Thursday. She was keeping every straw from every juice she'd drunk in a glass by her bed to mark the ever-so-slow passing of time.

So far she'd imbibed liquid kale, liquid cabbage, liquid spinach – each juice thinner, murkier and more bitter than the last. Her body had never felt worse: zero energy, constant hunger pains, her ankle throbbing again in protest, her teeth aching from underuse. Not eating solids was clearly intolerable, but she also had a cracking pain through her face, head and neck from caffeine withdrawal. More traumatic still: she'd realised she had not gone a day without alcohol for . . . well, quite some time now. She was officially one of those career-woman low-level alcoholics the *Daily Mail* was always writing about and she was now experiencing the horror of withdrawal.

Well, just because she was stuck in this glorified prison for four more days didn't mean she had to leave her bedroom. Every time she'd popped out to pick up her juice from the 'dining room' – huh! – she'd been trapped in one unwanted social interaction after another: Chandon, the helium-voiced PR girl from LA who had told Lenny how she was ultra-spiritual and even had the tattoo to prove it. Belles Carlton – Lenny would google her the moment she had Wi-Fi, she was sure she'd seen her on the cover of *Heat*. And Creepy Mike, who 'could feel Lenny's pain', but was in fact trying to feel her bum as she stood by the herbal tea station, silently weeping. They were terrible, awful human beings, every one of them.

No: she would hole up in her fluffy robe, sleep, read her book and pretend none of this was happening.

She turned off her light. The pain in her head flared up the side of her face. Eighty-seven hours, forty-two minutes and eight seconds to go.

* * *

Lenny woke on Monday with a new definition of the blues: a swollen throat, a giant spot on her chin, and her hunger, if anything, intensifying.

She went down to the dining room. She'd stopped making jokes about bacon sandwiches yesterday; the spirulina-sprout juice had somewhat drowned her *joie de vivre*.

'How are you getting on, sweetie?' said Chandon, cornering her by the juice table. 'Oooh, wheatgrass!'

The vicious green liquid looked to Lenny like it might glow in the dark.

'Wheatgrass contains more micronutrients than any food on the planet,' said Chandon. 'Plus, it cures cancer.'

'That's a medical fact, is it?' said Lenny, as she held her breath and tipped the drink down her throat: it tasted of intense liquefied grass with a harsh chemical aftertaste.

'I love fasting. I wish I never had to eat,' said Chandon. 'I find it so oppressive thinking, "what am I going to eat, what am I going to eat?" every single day.'

'I spend all day, every day, looking forward to my next meal.'

'You're totally joking?'

'Have you never tasted fresh crusty bread and butter?'

'Super-toxins!' Chandon shuddered. 'You British and your carbs. Did you know, the human body was designed to live on a liquid diet?'

'Bollocks, or how do you explain teeth?'

Chandon looked at her with pity. 'You should come hear Ian this morning – he's talking about Acceptance; tonight it's Self-Compassion. You seem like you'd totally benefit from it.'

'Chandon, I'm going to my room for a lie-down.'

Four p.m. Lenny was convinced she could smell onions being fried. Her stomach let out a persistent mewl of complaint, like a cat locked out of a house at night.

She'd finished reading her novel two hours ago. Her concentration was shot. She'd had to re-read several passages, and skip several others in which the heroine discussed in luscious detail how to cook the perfect spaghetti Bolognese.

She picked up the phone.

'Hey, Lenny . . . ' said Estella, warily.

'Estella! I know you said there are no exceptions but please, stay on the line: I don't need food but I medically do need coffee.'

'I'm not allowed to, Lenny.'

'Sure, sure, let's talk cash. Fifty euros. For one cup. Trust me – coffee is not the biggest problem in my life, so I can personally guarantee that *you* procuring *me* some *coffee* will in no way set back my progress of wellness or happiness or spirituality or whatever crap you guys are flogging . . . '

'Have a drink of hot water.'

'Estella, that's like saying watch a blank video. Hot water is not a drink, a drink must have content.'

'Lenny, did you go to Ian's lecture earlier?'

'I *cannot* bring myself to listen to a guru named Ian Bottomsley.'

'Go tonight. Your mind needs the spiritual nourishment we provide, as well as the vitamins in the glass. Your body is currently experiencing intense detoxification. This programme is holistic – it's designed to flush out your mental pollution, to overload your system with positivity. It only works if you embrace it mentally too.'

'Playing hardball, I see. Nice. OK then – one hundred euros! For a single cup. No one will offer you a better deal in your whole life. I swear I won't tell the others, it can be our little secret.'

'Lenny, if your body wants coffee that much, go down to the colonic chamber and—'

Lenny slammed the receiver down.

That night Lenny counted the straws in her glass marking the slow passage of time over and over again. This place would not break her. She picked one up and gnawed the end. They could remake that Tim Robbins prison movie starring Lenny . . . call it The Strawshank Redemption . . . She laughed – a bitter, hungry sound – then checked her handbag for any stray M&Ms.

She slept fitfully, dreamed of walking in the surrounding hills and gazing up at clouds of mashed potato. In her dream, a local goat approached her, bleating plaintively. Lenny had to stop herself from strangling it and eating it raw.

38

An hour after her broccoli and ginseng juice on Tuesday morning Lenny sat at the end of her bed, shoulders hunched, head down. There was literally nothing to do, nothing to read, no TV to watch, no Internet to surf, no meal to punctuate the day – absolutely nothing left to distract Lenny from her self.

She lay back, but her thoughts started spiralling rapidly downwards, so she picked up the brochure from the bedside table and flicked listlessly through it: 'Tuesday 11 a.m. – yoga studio – Guru Ian on Healing The Self'.

Lenny checked her watch: she could probably make it if she left now.

Ian was short and wiry, with heavy eyebrows and a face that looked like he'd spent every summer in Ibiza wearing no SPF, and doing all the narcotics in the Balearics and most of the ones in mainland Spain. He sat cross-legged, a stick of burning incense and three pieces of crystal on the floor in front of him. Lenny lingered with one hand on the studio door – could she back away now, pretend she'd got lost looking for the sauna?

Ian gestured for her to lie down and she reluctantly joined the others as Ian spoke to them in a low, soft voice. 'The world is not what we think it is – it's a mere projection, a world of phenomenon.'

The world felt pretty real to Lenny: the hard wooden floor digging into her spine, the caffeine headache which had taken up residence in her eyeballs, the gargantuan effort it was taking her not to fart.

'Your self is not your true self . . . it is not doing . . . it just is . . . being . . . so are you.'

Either Ian was on acid, or the absence of protein in Lenny's diet had melted her brain – it sounded like utter gibberish.

'The eternal exists outside of you, behind the defence of you.'

She lay back and let his sentences waft over her, along with the smell of incense. It reminded her of her local curry house and she found herself fantasising about a chicken curry, tender cubes of potato, a pile of fragrant rice. Oh, to feel the crispness of a papadum between her teeth.

'Your mind is not you; nor is your body.'

Her stomach made an angry gurgle of dissent.

Lenny returned to the studio for the evening session. The view out over the snow-peaked mountains was marginally better than the view of her bedroom wall.

'It's a little chilly tonight,' said Ian. 'Feel free to grab a blanket.'

Lenny was last in the queue and watched in disbelief as Chandon, in front of her, took the last two.

'Can I have one of those, please, Chandon?'

'I'm from southern California, I feel the cold super-majorly,' said Chandon, returning to her mat with both.

'Relax and breathe,' said Ian. 'Tonight we're going to think even more intensely about the self.'

Chandon's got that covered already, thought Lenny.

'We talk of wanting freedom,' said Ian. 'Yet we are all prisoners of our own minds. Emotions come and go, yet we attach to them like they are real. None of it is real – it is not the essential us.'

Everyone around her was nodding like a disciple. Lenny lay back and tried to sleep without snoring.

'If anyone wants to go deeper into the practice, I'm here,' said Ian, as the rest of the group filed out. Lenny lingered at the back. 'Lenny! Don't be shy. You look like you want to ask something?'

'I still don't get it – why aren't we allowed to eat?'

'Ah!' said Ian, as if he'd just revealed a winning scratch card. 'The universe gives you bread and you throw it back and ask for toast.'

'But there *is* no bread!' said Lenny. 'That's my point.'

'And that is *my* point. Your soul is being nourished and all you can think of is your stomach.'

Lenny frowned.

'You'll never find inner peace until you stop your resistance,' said Ian.

'I'm not resisting. I just don't know what on earth you're talking about.'

'Which is a form of resistance. This isn't about logic. Your brain is not your thoughts, your thoughts are not you. For the self to be reborn you must surrender the toxic self.'

'Nope, still don't get it.'

'Sleep on it.'

Lenny stared at her bedroom ceiling. It seemed lower than it had been five days ago. If her thoughts weren't hers – and she'd happily disown most of them —who did they belong to, and what were they doing in her head?

One fifty-eighty a.m. It was no use – she felt too hungry, too troubled and too miserable to sleep.

She headed to the dining room; she'd be safe from the others at this time of night. She made a hot water with lemon, sucked every last morsel of flesh from the pulp, then took a seat and gazed out into the night. The air up here was so clean, the sky bright with a thousand stars. The more Lenny looked, the more seemed to appear. She never looked at the stars in London anymore, why bother? There was so much pollution, even when there weren't clouds. If only she could be enjoying this view with a glass of Rioja, and Pringles.

She jumped at the sound of footsteps, turned, and saw Ian, carrying a laptop and heading over to the yoga studio.

'Is that you, Lenny?'

'I couldn't sleep.'

'May I sit with you?'

She shrugged.

'See there?' said Ian, pointing to one of the brightest stars. 'That's my favourite star, Sirius. And there, that's Venus, and that's Neptune.'

Lenny couldn't help but be impressed. 'You never see planets back at home.'

'You do – you just don't know you're looking at them.'

She turned her head to get a better angle. 'Venus and Neptune look pretty close together.'

Ian chuckled. 'They're usually around thirty astronomical units apart.'

'What's that, in miles or light years?'

'It's thirty times one hundred and fifty million kilometres.'

Lenny did the sum in her head, got lost in zeros, felt keenly the sense of her own nothingness.

Her gaze drifted to Ian's computer. 'Why are you up so late? Are you working?'

'I'm heading to the yoga studio to watch a live webcast by my spiritual guru.'

'You *what?*'

'My Zen master is doing a session from his Tibetan monastery. He does a three-hour masterclass every week, webcast live to his followers.'

'How on earth is that possible?'

'Oh, technology's marvellous. They have a satellite link—'

'No, I mean how is it possible if you don't have Wi-Fi?'

Ian smiled as if he alone knew all the answers. It was most annoying. 'You can only access the Wi-Fi in the yoga studio. Besides, if we gave you the code, you'd spend the whole time here distracted from your job.'

'I swear to you, I would not check my work emails!'

'No, I meant the job you're here to do – the job of becoming you. Lenny, you look to me like someone who's in pain.'

She couldn't deny that. 'My stomach feels so hollow, it's like an aching cave. Do you think you could possibly find me a snack?'

'Lenny, I mean spiritual pain.'

He looked deep into her eyes and kept looking. It was the strangest sensation. The more he looked, the more he seemed to see straight through her. At first she felt her face flush, then her bottom lip started to wobble, and then with a sudden, fierce rush the tears started to flow.

'I'm hungry, that's all,' she sobbed. 'It's lack of bloody carbs!'

'Lenny, it's OK to be human. We're all the same on the inside.

Why don't you watch the webcast with me, it might help you understand a little better.'

She followed Ian meekly to the yoga studio and they sat side by side in front of his laptop. On screen a monk in maroon robes sat on the floor, speaking in a voice barely audible. At first Lenny was bored at his talk of harmony and nature. But then he spoke of compassion, of kindness, and how the path to happiness is reached through self-nurture. The way he explained it somehow managed to bypass her brain and touch her very core. She felt her defences fall, felt herself finally willing to surrender to the universe – if it meant she could get what she wanted.

She listened to him speak of the deception of the ego, and again she felt tears falling, washing away her illusions. She experienced a clarity the like of which she'd never experienced before. Truths she'd been avoiding for so long presented themselves like a relentless, inescapable spiritual PowerPoint presentation:

She wanted love, yet wasted herself on Ellis. Ellis would never love her – how could he? She didn't even love herself.

She relied on booze and food to suppress her feelings, yet her sadness followed her always, like a shadow.

She was scared of absolutely everything: being single, being in a relationship, missing out, getting old, dying alone, failure, failure, failure.

She was still the girl she'd been when she was a teenager. The reason she was so harsh about Danny and Ellis was because she was just as bad as they were – she too had never grown up.

Her whole life was based on things working themselves out at some unidentified later stage but this moment – this very moment, sitting cross-legged on the floor next to the prematurely sun-damaged Ian Bottomsley – this was all there was! This present moment was the world.

But what this also meant was, the past didn't matter. She could go home and be a better Lenny. She could be brave, she could be fearless! She could go out into the world filled with love for humanity.

By the time the webcast ended, the sun was rising, pale gold over the mountains. Her brain was buzzing. Perhaps Lenny was being reborn – or perhaps it was just the final stages of caffeine withdrawal.

She slept for three hours but woke feeling entirely alive. Her spinach and celery juice was delectable, and when she cleaned her teeth she noticed her complexion was radiant, her eyes clearer than they'd been in years. She had so much energy, her body needed to move! She could hardly wait for the 11 a.m. talk, but first she searched the drawer for the map of local hikes and headed out the door.

She set off up a rocky path, felt the stones beneath her feet, the crunch of branches. She climbed through a forest of pines to the top of the nearest hill and at the summit stood looking out towards a lake in the distance, the waters still and dark and green. She breathed in deeply. Such clean air. Such peace, such quiet. She felt her heart expand with joy. This is what people meant when they talked about connection to a higher consciousness.

She couldn't wait to get home and start being the new Lenny.

At the morning session Lenny sat on the front row, straight backed, absorbing Ian's every word: 'We are – you is – you are not I' – now it made perfect sense!

She spent the afternoon with Chandon discussing which juicer to buy – centrifugals were cheaper, but masticators would squeeze every last drop of kale juice from the leaf!

The evening's lecture was terrific! Ian told the tale of an ancient farmer in a remote village. One day the man's horse dies. The man weeps, for his beloved son cannot ride to the neighbouring village to sell millet on market day. The man and his son go hungry. But then news arrives that the neighbouring village has been attacked by bandits and everyone slaughtered. The man rejoices – his beloved son has been spared!

'The tale is teaching us we are often too quick to judge,' explained Ian, lighting the incense. 'Do not presume to know the whole story until it is done. What at first appears to be a curse may be a blessing: your darkest hour is a gift: only then do you discover your true self.'

* * *

When it came time to leave on Thursday morning, Lenny felt bereft. She'd write a cheque right now for £4,000 to stay another week! Hope and good intentions were seeping from her every pore.

She gave Ian a huge hug goodbye. 'You've literally changed my life.'

'Mind how you go,' he said, gently. 'It's when you think you have it all worked out that the universe tends to present you with the greatest challenges – that's when you'll truly be tested. You don't change a lifetime's behaviour in one week. Keep up the practice.'

On the way back to the airport she ordered the juicer Chandon had recommended, Amazon express delivery, arriving tomorrow!

At the airport she walked straight past the coffee shop with its rows of cakes and tarts without even flinching. The cakes looked trapped behind glass – like Lenny had been trapped in her old ways of thinking, her old self-destructive habits. No more, no more!

As she waited to board she dropped Occy an email:

Wow! It was the most incredible experience. Thank you – I'm profoundly grateful. I must admit initially I was dubious, but I feel like a new person. Resilient, strong and ready to face the challenges of the next six months.

She received an out-of-office reply:

I am currently in New York, returning on Monday.

On the plane home the six year old sitting behind Lenny maintained a relentless drumbeat with her foot in the back of Lenny's chair. Old Lenny would have turned and given a stern look, but new Lenny paused. This child was clearly excited. Perhaps it was her first time on a plane. Perhaps she was bored. Her poor mother must be exhausted. Lenny left it a whole twenty minutes before gently asking the girl to refrain. The girl's mother called Lenny a word in Spanish that did not sound remotely serene. The girl kept kicking.

The plane landed to a typical Gatwick December day: grey sky, icily cold. No matter! Lenny had left London bruised and battered

– she returned whole. As she strode into the terminal, admiring her slightly slimmer reflection in the windows, pure sunshine shone from within her.

As the train lumbered through Croydon she could feel the very top layer of her mood washing away like silt in the drizzle. Her sense of smell had sharpened noticeably and the man sitting next to her stank of nicotine and greasy hair. Her train got delayed on the track for an hour, then at King's Cross Lenny realised that not only had she been sitting on chewing gum but she'd forgotten her Oyster card. Ian was right, though – this was precisely what he'd predicted: the minute you thought you had it all sussed, the universe starts chucking little spanners in your direction. She popped into Pret, ordered a hot water and lemon, massaged her temples and re-centred herself.

It was noon. She wasn't due back at work till Monday but she pictured the mounds of paper on her desk and felt a strong urge to tidy them once and for all.

When she walked into reception, she knew instantly from Fran's face something was up.

'What's wrong?' said Lenny, her smile falling. 'Has somebody died?'

'You haven't spoken to Occy yet?' said Fran, nervously.

'About what?'

Lenny sat in the coffee shop with her jaw grinding, holding Fran's copy of the all-staff memo in her fist.

'Fran. Do me a favour. Take back this hot water and ask them to put three shots of espresso in a cup for me. Do it. Do it now.'

Lenny could feel her lip going into spasm as she re-read Occy's words:

Wappen London is delighted to announce the appointment of our newest board member: a team player who embodies the Wappen brand; a visionary and natural networker who creates effective peer-to-peer relationships. The new role of Chief Happiness Officer goes to Nick Cooper. In addition, as a reflection of her contribution to the business, Leonora

Dublonsky is being promoted to Regional Head of Research, Eurasia, based in the brand new Wappen office in Guangzhou.

Lenny necked the coffee Fran brought her, felt the hot, dark bitter liquid burn her throat. Ah, it felt good to be back on the caffeine train.

'What will you do?' asked Fran. 'Are you going to kick off?'

Lenny stared at the bottom of her coffee cup. She thought back to the last seven days, everything she'd learned. Standing at the top of the hill, looking out across the mountain, the air so cool and crisp. That feeling of truly being at one with the universe, serenity, forgiveness, grace, peace, acceptance and, above all, love.

'You epic little prick!' said Lenny, as Cooper sat at her desk readjusting his line-up of toy robots. 'You couldn't even wait till I'd gone before you stole my office!'

'Occy was going to call you later – you weren't due in today. All your stuff's been neatly packed and you're getting two weeks off to sort out relocation stuff.'

'So she sends me to juice camp to get me out of the picture, then hides in New York so she doesn't have to fire me to my face!'

'*Fired?* You're being promoted.'

'Really? I bet you can't find Guangzhou on a bloody map.'

Nick shrugged. 'I don't have to. But seriously Lenny, it *is* a promotion!'

'*Peer-to-peer relationships* – I know a euphemism when I hear one. Your ping-pong balls? Is that what this is about?'

'Lenny, trust me, I have never slept with Occy.'

'Trust *you*? You literally have your feet under my desk.'

'Lenny, the added value I bring is worth a quantifiable amount to the Wappen brand. Equally, your skill-set will be invaluable in Asia.'

Lenny stared at Nick's robots, the yo-yo meticulously placed in the corner of his desk. 'Look at your stupid little toys, you're basically just an over-sized child.'

'And is that better or worse than being an over-sized stroppy teenager?'

How dare he! Lenny grabbed the nearest robot – a tin Dalek with little red and blue lights on its chest – and threw it to the floor.

Nick stood up rapidly. 'Not Robby the Robot, he's original, he's vintage, he's Japanese!'

Lenny lifted her foot and was about to stamp on the robot's head when she realised it was her left foot and she'd be wiser using her right.

'You know what, Cooper?' She put her foot calmly back on the floor. 'I hope you are blissfully happy in your new job. I'll spare your little robot friend because like me, he's the innocent victim in all this, but I am calling Occy right now and explaining to her why she cannot possibly do this to me.'

'I'm surprised and quite frankly disappointed,' said Occy. 'Hold on! *Double shot skinny latte, almond milk, and tell Jared I'll only be two secs? Yup, a London issue, yep yep, exactly! Thanks.* Lenny, listen, can this not wait till I'm back on Monday?'

'Octavia, I do not want to move to China.'

'It's not like you have a partner or children. A single woman with no dependents should jump at an opportunity like this – the market is huge! And you're right near Hong Kong – the shopping, the life-style. I know you love travelling.'

'My life is in London.'

'Guangzhou is a vibrant city, it's a key emerging hub for Wappen.'

'I've checked online, it's the most polluted city in China, it's worse than Beijing.'

'It's only polluted because there's so much exciting growth!'

'Octavia, please!'

'I can't believe this Lenny – after what you said earlier?'

'What? Said to who? When? What did Nick say I said?'

'After what *you* said to *me* – *today* in your email. "I'm resilient, strong, ready for the challenges of the next six months" . . .'

'I didn't mean *these* sort of challenges.'

'Look, Lenny, my hands are now tied.'

'What does that mean?'

'It means as part of the wider global restructure, I've planned resource with you as lead researcher in Asia. If you are turning down the role, that gives us both a problem.'

'Why? I'll just stay in London.'

'That's what I'm saying. Within the new structure, UK research falls under Nick's remit.'

'What?'

'We're splitting your role into three more junior roles, reporting into Nick.'

'So you're saying I move to China, or stay here and work for *Nick*?'

'Actually, legally you'd need to apply for one of those roles, we couldn't just hand it to you.'

'So *China* – or apply for a worse paid, more junior role with Nick *as my boss*. Or *what*, exactly?'

'Well yes, Lenny, that's my point. If you don't like the proposal on the table, I fear we're looking at *or what, exactly?*'

39

Lunch with Mitchell and Celina. The invite had only taken five and a half years to come but now, as Juliet sat alone at a table for three in The Wolseley, she was starting to think she'd imagined it. She'd already been waiting for forty minutes. She'd have ordered a drink if she'd known they'd be this long. She checked her phone again – nothing from them, but a text from Martha about Christmas plans – did she want to join them at Nate's parents? If not, she and Nate would come down and cook for her. *Happy either way* she replied, then beckoned the wine waiter over.

Juliet had mentioned to Mitchell she was considering selling her bread at local delis but assured him it wouldn't interfere with the new comfort food book. She believed in this book wholeheartedly, but she was planning on asking for a pay rise today. On set she'd worked out that with the extra hours she routinely put in, she earned less than minimum wage. Not Mitchell's fault – her own, entirely, for not having checked the numbers properly – but she'd checked them now.

Mitchell and Celina finally appeared through the revolving door at 1.55 p.m. Celina hugged her so intensely Juliet thought she might actually leave an imprint on Celina's cream Victoria Beckham dress.

'Babe!' said Celina. 'We never get to do this. Why are we only doing this now, Mitch?'

Mitchell shrugged jovially. 'Champagne, ladies?'

They toasted, 'To the best book ever!' and Juliet was considering when she should mention the pay rise when Celina saved her the trouble.

'So babe, the new book,' said Celina, rubbing her hands in delight. 'Me and Mitch have been chatting and I'm beyond excited!'

'Great,' said Juliet. 'I've been working on some recipes—'

Mitchell coughed gently and opened the wine list.

'We can talk about that later if you want,' said Celina. 'But I meant the next book.'

'The comfort food book?'

'When Mitchell pitched it? That integrity stuff? I've realised who I am at the moment is like kale.'

'Like kale? Or actually kale?'

'Total kale. Kale soups, mains, desserts, kale brownies. And I know Sef's a master of make-up, but she's really up for food styling, I mean it's the same as clothes, right? So I thought she could co-style, take some of the creative parts off your hands.'

Juliet took a sip of Champagne.

'And you know that expression Epic Fail?' said Celina.

Juliet suppressed a smile. Martha used to say that – in 2012.

'So, we're going to call it Epic Kale,' said Celina. 'Because it rhymes!'

'Not with itself,' said Mitchell. 'But it resonates. With millennials.'

'And the other thing,' said Celina. 'If Sef's co-stylist, that will impact your day rate but then Mitch said you'll be selling bread in shops or something?' Celina raised her glass to Juliet. 'So, how quickly can you get me recipes?'

Juliet looked down at the linen tablecloth. Such a shame to leave before her prawn cocktail had even arrived. 'Can I just clarify – you're not interested in my book idea now? Or ever?'

Celina pulled a face as if she'd sniffed off-milk.

'Will you excuse me?' said Juliet, placing her napkin on the table and heading down to the toilet. She locked herself in a cubicle, sat on the closed lid, then took out her pen and notebook. If she started selling one hundred loaves of bread a week, retailing at say, £3.50 a loaf, at an 80% margin . . . No, that wouldn't make enough. Now that Matt's stupid Porsche was gone for good, she could use the garage, turn it into a micro-bakery, maybe look at hiring a bigger oven? She could increase her capacity and potentially do forty loaves a day, sell them at farmers' markets and that fancy new deli in Highgate. She flicked back in her notebook and reread her notes from the last few months: *Turn a negative into a positive . . . think less, do more . . . food should be delicious . . . be brave . . .*

She remembered being high up on that trapeze platform, standing at the edge. Lenny had been so scared, and she'd wanted Lenny not to be scared, and so she'd taken a deep breath and grabbed the bar and just jumped. It might have looked from ground level like she was fearless but she was just as scared as the next person, but she did it anyway and it turned out to be the most fun she'd had in a very long time.

She scribbled down a few more sums, took a deep breath, then returned to the table, where the starters had just arrived.

'Thank you so much for lunch, Mitchell, and I'm sorry I can't stay, but it's two fifteen already and I was expecting you at one,' said Juliet. 'I've run out of time. On which note, I think now would be the perfect time for us to go our separate ways.'

'Babe, what?' said Celina, warily putting down her fork.

'Celina, I'm sure Epic Kale is the book you were meant to write. But not with me.'

'But we're a team.'

'You and Sef will make a better one.'

'Not without you!'

'Celina, I can play second fiddle but I can't play third. Anyway, I've decided, I'm on my own team now.'

'We can look at working something out on the money front,' said Mitchell, rapidly. 'If you give me a few days, there might be room for some flex.'

Juliet smiled – she was a little sharper on bullshit detection nowadays.

'Please sit,' said Mitchell, reaching his arm out. 'Eat your starter at least! I've paid for it.'

'Don't worry, I'll grab a sandwich on the way to the Tube.'

Celina poked Mitchell so hard he winced.

'Sweetheart!' he said. 'Think of all those beautiful books you ladies have done together.'

Juliet thought of all the hours, the effort, the care and love she'd put in. Time to put that into something of her own.

'If you'll excuse me,' she said, 'I don't want to be late for my first board meeting.'

'Sweetheart, I'm disappointed,' said Mitchell. 'Six years together: six! That's longer than some marriages. Doesn't loyalty mean anything to you?'

Juliet had turned to leave but paused and turned back to the table. 'I'm glad you asked me that, Mitchell: *doesn't loyalty mean anything to me?* Why yes, absolutely it does. It means everything to me.'

Then she smiled, turned her back on them and headed for the door.

PART SIX

SIX MONTHS LATER

'Let go, or be dragged'

Zen proverb

40

Happiness, shmappiness.

Lenny lay on her sofa, pencil in hand, assessing the sheet of A4 on her lap. Scattered below her on the floor were six balls of scrunched-up paper: perfect circles were extremely hard to draw. Outside the rain was horizontal – May this year was a washout. Any day now she'd need to meet up with Fran for more stationery and a gossip but today was not that day and this circle would have to do.

She carefully traced her pencil from top to bottom, left to right, and in the top left quarter wrote WORK. There was still some settlement money left – with a few further economies she could make it last till autumn. Of course Lady of Leisure was not a viable long-term option, but then nor were the briefs her headhunter kept sending her: *Creatalyst?* – Not a real word. *Full Stack Cloud Architect?* Not a real job.

Lenny contemplated turning forty next year, with another two and a half decades of work still to go, jumping from one miserable option to the next – *if she was lucky*. The nineteen interviews she'd had since parting company with Wappen had made her, well, not depressed, but not exactly un-depressed. Job hunting had officially replaced online dating as the primary source of rejection in Lenny's life.

On which note, top right: LOVE. Technically she should make that quadrant less prominent, given how negligible the love in her life was. But to revise the circle, to arise from the sofa, locate a rubber, erase the line and then transport the little shrinkles of used rubber to a bin without spilling any on the carpet? Lenny definitely wasn't up for hoovering – why, just thinking about it exhausted her. Besides, the love part was simple: she'd carry on shagging Ellis until his band had a hit, at which point she'd lose him to a twenty-three-year-old groupie wearing high-waisted denim and those trendy earrings that crawled up the side of your ear like a spiky golden bug.

Bottom left: FOOD / BODY. Lenny had sagely lain down her own layer of winter fat to save on heating bills. There'd been quite a lot of comfort eating recently; she could draw a pie chart of the pies she'd eaten over the last month alone. The bread samples Jules brought every week were not helping. That classic sandwich loaf, with its crisp crust and soft, pillowy insides – it was hard to not eat it all in one session, especially when it arrived oven-warm. And that rosemary focaccia last Friday, dripping in fruity olive oil, springy, light, dense, salty . . . Lenny poked her finger into her thigh. Something must be done. And would be done, soon. But Jules and Amy did their 10k thing most Sundays, and Lenny wasn't going to be chasing after them in a hurry.

Ah. The final piece of the pie: the corners of Lenny's mouth drooped: FRIENDSHIP. Andrew had been seeing Fiona since Christmas and had become incapable of doing anything unless Fiona came too – and a night out with Andriona involved excessive PDAs and the odd look of pity. Amy was still Amy, nagging Lenny to go drinking to chi-chi bars even though she knew Lenny was on a restricted budget. It was all very well Amy saying 'just get another job', but Amy hadn't just battled through eight separate interviews at IncaTech, including a full day of meeting the board, only to be told the job had been given to a guy who already worked there. Who was born in the nineties.

And then Juliet . . . Juliet's life had turned on its head again – this time for the better. She did dough shifts Monday to Thursday in the micro-bakery in her garage, then from Tuesdays to Fridays woke at some hellish hour and baked till 7.30 a.m. when Danny would drive the bread round to her customers and she'd grab a few more hours sleep. Lenny had kept her company a few times, and ended up mesmerised by the industrial mixer, its giant spiral hook spinning gently through the voluptuous dough. Eventually she'd realised she was getting in the way, but Juliet had been too polite to say. So now Juliet popped in every Friday with bread, which made Lenny feel like a grandma. At the weekends Juliet was with Robert. Lenny was a huge fan: Robert was warm, genuine and utterly smitten. And Lenny was relieved to see how well he and Martha had got on when she'd been down at Easter. Yes, that was all excellent. Juliet's business was growing, she had a man – two if you counted Danny still in the spare room – she was firmly in control of her life again. And Lenny had Ellis – occasionally – and her telly, and her anger that she clung to like a raft in a storm.

Was it anger? Sometimes it felt that way, though Fran had asked Lenny why she was angry, when Fran thought she'd caught a lucky break. Yet somehow Lenny felt betrayed; even though she'd negoti-ated herself a pay-off from Wappen it had not felt much like her choice.

Or maybe the feeling wasn't anger, but more like sadness? Or a total loss of confidence? Or 360 degrees of fear about her future?

Tomorrow – *if* she had time – she might draw a Venn diagram of all these troublesome emotions and try to understand their over-laps better. Or she might just get Ellis round and then she wouldn't have to think about her life at all.

Happiness was vastly overrated anyway. Lenny had everything she needed: Netflix, a card for free daily coffee from Waitrose, and loo roll. Netflix, free coffee and loo roll – what else was there anyway?

41

Juliet stood at the worktop in her garage, scanned the sheet of paper in front of her, then pressed one palm to her forehead and let out a small, strangulated noise. Attempting five different breads today and committing to brioche tomorrow was too much, and she wasn't even done yet! She picked up her pen and added to her list:

Order more loaf tins
Call Maisie's deli re granary rolls
Order rye + spelt flours & more advanced colour-coded weekly planners
Do accounts / admin from April onwards
Go for a run??
Get a life / Get an extra pair of hands to help out??

Juliet had learned a lot in the last six months and was still learning – but one thing she'd known before she began was that the essential ingredient for great bread was time. Leaving the dough to rest for twelve hours transformed simple ingredients into magical loaves. So on that basis she was willing to get up at 4.30 a.m., four days a week, to turn on the second-hand deck oven Danny had helped her buy, which took ages to heat up, but gave her a capacity far greater than anything she could've had in her home kitchen.

In her first week of trading she'd had two customers and orders for twenty-five loaves. She'd been in a state of near-constant anxiety. The hours, the cobbled together production line, trying to guarantee consistency scaling up – but more than anything the responsibility of having customers pay their hard-earned cash for something she'd made. Yes, it was 'only bread', Matt, but in her opinion, good bread was one of life's greatest pleasures, which made it kind of important. That first time she'd struggled to lift a 16kg bag of flour from

Danny's van to the new IKEA racking system she'd thought: I've made a stupid mistake, I cannot do this. But she'd looked in her yellow notebook and reread her notes about working hard, being brave, and making food with integrity. And on Day One she'd baked seven sourdoughs, ten sandwich loaves and eight multi-grains – they'd looked good and tasted even better. She'd done it the next day and the day after. And a fortnight later, Maisie's deli had increased their order from eight multi-grains to a dozen. And the following month, when Matt submitted a revised financial settlement proposal that was laughably short, Juliet was grateful she had an order for a dozen fig and walnut loaves – and so consumed was she with getting the balance of fruit to nut right, that the unpleasantness of their subsequent row wasn't half as stressful as it might otherwise have been.

Things had evolved considerably since then. Juliet now had nine customers, a second-hand industrial mixer and fridge alongside her oven, and she was baking up to seventy loaves a day. Things with Matt were less evolved, they were still back and forth on financials, but she'd worry about that next week, or perhaps the week after. She looked at today's list again and took a deep breath. Her lower back was aching, her knees hurt, she was brutally tired, but she felt the familiar twitch of excitement in her fingers as she reached for the flour and the scales.

She'd done a lot of experimentation with flours, and during her research she'd found a fantastic stone-grinding mill in Berkshire that supplied directly to other micro-bakeries in the area. With Juliet's increasing volumes it now made better sense to buy their bigger bags – the 25kg ones, she was getting through nearly twenty every week! Whenever the delivery guys arrived at her door, they'd make a fuss and try to stop her going near the bags, because the bags were really heavy. But Juliet had more muscle now; she was stronger than before. And yes those bags really were heavy – but she could lift them, help carry them, and she did.

Juliet checked her watch as she went back into the house – 7.30 p.m. already! She'd overrun – the mixer was playing up again, she'd have to ask Danny to take a look at it later, if he wasn't too tired after college.

It was such a beautiful early summer's evening, she'd have liked to go for a drink with Lenny – they never hung out anymore – but all Juliet had the energy for tonight was a long hot bath with some Epsom salts. A phone call would have to do.

'Lenny, you sound like you've just woken up!'

'Don't be silly,' said Lenny, opening her eyes, then hurriedly grabbing the remote control and pressing pause on *House of Cards*, still running in the background; had she missed an entire episode? What, she'd been asleep for *three*?

'I've been applying for more jobs,' said Lenny, clearing her throat. 'It's pretty tiring. Have you just finished your shift?'

'Yes, those chocolate-chip brioche I brought you last week – Laith's have called and doubled their order.'

'I'm not surprised, they were amazing.'

'I'll bring you more on Friday, you can always freeze them. You won't be out at an interview will you?'

Lenny grabbed the copy of *Grazia* from the floor and noisily flicked through it. 'Looks like Friday I should be here . . . '

Juliet looked at her schedule for the rest of May, pinned to the kitchen wall. She was getting busier every week. 'Lenny, if you're still looking for a job this time next month, how would you feel about helping me out in the bakery?'

'Doing what?'

'The Bread Association's put me in touch with their apprentice scheme, but I wondered if you'd be up for learning how to bake? I'd pay you, of course.'

Lenny laughed. 'Jules, every time I had a grad work for me it took forever to train them. That's fine in a big company but trust me, if you need a baker right now who's not going to destroy your business overnight get someone who knows how to bake.'

'Lenny, it's really not hard, and it's fun. I mean it's a little challenging physically but not mentally.'

'You'll have us all on the payroll soon – me, Martha, Danny—'

'He was asking after you the other day.'

'Was he? How is the old git?'

'Honestly, Lenny, I don't know what I'd do without him. I don't have to think about the delivery stuff, he's such a godsend.'

'How do you live with a bloke like that, though? I bet he never buys loo roll and leaves the toilet seat up all the time.'

'Danny? He's far better house trained than Matt ever was.'

'Seriously?'

'And he's a great cook – actually he mentioned doing a Thai curry this Sunday.'

'You and him?'

'And *you*, and Robert – the four of us.'

'This Sunday?' Lenny froze. 'I think . . . I think I'm with Ellis . . . '

'Oh,' said Juliet. 'Really? Well you could bring him too, of course. I'd really like to meet him one of these days.'

I'll never get Ellis to do happy couples stuff, thought Lenny. And besides, he's up in Hull on tour with the band this weekend.

'Another time,' said Lenny. 'We've sort of already got plans.'

42

Savage Sunday yet again. Lenny was a fool, she should've turned that concept into some sort of business months ago; she'd be rich by now. What to do today? She picked up her phone. Maybe she could have lunch with Juliet and Robert? Oh, but no . . . Jules had gone with Danny to help Martha pack her stuff up and bring it home now summer term was over. Where had the last month gone, how was it June already?

She scrolled through her phone. Andrew? She could probably handle Andriona if it was Andriona or nothing.

The phone rang out, and eventually Andrew picked up, sounding horizontal.

'Hey!' said Lenny, forcing some pep into her voice. 'What are you guys up to today?'

'We're just having a lazy Sunday.'

'Do you want to meet up? We could go to the park?'

'I think Fee just wants to snuggle up under the covers.'

'But it's nice out. Sunny.'

'Fee's knackered. Did I tell you she's been promoted? She's been working late all week.'

'Right, then Fee can stay in bed. You can come out on your own for once, can't you?'

'I kind of fancy an afternoon of doing nothing too.'

'Then how about tonight? The new Cate Blanchett film's out. I can come to your neck of the woods if you guys don't want to move far.'

'Next weekend, maybe? I'll need to check with Fee what our plans are.'

'Don't worry. It's fine,' said Lenny, hoping she didn't sound quite as pissed off as she felt.

Amy had gone quiet recently. In fact, now Lenny scrolled back through their texts, Amy hadn't replied to her last three messages! She texted: *Why are you ignoring me?* – then cringed as she realised she sounded passive-aggressive and needy and a lot like Amy.

Found the last hot single man in London – he existed and I've got him!! Oliver, tall, handsome, funny & filthy in the sack, I could not be happier xx

Typical – always ditching her mates for a man. No, that wasn't fair. Lenny wanted Amy to be happy. But more than that, Lenny wanted *Lenny* to be happy and that was nigh on impossible when she was reduced to the last desperate scrapings of the Netflix barrel. She'd watched all four seasons of *House of Cards*, all the Scandi crime shows and their inferior American remakes, she'd even resorted to some Anime.

There must be something she hadn't seen . . . She listlessly scrolled through the menu. No? No. Hmmm. She flicked on to ITV Player, then hurriedly turned the TV off. If you were watching Jeremy Kyle you were in deep, deep trouble. Even the thought of how close she'd come to seeing his hate-fuelling face was enough to propel her from the sofa into the kitchen.

Her expensive top-of-the-range juicer lay dormant on the counter. She slowly traced her finger through the dust on its surface. Perhaps if she was still unemployed in July she'd sell it on Gumtree, even £30 would help. She'd switched Internet providers two weeks ago so that she wouldn't have to pay for a landline. And with her free coffee and Juliet's weekly bread she'd be fine till she found the perfect job, or at least one she could bear to do and that would have her . . .

Ellis. That's what she'd do today. Go to Waitrose – maybe Janice would be on the till, she liked Janice. Then she'd come home and call him. If he wasn't up yet, she'd sort out the stuff under her bed. There were at least twenty-five VHSs stashed under there that had escaped Juliet's over-zealous attention in the purge. She'd find something to watch, and then, when Ellis surfaced, she could hook up with him.

43

Matt had developed an annoying habit of calling Juliet in the middle of her dough shift. She'd stopped taking the calls but he'd rung three times in a row this afternoon and she panicked that something might have happened to Martha – though she doubted whether Martha would have called Matt in an emergency, she'd only just started speaking to him again.

'Oh, you've picked up, have you?' he said cheerily.

'Er, yes, evidently. I'm right in the middle of pre-shaping. I have asked you not to call during my shifts.'

'You know I can't call you in the evenings. I think Tasha's a little jealous of you if I'm honest.' He said this as if he were paying Juliet the highest of compliments and expected her to sound suitably flattered in response. 'Jules? Are you still there?'

'Why are you calling?'

'I just wanted to find out how it went at the weekend, bringing Martha's stuff down.'

'Fine.'

'Ah, good. Is she . . . is she there now?'

'She's gone out, try her on her mobile.'

'She doesn't always answer when I call.'

'Doesn't she?' said Juliet, slapping a ball of dough down on to the counter and digging her knuckles into it hard. Ooh that felt good. 'Well, she's a busy girl. Try calling her anyway.'

'You didn't go up to collect her things with your new *friend*, did you?'

'No, I went up there with my *old* friend: Danny.'

'You're joking?'

'Why would I be joking, Matt? We needed a car big enough to move her stuff and Danny offered the van.'

'It's bad enough he's living rent-free in my house but I don't want him spending time with Martha when I've only seen her once myself this year.'

'Matt, none of this is my problem. I'm going to hang up now.'

'Wait! Actually, that wasn't the only reason I called.'

'You don't say . . . '

'Listen, my lawyer says your lawyer says you haven't come back on the revised proposal. This isn't your new friend getting involved is it?' he said, struggling to sound relaxed.

Juliet sighed. 'Robert is not involved. Yet.' Juliet wouldn't dream of involving Robert. Still, Matt's paranoia was proving far too much fun not to play with.

'Then what's causing the hold up?'

'Matt, I don't think you appreciate how little spare time I have. My priorities no longer overlap with yours. This week I'm meeting up with two potential apprentices, and I'm seeing another one next week, and until I've sorted all that out I don't have time for the non-urgent things.'

'You're taking on staff? How much bread are you actually selling? You're not making proper money from it, surely?'

'Listen, I've got a call on the other line,' said Juliet, pulling the phone from her ear to check who it was – oh, Mitchell again, she could ignore him.

'Jules, I really, really, really want the settlement agreed by September.'

'And I've just told you I will get round to it as soon as it's convenient for me. Anyway, if you hadn't lied on your original disclosure forms, this could have been sorted months ago.'

'I didn't lie; it was an unfortunate accounting error, as I have previously explained to you. Look, Jules, to be honest, Tasha's putting a lot of pressure on me. She's pretty uncomfortable with the fact I'm still married.'

'The fact you were married didn't seem to trouble her much when she met you.'

'I need to explain this delay, what am I going to tell her?'

'Tell her what you used to tell me.'

'Which is what?'

'A pack of lies.'

'Jules.'

'Matt.'

'Jules!'

'I mean it. Tell her that your soon-to-be ex-wife is jumping entirely to your tune. Or tell her the truth, which is that you're going to have to be patient. I don't care what you do – just don't do it on my time.'

'Juliet, I don't understand you any more. You've clearly moved on, with this bloke and your bread stuff, so why are you so bitter?'

'Matt, I'm not bitter. I'm angry and I'm busy and I'm sorry you find those qualities problematic. I know you're not used to them coming from me – but tough shit.'

'Jesus, Juliet, you've been spending too much time with Leonora.'

'What? Because I said the word shit? Yep, it's true, Lenny's been a terrible influence. On which note, what I actually meant to say was, I'm right in the middle of my country whites so could you please just fuck off.'

Juliet hung up and felt her jaw clench with rage. She glanced over to her yellow notebook on the shelving rack. She tried to calm her mind, took a deep breath in – out – and in again: progress.

44

Who on earth was that at the door, waking Lenny in the middle of such a delightful snooze? She checked her phone. Nope, no calls made to Domino's before she'd nodded off. *Juliet*? On a *Thursday*?

'I thought bread day was Friday?' said Lenny, opening the door and giving Juliet a hug.

'It *is* Friday.'

'It's Thursday?'

They stared at each other in confusion, then Juliet took her rota out of the back pocket of her jeans. 'No, it's definitely Friday – July the fourteenth, Bastille Day. I've just baked a *lot* of baguettes,' she said, holding up the bag she was carrying. 'Lenny, why aren't you dressed yet?'

'Me? I've been researching, I haven't had a chance.'

'Researching jobs?'

'Mmm. More general knowledge.'

'Lenny,' said Jules, placing her bag on the small patch of Lenny's carpet that wasn't covered in VHSs. 'What are all these?'

'Yes, exactly! My research – *Civilisation* – it's a documentary series, quite brilliant. This morning I learned about an amazing Bavarian Rococo church and some fascinating facts about Bach. Kenneth Clark sounds posher than the queen!'

Juliet looked at her suspiciously. 'You don't actually mean Jeremy Kyle?'

'Er, the diametric opposite of Jeremy Kyle. If you plotted a central-axis graph with Jeremy Kyle at one end, Kenneth Clark would be at the other, Paxman would be—'

'Lenny, why aren't you job-hunting?'

'Look, Jules, the last interview I had—'

'Which was when?'

Lenny turned her gaze to the floor. 'A week ago.'

'What did you wear?'

'What?'

'What did you wear to the interview?'

Lenny shrugged. 'My yellow sundress from Topshop and a cardi?'

'Lenny . . . '

'What?'

'You're giving out all the wrong signals – you don't even *want* these jobs.'

'Jules, there's no point investing in fancy clothes. Besides, the dress wasn't the reason I didn't get the job. They said they were looking for a Digital Native, which is a polite way of saying I'm too old. Anyway, I've told my headhunter I don't want any briefs in companies that employ Disruptionists or Visionaries or Fun Boy Three Monitors. I just want a nine to five with normal colleagues.'

'Lenny, can you afford to wait for the perfect job?'

'Jules, I've got . . . some cash left. I just need to downsize my lifestyle. I've already got rid of my landline, and taken Uber off my mobile.'

'Lenny, get a part-time job at least – even a bar job. Actually maybe not a bar job, but something local,' said Juliet, shaking her head and opening a window. 'It's so lovely out there, you need to get yourself out of this flat!'

'I *have* been out. To Waitrose. Earlier. Oh, yeah, so there was this guy in the queue in front of me, he looked a lot like Bradley Cooper! I was thinking you're way too hot to be in my local supermarket, but then he ordered a half shot latte with soy milk and caramel syrup. *Half shot? Soy milk? Caramel syrup?* What are you, an eight-year-old girl?'

'Lenny, it is irrelevant to me *or you* what type of coffee the man in front of you is ordering.'

'I'm just saying it was not a sexy coffee order for a man.'

'And I'm just saying the longer you sit here doing nothing, the more demotivated and slightly insane you'll become.'

'Jules, I've worked in offices for nearly twenty years. I watched a TED talk the other day about executive burnout – it said it's important to take time out to recharge.'

'Recharge – not fall asleep in front of the TV. How about learning a new skill?'

'What, some nonsense hipster *Time Out* magazine hobby like mouse taxidermy or beekeeping?' Lenny snorted.

'No, something practical, like *book*keeping? I'm snowed under on my paperwork, and Danny could use some help with his accounts too.'

'Me, work for Danny? Can you imagine the smugness?'

'Forget Danny – do it for me? I'll give you fifteen pounds an hour, two half days a week, just till you find a job again.'

'I couldn't take money off you. I feel bad enough about the bread. I can afford to pay for it, you know.'

'Lenny, I give you bread because I want your feedback.'

'You could get feedback from Danny.'

'Boys will eat anything, I *trust* you. Look,' Juliet said, her voice softening, 'you can't just sit around waiting for something to happen.'

It's all right for you, thought Lenny. You're good at something. You're good at everything. 'Anyway!' said Lenny. 'What's going on with you?'

Juliet rolled her eyes. 'Matt's being a dick again. Oh, but Eddy – the apprentice I liked best – said yes! He's starting next Monday, helping with a couple of dough shifts a week.'

'And how's Robert?'

Juliet smiled automatically, but then looked suddenly worried. 'He's great, but . . . he's asked me to go to Amsterdam with him in a couple of weekends' time. It's where his son Jack lives.'

'Great, yeah, I know. So?'

'I've got eighty loaves ordered for that last Friday in July. It's my busiest bake yet.'

'All the more reason to have a little break after. What's wrong?'

'Oh, I don't know . . . '

'Jules, it's a weekend away, enjoy yourself. But promise me one thing,' said Lenny.

'As long as it doesn't involve smuggling drugs.'

'You're such a spoilsport, Jules – you'd make the perfect mule. They'd never suspect anyone as squeaky clean as you.'

'Lenny!'

'Oh please, of course it's not. Look, you know I love you, and your bread, but promise me you won't drop off anything that Friday if you're busy.'

'Fine, well promise me one thing too. Will you at least go out for a run or something? Even if it's just a ten-minute jog. I think some exercise would do you good. One of the best things about HappyGuru was that it started me running.'

Lenny made a loud snoring noise, but then promised anyway.

Lenny lay on her bed that afternoon feeling pretty guilty. She hadn't *lied* lied to Juliet, it was just . . . well . . . that last interview had been three weeks ago, not one. Lenny didn't have the heart, or the guts, to admit that the briefs were getting fewer and fewer, as were Lenny's hopes of gainful employment.

The best way to redeem herself would be to keep her promise of a run. She looked out of the window at the beautiful summer's day. She reached into her cupboard for her fancy gym kit. She'd only worn it that one time. How strange, she must have washed it on a sixty; it was way tighter than she remembered.

She put on her headphones, pressed play on 'Shake It Off' and cautiously set off down her street. Oh god, it was hot out, she was running much too fast, she needed to jog to something with fewer Bs per M. She paused outside a neighbour's house while she flicked through her song list. Turin Brakes, yes, good, she loved Turin Brakes! 'Underdog' was her favourite, that chorus was so obviously written about her life.

She pressed play and resumed her jog in time with the music, but two minutes later ground to a halt, this time taking a seat on a bench.

Google: *how many BPMs 'Underdog'?*
Answer: *77*
Google: *Optimum BPM for beginner runner who hates running?*
Answer: *150*

She switched back to Taylor Swift and made it a whole additional two hundred metres down the street before she was sweaty, totally out of breath and had developed a mild stitch. She'd been out of the flat for a total of nine minutes.

She calculated: by the time she walked back to her front door, that would make it at least fourteen minutes, more like twenty if she went via the newsagent for an ice lolly.

That was more than enough to make good on her promise to Juliet.

45

Juliet had definitely made the right choice with Eddy the apprentice. When she'd interviewed him over a cup of tea in her kitchen, he'd been shy on the verge of mouse-like, until she'd got him talking about the crumb of his ideal loaf and then she couldn't get him to shut up.

At the start of Monday's session she'd found herself watching him very closely, but after a few hours she began to relax. She'd been stretching the truth when she told Lenny anyone could make bread. Of course anyone *could* make bread, but not necessarily great bread. You had to be a little bit obsessive about it – and Eddy, testing and retesting the springiness of the dough, clearly was.

Today, Wednesday, was his second session and Juliet felt so confident he could do the job that she'd popped back into the house for a twenty-minute nap. She'd forgotten to turn her mobile to silent though, and just as she'd fallen into a light doze it rang – Mitchell again. This was the fourth call she'd missed from him in the last fortnight but he hadn't left messages, and she'd been too busy to get back to him. She debated ignoring it but then curiosity got the better of her. 'Mitchell! How nice to hear from you. How is everything?'

'Hectic – just done *This Morning* with Celina, I don't know if you saw it?'

'I didn't, I've been flat out.'

'Ah, sweetheart. I bet you're giving *Bake Off* a run for their money.' There was a pause on the line before Mitchell let out an elaborate sigh. 'Listen, Jules, I don't know what happened last year, I think Celina was . . . a little exhausted from the summer and lost her way a bit. Anyway, water under the bridge, right?'

'Sure.'

'Great, because we were wondering whether you might be able to help us out on a little job later in the year?'

'Oh. Right. I do work full time on the bread now.'

'Sef's done some recipes but if I'm honest, off the record, I'm not quite sure she's up to the challenges.' He paused to give Juliet the opportunity to make a smug comment but Juliet said nothing. 'Anyway, Celina and I wondered if you could perhaps cast your eye over the recipes, test them maybe?'

'These are the kale recipes?'

'Ah no, the publisher wasn't fully convinced by the proposal, so we're doing a vegetarian book. Sef did a sterling job on recipes in this year's Easter pull-out. I don't know if you saw it?'

'No. I was up to my knees in hot cross buns, almost literally.'

'Ha, ha, well anyway . . . yeah, a sterling job but I don't think she quite has the panache that you always brought to the job, do not quote me on that.'

Juliet felt like she might drown in the syrup.

'So yeah,' said Mitchell, hurriedly. 'She's done forty recipes already, we need those tested and then we might need another, say, twenty to forty by October? The annoying thing is that the publisher's asked to see all the recipes before they'll sign off on a shoot.'

'That's unusual – they're normally not that cautious, are they?'

Mitchell sighed. 'New editor. Reading between the lines, I think they prefer the style they're used to from Celina. What do you think? You've got a couple of months to play with.'

'I'm sorry I can't be more helpful but I'm afraid I really don't have the time.' Or the inclination. 'I can barely keep up with my orders; I've just taken on some help myself.'

'I see . . . I figured maybe a chat about your day rate might help. If we look at doubling it, might that free up any time at your end?'

Juliet bit her lip. 'Thanks, but that wouldn't make any difference.'

'Crikey, you must be shifting a load of bread! What you charging for it, anyway?'

Juliet laughed. 'Different customers charge differently – I think between two pounds fifty and four pounds. How about I give you the names of some recipe developers I rate, though the good ones are usually booked six months in advance.'

'Jules. You know I wouldn't be making this call if we didn't really want you.'

Juliet knew he certainly wouldn't be doubling her day rate and complimenting her panache unless he absolutely had to. 'Mitchell, that's very flattering – but I can't. Let me know if you want those names.'

She switched her phone to silent, rearranged her pillow, closed her eyes again and went to sleep.

46

'So, basically a nine of hearts or diamonds means you change direction, a one-eyed Jack is wild and the three of clubs clears the deck.'

'Got it,' said Ellis, nodding. 'And if you lose this round, you're taking off your bikini top and those denim shorts?'

'And just sit here in my pants?'

'We'll be twins!' said Ellis, gesturing to his boxer shorts as Lenny's gaze drifted slowly over his torso.

Ellis had been here for at least forty-eight hours, maybe more, Lenny had lost track of time recently. Nowadays every day felt like a Saturday night, if she was happy and doing something bad for her (Ellis, junk food, wine). Or like a Monday morning, if she was doing something sensible and displeasing, such as checking her bank balance.

She and Ellis had been getting on brilliantly recently. She'd hate to have a job right now, a job would mean she couldn't sit around in the middle of the day like some cool Brooklyn girl on Instagram, playing cards with her musician almost-boyfriend, smoking and pretending that wasting her time didn't matter.

Lenny had just picked up a one-eyed Jack, her fist clenching in glory, when the doorbell rang.

'You expecting someone?' said Ellis.

'What day is it?'

'Dunno.'

Lenny checked her phone. Friday, but it was the weekend Jules was going away and she'd sworn not to pop over.

'Must be for upstairs.' Lenny shrugged as she jubilantly laid down her card on top of the deck.

'Does that mean I have to take these off?' said Ellis, pulling at the waistband on his boxers as the doorbell rang again.

'Who *is* that?' said Lenny, standing and reaching for Ellis's Bob Marley T-shirt.

She spied through the peephole the back of a man, a tall man wearing blue jeans and Timberland work boots, with newly shaved hair and a familiar stance. Oh bloody hell! Why him, and why now?

'Lenny, I can hear you're in there,' shouted Danny. 'Open up, sweetheart.'

Lenny opened the door and stood, staring at her toes, feeling the heat rising to her cheeks.

'I see you've dressed for my visit,' said Danny, walking past her, carrying two large paper bags. 'Bob Marley T-shirt? Gearing yourself up for Freshers' Week, are you?'

'What are you doing here?'

'Special delivery, two black olive sourdoughs, a pain de campagne and a sandwich loaf. Jules wants feedback on what the sourdough's like after a defrost.'

'Aren't you busy with work?'

'Busier than you by the looks of it,' said Danny. 'Nice legs, Dublonsky, you should get them out more often.'

'Give me those,' said Lenny, lifting the bags of bread from his arms.

'Aren't you going to ask if I want a cup of tea?' Danny looked her up and down again and grinned.

'You just said you were busy.'

'I can spare five minutes, I haven't seen you for ages.'

Lenny sighed, then marched back to her bedroom where Ellis was sitting, rolling a cigarette.

'Who was it?' he said, squinting at her like she was the sun.

'More bread, Jules got her delivery guy to drop it off. I'll be back in five, do not move.'

She popped to the bathroom and checked the mirror. No doubt Danny would report back to Jules on the state of her. She splashed her face, quickly scraped some of the make-up from under her eyes with her fingertips, then went back into the living room, where Danny was looking through her DVD collection. '*30 Rock?* I didn't know you liked Tina Fey?'

She shrugged.

'She's awesome. Wow, and you're the only person I know who still has a VHS player!'

'Whatever.'

'Lenny, I think it's cool. *Civilisation*! I used to watch that with my granddad. I'd love to watch it again.'

'How do you take your tea then?'

'White, no sugar.'

Lenny paused and stared at him. 'You've had all your hair cut off.'

'Wow, Lenny, your powers of observation are second to none. If you can't find another research job perhaps you should consider detective work?'

'Oh shut up,' she said, laughing. 'Do you really have to have a cup of tea?'

He raised his eyebrows. 'The hostess with the mostess. Now I know it's such a colossal effort for you I'll have a sandwich too,' he said, heading through to her kitchen before she could stop him. On the kitchen counter were two wine glasses, four empty beer bottles and an open pizza box. Danny glanced at them, then tidied them neatly into one corner before opening her fridge. 'What's in here that goes on bread?'

Lenny thrust her hands into her pockets. 'A bit of ham, some Cheddar?'

'Garlic mayo?' he said, reaching for a jar, then pulling a face.

'Oh god, you're not one of those men who makes a fuss about garlic, are you?'

'You could make this yourself in two minutes flat. Homemade's so much better.'

'Danny, you know I can't cook.'

'It's easy, I'll show you. You got eggs and garlic?'

Why hadn't she just told Danny she had a friend here? Though the thought of those two meeting made her feel weird. 'Danny, I am in the middle of something . . . '

'Something like doing nothing?' he said, winking, then opening the cupboard for a bottle of olive oil and a bowl.

Lenny glanced over her shoulder. 'No actually – I am busy!'

'What, job hunting?'

Lenny made an indeterminate mumbling noise.

'You still looking for research jobs?' he said, cracking an egg, then confidently separating the yolk from the white.

'What of it?' Lenny tried not to stare at the fleck in his biceps as he whisked.

'At dinner round at Juliet's that time, you made a whole big fuss about how you hated your job.'

Lenny sighed, exasperated. 'I don't like big offices, and I don't like technology, but it's what I know so I have no choice.'

'Lenny, much as it pains me to admit this, you're smarter than I am – slightly – and I've managed to retrain. Did Jules mention she needs help with her accounts? And I could use some help too?' He held out the mayonnaise for Lenny's inspection but she stared at him, her eyes narrowing.

'Is *that* why she sent you?'

'Don't get annoyed, Lenny.'

'To check up on me? Is that it?'

'No, she wanted you to have your bread, you daft cow.'

'You're the social worker and I'm the lost cause?'

'For goodness sake, Lenny, get over yourself. Oh!' he said, looking suddenly startled. 'Who are you?'

Lenny's heart sank.

'Hey, baby,' said Ellis, resting his hands on Lenny's shoulders. 'I was gonna pop downstairs for a fag, I've borrowed one of your sweatshirts. All right, mate?' He reached to shake Danny's hand. 'You must be the bread delivery guy?'

Danny raised his eyebrows. 'I guess I must be . . . '

'Shit, that looks good!' said Ellis, eyeing up the loaf on the counter. 'I'll go smoke this and see you in a sec, yeah? Make me a sandwich, would you?' he said, pinching Lenny's arse on the way out.

'So,' said Danny, after they'd stood awkwardly in silence waiting for Ellis to shut the front door. 'Is that what applying for jobs looks like?'

'It is literally none of your business, Danny Freeman.'

Danny shook his head. 'Lenny, you're a grown up; waste your own life. Jules just wants to see you happy.'

'And I couldn't be happier, thanks. Jesus, Danny, you're not my mother!'

'Oh, that's right, I remember now, you always were really scrappy with your mum, weren't you?'

'So?'

'Did it never occur to you that the people who give you the hardest time are the ones that love you the most? The ones that actually want what's best for you?'

'Oh my goodness! It's Oprah bloody Winfrey in my kitchen making me my mayo.'

'No,' said Danny, reaching for his van keys. 'It's not Oprah bloody Winfrey, it's just "the bread delivery guy". I've got to get back to my day job, because unlike you I actually do have a day job.'

When Ellis came back up, the first thing Lenny did was drag him to the bedroom.

She did not need Danny Freeman's patronising concern. She did not need him pretending to care. She needed half an hour of rampant sex, half an hour where she could get lost in sensation, half an hour where she did not have to be herself.

47

Juliet lay naked in bed in the crook of Robert's arm, her heartbeat slowing back to normal. She shouldn't have given Lenny a hard time about not seeing enough of Amsterdam, when all she'd done since she and Robert checked into this hotel was have sex, order room service, have sex and more sex.

It wasn't that she hadn't had a good sex life with Matt – they'd had a very happy sex life – but sex with Robert was something entirely different. And better. Maybe it was the newness, or maybe it was the way he wanted her, or maybe she realised quite quickly into being around Robert that he was a grown up, comfortable in himself, with nothing to prove. And in retrospect, her husband wasn't.

She'd been so very adapted to Matt's ways, she could only see them more clearly now she had someone else up close to compare them to. It was the little things. Like every time they went to a restaurant, Robert was friendly and sincere not just to the female staff but to the male ones too. He was confident without being arrogant, he was interested in everyone, not only in people who could do something for him. He tipped generously, even when he thought no one was watching. Maybe these weren't little things at all.

'We've got a couple of hours before we're meeting Jack at the restaurant,' said Robert, picking up his watch from the bedside table. 'Do you want to go for a drink somewhere, there's a great bar in The Dylan hotel?'

'Actually,' said Juliet, turning sideways to face him. 'Can we do a quick trip to the food hall I went to with Lenny? I wanted to take another look at one of the stands.'

'Whatever you want, lovely. It's out west? That'll take about fifteen minutes in a cab,' he said, putting his watch on.

Juliet picked up his wrist and looked at the time. 'Fifteen minutes isn't far at all, is it?' she said, slowly undoing his watch and placing it back on the bedside table. 'I think that gives us at least half an hour staying right where we are . . . '

He grinned, kissed her softly on the neck, then harder on the mouth and rolled back on top of her.

Juliet sat in the airport with Robert, waiting for their flight home on Sunday night, staring into space. She'd had such a great weekend. Jack was a lovely kid, and he looked so much like Robert – except with a full head of dark curls. He'd made her feel so welcome and relaxed. Like his father, he was warm and funny and had no edge to him.

She'd been nervous about this weekend because, in a post-Matt world, she was nervous about a lot of things – primarily her own judgement. When she was with Robert she felt safe, but alone she worried: what if he was another liar? A cheater too? How could she have met someone great so quickly? Surely she was too lucky? Lenny had said luck had bugger all to do with it and that Juliet *deserved* someone good, which was why she'd met Robert. But did that mean Juliet had *deserved* Matt? Or that Lenny didn't deserve someone good too? Juliet had long ago learned that people don't really get what they do or don't deserve in this life.

'Are you OK, darling?' said Robert, taking her hand and kissing the palm of it. 'You look a bit dazed.'

'Happy, that's all,' she said, giving his hand a squeeze.

'What's your week looking like? Do you want to try and grab dinner one night?'

'Can we play it by ear? I've got so much on.'

'We can leave it till the weekend. Maybe drive out to that pub in Essex with the great fish and chips?'

'Actually, next Sunday is Lenny's birthday.'

'Oh right, has she got plans?'

'That's the thing. She usually has a party, even if it's only a small one – but I asked her the other day and she totally side-stepped the question. Robert, I'm worried about her – she's just sitting in that flat, festering. I thought maybe I could do a little surprise lunch.'

'Do you think she'll be up for it?'

'Well, it's a surprise. I can't ask her, but I don't mean anything big. Danny, Martha of course, Nate? Andrew and Amy and their other halves . . . Ellis? We could do a barbecue if the weather's good?'

'Sounds great.'

'And also, as a present, I was thinking maybe I'd buy her a course – on bookkeeping. She's so good with numbers, it'd be easy for her to learn, and then she could start doing my books. I need the help but I think it might help her too – not just having a bit of cash, but having a sense of purpose.'

'I'm sure there are loads of courses in London. I could ask our finance guy if his team know anywhere in particular?'

'Why not? Could you ask him tomorrow? And then I can book it straight away.'

'Do you have a budget in mind?'

'Robert, I don't care what it costs. I owe Lenny so much I can't even begin to tell you.'

48

Lenny hung up the call and rested her mobile beside her on the sofa. She took a deep breath and tried to calm herself as the dark thoughts swarmed back into her mind, preparing to sting.

She'd been unemployed for eight months now, and her headhunter had just informed her that the market at her level was bad and unlikely to pick up till next year. Lenny had always had such a troubled relationship with her day jobs, she'd never realised quite how much her sense of self was defined by them – by being a person with skills that others were willing to pay her for. Without a job, who was she? This must be her punishment for heaping such scorn on to Danny about his non-career.

Where *had* all her money gone? It was impossible to sit still in London without spending cash. Leaving the flat for a pint of milk seemed to involve spending £50, better never to leave the flat in the first place. Lenny found it inconceivable she'd ever had an app on her phone that ordered taxis with the push of one button!

In retrospect she'd been hasty telling Occy her life was in London: what life, exactly? That bloody retreat. It had messed with Lenny's head, made her believe that life could be different, could be a life she chose. It had given her wildly unrealistic hope about her possibilities – if only for a heartbeat – and so her fall had been that much steeper than if she'd never had hope at all.

She went to the kitchen and made a classic toastie, the way Juliet's mum had taught her to thirty years ago – butter on the outside and in, cheese slices stopping three millimetres from the crust. As she waited for the light on the Breville to turn green she lovingly prepared her plate with a dollop of ketchup at the edge and some mayonnaise. Danny had been right about one thing – homemade mayo was better than shop bought.

As her teeth sunk through the crisp, buttery bread and her tongue touched the warm melting Cheddar, she felt momentarily blissful. All her friends who were happier than her, all the employers who didn't want her, they didn't matter, she had her sandwich.

But then she ate the last bite and the negative thoughts returned, so she cut another two slices of bread and turned the Breville back on. And while she was eating toastie two she felt temporarily lifted, and also while she ate its successor. She had to force herself to go and clean her teeth as a precaution against making a fourth.

It was Friday. Jules would be round later but for now . . . She flicked on the TV, changed channels several times, then settled back into the loving embrace of the sofa and experienced an epiphany. What was it Ian Bottomsley – that *utter* charlatan – had said on the final day of the retreat? 'Your darkest hour is a gift: only then do you discover your true self.' Incorrect, Ian! Your darkest hour is a gift: only then do you discover that Jeremy Kyle is almost-watchable TV! It's logical, think about it: how else could the man have sustained a career on prime time television for more than a decade if his show wasn't incredibly well constructed?

Urgh, Juliet at the door, at the very moment Jeremy was about to reveal the results of Kayleigh's lie detector test – though you can tell Kayleigh's lying, just look at her! She can't even look poor Jayson in the eye.

'Just a sec!' Lenny shouted, turning off the TV, racing to her bedroom, pulling off her nightie and pulling on a sundress. 'Sorry, Jules, I was in the bathroom, come on in.'

Juliet noticed that the seams of Lenny's dress were on the outside, but said nothing. 'Brand new banana sourdough, and the classic sandwich loaf,' she said, handing Lenny the bags of bread and taking a seat on the sofa.

'How's everything?' said Lenny, cheerily. 'How's Robert? How's your new apprentice?'

'Yes, everything's good. How's your week been?'

'You will *never* guess what happened!'

'You found a job?'

'There was a fight yesterday in Waitrose! Coffee machine two was down, it had that "empty the grounds" message on the screen, and this bloke – obviously not a regular – didn't realise. So! He went to machine two, then tried to go back to machine one just as this super-aggressive American woman was about to press the button on her latte. He was hovering. I don't think he was actually trying to push in or anything, just waiting, but she was clearly spoiling for a fight – she had that pinched, angry look – and then suddenly she *lost her shit!* She called him a bully, said he was a typical white male, trying to dominate her. I mean, she was white too! Then *he* said she should go home and take her HRT tablets, and then they had to get the manager over! I swear it was like a really middle-class episode of Jeremy Kyle, live in front of me! Er, so yes, no, it was . . . it was all pretty dramatic, and—'

Juliet sat listening to Lenny's story till she could take it no more. 'Lenny, I do not want to hear another story about your daily trip to the supermarket. Your life is so small now. You used to travel and do fun, interesting stuff.'

'Jules,' said Lenny, tightly. 'I cannot travel or have a big, fun, sexy life without money and . . . well, I'm now having to be extremely careful about money.'

'Lenny, get a job!'

Lenny opened her mouth to explain – yet again – that the reason she couldn't find a job was because of the market, and because of her age and so forth, but realised, perhaps for the first time, that this was absolute bullshit. The truth was, she was totally lost. She did not want to keep going in her old life, but she was far too terrified to do anything else – and that was why she'd messed up the last eight months of interviews and why she was now paralysed by fear. She was standing on the edge of the trapeze platform without any safety net, and it felt very much like Juliet was trying to push her off.

'Sorry,' said Juliet, looking at Lenny's crestfallen expression. 'I didn't mean to sound so harsh, really, I didn't. Lenny, do you think you might be depressed?'

Lenny frowned but made no answer.

Juliet reached for her handbag and rested it on her lap. She really wasn't sure if this was the right thing after all. 'Lenny, what are your plans for Sunday?'

'Thirty-nine? Not really an age to celebrate, is it?'

'How about a little lunch at mine? You haven't been round for ages.'

'Just the two of us?' said Lenny, hopefully.

'Maybe Robert. Martha and Nate – or she doesn't have to invite him but he's down this weekend?'

And have everyone ask Lenny what she'd been up to? And all she had for conversation was coffee wars and Kayleigh's lie detector results?

'Say yes, Lenny. It's only lunch. I'll make something nice. It'll be fun. Time to leave your postcode. No lycra involved this time!'

It was an echo of what Lenny had said when she was persuading Juliet to try the app, but Lenny just stared at her blankly. 'What sort of time were you thinking?'

'I'll text you when I've figured out the menu.' Juliet reached into her bag, her fingertips brushing the envelope. She shouldn't have gone ahead and booked the course for Monday – she should have waited until she'd had more time to gently nudge Lenny. Still, she couldn't bear another week of watching Lenny shrink. 'I've got you a card,' she said, taking it from her bag. 'There's a present in with it.'

Lenny's eyes widened in delight. 'Ooooh, you shouldn't have!' she said, putting it on the side table.

Juliet hesitated. 'You should probably open it now . . . it's sort of time sensitive.'

'How exciting!' Lenny ripped open the envelope, and admired the card – Van Gogh's painting of pink almond blossoms on a turquoise background. 'Very pretty!' Inside was another smaller envelope, which Lenny put on her lap while she read Juliet's message:

Close friends are truly life's treasures. Sometimes they know us better than we know ourselves . . . They are there to guide and support us, to share our laughter and our tears. Their presence reminds us that we are never really alone.

'Ah Jules, that's a lovely thing to write.'

'It wasn't me actually,' said Juliet, laughing. 'It's a quote from Van Gogh.'

Lenny reached over and gave her a hug. 'And what's in this envelope?' she said, pulling out the leaflet and reading the printed voucher in confusion.

'I know it's not the most exciting present, but I thought it might be useful,' said Juliet. 'It starts this Monday, it's twenty-five hours of tuition across five days.'

Lenny stared straight ahead, feeling the colour rise to her cheeks.

'It's meant to be a good college,' said Juliet, in an attempt to change the expression on Lenny's face. 'Robert said so – some of his team have done courses there.'

'Right,' said Lenny tightly, putting it on the side table. 'Well, thank Robert and his team for their input, I'm so glad they were all consulted.'

Now Juliet was the one looking wounded. 'I guess it's the thought that counts.'

And what thought would that be? Lenny is useless, Lenny's the poor little charity case, let's spend . . . Lenny picked up the leaflet again . . . £500 on a bookkeeping course! Lenny wasn't sure if she was angrier about the fact Jules and Robert had pillow-talked what a loser she was. Or at how utterly extravagant and wasteful that £500 was. Or perhaps she was plain ashamed that Juliet had been so generous and she was acting like a total brat.

'I don't suppose you could get a refund? I could really do with the cash.' Lenny meant it as a joke, except the way she said it, it sort of sounded rather like the truth.

Juliet's smile faded and she checked her watch. 'It's one o'clock already. I'd better go. I've got the Environmental Health guy coming at three and I can't be late.'

'Er, yeah, OK,' said Lenny, standing awkwardly. 'You'll text me about Sunday then?'

'Yep,' said Juliet, distractedly. She sounded tired, or disappointed, or both.

When Lenny went to the bathroom later, she caught sight of her reflection and realised her dress was on inside out. She turned away from the mirror as her cheeks burned scarlet again with shame.

49

Some birthday this was turning out to be.

Maybe Juliet had had a better offer from Robert. Or maybe she was still pissed off from Friday. Fair enough, Lenny had behaved quite dreadfully. Even so, she might at least have called to say lunch was off. Or happy birthday. Andrew had obviously forgotten, because Andrew's entire life was Fiona nowadays. And she wouldn't expect Amy to text because Amy was a shit friend and always had been.

At least Ellis was here. She glanced over at him, lying asleep with his back to her. Ellis slept like a teenage boy, whereas Lenny's sleep pattern these days involved waking in cold fear at 3 a.m., then napping throughout the day. Which was *not* a sign of depression – merely of tiredness.

She got out of bed and checked her phone again: nothing. She felt a dull pain in her chest. Oh, silly girl. What was she feeling down about? She'd forgotten her little present to herself. There it was, by her TV. Such serendipity, Amazon had dropped the price of the *Game of Thrones* box set only two weeks ago, so maybe the universe was looking out for her after all.

She made two cups of tea, went back into the bedroom, and gently poked Ellis's arse through the duvet. He grunted in response.

'Ellis, time to get up. *Wake. Up.*'

'I'm asleep.'

'We have work to do.'

'It's Sunday?'

She pulled the cover back from his face. He was starting to look quite haggard, but then he opened his beautiful blue-green eyes and she smiled. '*Game of Thrones* box set, ten hours, we can do it all today if we start now.'

He wrinkled his nose. 'That's some weird, nerdy sci-fi shit, isn't it?'

'Everyone says it's amazing.'

'But it's got dragons?'

'And sex – a lot of sex.'

He raised himself up on his elbows, more alert now. 'You're not just saying that to trick me, are you?'

'Get out of bed, come on. It's going to be a good day.'

The sun was high in the sky, the garden table laid with a jug of Pimms, chilled rosé, and a mini-feast of salads, the barbecue lit and ready for action but the birthday girl was nowhere to be seen.

'Shall we start without her?' said Danny.

'She's only twenty minutes late,' said Juliet, setting down another bowl of potato salad and counting the number of dishes on the table.

'This looks fantastic,' said Robert. 'I thought you said it was going to be low-key?'

'Yeah, well, low-key for mum means six salads instead of twelve, right?' said Martha, laughing.

'You don't think it's too much food, do you?' said Juliet.

'It's perfect,' said Robert. 'Better to have too much than too little.'

'A man after my own heart,' said Andrew, pouring two glasses of Pimms, and handing one to Fiona as the doorbell rang.

'She's here, I'll get it!' said Martha, running back into the house.

'Right, I'll get the burgers on,' said Danny, grabbing the tongs and heading back to the barbecue.

'See? It's all OK,' said Robert, putting his arm around Juliet as she gave a sigh of relief and poured a glass of Pimms for Lenny.

'Should we hide behind a tree or something?' said Nate.

'Looks like there's no need,' said Danny, as his gaze turned to Martha, returning to the garden with a confused look on her face and Amy and her boyfriend following in her wake.

'Darling,' said Amy. 'I know I said we couldn't make it but Oliver and I figured we'd swing by just for an hour to say hello and give Lenny her present. Where is the old trout anyway?'

'Jules, let me at least put the burgers on,' said Danny.

'No,' said Juliet. 'She'll be getting two buses over here, you know what Sunday traffic's like.'

'I'm properly starving,' said Andrew, finishing the dregs of his second Pimms and pouring a third. 'It's nearly two o'clock.'

'Have some more salad,' said Juliet, impatiently.

Danny shook his head as Robert checked his watch too. 'Is she normally quite punctual?'

'Look, ten more minutes, OK?' Juliet snapped, then walked back into the house.

Danny and Robert moved to go after her but Martha shook her head and followed her in.

'Mum, what's up with Lenny? Where is she?'

'I don't know,' said Juliet, taking the bottle of kitchen cleaner and wiping down the counter for the third time.

'Shall I give her a call?'

Juliet sighed and shook her head. 'I sent her two texts yesterday, another three this morning, and I've called.'

'Maybe she's lost her mobile?'

'She doesn't go *out* anywhere to lose it.'

'Try her landline?'

Juliet shook her head. 'She doesn't have one any more.'

She hadn't actually spoken to Lenny since Friday, when Lenny had been at her worst – prickly, aggressive and angry. Juliet had only ever seen Lenny in that state when a man was involved, and then it was best to let her calm down on her own.

'Are you sure she's coming?' said Martha. 'Mum, why do you look so stressed?'

'Oh Martha, Lenny and I had this really awkward conversation on Friday. I must have upset her.'

'How?'

'I think she felt I was patronising. She's been quite down since she's been out of work.'

'What's going on?' said Danny, coming into the kitchen, his brow creased. 'Andrew's going to hijack the barbecue if I don't put some meat on it right now. Come on, Jules, this is ridiculous. She knew the party was happening, she's clearly not coming.'

'I'm going to try her once more,' said Juliet. 'Martha, give me your phone?' Just in case Lenny was ignoring Juliet's number. 'It's just ringing out. Do you think I should go round there?'

'Absolutely not!' said Danny, turning as Amy came into the kitchen.

'Mum, don't. She'll be OK. She's probably . . . I don't know,' said Martha, shrugging.

'What are you guys talking about?' said Amy.

'Nothing,' said Juliet, quietly. 'Everything's fine.'

'Right – that's it,' said Danny. 'I'm going round there to have a word. I'll be back in an hour. Get Andrew on that barbecue. Start eating. Don't let all that food and effort go to waste.'

'Ooh, he's very sexy when he's angry!' said Amy to Martha, as Danny stormed out of the kitchen.

'Wait!' said Juliet, chasing after him. 'If you're going over there, take some cake at least. And a bottle of something. And I don't think she eats vegetables anymore, I'm surprised she hasn't developed scurvy, hang on, I'll put together a little picnic.'

Danny stood in the hallway, arms tightly folded. Juliet went back to the garden with a collection of Tupperware and foil and returned ten minutes later with a large paper gift bag tied with a ribbon.

'I don't think she deserves this generosity,' said Danny.

'Danny, you have no idea what Lenny's done for me,' said Juliet, handing him the bag.

'Christ, this is heavy! What have you got in here?'

Juliet looked upwards, as if doing a calculation and then paused. 'Hang on, there's one more thing . . . '

She went to fetch her handbag and returned a minute later. 'Give me a minute, Danny, I need to quickly repack this.'

'You were right, there is a lot of sex in this show,' said Ellis, approvingly, as Lenny pressed pause on the DVD player.

'It's half past two – time for a food break.'

'Shall we get a pizza?'

'Ellis, I can't afford any more takeaways.'

'I'd buy you one if you could lend me a tenner; I'm a bit brassic myself. But no worries. What have you got in the flat?'

'Loads of nice bread. Butter. We could have cheese and bacon toasties, but we need bacon.'

'I'll pop down the shops and get some. I've got . . . ' He counted some change. 'Two pounds thirty on me, will that be enough?'

Lenny went to her wallet and found another £2.40. 'Get the good stuff, don't buy the value line. Back bacon, and maybe a small packet of mozzarella – for extra meltiness.' What the hell? It was her birthday, after all.

'Back in a sec,' Ellis said. 'Don't watch any more without me.'

Lenny picked up her phone and stared at it. No one, not one person! She thought about calling Juliet, to say hi – and sorry. Would that look passive-aggressive, like she was actually saying: *where the hell is that birthday lunch you promised me?* She would apologise for the fuss she'd made about the course. Though she had no intention of actually going on it – and it still annoyed her, all that money wasted.

She heard Ellis at the door.

'I tried calling,' he said. 'I couldn't remember whether you said streaky bacon or the other kind.'

'I quite clearly said back bacon.'

'Oh. Sorry. My bad.'

Lenny sighed deeply.

'Don't be moody. I did try calling you to ask.'

'No you didn't!'

He held out his phone: three dialled calls to her in the last ten minutes. Lenny checked her phone again – no incomings. She took his phone and dialled herself, her jaw setting in fury as her phone remained obstinately unresponsive. *Not again?* Those utter, utter wankers!

'Baby, I have to concentrate on what's going on in this episode and that hold music's kind of annoying, can you turn it down?'

'No, I might miss it when they pick up . . . it's been an hour and a half already, they'll pick up any minute now, ooh, see? Hello! Yes, I wonder if you could possibly please help me?' Lenny put on her most sickly-sweet voice and explained the problem. 'Yes, and I'd really appreciate it if you could fix it in the next, I don't know, twenty minutes or so because it's my birthday and . . . yes, that's right, yes, yes, today! Oh, well, thank you, Ranjit, that's so sweet of you. Yes, great, you can? Excellent, thanks so much for your help.'

She hung up and nodded in satisfaction. Lesson learned: be less of a bitch and you get what you want.

'Oh, baby,' said Ellis, taking her hand and looking sheepish. 'Why didn't you tell me it was your birthday?'

'Oh Ellis, I don't care about birthdays, really, I don't.'

'We should do something to celebrate,' he said, putting his arm around her.

Lenny snuggled into him. 'Come on, press play again. I want to know what Tyrion's plotting.'

Twenty minutes later her phone started to ping. And ping. And ping. Messages from Saturday lunchtime onwards.

Juliet: *OK, 1pm at mine tomorrow. Can't wait to see you. Sorry about yesterday xx*

Juliet: *There might be a few old friends, hope that's OK?*

Andrew: *Happy birthday, Len. Love you. See you soon, maybe!!*

Amy: *Happy birthday xx*

Fran: *Happy birthday, granny! I'm taking you for cocktails next week.*

Juliet: *Happy birthday, my love. Just checking you're OK for 1pm?*

Juliet: *Are you on the bus? We're just going to start the sausages but come whenever.*

Andrew: *Well – it was a surprise party but it isn't anymore – hurry your lazy arse round here NOW! x*

Martha: *Lenny! Where are you? The food's getting cold and I want to see you!*

Juliet: *Are you OK? If you get this, just come along anyway, we'll be in the garden all afternoon.*

Ellis: *Streaky or the other stuff? Let me know!!*

Danny: *Eight disappointed guests, one gutted Juliet – I hope you're happy now.*

Lenny felt mildly sick. She pressed stop on the DVD player. 'Ellis, we're going to my friend Juliet's for a drink and a bite to eat.'

'We're mid episode!'

'Ellis,' she said, getting to her feet. 'It's four thirty now, we'll be there by five thirty.'

'Where are we going? Who's going to be there?'

'I'm not sure . . . ' said Lenny, checking her phone. 'Andrew and his girlfriend, Juliet and her boyfriend, Martha – Juliet's daughter . . . '

Ellis made a face like he'd just seen a millipede crawl from his shoe. 'Baby, you know I don't do big family get togethers . . . '

'Ellis – it is not a big family get together, it's a few of my friends, and I'm officially playing the "It's my birthday" card, so get your T-shirt and shoes on.'

He was shaking his head to say no again when the doorbell rang. 'Who's that?'

'Must be Interflora with the huge bouquet of roses you ordered for me,' said Lenny crossly, as she went to the bedroom.

'Are you going to get it or what?' Ellis called out.

'It won't be for me, ignore it. Get yourself ready.'

Lenny opened her wardrobe. She hadn't bought anything new this year and everything in here looked like she felt: old, tired and past its best. That lovely silk Whistles dress would have been perfect . . . bloody Ellis, that bloody Oxfam bin . . . what to wear, what to wear?

'Baby . . . '

'Hurry up,' said Lenny, flicking through dress after dress.

'It *is* for you. That guy with the bread again. He's got a big bag of stuff.'

'*What?* Look, you get dressed, I'll be two minutes,' she said, hastily putting on an old sky-blue H&M dress and striding to the front door.

Danny was standing in her hallway, holding a large bag with purple tissue paper sticking out of the top, tied with a huge ribbon. There was a look of utter disappointment on his face.

'If you've come to give me a bollocking, don't bother!' said Lenny, hands going straight to her hips in pre-emptive fury.

Danny frowned but said nothing.

'My phone was *broken*. It was! This has happened before and it's not my bloody fault!'

Danny stayed silent.

'*What?* She said she'd text on Saturday and tell me the details. As far as I knew until five minutes ago, she'd done nothing of the sort. She never told me there were so many people invited, it was all a very casual arrangement.'

'Didn't look casual from where I was standing.'

'What's that supposed to mean?'

'She did crazy shifts all week, then spent all of yesterday in the kitchen. Cooking for you.'

'Don't you dare try to guilt trip me! I thought she'd probably decided to sack it off and do something with Robert instead.'

'As if! Or are you the one who had a better offer? Is that what happened? Lover boy in there take you somewhere nicer for lunch, did he?'

Lenny felt her face flush scarlet. 'You're not listening to me! She said she'd text, the texts didn't come through – I just explained to you it's my phone's fault.'

'Of course, Lenny – it's not *your* fault. It's not *your* fault you can't get a job. It's never *your* fault.'

Lenny barked a laugh. 'Marvellous! Danny freeloading Freemason, staying rent free at Juliet's and turning up at my door to lecture me about personal responsibility!'

'She's your best friend. You've totally let her down.'

'Amay-zing! Now you're preaching to me about being a good friend to Juliet, please do remind me why you kept her husband's first affair secret for fifteen years!'

'Happy birthday, Lenny,' he said, placing the bag at her feet and turning to leave.

'Well hang on a minute. Am I meant to go round there now or not?'

'You're not.'

Lenny stood for a moment, chewing the inside of her cheek. 'Danny,' she said quietly, 'it *was* a very vague plan. And my phone was broken.'

'It's not me you need apologise to, Lenny.'

'I wasn't apologising to you, you arrogant idiot! Why would I apologise to you?'

'Grow up, Lenny. Or don't, what do I care? Carry on hanging out with that muppet,' he said, shaking his head. 'I'm sure he's perfect for you.'

Ellis makes me happy. Ellis loves me. Ellis did something really wonderful for me for my birthday but I can't think quickly enough to make something up . . . Lenny stood in silence, feeling her throat constrict. She felt a tear roll down the side of her nose, but to wipe it away would draw more attention, so instead she lowered her gaze to the floor. She sensed Danny reaching out his arm towards her but then stopping himself. He was hesitating, on the brink of saying something. But then he wasn't, and by the time she looked up again he'd gone.

When she went into her bedroom, Ellis was standing in front of the mirror fiddling with his hair. 'I'm ready, baby, but can we just go for an hour? It's nice chilling here with you, that's all.'

'Don't worry, you're off the hook,' said Lenny, wiping away her tear-smudged mascara.

'So we can carry on watching *Game of Thrones?* Result!'

'No, Ellis, it's not a result, because you're going home.'

'What, why? Are you going somewhere?'

'I'm going precisely nowhere and that's why you have to leave.'

'Baby, is that a dig at me? Have I done something wrong?'

He'd done everything wrong from the very start, and Lenny had allowed every second of it. There'd been so many times when she'd fantasised about the moment when she'd finally feel strong enough and happy enough to dump Ellis. This would be when she had a better option, was looking tanned and slim and was hopefully dressed in some Dolce and Gabbana finery rather than a £10 H&M dress. In her mind this scene would be dramatic and impressive. She'd berate him fiercely with extensive and eloquent use of the English language over the fact he'd never valued her true worth. Then she'd leap into her new boyfriend's convertible vintage navy blue Mercedes and drive off into the sunset. She had not imagined the scene would be calm, sad and totally anti-climactic.

'I'm sorry, Ellis, but I can't do this anymore.'

'What do you mean?' he said, grabbing her hand in plaintive

confusion. He knew exactly where the power lay in this relationship and it was *not* with Lenny.

'If all you can ever give me is half-hearted nonsense or nothing then I'll take nothing.'

He put his hands on her shoulders and gently pulled her closer. 'But baby, why? We make each other feel so good.'

In spite of what she was trying to say, her body moved to his, but she paused. She remembered last year, when he'd gone to that rave while she was in bed with her sprained ankle, and he hadn't called once to check up on her; the time he'd failed to turn up at her birthday two years ago despite promising he'd show for at least an hour. And all the times he'd left her feeling not at all good – in fact the opposite of good – in fact the word was bad.

'I'm sorry,' said Lenny. 'But I'm done.'

And it didn't matter that she hadn't found the perfect, most victorious words with which to say it. All that mattered was this time she knew – in her bones – that the words she had found were the ones she meant.

After Ellis had gone she took a bottle of wine from the fridge and poured herself a large glass. She started to unpack the bag Danny had brought, her heart sinking with every item she laid on the kitchen counter. Carefully wrapped in wax paper were two burgers, two sausages and a steak. There was a Tupperware box of potato salad, her favourite, made with bacon and spring onion; another with green salad and when Lenny lifted the lid she saw a generous amount of avocado on top. Juliet must have sliced that freshly for her because it had no trace of brown around the edges. And more! A bottle of Prosecco, two packs of Hula Hoops, Lenny's crisps of choice, a slice of birthday cake with a dark chocolate L piped on to white icing. And still more: in the bottom of the bag were two gift-wrapped presents – one from Andrew – vouchers for her local cinema; and from Amy, a pedometer and a £50 Topshop voucher.

Lenny put all the food except for the cake in the fridge. She stuffed the wrapping paper back in the bag and moved it to the floor, but as she was doing so felt the weight of something else in there. She took the wrapping paper back out and underneath, tangled up in the tissue paper right at the bottom, she discovered Juliet's Oyster card and her yellow notebook.

Lenny put them to one side, took a fork and tried to eat the cake. It was delicious – icing made with cream cheese, not too sweet – but she felt a tight lump at the base of her throat. She should text Jules, tell her that her notebook and Oyster card had slipped into the bag.

She picked up the notebook and flicked through it, Jules's neat handwriting forming perfect straight lines across the unlined paper.

There on the first page was written: *HappyGuru - stage one! Positive thinking.* Lenny smiled in spite of herself. That Dr Toss Bag with his talk of vibrations . . . She noticed Juliet had circled various words in red ink: *Opportunity in the negative. Think less. Do more.* She turned the page and noticed all the words that were circled.

2 – Move! Stretch.

3 – Do things properly or not at all. Lenny thought back to the vegan dinner party. Danny *had* been pretty flirty with her that night. Nowadays he just looked at her like she was an idiot. She really wanted him to stop looking at her that way.

4 – Infinite possibilities. Make something beautiful. That must have been something Juliet had been up to while Lenny was stoned.

5 – Be brave. Jump! Lenny shuddered at the memory, and reached for her wine glass.

6 – What do you truly love? Everything else is in your way! Well she'd finally decluttered her most cumbersome baggage: Ellis.

7 – Focus. Joy in small things.

Lenny flicked to the end of the notebook and noticed Juliet had written more notes, starting on the final page and working her way back in again. They were lists, each with a date on, and Lenny started to read but then stopped herself. Was reading Juliet's gratitude lists akin to reading her diary? Lenny hoped not, as curiosity got the better of her and she picked up the notebook again.

She was amazed at some of the entries. Even on the bleakest days of last year Juliet still managed to find joy, in the smell of bonfires, a lack of rain, a perfectly turned out brioche. There were so many lists in the book, of all things big and small: twenty, forty, sixty lists

– some with a dozen entries, some with just three. And as she turned the pages she felt a rush of gratitude in her own heart for there was one word that appeared on every single one of those lists, and that word was Lenny.

Lenny lay in bed that night in a state of confused agitation. She'd spent far too much time over the years comparing herself negatively to Juliet – from the length of their noses to Juliet's culinary skills. The only area in which she felt remotely superior to Juliet was in her emotional temperament. She'd thought Juliet's default of only seeing the good in people was a weakness verging on naivety, and that her own cynicism was a smarter defence against life's relentless threats. Yet for all the trauma Juliet had suffered, she'd emerged in far better shape than Lenny. Dr Toss Bag was right, positivity had helped Juliet to deal with far greater problems than Lenny's trivial ones.

Lenny had considered herself the tough one. How wrong she'd been! She was an utter wimp, a moron, the world's biggest idiot!

All the anger she frequently felt, channelling in all directions . . . She was never comfortable unless she was metaphorically beating someone up – Occy, Nick, Matt, Ellis, bloody Danny – but the one person she loved beating up the most was Lenny. And this was the key, the greatest difference between her and Juliet, the reason Lenny was a mess and Juliet really wasn't. Juliet knew which battles to pick and they were rarely with herself.

Lenny turned on to her side, turned out her bedside light and decided that right now, at 10.34 p.m. on the evening of her thirty-ninth birthday, would be the moment she let go of her anger, let go of the past. This would be the moment she finally grew up.

PART SEVEN

'Some pursue happiness, others create it.'
Ralph Waldo Emmerson

50

Lenny had never met a Nimrod in real life before, but here she was in a Debtors and Creditors Ledger Control Account Reconciliations session, listening to Nimrod Davies recapping the basics of double entry. Juliet was right, Lenny was learning stuff; stuff she wasn't much interested in but it had got her out of the flat for the last three days in a row and she could feel her brain slightly aching – a sign it was getting used again.

Her brain wasn't the only part of her body aching. Her thighs and bottom were in a certain amount of distress, a consequence of her bounding out of bed on Monday morning for a run. She had planned to take it more slowly this time, but then she'd put on the Chemical Brothers 'Galvanize' and got all charged up. It seemed like someone was looking out for her: the sky was a little grey but halfway across the park Lenny noticed the high, wide arc of a perfect rainbow, vivid in the sky. Rainbows – one of nature's most brilliant inventions, thought Lenny, taking a gulp of air. But then she remembered that rainbows appeared for reasons other than to look pretty and to reward Lenny for having put her trainers on. Within minutes heavy, cold drops were falling from the sky, and by the time she got home she was drenched.

And one other part of her was aching slightly: her heart. She'd been such a complete and utter bozo for such a long time: self-pitying, lazy, fearful, a rubbish friend. She'd apologise to Juliet by actions, not words! She wasn't going to apologise to Danny. What for? Holding up a mirror for Lenny to look into during her ugliest moments? No, thank you very much – he should be the one apologising to her.

Lenny popped over to Juliet's on Thursday on the way to her course.

'Jules, I'm sorry I've been such a complete arse—'

'Lenny, please. I was being insensitive and patronising and I'm sorry Danny gave you such a hard time, he shouldn't have.'

'You know I don't do big cheesy "I love yous", but if I did, this is the bit where I'd do that. Anyway, sorry – really, I am.'

Juliet waved her hands to stop her. 'I called the college to see if they could move you to another course on a different date—'

'No need, I'm on day four already. Go on, ask me a question about VAT thresholds, ask me!'

'Oh, Lenny,' said Juliet, her face lighting up. 'Is it insufferably boring?'

'Actually, it's getting more interesting,' said Lenny, looking at the pudgy balls of dough lined up in row upon row on the counter. 'What are you making today?'

'I'm about to start on sourdoughs, then soda breads, then granaries, then fougasses.'

'All in one day? I'd better let you get on. I was going to suggest I come by next Monday and start looking at your accounts.'

'Deal,' said Juliet, shaking her hand.

Lenny turned to leave and then turned back. 'Oh, by the way, I nearly forgot, I found these on Sunday in the bottom of the bag – I should have brought them round earlier – your Oyster card and your notebook.'

'Ah, right, I was wondering where those had got to,' said Juliet, taking them from Lenny's hand and quickly turning away before the colour rose to her cheeks.

Juliet really was a terrible liar.

51

'OK, so the ones on top are customer receipts, the ones underneath are supplier invoices, they've all been paid already – but there's no real filing system from April onwards,' said Juliet, placing her files on the kitchen counter on Monday morning.

'Leave it with me,' said Lenny. 'Do you want to go and have a nap or something?'

'I'm fine. I don't bake on a Monday, but thanks anyway. Though actually . . . ' She looked outside at the cloudless sky. 'Would you mind if I went for a run? I haven't been for a week.'

'Go, go,' said Lenny, waving her away.

Lenny sat down to work but almost immediately came unstuck. There was a pile of receipts with figures scribbled on them but a bunch had no dates. She didn't want to disturb Juliet five minutes into her run, so she grudgingly picked up the phone and called Danny.

'Lenny, how nice to see your name in lights! Are you finally calling to apologise?'

'Listen, I'm trying to make sense of these receipts but half of them don't have dates on.'

'You're doing Jules's receipts? Interesting. So you actually got off your arse and left your flat, congratulations.'

'Why haven't you put dates on some of these receipts?'

'Anything without a date on is on blue paper, isn't it?'

Lenny shuffled through the pile. 'That's correct.'

'So blue paper, no date is August. Yellow paper is July, they should have dates on, and I think June was on green.'

'Seriously – that's your accounting system?'

'Lenny, we're getting busier and busier every week. I have about ten seconds to get cash off people while keeping one eye on the van so I don't get done for double parking. I'm sorry I don't live up to your exacting accountancy methods, Madam Chancellor of the bloody Exchequer, but it's a small homemade bread business, not Enron. You know you should—'

Lenny put the phone down. OK, so blue . . . August, then July, June . . . back to April. Lenny made neat piles of all the receipts and started going through them methodically. By the time Juliet returned and had done her full dough shift, Lenny was still only halfway through.

'Go home, Lenny – you've done six hours already.'

Lenny checked her watch. 'Fine, OK, I'm going to come back tomorrow to do the rest.'

'It's hot in here today,' said Lenny, fanning herself with a sheaf of papers as she walked into the garage to find Jules resting against the fridge door. 'Are you OK? Do you want a cup of tea and a break?'

'If I sit down, I'm not sure I'll ever stand up again,' said Jules, rubbing the small of her back.

'Something smells amazing – are you baking *now*?'

'Testing the second deck of this monster,' she said, pointing her thumb towards the oven. 'It's running too hot. Danny thinks it might be the circulator – if I'm lucky. And if I'm not, it's caput. How's it going?'

'I've put all the transactions on a master spreadsheet. I'm just trying to figure out your overheads – do you have your electricity bills for the last eight months?'

'In the lavender box file in the study.'

'By the way, how many orders have you got going out tomorrow morning?'

'Six?' Juliet checked the list on the wall. 'No, seven now, we've got a new customer in Cricklewood.'

'And what time does Danny head off on his rounds again?'

'Six forty-five tomorrow morning – the café in Cricklewood need their bread by seven thirty. Why?'

'If he doesn't object too violently, I was thinking I might go with him.'

* * *

The following morning Lenny arrived as Juliet and Danny were packing the hot loaves into bags. Lenny picked up a crusty white bloomer, squeezed it gently in the middle, then brought it lovingly to her nose.

'Stop kissing it, start packing it,' said Danny, glancing up at her briefly.

'Ooh, somebody's not a morning person!' said Lenny, putting the loaf into a paper bag, then helping to pack the rest.

'We've got oven problems,' he said, frowning. 'Jules, I'll call the guy in Bristol later but you're going to have to work around it for now. Right Lenny, if you're coming, we're leaving now.'

They were ten minutes down the road heading towards Cricklewood, Danny happily nodding along to Absolute Classic Rock, Lenny struggling to keep her mouth shut.

'Sorry, Danny, I can't take it any more,' she said, changing the radio station 'It's too early in the morning for monsters of rock.'

'You're a guest in this van,' said Danny, his finger moving back to the car stereo like lightning. 'You don't get to choose the music.'

'Wow, Danny, fastest fingers in the west!' said Lenny turning to stare out of the window, while surreptitiously edging her finger back towards the radio.

'Fastest fingers, and the three hundred and sixty degree vision of a chameleon,' said Danny, intercepting Lenny's hand just as it was an inch from changing stations.

'Oh Danny, can we please have some Heart FM? I know you secretly love Bonnie Tyler.'

'Go on then, just for one,' said Danny, his voice softening. 'But don't expect me to sing along, even if I do know all the words, you know I have my reputation to think about.'

They drove around the cafés and delis and found a reasonable compromise with BBC6 Music. Lenny watched as Danny dropped off the bread, lugging the bags to each customer, hurriedly taking the cash and handing out receipts, then racing back to the van.

'I really think it would be a lot quicker and more sensible if you let me drive,' said Lenny.

Danny laughed and simply turned the music up.

'What, Danny? I'm a good driver.'

'When was the last time you drove a van?'

'I've driven a lot of cars. Lots, in my time.'

'This is a van, not a car. Thanks for the offer but let's stick to you checking for traffic wardens.'

'They don't even work this early,' she tutted. 'Why are we going back *this* way?' she said, as he started heading north again.

'Look at the list in front of you. Last delivery's in Crouch End.'

'But why didn't you do it first?'

'Because I'm a moron, Lenny.'

'Well obviously you *are* a moron or you would have dropped off in Crouch End first.'

'Really, Lenny? You're going to flounce into my van for five seconds and tell me how to do my job better? I'm dropping off there last because they don't need their delivery till ten – and they don't open till eight a.m.'

'I don't think the word you're looking for is flounce, Danny. It's quite hard to flounce into a van, it's too high up to *flounce* into.'

Danny said nothing but Lenny could see the twitch of a smile at the corner of his mouth.

'Danny, if you factor in petrol and time this is not a cost-effective route. Next time there's a staggered order you could do two deliveries, plan the route more efficiently.'

'Except that I have a job to get to and I don't think Mrs Dunsmore in Enfield will be too chuffed if I'm three hours late to unblock her downstairs toilet.'

'But I don't have any toilets to unblock. I could do it?'

Danny laughed. 'Oh, Lenny, how the tables have turned.'

'What?'

'You, bumming around doing odd jobs, dreaming of the day you can drive your very own white van . . . '

Lenny sighed, and when Danny was steering round a corner, changed the radio back to heavy-duty power ballads.

52

Lenny spent that Saturday going over Juliet's numbers again. Even with her very basic understanding of the principles of accounting, something was not right. She double-checked, then triple-checked, then returned to the pile in the living room where she'd dumped her handouts from the course to reassure herself she wasn't doing anything obviously stupid. No, the numbers were straightforward but they were troubling.

She summarised her thoughts on to one page, then put her pen down. Her brain was fizzing again from overuse. She looked at the time – it was already 7 p.m. It was a gorgeous evening out there. She very much wanted to go and sit outside a pub and drink a glass of white wine; she'd earned it – but instead she put on her running gear and dragged herself to the park. So this was the joy of running? Putting one foot in front of the other? She paused to catch her breath, thought of how perfect that wine would taste – cold and crisp and dry – but then put one foot in front of the other again and carried on.

On Sunday she woke up and was disturbed to discover that the new and improved version of Lenny had disappeared overnight and that old Lenny had returned. Two afternoons a week bookkeeping wasn't going to save her, and now she didn't even have Ellis to take her mind off herself.

She made coffee, then scanned her wardrobe for something to wear. It was another annoyingly perfect day and she took out her old blue H&M dress. It reminded her of her birthday, and of Ellis. She took it off the hanger, crumpled it into a ball and chucked it across her room. Then she took out every other outfit that reminded her of unhappy times and watched her clothes fly through the air to join the dress in a heap. Before she could begin to have second thoughts she stuffed them in a bag and rushed them round to the charity shop.

Rejuvenated she returned home and took another look at the work she'd done yesterday, to check she hadn't made a mistake. She added up the numbers again – yup, same problem.

Lenny placed her pile of paperwork down in front of Juliet on Monday morning and handed her the one-pager.

Juliet's face lit up. 'You've worked it out with proper overheads and everything – that's great.'

'It's not great if you look at the bottom line.'

Juliet looked at the numbers to see what she'd missed. 'They seem OK to me?'

'But look – by the time you've taken off your fixed costs and tax, you're basically paying yourself less than minimum wage.'

Juliet winced. 'I hadn't taken into account this whole column – all the stuff like petrol and premises, because I'm not actually paying for them.'

'But you're not going to have this garage or Danny forever, are you? The way you're currently operating, you're never going to make money.'

'Lenny, I knew this business wouldn't make me rich.'

'I don't even mean rich – but if you want to run a sustainable business and pay yourself a viable wage, you're going to have to make some changes.'

'Like what?'

'I don't know yet,' said Lenny, her brow furrowing. 'Jules: why did you start this bread business in the first place?'

Juliet looked at her as if it might be a trick question. 'I love making bread. And I wanted to do my own thing and earn enough to live on.'

'OK, anything else?'

Juliet paused, then looked slightly embarrassed. 'This might sound arrogant but I wanted as many people as possible to try my bread, because I think my bread's pretty good.'

'Yes, you want to make them happy, you're a people pleaser – spread the love,' said Lenny, clicking her fingers. 'So basically you need to expand your output.'

'Expand? I can't afford more help. How am I going to expand?'

'I don't know yet but there must be a way. Give me a few days and I'll be back with a plan.'

That week Lenny went to bakeries, cafés, delis and farmers' markets all over town. London was a city of villages, and each one she visited gave her something new to think about.

As long as you used the word 'artisan' in Belgravia you could get away with charging nine pounds for a loaf, and the residents didn't even blink, though perhaps that was just an excess of Botox. In Islington customers were obsessed with sourdoughs, which they seemed to favour in combination with obscure Swedish berry jams. Outside one tiny bakery in Peckham the queue for multigrain baguettes snaked all the way past the jerk chicken shop and the 99p store to the station. She followed one customer round a Chiswick food hall for ten minutes, waiting to see what else he'd place in his basket alongside the six half-loaves of Poilâne.

She spent Thursday in the garage with Juliet and Eddy, studying their routine – timing how long it took to do the scrape down, the weighing, the turning out – and trying to calculate the ratio of time spent on each recipe to output. She asked so many questions about techniques Juliet had to send Eddy home early because he looked as though his head might explode. Lenny spent until midnight fiddling with the numbers, trying again and again to figure out a way in which to make the hours Juliet worked more productive. She tried altering the order Juliet made the recipes, shortening the dough shift by changing the schedule, then reducing it again – there had to be a way.

On Friday morning she visited Juliet's customers, introduced herself and chatted to them about their preferences and the possibilities for a slightly different set-up. She spent the afternoon googling micro-bakeries, taking notes of success stories, and of failures. There was a book mentioned that sounded invaluable, and she searched all the libraries in Camden and found one copy at a library two bus rides away. It was a miracle! *Knead to Know* was exactly where it was supposed to be on the shelf – that never happened, it must be a sign. Lenny grabbed hold of it like a winning lottery ticket, and joyfully checked it out. The book was 145 pages long but the font was big, and some of the pages were just recipes. Lenny had finished writing notes from it by 10.30 p.m.

Saturday was spent studying small business plans online and creating yet more charts. Lenny discovered that all the years she'd spent sitting in endless marketing and sales meetings, feeling like a bored goldfish swimming in murky waters, had not been in vain. She'd somehow managed to pick up a few ideas along the way and now her brain was firing them out in all directions. Even after she'd slept on them, some of these ideas still seemed quite reasonable. She put all her work into a master document, printed it out on her old black and white printer, raced to Paperchase before it closed and bought a jumbo pack of rainbow Sharpies, then hurried home to start colouring in her vision for a bright new future.

That night she went to bed with an unfamiliar feeling, one she hadn't had in a really long time: pride.

53

'OK, so: I've had a few thoughts,' said Lenny, laying out chart after chart for Juliet on the dining-room table. 'Your objective is to get your bread into as many hands and mouths as possible. We're not talking world domination, just a decent chunk of North London.' She drew a red circle covering a ten-mile radius from Juliet's house. 'Your average working week is sixty hours, split between dough shifts, admin and your middle of the night baking.'

'I can't ditch the overnight proving, that's what gives the bread its flavour.'

'Bear with me: sixty hours, baking up to twelve breads each week is, frankly, lunacy. You need to simplify right down – you're not big enough for so many varieties.'

'You're not suggesting I only make one kind?'

'I'd say three but with seventy per cent of production focused on one, and split the rest across the other two. The bestsellers in your catchment area are sourdough, granary and white.'

'Sourdough then – it's everywhere.'

'All the more reason to do sandwich loaves. No one's making anything as good as yours.'

Juliet looked at her sceptically. 'You don't think sandwich loaves are a little . . . boring?'

'They're classic! Anyone who doesn't like sandwiches is a weirdo. I've been stalking people's shopping baskets—'

'Who's the weirdo exactly?'

' – building up a customer profile. Look, here are the stats on price points, customer demographics and cross-purchase decisions.'

Juliet looked at the pie charts and couldn't help but raise her eyebrows. 'And you don't think I'll just end up selling less bread?'

'Quite the reverse. Strip the complexity, free up production time, move to a five-day operation and extend your customer base by selling on a Saturday. Same hours overall but significantly increased volume, turnover and profit. Also, you need to charge more. Look at the price elasticity of a quality loaf in London.' Lenny handed her another chart. 'I've estimated margin based on current raw material costs, and yes, I do know we can't do a price hike with existing customers – but when we've got new customers we can.'

'New ones?'

'Give me a month, I reckon I can get another dozen, and with that volume you can afford to extend Eddy's hours.'

'And pay you a little something?'

Lenny thought about it. 'Sure. And then there's distribution. I think you should consider selling directly to the public – farmers' markets, et cetera. Get out there and meet the end customer.'

'Lenny, I need a cup of tea to process all this,' said Juliet, turning to the kitchen.

'Hold on, I'm not done yet,' said Lenny, grabbing her arm. 'There's one more thing . . . '

'So let me get this right, ladies,' said Danny, as Juliet and Lenny stood in Juliet's living room, bubbling with excitement. 'Firstly, you're letting this one,' he said, pointing to Lenny, 'dictate what you sell your customers based on these charts?'

'Have you actually looked at the numbers?' asked Lenny.

'And Jules says you've been trailing people round the shops, like some James Bond of baguettes.'

'Basket analysis, Danny. That's how you get first-hand accurate data.'

'And now you're saying you'll sell forty per cent more without doing any extra work?' he said, dubiously.

'It's way more efficient. It's a pretty straightforward equation, Danny. In fact, I think forty per cent is conservative.'

'And then you want me to help you choose a name because you think a name will help sell more bread?'

'Yup,' said Juliet.

Lenny nodded in firm agreement.

'Am I allowed a cup of tea and a sit down while I read this list, or are you two just going to keep standing there staring at me like a pair of wide-eyed loons?'

He settled on the sofa with the tea and scanned the list, shaking his head, frowning and occasionally making a derisory snort.

'Fortytude?' he said. 'Spelled with a "y"?'

'She's nearly forty,' said Lenny. 'She has attitude, plus she displayed fortitude in surviving a marriage to Douchebag. It works on three levels.'

'Nope,' said Danny. 'It's dumb. And so is Rising Stars, and Bread Winners, and Something To Prove.'

'But it's about bread – you know, you prove it?'

'So then it's a bad name *and* a bad pun. As is Rise and Shine – sounds like an ITV cop show.'

'No it doesn't,' said Lenny.

'I kind of think it does,' said Juliet, sheepishly.

'Bread And Butter?' said Danny. 'You don't even sell butter.'

'God, Danny, you're so literal,' Lenny sighed. 'It's slang, for a job – someone's work?'

'No – too confusing. And *Happy* Bread? You don't think McDonalds would have something to say about that?' said Danny.

'They can't trademark the word happy,' said Lenny.

'It's nice and upbeat,' said Juliet. 'What about Happy Buns?'

'If you were opening a male strip joint,' said Danny.

'That's part of the five-year plan,' said Lenny.

Danny took another sip of tea and smiled. 'I've got a great name! Late Bloomer.'

'Late Bloomer?' said Juliet.

'I mean with all due respect, you started your business at a certain stage in life.'

'Rudeness!' said Lenny.

'Jules was happy to call it Forty-something?' said Danny in confusion. 'And Late Bloomer's also good because a bloomer's a type of bread.'

'Yeah, I think Juliet probably understands the double meaning of bloomer.'

'I'm not even baking bloomers in Lenny's new world order.'

'And bloomer's got Benny Hill big-knickers overtones,' said Lenny. 'It's definitely a dumb name.'

'And Spread the Loaf isn't?' said Danny. 'OK, fine, I've got it!' He clicked his fingers in a Eureka gesture. 'Lenny, get those guys you worked for to build an app that people can click on to order their bread, call the whole thing Bap! Bapp app! Genius! What? What's that face supposed to mean? You think I should stick to fixing toilets?'

'You said it, not me.' Lenny shrugged.

'Fine. Well, ladies, I'm sorry but I don't like any of these names.' Juliet looked to Lenny who was staring at the floor, dejected.

'I don't know,' said Lenny, under her breath. 'Maybe he's right.'

Juliet went back to the kitchen and Lenny went to take her charts from the table when Danny stopped her.

'These charts?' he said.

'What about them?'

'The way that you've analysed all this data?' said Danny.

'I've triple-checked the numbers,' said Lenny, wearily.

'Do you think, maybe, you could have a look at my accounts and come up with some ideas for me?'

Lenny turned to look at him properly. He smiled sheepishly at her and she blushed.

'I don't have the nous for this sort of stuff,' said Danny. 'And you've still got time on your hands. I'd pay you, obviously.'

Lenny thought about it. She really needed the money. And she'd had way more fun doing these numbers than she'd admit to. And also these last few weeks Danny had finally stopped looking at her like she was an idiot – and that felt pretty good too.

'Yeah, all right,' said Lenny. 'I suppose I could give it a go.'

54

They could tell after just ten days that the plan was moving things in the right direction. Lenny toured her hit list of delis armed with fresh bread, butter and a smile, and rarely left without the promise of a follow-up call. Meanwhile, Juliet rearranged her schedule, her shifts and her mindset. 'This all makes life so simple, I can't believe it didn't occur to me before.'

'You were busy doing the job,' said Lenny, typing up the list of invoices to go out that week.

'Do you think we'll have enough of a customer base to start doing five days a week by the end of the month?'

'Almost definitely,' said Lenny. 'I'm going to see these guys tomorrow.' She showed Juliet her latest list. 'And I might head down to Whitecross Street Market, near my old office. There's a posh sausage sandwich guy I used to buy lunch from. He's cool, he might be persuaded to give us a try.'

The following day Lenny had just finished dropping off samples with Signor Sausage and was about to call Fran to see if she was free for lunch when she heard a familiar voice calling her name. She turned round, then instinctively turned her head away, but there was no avoiding him now. Why couldn't it be Philpott, or Ravi, or anyone but Cooper, wearing his stupid metrosexual man-scarf so meticulously folded that Lenny still, ten months on, had a terrible urge to yank it.

'*Le*-nny! *Long* time no see,' he said, kissing her hello.

'Nick, this is Signor Sausage, Signor Sausage, Nick,' said Lenny awkwardly, as the two men shook hands.

'So, back in the hood!' said Nick, winking. 'I heard you were down to the last two for the job of Research Director at IncaTech?'

'Yeah, well that was a while back. It didn't work out.'

'But something obviously did. So who in Silicon Roundabout has the pleasure of your company now?'

'Actually I'm just helping a friend out with something completely different.'

'Ooh, sounds exciting! You know, we're always on the lookout for blue-sky game changing ideas.'

Lenny laughed. 'No, this is definitely not a Wappen sort of project.'

'You're not already speaking to someone else about it are you? Because I'd definitely be interested to hear whatever it is you're up to.'

Lenny looked at Nick cautiously. He wasn't actually mocking her. 'Er, thanks, Nick, that's quite decent of you, but no – it just isn't something you guys . . . ' She shifted to one side to make space for a customer ordering a chorizo bap. 'Yeah, it's not one for you . . . er, though actually . . . ' She turned to look at the sandwich being made behind her and hesitated. 'Actually you know what? Maybe it is. You haven't got rid of the work canteen, have you?'

'The canteen? No, of course not. Why?' asked Nick, catching her look of excitement. 'Is it a food app, the next Deliveroo? Anything game-ification related? We're desperate for narrowcast apps that deliver magical user experiences to the hearts and minds of consumers.'

'No, there's no pokes, no click throughs, none of that guff. My friend makes actual products you can hold in your hand.'

'Throwback Thursday!'

'I don't know what that means, Nick, but I do know that what she produces definitely makes people happy. And you're Chief Happiness Officer, in charge of all those people's well-being, frankly you'd be a fool not to get on board.'

'Oh Lenny, you're such a tease,' said Nick. 'Come on then. Let me buy you a coffee and you can tell me more.'

'So, Signor Sausage is calling back tomorrow, and you'll never believe who's agreed to try your sandwich loaves – but you'll need a Sunday dough shift as he wants them for bacon butties a week on Monday.'

Juliet looked up at Lenny, slightly shell-shocked. 'Sorry, Lenny, I wasn't listening to any of that.'

'What's wrong?' said Lenny. 'You look exhausted.'

'Matt's been pestering me about the paperwork. Until we sign off on the finances we can't get the decree absolute; it's hardly like I want to stay married to the cretin. But more importantly, that oven is on its last legs. Danny said the parts will cost more than it's worth and it still won't be totally reliable. I've seen a fantastic-looking ex-display one on Brook Food's site, but it's the best part of ten grand and I haven't got access to anywhere near that.'

'Ten grand?' said Lenny in alarm.

'Danny's been a total sweetheart, he's offered to give me three grand towards it from the rent he hasn't been paying, but he's been saving for a deposit on a flat. I couldn't possibly take it off him.'

'Yes you could. He's been living here rent free for ages.'

'I said he could do that. Plus he's been making deliveries for me for nothing for eight months.'

'Could he at least lend it to you till the divorce is finalised?'

'Perhaps, but it's still not enough.'

'What about a credit card?'

'Maybe for another few grand, but that would still leave five.'

'Make that idiot Matt give it to you!'

Jules raised her eyebrows. 'Lenny, it's a struggle enough getting the interim maintenance payments out of him. Besides, I'd never go begging.'

'I don't mean beg, I mean demand.'

Lenny could be a little naive sometimes, thought Juliet. 'Oh Lenny, if only it were that simple.'

55

Robert cleared the plates from the dinner table and brought two cups of coffee through to his living room where Juliet was on the sofa, checking her phone.

'Everything OK?' he asked, sitting down and putting his arm around her.

'Sorry – just looking at second-hand ovens online . . . ' she said, guiltily.

'Look, Jules, I think Lenny's right. If Danny's happy to lend you three grand then take it – but I wouldn't put any on a credit card if you don't know when you can pay it back.'

Juliet sighed. 'I just really wanted to see if Lenny's plan would take off. I thought it might actually free up a bit of my time if Eddy did more hours.'

'What are we talking – best part of seven grand?'

Juliet nodded.

'I'll lend it to you.'

Juliet started to shake her head.

'I don't think you're a flight risk,' he said, taking her hand. 'Let me help you.'

'I just . . . I don't want to borrow money from you.'

'Why?'

'Just because,' she said softly. 'Meanwhile, Matt's been on the phone again about finalising the divorce.'

'Are you sure you don't want me to have a look at the details?'

'No. Thank you though – it's nearly where it should be. The thing is, I know it's going to mean selling the house, and I just . . . ' Her shoulders drooped.

'It must be hard, having to say goodbye to all those memories.'

'It's not the memories.' In fact she was itching to be free of the ghosts. 'The thing I'm really attached to is the garage,' she said sheepishly. 'With the money I get from the settlement, I'll be looking at a two-bed flat, with no chance of any workspace. It's just so bloody convenient being able to go down there at half past four in the morning and bake in my pyjamas.'

'Ah, I see. And you don't think you could hire a workspace somewhere else and turn up in your pyjamas? I won't tell, as long as you let me come along and watch occasionally,' he said, grinning.

She laughed and kissed him, then smiled and kissed him again. She felt like a teenager with him sometimes – in a really good way.

He smiled, then looked away, and when he turned back he looked hesitant. 'I think I do know someone who's got a garage, and they're not too strict on dress code. They may even have a spare bed . . . or at least the left-hand side of one,' he said, his eyebrows raising in a hopeful question.

Juliet's smile stayed on her face, but she felt a pang in her chest. 'Robert, it's a very generous offer but . . . I can't.'

'We could work out a token rent for the garage, if it makes you feel better? You could write that off against the business.'

'It's not the money,' said Juliet, gently.

His smile faded and he looked suddenly perplexed. She took his hand, slipped her fingers between his and gave them a gentle squeeze. They'd had eight glorious months together and she hoped they'd have many more. Perhaps he'd turn out to be a great love, perhaps not, but either way she was happy right where she was for now.

56

'Jules, I can't believe you turned down the loan, and I really can't believe you turned down the workspace,' said Lenny, crossly. 'And free rent! What is *wrong* with you?'

'Lenny, believe it or not I do not want to be beholden to any man I'm in a relationship with ever again.'

'But Robert's a good guy, he's not going to shaft you.'

'No! I've said no. I'll borrow the three grand from Danny – that's a start, isn't it?'

'But what about the rest?'

'I've been thinking—'

'You're going to ask Matt?'

'No, I am *not* going to ask Matt! What is wrong with *you*?'

'Oh, nothing, I'm just fine,' said Lenny, throwing her hands up. 'I can't wait to see your business fail when you were on the verge of expanding.'

'Well if you hadn't gone and got me a load more orders that I can't fulfil, I wouldn't be under quite this much pressure right now, would I?' said Juliet in exasperation.

'And there's me thinking I was helping you!' said Lenny.

'Oh god, Lenny, I'm sorry. I'm just frustrated. Look, I do have one person I was thinking of calling . . . '

'Who?'

'It's not ideal. And I don't know if the timing will even work, but I think he might be worth a shot. And at this point I've got nothing to lose, I might as well go for broke.'

'Sweetheart,' said Mitchell, pulling her close for a double kiss. 'You're looking fabulous.'

Juliet smiled. She'd spent considerably longer than usual choosing her outfit and doing her make-up. If she was going to act like a warrior she'd better start dressing like one.

'No, really,' he said. 'You're looking five years younger than when I last saw you.'

'Amazing what shedding an excess husband can do,' said Juliet, taking a seat.

'Thank you so much for reaching out again,' said Mitchell, shaking his head sorrowfully. 'I cannot reiterate how much Celina regrets the way you ladies parted. Honestly, she was close to devastated.'

Not that close, clearly. 'Where is she?' said Juliet, arching an eyebrow. 'I thought she might have been here today?'

Mitchell coughed loudly. 'Er, she wanted to join us, of course she did, but she's got so much on at the moment,' he said, pushing the plate of brownies towards Juliet. 'Anyway, I know you're extremely busy with your own projects, clever girl, so shall we get down to business?'

'We can if you like, but before we do, I wanted you to know that I've been thinking over the numbers and timings you mentioned on the phone, and they're not going to work for me.'

'What, none of it?' said Mitchell, his smile dropping as Juliet nodded. 'Then if it's not a stupid question, why did you come in today?'

'I've had a few thoughts about how it could all work for me. Shall I take you through them?'

Juliet knew she was on safe ground because this was the only time in all the many years she'd known him that Mitchell had offered her the plate of brownies before attempting to grab one for himself first.

Juliet was buzzing with excitement by the time she left Mitchell's office. This was the first time in her life she'd been entirely unreasonable in her demands and, after only a small amount of to-ing and fro-ing, Mitchell had given her exactly what she'd asked for. My god, she wished she'd lived her entire life acting like such a diva!

She was about to call Lenny to share the good news but as she walked down Piccadilly she felt an urge to treat herself to a packet of posh chocolate biscuits from Fortnum & Mason. What the hell, she could afford it after that meeting.

She was admiring a box of Halloween mini ghost-shaped white chocolates when she heard a familiar voice behind her and instantly regretted having popped in to the store.

'Juliet? Juliet!'

Juliet's heart sank as she turned to see Danielle standing behind her with a tin of Earl Grey loose-leaf tea in her hand and a quizzical look.

'My goodness, it's been a long time. I don't think I've seen you since . . . your anniversary party. What are you doing in Mayfair?' Danielle's gaze scoured Juliet's face intensely, as if looking for signs of wear and tear. 'You look so well.' Juliet could have sworn there was a hint of disappointment in her tone.

'Thank you,' said Juliet. 'I am well.'

'Everything . . . all better now?'

'All better in what way?'

'Well . . . I don't mean to pry, but, obviously . . . ?' Danielle looked as if she were expecting Juliet to finish the sentence for her.

Juliet stared at her blankly. 'Obviously what, Danielle?'

'Obviously *I* know from being with Caspar how hard a divorce can be,' she said, touching her palm to her heart with a dull thud. 'Quite devastating. Really traumatic. Heart-breaking.'

'Oh, right, yes, it wasn't much fun,' said Juliet gently. 'Still, I'm not entirely convinced Caspar's experience was quite the same, was it? I mean Caspar chose to leave his wife. And the way my marriage ended . . . well, that wasn't my choice in the slightest.'

'It's hard for everyone involved, regardless of the particulars,' said Danielle, hurriedly. 'Anyway, Matt told Caspar that you've moved on quite significantly.'

'It has been well over a year now.'

Danielle paused, opened her mouth, then hesitated. 'Caspar said . . . No, actually, he must have got the wrong end of the stick . . . '

'No, go on, what did Caspar say?'

'He said —' Danielle's face crinkled in confusion. 'He said you were now living with Matt's best *friend*?'

Juliet broke into a laugh. 'Wow, yes! I *am* cohabiting with Danny. And yes, technically he was Matt's best friend – not anymore, obviously. Gosh, the grapevine's in bloom.'

'Really? I thought maybe Caspar had got confused,' said Danielle in wonder. 'So it *is* true?'

'Oh god yeah! Have you seen Danny? The man is gorgeous! Six foot two, great body – a surfer, plus,' said Juliet, leaning forward with a conspiratorial whisper, '*much* better endowed.'

Danielle's mouth twitched in confusion.

'Oh, and I do have another one on the go too,' said Juliet, warmly. 'His name is Robert. As you know, Danielle, career's never been my strong suit, but it turns out I am great at man-juggling – keeps it fresh, exciting, as you head towards your forties.' She checked her watch. 'Nice to chat, Danielle, do send Caspar my regards.'

'I love the fact you told that stupid witch Danielle you're now some sort of polygamous sex fiend,' said Lenny, putting down her wine glass just long enough to high-five Juliet.

'Her face!' said Juliet. 'I wanted to take a selfie with her and send it to you but I wasn't brave enough.'

'Brave enough? You're an absolute legend.'

Juliet shrugged. 'The Celina job is not entirely without its challenges. All of Sef's recipes are going in the bin, so that means starting from scratch.'

Lenny froze, mid wine refill. 'Er, not to put a dampener on this but haven't you already got enough on?'

'No, here's the thing,' said Juliet, grabbing her notebook. 'Last Easter, I did thirty-two recipes in ten days. I've negotiated an extension with Mitchell till Christmas, I can easily do eighty recipes between now and then, and with the money Mitchell's paying I can afford Eddy five days a week – and still have some left to pay you a little something.'

'How much is Mitchell actually paying you?'

Juliet mouthed the figure at Lenny.

'Twenty grand, are you *serious*? How much does *Celina* earn?'

'I saw her contract once on Mitchell's desk when he popped to the loo. Two hundred grand per book, and that's just UK, it doesn't even take into account foreign sales.'

'For *what?* *You* wrote all her recipes.'

'The power of the Celina brand . . . That's nothing – Mitchell just signed some girl from Instagram and all she does is take photos of avocados.'

'I don't want to hear this,' said Lenny, putting her hands over her ears.

'Photos of avocados, three times a day, and he's got her a million pound deal.'

'Oh good Lord,' said Lenny in fury. 'What a world we live in.'

'It's not all bad though, is it?' said Juliet. 'Now we can do everything on your plan.'

'I do hope you're going to tell Mitchell you want your own book deal.'

Juliet smiled. 'One step at a time, right? Oh for goodness sake, can't I just enjoy a glass of wine in peace?' she said as her phone rang and the name Wanker appeared on the screen.

'Who?' said Lenny.

Juliet held the phone up to her.

'Go on,' Lenny whispered. 'Make it an arse-kicking hat trick!'

'Why are you whispering, Lenny? He can't hear you.'

'And do it on loudspeaker, please?'

Juliet paused. She was slightly tipsy and not in the mood to speak to Matt, but what the hell, perhaps he was calling because Danielle's gossip had already filtered back to him. She put the phone on loud-speaker and raised her finger to her lips.

'Jules,' he said, sounding exhausted. 'Hey, how are you?'

'Fine. I was under the impression you couldn't talk to me in the evenings?' said Juliet calmly.

'I'm still at work,' he sighed. 'It's insanely busy at the moment. Anyway, I'm sure you don't want to hear my woes. Now Jules, as you know, I did very much want all the divorce paperwork tied up by September and it is now September, and before you say anything, I do entirely understand it's not your priority. I know you're very busy with your work and I think it's great your bread thing is going so well, I do, I really do.'

Lenny rolled her eyes in annoyance.

'So listen: Tash has fallen in love with a three-bedroom flat in Primrose Hill.'

'I bet she has,' mouthed Lenny.

'And it's nothing big or anything, but – it is on at a really good price.'

'How much is it?' said Juliet.

'A good price for Primrose Hill,' said Matt. 'It needs work, quite a lot of work.'

'How much?' said Juliet.

'I wasn't going to offer the asking price.'

'How much?'

'It is what it is.'

'I can just look the price up myself on Zoopla if you do buy it.'

'OK, fine, it's nine-seven-five, but we're only offering nine hundred.'

Lenny let out a snort of outrage, then mouthed 'sorry' at Juliet.

'What was that noise?' said Matt. 'Have you got me on loud-speaker?'

'Yes.'

'Oh. Look, Jules. We've already missed out on two other proper-ties this year because I don't have the equity. I know you're very attached to that house emotionally, I know you have expectations of maintaining your lifestyle – but realistically you can't go on living there indefinitely, you must have known that, surely, this can't be coming as new news.'

'You can put it on the market tomorrow, if you make it worth my while.'

'Do you really mean that?' said Matt, nervously.

'I mean you couldn't have picked a worse time for my business, but if you give me the cash to set up new premises, and a finder's fee, then absolutely, go ahead and call the estate agent tomorrow.'

'Hang on, slow down – what do you mean, a finder's fee?'

'I'll need a new workspace I can walk straight into without disrupting my schedule, so I'll need someone to scout appropriate production locations that have enough space for the kit. Plus I'll need someone here to manage the sale of the house. I presume you won't want to take time off work to help, and I'll need someone I can trust entirely so on second thoughts that wouldn't be you anyway.'

'Hang on a minute!'

'Selling this house will take at least two months – call it three – and I'll need help finding a new flat too. I'd say ten grand for relocation services might cover it.'

'Ten *grand*?'

'Who could I get to help, though?' she said quizzically. 'Danny's *so* busy nowadays—'

'*Danny*?'

'Oh yes, his business is flying – and by the way, while we're on the subject of Danny, next time you want to tell your friends I'm shacked up with him, implying *I'm* the one living in some sort of adulterous love-nest, you might want to choose your words more carefully.'

'What? Who've you been speaking to?'

'Irrelevant. Yes . . . so . . . Danny can't help but perhaps Lenny could if she's free,' said Juliet, raising an eyebrow towards Lenny, who had a stunned look on her face.

Matt made an indignant grunt. 'Lenny's never even owned a property! She won't know how to do it.'

'I think Lenny probably has the intellectual capacity to manage a process thousands of people do every day.'

'No, Juliet, I'm sorry but I'm not paying ten grand to your slovenly mess of a friend to—'

'Before you say another word, be aware that that "slovenly mess" is sitting right next to me,' said Juliet, furiously.

'Oh for Christ's sake, I thought you sounded like you'd been drinking. Do you have any idea what you're doing?'

'Yes actually, I do. You always told me to "play hardball" with Mitchell. Well guess what? I'm playing hardball. With you. I want ten grand for Lenny to project manage, I want you to cover the rental costs of the first six months of my new work premises, and don't even begin to tell me you can't afford it if you're looking at flats that cost more than this house—'

'Jules, I'm sorry but you cannot put me over a barrel like this, it's utterly ridiculous.'

'Matt – *it is what it is*. You've got forty-eight hours to think about it, which is more than generous. If not, the whole process will take as long as it takes, because frankly it suits me to stay right where I am.'

57

Juliet was not entirely surprised Matt had agreed to her terms – nonetheless, she realised as soon as he had done that she was in no rush to buy a flat. Her life had changed so much in the last year and she had no idea what changes were to come. Instead she'd decided to rent and had briefly entertained the idea of sharing with Lenny. They'd had a five-minute discussion – about the joys of mess versus the joys of clear work surfaces – at the end of which they'd both agreed wholeheartedly that it was the worst idea Juliet had ever had. Lenny was on the case scouting for premises for the bakery and the flat; in the meantime Juliet was hard at work. The new streamlining strategy was paying off. The shiny almost-new oven was sitting in her garage, baking up to 150 loaves, Mondays to Fridays every week, with an extra dough shift on Sunday afternoons. By mid-November her customer base had doubled and included four new delis, two market stalls, two local restaurants, and supplying Wappen's canteen with breakfast and lunchtime loaves. Having Eddy for five shifts a week had freed up so much of her time, she'd nearly finished writing Celina's recipes, ahead of schedule.

Lenny had gone from being unemployed to having three jobs at once: Juliet and Danny's accountant, Juliet's chief salesperson, and overseer of Juliet's property requirements. Lenny found it a lot easier spending her time persuading shops to try Juliet's bread than it was to spend that time at home engaged in the act of self-destruction. She was so busy every day she simply had no time for bad feelings. It helped that she was on a total man break. She was surprised now how rarely she thought of Ellis. When she did it was with neither fondness nor anger but a sense of regret at all she'd put up with to avoid loneliness.

By the end of November, they'd had an offer in on the house and Lenny had lined up three possible flats and a workspace she thought could be ideal – one arch in a stretch of renovated Victorian railway arches in Kentish Town. On weekdays the arches were home to a dozen independent food producers including Spector Coffee, Two Jakes Cheese and Kentish Brew Time. At the weekends the area in front of the arches sprung to life, forming an avenue of hip food stalls. She'd dragged Ellis there last summer and they'd had an amazing salt beef sandwich at one of the stalls, and then he'd insisted they go over to the Heath so he could feel her up under a tree.

Lenny had visited the arches on Thursday when it was just the producers at work but she wanted to see if the market encroached on the proposed space, and so she had it in her diary to visit on Sunday. She'd have asked Juliet to come with her – she was already excited when Lenny had described the space – but Juliet was head down, finishing recipes.

Lenny was washing her coffee cup and about to set off when she was assailed by a little stab of memory. That time with Ellis, he'd devoured his lunch with such gusto; she remembered him looking at that sandwich with the look he sometimes gave her – a look she'd hoped was adoration but was in fact merely generic hunger. All the more reason to go back and overlay that memory with a neutral one.

Then again, it would be more fun to go down there with someone in tow, someone fun who liked food . . . I mean it couldn't hurt to suggest it to him now, could it?

She picked up her phone and scrolled to his number. What was the worst thing that could happen if he said no? She'd feel foolish, but she was an expert at that.

Lenny's heart skipped a beat as he answered on the third ring. 'Danny?'

'Yes, it's me. Why do you sound like you've dialled the wrong number?'

'No, I meant to call you. I just didn't expect you to pick up so quickly.'

'Oh, OK. Well, I did pick up quickly. I'm by the phone. To what do I owe the pleasure on this fine Sunday morning? It's not month end for another two weeks.'

'Listen, I know it's your day off but I wondered if I could borrow you.'

'For what?'

'I'd really like some company – only for a couple of hours, it won't take long.'

'Ah bless you, Lenny, but there are escort agencies for that sort of thing.'

'I mean a friend. And you're the only person I know who's single and not doing couply things at the weekend.'

'What's wrong with your Bob Marley muppet boyfriend?'

'Who?'

'The muppet who's always in your flat?'

'Ellis? Ellis is not my boyfriend.'

'Boyfriend, friend with benefits – whatever you ladies call it nowadays. That guy.'

'Oh. Well that guy is no longer *that* guy. He hasn't been for a while.'

There was a pause on the line, during which Lenny cursed the fact she'd put herself out there. I mean she absolutely was not asking Danny out on a *date* or anything – so why did she feel quite so exposed, waiting for his response?

'I suppose you want my van, too?'

Lenny's heart leaped. 'Nope, just you. Meet me outside Kentish Town Tube station in an hour. I shan't be wearing a carnation.'

'You look . . . different,' said Danny, kissing her hello as Lenny tried to figure out if 'different' was a good or a bad thing. Perhaps the dress, ankle boots and double layer of mascara she'd put on were too dramatic a leap from her normal jeans and sweatshirt look.

'I do sometimes make an effort,' she said lightly as they started walking to the market.

'I can see that. So you're seriously telling me I'm the only man in your whole address book who's single?' said Danny, as they waited at the traffic lights.

'Pretty much.'

'Do you think you and I are the last two single people left in the world?'

Lenny blushed. 'Er, well, personally I'm on a man break so I don't currently think of myself as the last single woman on earth – but yeah, maybe? Are you . . . are you not seeing anyone at the moment?'

'I think Jules would have reported back to you if I was, don't you?' he said, grinning.

'Believe it or not we don't actually spend our whole time talking about men.'

'Lenny, I live with Jules. I am fully aware of the nature of what you girls talk about.'

'Yeah, well, if it sounds like we're talking about men, it's code – we're actually talking nuclear fission.'

'I forget you're MI5,' he said, laughing. 'On a man break? Why's that then?'

'Oh god,' said Lenny, shaking her head as they crossed the road. 'A million reasons.'

'A million's a lot of reasons.'

'You know what I mean. I'm no good at relationships. I muck them up, or they muck me up. I can't do it, Danny, I'm not like Jules.'

'I don't think Jules would claim to be an expert at relationships.'

'Of course she is. She was with Matt for ever and ever.'

'But not any more.'

'Right, but that's not her fault.'

'I wasn't saying it was. I'm just saying your definition of success is odd.'

'I think everyone would agree that being married, having a family, a nice house – all those are definitions of success.'

'So you'd say Matt was successful?'

'Well, yeah. He's got money, a great job, a fast car, some bimbo girlfriend.'

'And he's dishonest and a liar and his own daughter has no respect for him. I don't think he's a successful human being in the slightest.'

'Of course he's a giant dickhead. I'm just saying he is convention-ally successful.'

'And I'm saying the only definition of success that's worthwhile is one where you're good to the people you love, and you live life on your own terms. And if you make mistakes, you learn from them, right? Why do you look so confused, Lenny?'

'I'm surprised you have this all figured out, that's all.'

'I spent a lot of time thinking, sitting on all those beaches.'

'Don't you miss travelling?'

Danny shrugged. 'I'm loving work at the moment. And the beach will always be there.'

'So here we are,' said Lenny, as they came to the entrance to the arches. 'These food stalls are only here at the weekend but they bring in a lot of people.' They made their way through the crowds to the arch that was for rent, stopping outside the metal shutter door that was currently pulled down. 'So inside it's basically a huge high-ceilinged space, bare-brick walls. It's bigger than we currently need but you could fit two industrial ovens in there, the fridge, the mixer and way more racks. In an ideal world you'd have four bakers working quite happily.'

'Wow, get you, Alan Sugar,' he laughed.

'Sir Alan,' said Lenny. 'Anyway, it's got all the gas and electrics in place, we'd just need the council to give us sign off and we could be up and running as soon as the kit's in. I was worried the market would be disruptive, but if you look at the jam guys, they're using the front of their arch as a shop.'

'You guys should do that too.'

'In a year or two when the business is bigger.'

'Lenny, the space is perfect. I think you've found the one,' he said, smiling proudly at her.

She smiled back, then felt a tiny ache of disappointment as he checked his watch. 'Do you have to head off somewhere?' she said, trying to sound nonchalant.

'I'm going round to Dad's at three, but do you want to grab some lunch?'

'Yes! Yeah . . . if you like. There used to be a great salt beef sandwich guy here,' she said, leading him back through the market to the spot where the stand had been. In its place was now a stall selling Thai food and a queue of people waiting patiently for noodles frying in two huge woks.

'This looks good,' said Danny. 'I prefer spicy food anyway.'

'You know what?' said Lenny. 'Me too.'

Lenny didn't have to overlay a new memory on top of the old, or wilfully turn her back on the ghosts. Turns out they were no longer there.

'Thanks for coming with me,' said Lenny, as they headed back to the station after lunch. 'It's really helpful to get another opinion. I thought the space was great when I first saw it but you know Jules and I are so different.'

'Yeah, you are,' said Danny, then pondered the statement. 'Well, you were. And you still are in a lot of ways. But up until the divorce she was always kind of Miss Perfect, and you were always such a hot mess.'

Hot mess – was that a compliment? Did it mean hot? Or did it mean something quite rude?

'But people do change,' said Danny. 'I said that to you before and you got your knickers all in a twist.'

Lenny sighed gently. 'Nice weather, isn't it? This sunshine's more like September than November.'

Danny laughed. 'See? Wisdom, maturity – not rising to the bait. You've grown up a lot.'

Lenny's mouth opened, but before she could respond stroppily she realised he was right.

'So what'll you do, get Jules to see the arch this week?' said Danny.

'If I can get her down here on Tuesday, I can line up second viewings of the flats as well. The one in Tufnell Park's only five minutes away and it's got a really sweet garden – I know she'll miss her garden.'

'All change, hey?'

Lenny nodded. 'For all of us, I guess. If we do start the rental agreement mid-January, does that give you enough time to sort yourself out?'

'Oh, I'm fine. My mate Steve's got a spare room to rent off Cally Road, but I want to be in my own place by next summer. What about you, what will you do about work?'

Lenny shook her head and turned her gaze to the pavement. 'I've been too busy to think about it properly. There'll be stuff to do for another month or so till everything's settled. And then . . . ' she shrugged. 'I'll figure it out. Anyway, you'd better get on or you'll be late. Thanks again, Danny. For today. And for everything.'

'My pleasure.'

'Oh, and Danny?'

'Yes?' he said, looking at her with the sweetest smile.

'I really am very sorry.'

'What for?'

'Always giving you a hard time. And for being difficult. And stroppy.'

'Ah, Lenny,' he said, pulling her close for a hug. 'Being difficult and stroppy are your most winning qualities.'

When Lenny had been to the market with Ellis last summer, they'd gone over to the Heath for an hour, but then he'd rushed off to meet his mates down in Brixton. Lenny remembered sitting on the Tube home that day, replaying the memory of Ellis's mouth, and the weight of his body on top of hers on the grass, and it had given her a rush of excitement. But today she found herself thinking of Danny: of his kindness, his solidity, the way his eyes always had a sparkle to them. She remembered last year, that time he'd tried to fish her clothes from the charity bin, how hard he'd tried to make her laugh. She replayed the memory again and again and again – and each time she did it made her feel a warm glow inside.

58

Juliet stood in the living room of her new flat on Saturday night, surveying the remaining storage boxes still stacked against the wall. She'd planned to unpack everything the weekend she'd moved in, but moving the bakery had taken priority and she'd been unpacking a box here and there in between shifts for the last month. She checked her watch – 7 p.m. already. Robert would be round with a takeaway soon. She could do a couple more boxes before then.

She lifted the lid off the one closest to hand, some of Martha's books. She carried them through to the spare room – Martha could deal with them when she was down at Easter. Another box, containing recipes and research for Celina, and Juliet's notebook for the comfort food book that never happened. Juliet flicked through, stopped at one page in particular, and sat down to read her notes in full. She nodded, read them through slowly twice more. But of course! That made perfect sense. She smiled to herself, placed the notebook on the side table, then carried the rest of the contents through to her room. She'd need to rent a storage unit at some point, but for now under the bed would have to do.

Another box. Juliet lifted the lid, then replaced it sharply. She should have dealt with the large wooden box inside when she'd forced Lenny to declutter, but even looking at it back then had been so painful she'd actually thought about destroying it – burning it, symbolically, or throwing it away.

She stared at the packing box. Twenty minutes and it would be done. Twenty minutes was nothing. She lifted the lid again, then reached inside, removed the box and unfastened the metal clasp. Right there on top was the photo album. She brought it to her nose and sniffed the soft, heavy grained leather cover. She turned the album over to the back, then opened it at random, two thirds of the way through, delicately lifting the tissue paper to peek underneath.

A photo of Danny – skinny, and with his hair tucked behind his ears – with that girl from the year above draped all over him. Then one of Amy, holding a Champagne flute to the camera, having her neck kissed by some boy with a quiff. Ah, and one of Juliet with her arm around Lenny, Lenny wearing that pretty purple dress – both girls beaming. Reluctantly Juliet turned the pages back to the start of the album and there they were, page after page of her and Matt.

How very young they'd been – still teenagers, clueless about what was to come. There they stood, holding hands, arms entwined, ready to set out on their journey together. She'd had blind faith that their love would carry them through. Maybe she'd been naive; maybe over the years she had wrapped herself in a cashmere blanket of delusion. But not any more. The decree absolute had arrived in the post in the middle of December alongside an invoice from her flour supplier and a gushy Christmas card from Mitchell. A piece of A4 with a formal round red stamp printed on top of their names, Petitioner, Respondent, 'final and absolute . . . the said marriage was thereby dissolved'. How very peculiar that a single page should come to represent everything that she'd lost – and everything she now realised she'd gained. Not that she'd choose to repeat any of it, but she felt different now: like nothing could hurt her in that way again; somehow she felt safer.

Juliet stared at the photo, traced a finger softly over her smile. The day before the wedding, she'd gone off alone for a walk in the hotel grounds and had found herself sitting on a bench in the mani-cured gardens, bent double, sobbing over the fact her mother would not be with her to share tomorrow, would never be with her again. But on the wedding day itself Juliet had recovered her composure, she had been happy – nervous, excited about the future, slightly weirded-out by her new mother-in-law's decision to pull back on canapés – but definitely happy.

And Matt, what about him? She contemplated his face – eyes staring straight at the camera, his smile confident, untroubled by doubt. With the benefit of hindsight was his gaze challenging, enti-tled, arrogant – or was it simply and uncomplicatedly happy?

Juliet decided she would choose what it meant. Not that it made any difference to the past, but it made a difference to the present and to the future, and she chose happy.

One day Martha might actually want these photos. For now Juliet closed the book of memories, put it back in the box and filed it neatly under the bed. No need to destroy the album, the past was behind her – time for the next chapter.

59

Lenny gazed out of her window. It was a fiercely cold early February day but at least that sky was bright blue, not the heavy grey it had been all week. Lenny had been up since 7 a.m., when it was still dark, doing admin, and as she made coffee she marvelled at all those months of unemployment when she'd chosen to sleep till noon – all those wasted hours. She now had more done before 10 a.m. than she'd sometimes done in an entire day at Wappen, now that she was motivated. She probably owed guru Ian Bottomsley an apology: her exit from Wappen, so traumatic for her at the time, had turned out to be one of the best things that ever happened to her.

She was due to pick up some paperwork from the bakery at noon, and this afternoon she really should give her old headhunter a ring to see what new briefs were out there. She'd delayed it as long as possible because the thought of working in an office again made her want to crawl back into a dark space. She'd come to realise she could quite happily live on less money – most of her old salary had been spent recompensing herself with treats for how miserable she was in the day job. Still, she did need more work. Thinking about it now propelled her into her running gear and out of the flat to distract herself.

Lenny had come to the conclusion she'd never be a runner. She had to force herself to do it twice a week; she still found it hard and boring but there were times very, very occasionally, like today in the park, when she 'got it'. She looked around her, at the grass so green underfoot it was almost blue, at her own legs moving her forward as though they belonged to an actual runner, and she felt a small shiver of joy.

She arrived at the arches at noon just as Juliet and Eddy were turning the heavy plastic cartons of dough. 'Everything go out OK this morning?' asked Lenny.

'All good – and we're about to start the heart-shaped brioche for

Maisie's for Valentine's. Don't look so worried, Lenny, it's a one-off. They'll tweet about it; it'll be good for business. Anyway, we've got time – more than enough time actually. On which note, I wanted to have a chat. Eddy, can you man the fort?'

They walked over to Spector Coffee three arches down and made themselves drinks on the beautiful big chrome machine, then headed to the back of the bakery and grabbed a seat.

'So I was speaking to the cheese guys last week,' said Juliet, popping her coffee on the floor while she gave her hands a quick massage. 'The market's getting busier every weekend, the Jakes are going to start selling from the front of their arch when Big Jake's back from honeymoon at the start of April.'

'You should do that too, one day.'

'Why not now?'

'Not possible. You can't make Eddy work seven days in a row, and you'd have no life.'

'I wasn't thinking bread.'

'Then what?'

'I was unpacking at the weekend and I found the work I did for Celina's comfort food book – I'd done a whole chapter on hot sandwiches. Apparently there was a guy at the market who used to do salt beef bagels, but he's gone, so maybe there's an opportunity for us?'

'Doing what?'

'Hot sandwiches!'

'Far too complicated, the whole reason you've doubled your volume is because you've simplified.'

'I'm talking super-simple: North London's best toasties made with North London's best bread! We'll get the cheese wholesale from the Jakes, get one of those big panini-style grills like those guys in Amsterdam.'

'What guys?'

'In the food hall? The hot ones? One person taking money and orders, the other manning the grill. We could do that. We're going to do that.'

'We?'

'Lenny, you make a mean toastie. Just make a hundred of them – every Saturday and Sunday.'

'Oh Jules, don't be ridiculous.'

'It's not like you've got anything better to do at the weekends.'

'Even if that's true, *you* can't do seven days and help on a stall.'

'Lenny, first of all you need to stop telling me what I can and cannot do.'

'Jules—'

'Secondly, toasties are better made with day-old bread, so we just add ten extra-long loaves to Friday's schedule and do a small bake on Saturday for Sunday's trade.'

'But—'

'And thirdly, we can do the stall together on Saturdays but I want a lie-in on Sundays.'

'You just said it's a two-man job?'

'Right. So perhaps a man like Danny could help?'

Lenny stared at Juliet in disbelief. 'Have you already spoken to him about this?'

'We wouldn't have him as an actual partner, but he's up for it, as paid staff.'

'A partner? What do you mean?'

'Lenny, we're going into business – we're going to sell toasties. We won't get rich, but we might get happy.'

Lenny shook her head. 'Guaranteed way to ruin a friendship, a recipe for disaster.'

'Let's agree not to call ourselves Recipe for Disaster,' said Juliet, conspiratorially.

'No, seriously—'

'Lenny, they say only work with people you trust – I trust you more than anyone.'

'Look, Jules, I don't think either one of us is going to abscond to Rio with the takings. It's just . . . I don't know if we could actually run a business together.'

'We've been working together for months now.'

'Yeah but that was different, that was unofficial. I was helping you, it wasn't my real job.'

'I wouldn't be here in this arch, freezing my arse off today if it wasn't for you. I wouldn't have a business, because I'd still be on my kitchen floor crying. Lenny, you did more for me than you'll ever know.'

Lenny stared into her coffee and frowned. 'Is that why you're suggesting this? Because you think you owe me?'

'No.'

'I helped you because it wouldn't have occurred to me not to help you.'

'Lenny, I believe in you as much as you've always believed in me.'

'I know we're not talking millions here, but any venture is still a risk—'

'Look, I'm not interested in running a business with a mouse. If you don't stop finding problems I'm taking my offer off the table.'

Lenny quietly sipped her coffee. She'd always moaned that the businesses she'd worked for were so frustrating. What did they sell? Intangible concepts: 'aspiration', 'connection', the promise of 'happiness' – a piece of digital code could never deliver that. But a perfect toastie? Now that was solid and real and could bring cheer to almost anybody.

'So,' said Lenny cautiously. 'How much money do you think we'd make, if we did sell a hundred a day? How much would we have to charge?'

'You figure out the numbers and tell me.'

Lenny did a quick calculation in her head. If they were lucky they might clear £300 profit a day. 'How many different fillings would we sell?'

'You're the researcher – research it!'

'I think I'd need to do it at least four days a week for it to be a viable full-time job.'

'So if it goes well, in three months' time you look at getting someone to help, and you do it weekdays at a food market, like the one near your old office.'

'But what would we call ourselves? You still haven't chosen a name yet.'

'God, Lenny, you do like finding problems. Look, we'll figure it out along the way but let's get moving. The cheese boys are starting their thing in five weeks – they'll be doing some PR and we might as well jump in and do it with them.'

60

Was this work, because it didn't feel much like work to Lenny? Every morning for the last month she'd woken with the same thought: she had finally joined that mythical group of people who looked forward to getting out of bed, who had jobs like 'chinchilla stroker' – dream jobs that were for the likes of others but not for the likes of Lenny. Until now.

How to build the perfect toastie? Butter on the outside and in, that was non-negotiable. A generous but not too overwhelming filling of comforting, melty cheeses – she didn't know which ones yet, that was its own universe, but they would need to ooze from the middle of golden crispy crunchy bread. Which bread? She thought of Juliet's mum's granary bread. Lenny remembered watching the minute hand on the clock in double physics move backwards, all thoughts on when the bell would ring and they could race back to Juliet's for tea. Even those compressed chewy crusts were fun to eat once you'd made short work of the lush interiors. Other favourites over the years, some on white bread, brown, challah, rye; some with bacon, mustard, baked beans, Marmite, one crazy drunken one in New York with a slice of cold pizza in the middle. Oh, and Pranza in Rome! Their sandwich had the greatest mozzarella stringiness, and they cut it in three long strips, not triangles or halves, stacked in a brown paper bag, hot in your hand as you left the shop. Where else? Last year – no! – it was the year *before* in Lisbon, she'd had a beauty: three millimetre-sliced bread, smoked ham and one nutty, mellow cheese; the bread grilled with lovely char lines. Where else? India! In a café in Mumbai Airport she'd had one with green coriander chutney and fresh chillies, better than anything she'd eaten in her five-star hotel.

Of course it wasn't just about *her* preferences, but the more people she spoke to the more overwhelmed she became – Branston pickle, Worcestershire sauce, black olives? When she'd mentioned fresh tomato to Danny, he'd recoiled. But two weeks later, he'd been passing by – he seemed to be doing that a lot recently – and she'd whipped him up a prototype with slow roast tomato chopped so small it was unidentifiable and he'd eaten every last crumb.

Lenny researched the hottest food trends: fermentation, kimchee, ramen noodles, Peruvian, kale? Everybody was obsessed. Lenny wrote down 'healthy toastie?' Then 'vegan??' Toasties were classic, they were all about comfort – they were no place for pickled kale. She crumpled the entire list of fashionable foods into a ball.

She looked at her stack of ideas that had made the grade – fifty already. Still, a conceptual exercise was meaningless when she hadn't even worked out her cheese blends! She spent five nights with Little Jake, getting a masterclass on flavours, textures and melt times. The Jakes' arch was so cold at night the tips of Lenny's fingers burned like they'd been dipped in acid, but Lenny sat entranced as Jake talked her through the rows and rows of every shape and size cheese: vast, ancient looking rounds of Cheddar; smooth amber slabs of Gruyère; cartoon-cratered Emmenthals. She experimented with colour and flavour combinations: red Leicester looked so pretty, but would it work with Ogleshield because their sandwich had to contain Ogleshield, made with Jersey milk – the finest melting cheese known to man.

And of course the signature cheese blends were not merely about cheeses. Amy had warned her not to go near onions, 'too polarising! Breath factor'. But surely you needed an onion – perhaps multiple snippets of onions – to cut through the richness, and for texture and colour. Which ones, though? Leek, spring onion, shallot, red onion, white? 'Know your onions' – no, don't get distracted and google the phrase's origin, Lenny.

Every time she brought an idea or a sample to Juliet, Juliet would give it ten seconds' concentrated thought, nod or shake her head, and then Lenny would get back to work. They bought a second-hand commercial double panini-style grill and Lenny retired to the back of the bakery with a long shortlist of fifteen fillings, three breads and five cheese combinations. It was time to start field tests. Each morning she made her pile of sandwiches with Zen-like focus, painstakingly changing the variables to determine which elements contributed to maximum deliciousness, plotting her results on a graph. She compared the same filling on different breads, tweaked the onion, tweaked the cheese mix, tested ratios of bread to cheese to butter. Every sandwich from the grill underwent Lenny's meticulous user test. Pressing her fork into the toasted bread, she'd check for the slight eruption of golden butter to rise to the surface like a geyser. Then she'd lovingly make a cut – the sound of the knife through the bread like music to her ears. The strings of cheese would boing together as she separated the halves, like they couldn't bear to be parted, which was how Lenny was beginning to feel about her sandwiches.

Every day she'd take them to her neighbours in the arches. She watched their faces as they ate, trying to discern from their pupil dilation which combinations would become the toasties people obsessed about, versus those that were merely delicious. Once she'd narrowed her list, she re-made everything, weighing each element precisely, working out costs and margins. She and Juliet had agreed not to stint on ingredients; still, she was relieved the shortlist was reasonably priced. She practised her technique again and again, getting faster and faster. She discovered that wrapping the sandwiches in parchment not only meant you could stack a pile neatly, but you could then grill directly in the paper. It was easier, cleaner and quicker.

They'd decided to launch with three varieties. She was down to nine fillings and a choice between sandwich loaf and sourdough. At Wappen they'd fiddled their research all the time. Lenny would not be doing that, oh no, she had her own bespoke methodology. She'd always found that the best way to discover what people really felt about anything was to get them quite nicely drunk before you asked them.

61

'What are *these?*' said Juliet, her brow crinkling as she tried to make sense of the stapled stacks of papers on Lenny's kitchen counter: boxes, line graphs, tables of words, blank pie charts and scatter plot graphs, all with lengthy paragraphs of instructions prefacing them.

Lenny was too busy meditatively crafting a Triple Cheddar to look up. 'Questionnaires,' she said, frowning at the plate. She'd felt sure sandwich loaves were the way forward, but each time she put the roof on a sandwich that wasn't sourdough, she missed that beautiful open texture and seeing the shreds of cheese peeping through the gaps in the crumb.

'Lenny, these things are four pages long.'

'They're not *things*, they're precision-honed research tools, and up until last night they were six pages long so actually they're succinct,' said Lenny, wrapping the sandwich in parchment. Wow, she was getting good. If this business failed she could walk into a senior job in origami tomorrow.

Juliet shook her head as she read out loud. '"Rate which of these adjectives best describes the cheese blend in samples A, B and C in order of preference. Take into account all organoleptic elements, i.e. flavour, mouthfeel, colour, etc.: melting, tangy, oozing, mellow, sharp, strong, mild, creamy, buttery, supremely damn awesome . . . " Lenny, it's Saturday night. You didn't invite people round to sit an advanced degree in organoleptography.'

'That's not a word, Jules.'

'This is meant to be a party.'

'No it's not. It's a research group that happens to have wine but let's be clear – tonight's objective is results, not fun, Jules.'

'Lenny, I'm delighted you're taking this so seriously but this form is too complicated. By the time people have figured out what to write on page two, they'll have forgotten what they were eating in the first place.'

'We're using these forms.'

'Just look at their plates. Whatever sandwiches disappear fastest are the winners. Now listen, I want to talk to you about what's going on next door . . . '

Lenny followed Jules through to the living room. Lenny had cleared the sideboard of all her piles of clutter, and in their place were bottles of wine, plates, kitchen roll and her crockery collection.

'Now, Lenny, am I right in thinking you don't own any two glasses that are matching?'

'Oh I'm sorry. I didn't realise this was the ambassador's reception.'

'Are you literally expecting nine of our guests to drink out of cups?'

Lenny sighed. 'I can ask Andrew to swing by the pound store and buy paper cups, if you think that'll be classier?'

'No, I doubt that'll be classier. Shall I ask Robert to bring some of his glasses?'

'Nah, they might get smashed.'

'On the subject of wine, how many people have confirmed?'

'Twenty-eight.'

'You've got *one* bottle per head?'

'Don't worry, I've told everyone to bring one too.'

'Fifty-six bottles? Lenny, you'd better get those results in early because this party is going to get messy.'

'It's *not* a party,' said Lenny, checking her watch. 'Shit, it's nearly seven o'clock. I haven't even started the ham and cheese. Can you do that thing you do to cushions to make them look nice, please?'

The guests started arriving, armed with booze and gifts. Andrew brought Champagne and wine and a huge bunch of tulips. Fran brought a bottle of Jägermeister, and her husband with an IOU for a logo he'd design once they'd finalised their name. Amy brought Oliver and his younger brother, a freelance journalist who Amy claimed would get them into *Time Out*'s food section as soon as she clicked her fingers. Martha had brought Nate down, and they'd both asked if they could work on the stand once they'd finished their finals in the summer.

Juliet made sure everyone was set up with a glass or mug of booze. Lenny distributed the questionnaires and a set of Barclays' free biros she'd procured, then headed back to the kitchen. Juliet looked around at the confused faces, then gathered back all the papers and filed them neatly under the sofa.

Lenny was wrapping the last of the mozzarella and roast tomato with basil oil on sourdough in baking parchment when Juliet returned to the kitchen. 'Len, it's nearly eight, people are getting pretty hungry and tipsy out there.'

'Hunger's the best sauce,' said Lenny, crossing off another variant from her list.

'You ready for action?' said Juliet, looking at the toastie machines lined up on the counter – hers, Lenny's and the bigger one they'd bought for the stall.

Lenny reached towards the plug sockets and pressed all three switches to on. 'Oh, I'm ready, Jules, I could not be more ready.'

Half an hour later Lenny had cooked her way through eighty sandwiches, only stopping for one small glass of wine and a brief chat with Martha and Robert. Lenny surveyed the round she'd just made – bubbling golden outsides, lush, melting pale yellow slowly oozing from the middles. She really should eat one, or the next glass of wine would go straight to her head. Still, her research was not yet complete. She cut each into quarters and stacked them on to plates and carried them through to the living room, which was now full of tipsy people laughing, flirting, chatting and getting more drunk. It did feel rather a lot like a party. Whether it was the booze or the sense of festivity, or just the rather small layout of her flat, the guests had fully intermingled – every cluster a mix of old and new friends, from work, from the arches, from school.

She noticed Danny leaning against the wall talking to Philpott, Robert, and Andrew's girlfriend, Fiona. Danny had made a double-decker of two Italian toasties and was merrily chomping away while he chatted. Over the last month it had become evident from his frequent visits to the bakery that Danny was very fond of toasties. And it had become equally evident to Lenny that she was very fond of Danny.

'Look at you, eyeing up Danny Freeman,' said Amy, sliding over to Lenny with a half-empty pint glass of wine.

Lenny rapidly turned her gaze from him. 'Ah, Amy, how are you getting on with your questionnaire? Where is your questionnaire?'

Amy blew out a puff of ridicule. 'I didn't come to your party to write a thesis. Still, I'm glad you took my advice and left the onions out.'

'Hmm. You can't really taste them, can you? Maybe I should put more in. Now listen, I have to go and count what's left on those plates,' said Lenny, frowning at the sideboard which was now covered in empty plates.

'Oh my effing gee,' said Fran, staggering over to grab Lenny by the forearm. 'Are you putting crack in these things? I cannot stop eating them?'

'Hang on – which one is that?' said Lenny, squinting at the remnant in Fran's hand.

'Dunno, but it's deliiii-cious,' said Fran, downing her wine, then handing her glass to Lenny as she staggered towards the toilet.

'What's inside, though?' said Lenny, following after her. 'And which bread is it on?'

'Lenny! Len! Lenny!' said Juliet, waving at her from across the room.

'Fran, make sure you fill in the questionnaire . . . ' Lenny called out after her, then hurried back to Juliet. 'What is it? Are we nearly out of booze?'

'Booze is fine, but we're totally out of the Italian and the spicy one. Have you got some more wrapped and ready to grill?'

Lenny came back to the living room with another six rounds to find everyone had moved from being mildly tipsy to really quite drunk. This gathering was less than an hour away from descending into chaos. Across the room she saw Andrew standing with Danny, rifling through her vinyl collection and before she could weave through the crowd to stop him, Andrew had fished out *Now That's What I Call Music 12* and was putting on record one, side one, Wet Wet Wet's 'With a Little Help From My Friends'.

She shouted for him to stop, but even if he'd heard, he paid no attention. Lenny nudged through the guests and tried to get to her record player, but he gently blocked her.

'Andrew. Take this off right now – it's an insult to The Beatles.'

'Oh shut up,' said Andrew, laughing. 'We know you listen to this record all the time – it was first on the left in your filing system.'

'Filing system? You think *I* have a filing system? Anyway, if it was on the left that means it was at the back because it's my least favourite record.'

'That would surely be "Push",' said Danny, fishing out her Bros album as Lenny felt herself blush deep scarlet. 'Though by the wear and tear on this cover, it does look heavily manhandled. Still falling asleep with Matt Goss's face on your pillow, Len?' he said, struggling to contain his giggles. 'Which one wears the red leather jacket, Matt or Luke? Surely you can tell them apart at twenty paces?'

'Two words for you, Danny, neither of which is Matt or Luke.'

'Oh come on, Lenny, stop being too cool for school,' said Andrew.

'*Me?*' she said, incredulously. 'Andrew, don't you remember? Danny used to think we were so uncool he used to call us The Mathletes – and now you're ganging up with him, saying *I'm* too cool!'

'Too cool for school doesn't mean you're actually cool,' said Andrew, laughing. 'It means you need to relax.'

'I *am* relaxed, I just don't want this horribly cheesy track on during my research group.'

Danny turned to Andrew with a serious expression 'Surely you need cheesy music at a cheese research group?'

'Research group!' snorted Andrew. 'Fran is currently teaching Philpott to do that Beyoncé move from the "Ring on it" video, and Nate has put Robert in some milkmaid's wig he found in your coat cupboard, and they're forcing everyone to do shots of all the weird booze in your collection. All the Jäger's gone, they're down to Madeira, cherry brandy and the Pisang Ambon.'

'Oh, it's all very well for you guys, you've just been getting hammered while I've been slaving away at the toastie deck.'

'Ah, poor Lenny,' said Danny, reaching for her hands and rubbing his thumb over her palms. 'Are those tender little paws suffering from a whole three hours hard work?'

Lenny was conflicted. She very much wanted Danny to keep stroking her hands, but not in public, and not purely because he was teasing her.

She took her hands back and rested them on her hips. 'None of you has filled out the questionnaire. I have no idea how we're supposed to make a decision, given that all the sandwiches are eaten, and that you two are the most sober bastards in my flat right now.'

'Sounds to me like someone's in dire need of some Pisang Ambon,' said Danny.

'What the—?' said Andrew.

'Green, boozy, tastes of banana and desperate times,' said Danny, heading to the sideboard.

'Bring the bottle back with you!' shouted Andrew, then nudged Lenny. 'Maybe you guys can play Spin The Bottle again when you're done.'

Lenny punched him in the arm. 'What is wrong with you?'

'What is wrong with *you*, divvy? He's so into you, he can't stop trying to impress you.'

'Don't be silly. It's Danny, he's like that with everyone.'

'Just grab him and snog him.'

'I have far more important things to be getting on with.'

'Order! Order!' shouted Lenny, clinking her spoon fruitlessly against her mug. 'Or-der!'

'SHUT UP EVERYBODY!' bellowed Juliet. 'Can we have some quiet, please? You at the back with the wig on, thank you! Right. It may have skipped your notice, but we invited you here tonight to get your opinions on the all-important subject of cheese toasties.'

'Fucking love them!' shouted Fran.

'Thank you, Fran, we're hoping for something a little more specific,' said Lenny. 'OK, so, if you could take it in turns to call out your three favourites in order of—'

'One!' said Juliet. 'Call out your one favourite.'

'*One*,' said Lenny, grudgingly. 'Name the filling and the bread it was on.'

'The meat one!' shouted Andrew.

'Meat, meat!' said Philpott.

'Which meat? The bacon or the smoked ham? Which bread?' said Lenny, turning to Juliet in frustration.

'The spicy one,' shouted Nate.

'The one with caramelised onions,' said Little Jake.

'The Cheddar The Better?' asked Lenny. 'The one with four cheddars, Jake?'

'The chewier white bread,' said another voice.

'The stringy Italian one,' said another. 'Pesto!'

'Il Toastio,' said Lenny. 'It's currently called Il Toastio. Do you like that as a name?'

'The Toastie With The Mostie,' shouted Amy's boyfriend. 'That's snappier.'

'Cheesed To Meat You,' said Andrew. 'How about that?'

'Name one after me!' said Fran. 'Call it The Fran-bloody-tastic!'

'This is utter chaos,' said Lenny, turning to Jules in despair.

'Embrace it,' said Jules, putting her arm around her. 'It's good news – it means they like them all.'

'What are you guys called?' shouted Andrew.

'I'm Lenny, she's Jules. Have another cherry brandy, you big drunk.'

'No, dummy, what are you calling your business?'

'Well, we do have a name we like,' said Juliet, smiling at Lenny, then being momentarily distracted by Robert who was beaming proudly at her from underneath his milkmaid's wig.

'It's not a pun,' said Lenny, 'but it does have some meaning.'

'Lenny discovered that the word Company comes from the Latin *Companio*,' said Juliet. 'Companion, the person you break bread with – *com pane*.'

'And you guys are mates,' said Danny.

'And you make bread!' said Andrew. 'Nice! Still, you can't call a company Company.'

'We can do what we like,' said Lenny. 'We're the bosses.'

'Are you Cheese Executive Officer?' said Andrew.

'Andrew, stop it now,' said Lenny.

'We're calling ourselves Good Company,' said Juliet. 'And if you don't like it you can keep it to yourself. Right, I believe the naming of a business calls for some celebratory shots. Robert, Danny, you're our barmaids – please, do your worst, and make Lenny's a double, she has some catching up to do.'

Lenny was lying on her living-room carpet, staring at the ceiling. She raised her watch to her eyeline – 2.15 a.m. and there were still a dozen people here, most of them slumped on her sofa or the floor.

'Results, not fun,' murmured Juliet, who was lying next to her. 'Results. Need to go home, Lenny. Can't let Martha see me this drunk . . . '

'She and Nate got a cab home an hour ago,' said Robert. 'I guess I should call us one too?'

Lenny tipped her head back. Robert was sitting on the floor, knees up, back against the wall, his wig now on sideways.

'That wig,' said Lenny.

'Reminds me of how my hair used to be,' said Robert, turning it ninety degrees so it was now on backwards.

'Keep it, if you like?'

'Lenny!' said Andrew, bounding into the room from the hall. 'Lenny – me and Danny have invented this amazing new drink.'

Lenny propped herself up on her elbows. 'It's Danny and I, not me and Danny – Danny and I. Danny and I . . . '

'What's Danny and you?' said Danny, coming in from the kitchen looking hopeful.

Lenny squinted at the saucepan in his hand. 'What are you cooking?'

'You don't have a cocktail shaker. I'm just mixing a round of sherry and lime cordials. Honestly, it's delicious – try some, I insist,' he said, pouring it from the pan into the nearest pint glass available and bringing it over to Lenny. 'In fact I think I'll pour myself one and come and join you.'

'Who was that?' said Lenny, as she heard the front door close yet again.

'Andrew and Fiona, I think,' said Danny, raising his head to check. 'Yeah, I guess it was them, there's no one else left.'

'Really?' said Lenny, sitting up. It was true, there was no one else in her flat – just her and Danny lying on the living-room floor. She needed a glass of water but she didn't want to move because if she did, Danny might move too and then he might decide it was time to go home, and she really was enjoying the feeling of the entire right side of her body touching the entire left side of his, and if they stayed down here long enough, there was a reasonable chance he might kiss her.

'What time is it anyway?' She lifted his left arm, bent it at the elbow. 'Only four a.m.? My friends are a bunch of lightweights!'

'Aren't they just?' he said, laughing. 'Is it time for another drink?'

'Are you trying to get me drunk, Danny Freeman?'

'I think you've done a decent job of that yourself, Lenny D.'

'You're going to have to start calling me Boss, this time next week.'

'Boss!' he said, trying not to choke on his giggle.

'Hey! Actually Jules gave you that job without consulting me – she shouldn't have done that.'

'Do you want to interview me now?' he said, turning on to his side to face her.

'Yes, I do,' said Lenny, turning to face him and feeling a deep ache of longing pulse through her. They were lying face to face on the floor. If he didn't make a move now with this much encouragement then he would never make a move.

'So? Ask me a question,' said Danny, smiling at her.

'I can't think of anything on the spot,' said Lenny, trying to stop herself from inching even closer to him.

'Shall I interview myself then? Danny, are you an amazing bloke? Yes, I'm the best. Have you worked in the service industry before? Why, yes I have – I'm a real people person. Are you capable of calculating the change from a tenner? Indeed I am!'

'Hang on, stop a minute,' said Lenny, putting her finger to his lips. 'I've got something. Hold on . . . what was it? Yeah, OK, that's it! We did this thing at Wappen . . . Nick Cooper had this thing about employing people who you'd like to be stuck in a lift with.'

'Easy, a young Sophia Loren. And you?'

'What? No, that wasn't the question.'

'But who would you like to be stuck in a lift with?'

'Er, no idea.'

'Take your time, Lenny. You can have both Goss twins if you like?'

Lenny shuddered. 'You know what? I would hate to be stuck in a lift full stop. I have a fundamental fear of being trapped.'

'Hmm, interesting,' said Danny, stroking his chin and inching a tiny bit closer to her. 'That's why you used to change jobs every few years, isn't it?'

Lenny paused. 'That might be true, actually. I never thought about it.' And she'd never thought Danny had been paying much attention to what she was up to over the years.

'And that's probably why you're not married,' he said, raising an eyebrow.

Lenny thought she was single because she was a serial attractor of chronically useless men, but maybe it *was* because she was a commitment-phobe? She liked that thought far better. 'I'm meant to be interviewing you, Mr Freeman, so could you please stop analysing *me*? Yeah, so . . . you've made me forget my point . . . '

'Stuck in a lift . . . ' he said, patiently.

'Yeah, so, that's right. The way you do that,' said Lenny, poking him gently in the chest. 'The way you do that is to ask people what they like and don't like and then you choose people who like exactly the same things you do.'

'That sounds a bit self-obsessed and weird,' said Danny.

'No, no, there's a brain science theory to it or something, so just do it,' said Lenny, nodding. 'Right, so, tell me something random you like.'

Danny's face furrowed in thought. 'What, like anything?'

'Yeah, anything that comes to mind.'

'Er, Ben and Jerry's Phish Food ice cream, especially the chocolate fish bits?'

'Oh, I like those bits too! Right, now something you don't like.'

'People who are on their phones the whole time.'

Lenny nodded – good, good. 'Now another like, it should be a bit quirky or whatever.'

'Really? OK . . . being tucked up warm in bed, listening to the rain outside.'

Lenny closed her eyes briefly and imagined herself tucked up warm in bed with Danny on a rainy winter's day – what a lovely thought. When she opened her eyes again, she could swear he'd moved a little closer.

'Another dislike,' said Lenny.

'I dislike . . . too many questions,' he said, grinning.

'Go on, just one more of each,' she said. 'Make it as random and specific as you can. Be totally honest, it doesn't matter if it's weird or embarrassing.'

'OK, give me a minute.'

Lenny found herself staring into his eyes, but every time she did she felt such an overwhelming desire for him to kiss her, she had to keep looking away.

'OK,' said Danny. 'I've got one. I really don't like it when there's something you really, really want, and you've spent an awful lot of time thinking about it and wanting it – and then there's that horrible bit when you don't know if you're going to get it or not because it could go either way. I don't like that,' he said, shaking his head. 'I don't like that at all.'

'When you say wanting *it* . . . ' said Lenny, trying to keep her voice calm. 'Does the *it* mean, like, wanting a second-hand van . . . or something?'

Danny shook his head and smiled. 'It means "or something".'

Lenny caught her breath as Danny's hand reached for hers.

'Are we done with the questions yet, Len?'

Lenny swallowed hard. 'Nope. One more: one more thing you like.'

Danny stared at her and she thought her heart might stop she wanted him so badly.

'And I'm not allowed to say sherry and lime cordial shooters?' said Danny.

'You are not.'

'What do I like, what do I like . . . ?' said Danny, his gaze drifting from her eyes down to her mouth, then back up again. 'Well, Lenny, I like you.'

And then he leaned in even closer and their lips met and she was finally, finally kissing Danny Freeman.

Lenny woke up with a stonking hangover and a strange sense of déjà vu. She was pretty sure it wasn't a burrito sharing her bed this time but nonetheless she held her breath as she gently rolled over and opened her eyes. Nope – not a Mexican wrap, and not a useless man who was incapable of loving her, but instead a six-foot-two adult male with a real job, who liked spicy food, and, more to the point, who liked Lenny.

'Morning, Lenny Dublonsky,' said Danny, his eyes still tightly shut as he pulled her closer to his warm, almost-naked body and let out a sigh.

She looked at his face in the bright morning light, the line of his dark lashes, the trace of stubble starting to appear on his strong jaw, his beautiful mouth.

'Danny Freeman,' she said softly, resisting the urge to trace her finger over the tiny bump at the bridge of his nose. 'Who'd have thought it? After all these years, Danny Freeman from school . . . '

'Danny Freeman from Good Company,' he said, raising his hand in a mini salute.

'It's an HR nightmare!' said Lenny, rolling on to her back. 'In bed with the boss already and you haven't even done a day's work.'

Danny laughed, opened one eye, then groaned as he rapidly shut it again and shook his head. 'Ah. Ouch. Jees, Danny, this is not good.'

'What's not good?' said Lenny.

Danny let out another pained noise. 'I think . . . perhaps . . . the sherry and lime cordial was a drink too far, don't you?'

Oh please, don't turn around now and say this was just the alcohol, thought Lenny. Please don't be that guy.

'Do you think . . . ?' he said, sheepishly. 'That maybe . . . '

'What?' said Lenny, warily. Do I think this was a bad idea? Do I think this will get in the way of our friendship? Do I think we should forget this ever happened and act slightly awkwardly around each other for the next two to four weeks?

'Do you think there's any chance of a cup of tea and a Hangover toastie?'

'Oh,' said Lenny with relief. 'Yeah, it is a possibility. At some point. Not now. But maybe later. If you play your cards right.'

'Ah, good. OK. That's good,' he said, nodding contentedly to himself as he shifted the pillow under his head and pulled her closer. His skin held the not unpleasant smell of last night's alcohol, and of clean laundry and the trace of an aftershave – something cool and woody. She felt his arm move slowly down her back. She opened her eyes to look at him, just at the moment his smile turned into a look of mild confusion.

'Lenny?' he said, gingerly.

Oh god, *what*? She knew all this was too good to be true, something sinister was about to come out of his mouth, she could tell by the furrow of his brow.

He reached and tucked a stray curl of hair behind her ear before running his finger down her nose. 'That "man break" thing you were so adamant about?'

'Oh, that old thing?' said Lenny, relaxing back into a smile.

'Are you still on it?'

'Er, it would appear not,' she said, letting her foot slip between his as their lower legs entwined.

'Yeah, clever clogs, I can see that. I meant are you intending to go back on your man break?'

'Why do you ask?'

'Well, I was kind of hoping you might stay off it for the foreseeable future.'

It was another Sunday – but this time not a savage one. In fact it turned out pretty wonderful in the end.

62

The following Saturday, Lenny's alarm went off at 7 a.m. She was due to meet Juliet at the bakery at 9 a.m., which would allow three solid hours of sandwich making before they opened for business. It was a bright spring day and Lenny decided to walk. As she headed up through Camden she felt the early morning sun on her face and a growing sense of nerves mingled with excitement. Day one: their creation was real.

Camden High Street was busy even at this hour. A scattering of last night's revellers were still drunkenly hovering outside the minicab office, and Lenny caught the occasional whiff of a joint. The morning traders were setting up their stalls: racks of DMs, and rows of T-shirts with fake Chanel logos and more variations of Keep Calm and Carry On than she could count. As she headed towards the station a stocky bloke in a leather jacket was walking towards her, picking his nose with one hand, texting with the other. Lenny involuntarily scowled as he headed straight for her, his gaze fixed on his screen. If he took off those ridiculous yellow Bono sunglasses he might stand a better chance of seeing where he was going. Lenny paused, took a breath, then side stepped around him and carried on marching towards the road that led to the bakery.

When she arrived Jules was already busy slicing yesterday's loaves into the agreed 1.5 cm width slices. Lenny washed her hands, put on her apron and joined her at the table, buttering the slices on both sides, carefully piling them with the cheese mix, then deftly wrapping them in parchment. They worked silently, side by side, the radio playing in the background. Every so often one of them would turn to the other and they'd both break into broad grins, then carry on with the work. Lenny thought back to all those patronising little lectures Occy used to give her. Occy was wrong, Lenny *was* a team player, a *great* team player, she just hadn't been on the right team until now.

At 10 a.m. Danny arrived and started hauling the makings of their stand from his van. It was a simple set-up: a long folding table from where Juliet would serve the customers; a separate prep table to the side for Lenny to grill the sandwiches; a large yellow and white striped umbrella in case of a shower – though by the looks of it they'd be safe today.

As the clock ticked down Lenny started to feel the nerves she used to feel when she was due to go on stage and speak at a conference: dry mouth, adrenalin coursing through her. Actually it felt more intense than that – she hadn't been this nervous since she was standing on that blasted trapeze platform, terrified for dear life. She grabbed a glass of water, took a sip, then another, then started to move the sandwiches on to her table, arranging them in six neat stacks of twenty.

She turned the grill on, her hand hovering over the cast-iron plate waiting to feel the heat rise. Come on, come on, come on! She breathed a sigh of relief as the light turned red and she felt the warmth against her palm – the plate hot and ready for action. Juliet was already standing by the till, everything in its right place. Lenny checked her watch: 11.59 a.m. She swallowed hard, checked her watch again and now it was noon! They were officially open.

They stood together, hands behind their backs, smiling awkwardly as people drifted by. The occasional browser would pause, look the stall over curiously, then nod and move on.

'What if no one comes?' said Lenny, quietly.

'They'll come,' said Juliet, smiling warmly as a couple walked by and stopped to squint at the menu on the blackboard before exchanging a glance, shaking their heads and walking on.

'It's my handwriting – it's too messy,' whispered Lenny. 'You should have done it, yours is so much neater.'

'Lenny, your handwriting's fine.'

'Look at them, all just hanging out, drinking fancy coffees, being trendy. None of them looks hungry, they're all too cool to do something as boring as eating.'

'Lenny, it's lunchtime. They're hungry.'

'We should have done something with kale—'

'Lenny.'

'What if they don't like toasties?'

'Then I know what we'll be having for supper from now until Tuesday.'

Lenny felt panic slowly rise in her chest. 'I need to check the grill,' she said, moving back to her table. Her heart started beating faster as she scanned the piles of sandwiches, her gaze drifting up and up – these piles were so high. She reached out to the first stack and straightened it, shifted it along the table to the left a bit – then right – then back to its original place. Forty of each flavour, 120 in total. Not even Lenny, drunk, could eat 120 toasties. Maybe five, at a push? Danny could probably do seven; that only left 108 to freeze . . . Would they freeze? And if so, should she freeze them in the paper? And in whose freezer?

'Lenny? *Lenny?*'

Lenny turned, startled, and felt a sudden electric surge of joy. Juliet was smiling at her, a tenner in one hand, two customers behind her and another three behind them forming a small queue. 'Lenny, two classics, please?'

Lenny took a deep breath, exhaled slowly, then smoothed down her apron. She took the first two wrapped sandwiches from the stack and positioned them in the centre of the grill, her heart fluttering as she did. She laid a palm briefly on the papers, pressed down gently, bought herself a moment's calm. Then she reached for the grill's handle, gripped the bar tightly in both hands and pulled the lid down. She took a step back, turned the timer to max and double-checked the temperature. The grill was fine, the sandwiches were fine, Lenny was fine – in fact a whole lot better than fine. It might have looked to the outside world like she was just a girl with a secret smile, standing patiently with her arms folded waiting for two toasties to cook, but on the inside Lenny was flying – flying.

Acknowledgements

I owe immense thanks to so many people for their help with this novel. Once again to everyone at Headline: my fantastic editors Emily and Mari and the rest of the dream team, particularly Fran, Vicky, Frances, Sara and Yeti. To my wise, patient agent Victoria, and the lovely Pippa – for straightening out Lenny, and on occasion me too.

Researching my books is always an immensely pleasurable (and fattening) endeavour. I learnt about great bread from two wonderful bakers – Fergus Jackson of Brick House, East Dulwich, and Tami Isaacs Pearce of Karma Bread, Hampstead. Thanks to Nisha Patel and Nishma Chauhan of Grill My Cheese for sharing their experiences of starting a (phenomenal) cheese toastie business. Steve Sanders at Brook Food for info on kit, and to the Real Bread Campaign and their helpful guide – *Knead to Know: The Real Bread Starter*.

For all things technological – Lucia Komijen, Jonathan Abraham and Sally Heath Minto. Dr Andre Spicer, author of *The Wellness Syndrome* – for his brilliant insights. Graeme Dunn, for medical advice and chicken soup. Belinda Kutluoglu for braving juice camp with me. Helena Fleming for Amsterdam adventures. Rosie Stewart for the chat and the lingo. Felicity Spector for babka and myriad treats. Isabelle Broom, fellow author and pub quiz queen for relentless support and good times. Heather Ingram, the best thing to come out of Eversholt Street – brave, beautiful woman. My writing group, the most talented bunch of authors I have the privilege of regularly drinking with: Kathryn Stokes Arbour, Jess Kimmel, Courtney Clelland, Camilla Hill, Tash Bell, Irena Brignull and Michelle Aland. Dominic Fry for your wonderful attention to detail. The gas-safe, rather gorgeous Patrick Read for help with my plumbing. Elizabeth

Watkins for providing me, yet again, with a peaceful yet booze-soaked writer's retreat. Ben and Gabi Kay for letting me borrow an entire house to work in. Adam Polonsky for your burrito. Thanks to my friends who read the first draft – Dalia Bloom, Debbi Adler, Anna Potts, Michelle Gross, Ali Bailey again, Ann Farragher. Clive Jones, as ever. Dan Simmons for keeping Le Product in check. Jenny Knight for wisdom and support. Andrew Hart for being a loyal and generous compadre. Rizwana Khan, for keeping me fed and amused. Alexandra Emerson-White for so much, the K-town car rap still makes me laugh. Nathan Mosher, for making me at least 7% more joyful (p.s. it's AUGUST 19TH – it's here now, published, as a reference for you for next time). My family, for everything.

And finally, immense thanks to my readers, old and new, for your support both digitally and in real life: it makes me very happy.